Moscow Misdirection

Book 2 of the Moscow Nights Series

By

Beth H. Macy

Copy edited by Dori Harrell

Line edited by Ellie Nall

Acknowledgments

I want to thank "Egor" (Rick) and Dan for their excellent preliminary reviews and feedback. And most of all, Chris, for her patient support.

Chapter One

Elda Ainsworth tore through the woods. The sun painted dabbled spots of brightness on the underbrush, making it more difficult to see ruts and holes. The sound of her feet crushing branches and leaves echoed loudly in her head, as her lizard brain urged her feet along. She skidded to a stop for a brief moment and listened. *Yes*—she could hear the distant din of muffled directions and broken twigs, revealing her chasers crashing through the woods behind her.

Speeding up, she wove between trees, to not leave a direct trail to follow. She careened around a sapling, tripped over a root, and jerked to stay upright. Her foot crushed a branch, and the sharp sound of the dry wood breaking reprimanded her woodsman skills and Native American heritage. If she could hear her pursuers, then they could also hear her. She ripped off her boots, tied them around her neck, and continued in her stockings. As she raced on, she could feel the twigs and branches scraping the bottom of her feet, but the sound was muted and she left fewer markers to follow.

Blood oozed from the swollen gums around her new crown, which hid a securely embedded microdot. She resisted the urge to spit out the metallic taste of blood and instead forced herself to swallow and not leave a trail. The pain in her mouth throbbed in time with her heartbeat and offset the pain in her feet. Her toe hit a hidden rock. She went down, barely suppressing the sound of the air leaving her body. She pulled herself up into a quick squat and jerked all the way back upright, moving her feet before she even reached fully vertical.

Her pursuers were gaining on her.

Spying a hollow behind two trees, Elda willed her body toward it. Sweat ran down her face and along the sides of her body. She dove into the hollow and covered herself up with dirt, leaves, and twigs. Her heart pounded in her chest as she slowed her breath to a whisper. She was grateful that she was wearing dark clothing that would blend in well with the forest undergrowth and debris. She took a deep breath and pressed her head down into the dirt below.

Two hunters raced by, dressed in camouflage and carrying black, steel OTs-02 Kiparis semiautomatic machine guns. The large magazine capacities, laser pointers, silencers, and steel butts folded up against the guns told her all she needed to know—these men knew what they were doing. They stopped a short distance away. Elda could hear them arguing in Russian over which way to continue. Closing her eyes, she silently recited the Lord's prayer. She prayed that she would deliver the vital information she carried, knowing it would save many lives.

Desperate for air, she slowly turned her head to take in shallow breaths, keeping her body perfectly still. After what seemed like an eternity, the two men started up again. She could tell from their retreating footsteps that they had veered off in the direction she needed to head.

Elda waited until she could no longer hear any sounds, forced herself to count to sixty to ensure all was clear, and lifted her head up. She rose and took a moment to orient herself. Realizing that the two assassins had gotten ahead of her now—and that others could follow—she calculated a different route to the extraction point. She took off at a rapid but quiet pace, perpendicular to her previous path.

***

Elda sat in a small interior room with a bright light focused on her face. She braced herself to handle the agony that would soon ensue. The man came closer to her with a set of dental instruments.

He stated, "I'm sorry that we do not have the facilities here to properly numb your mouth. We will need to yank the crown off and remove the information beneath it. After doing that, we will replace the crown."

Elda nodded at the embassy doctor, closed her eyes, and mentally transported herself to a different world. She tensed her neck to keep her head from turning as he twisted, and braced her head against the back of the chair to combat

3

the yanking. As the pain intruded on her thoughts, she focused on it, softened it, breathed deeply, and allowed herself to float back to a state of lower pain. The grinding sound reverberated in her head as the doctor wrenched the crown off. The crown clinked into a metal tray—the first half of the procedure was over.

An intelligence officer standing by the doctor murmured his approval, as he collected the tiny data-chip in a small cup. He left to clean the chip and gather its information. The sharp smell of dental adhesive assaulted Elda's nostrils as the doctor pushed again and again on her jaw, forcing the crown back on.

"*Finito.*"

Elda opened her eyes and took a deep breath. She waited a few minutes to ensure she could stand without showing signs of weakness. "*Grazie.*" She shook his hand and checked her watch. *Just enough time to make it.* She jogged out of the room, her mouth pounding with each step.

She dashed out of the embassy and flagged down a taxicab. "*Museo dell'Opera del Duomo, per fovore.*" As she hopped out of the cab, having thrown a generous tip in with her payment, she pulled the bloody cotton wad out of her mouth and tossed it into a nearby trash receptacle.

"*Stiamo chiudendo!*" a guard shouted to inform her the museum was closing. Elda brushed by the guard and rushed to get through the doors before they shut. He shouted, *"Fermati o sparo!"* and reached for his sidearm.

The angry words floated up to her, causing her to stop in her tracks. She turned, looked at the guard beseechingly, and showed him the palms of her hands to signify she wasn't a threat, while adding her most engaging smile, *"Si, Si. Cinque minuti per favore. Voglio vedere Maria Maddalena."* She held her hand to her heart, cocked her head and raised both her hands in front of her chest, fingertips touching, as if in prayer.

"Si." The guard, recognizing the imitated stance of Donatello's statue, smiled at her and waved her on.

Panting from her dash into the museum, Elda stood admiring her favorite piece of art, the wooden Donatello statue of Mary Magdalene. Years of deprivation and suffering were etched on her craggy, but beautiful face. Standing there, for a brief moment Elda felt understood and accepted. Her own physical pain temporarily eased. Then, she tamped down her feelings of peace and assumed her mantle of alertness and callousness. She wished she could stay longer, but she had to return home and face Dawn.

Elda grabbed a taxi to the Florence airport and boarded the Alitalia flight to Boston. Once seated, she checked the backdated stamp on her passport. If Dawn checked that passport, it would show that she had been in Italy the entire time. She hated lying to Dawn. Elda's restricted clearance forbade her from sharing information with those who did not have the same access. The fewer details Dawn knew, the less likely she could become a target, and the safer she would be.

***

Elda snapped to a sitting position in bed, panting and in a cold sweat. Her hands shook. She glanced to her left and noted that her partner, Dawn, was soundly sleeping. Dawn's short, brown hair was tangled from their bedtime activities just a few hours earlier. Her hands were folded across her chest. As Elda looked at Dawn, her heart filled with warmth

She envied Dawn's ability to sleep so soundly—*when had she last been able to sleep through the night?* She wondered if she should try that meditation class Korinna and Dawn kept asking her to go to. It just seemed so frivolous and 1970s-style hippy-ish to Elda.

The aches from her trip still present, Elda slowly crawled out of bed. Dawn stirred and reached for her. Elda patted Dawn's hand and murmured, "Go back to sleep, honey."

Dawn groggily replied, "Dear, stay in bed. You were gone for days on your Italy vacation."

"I can't sleep. But I wish you liked to travel more. I'd love to show you Italy."

"You know I hate flying. Move it closer to us and I'll go." Dawn rolled over and was immediately back to sleep.

Elda whispered, "I so wish I could fall asleep like that. Sleep well, honey." A wave of guilt washed over her. She justified in her head that she didn't *actually* lie to Dawn. After all, saying that she'd love to show Dawn Italy *was* the truth. She had left her duplicate passport out on the counter when she returned home. When she went to put it away, it had been moved slightly. Dawn must have checked the stamp on it.

Feeling better after her rationalization, Elda grabbed a black and red flannel shirt to put on over her T-shirt and padded barefoot down the oversized wooden stairs to look for something to distract herself from her memories. Her feet recoiled at each step as the hardwood met the bruises from her escape through the woods. The clicking of nails on the floorboards brought her attention to her small black and white dog, Vee, trotting behind her, happily wagging her tail. At the foot of the stairs Elda glanced at her Garmin GPS watch. It was only 22:00. She hoped she could get back to sleep after drinking a cup of warm milk. Perhaps a Tylenol would also be in order.

She strode across the wide planks of the well-worn wooden floor and across the tan-and-brick-colored natural stone tile floor in the kitchen. She flung open the stainless-steel refrigerator, grabbed the milk, and filled and heated a cup in the microwave. Stepping into the living room, she threw together some crumpled newspapers and small twigs and laid on top three small logs in a teepee position to start a fire in the fireplace. Once the fire was roaring, she plopped down onto the well-worn brown leather couch with her Apple MacBook Pro laptop.

Elda sipped her warm milk and logged in over the secure VPN into the government network to check her encrypted messages. One stood out—a high-priority message sent that morning from her boss in DC, Ed Wilson, 1 March 2019 at 18:00. *Darn it.* She opened it and read, CALL ME THE MINUTE YOU READ THIS, NO MATTER WHAT TIME OF DAY OR NIGHT. IT'S URGENT.

She scratched her head and frowned. There went tonight's sleep. She snuck over the creaky old pine floors to the spare room downstairs, so she wouldn't wake up Dawn by using the secure phone in the bedroom.

Walking past the mirror hanging over the bureau in the room that contained her tiny makeshift office, Elda caught a glimpse of herself. Her naturally curly hair was all askew, jutting out at right angles from her head, and her brown eyes were wild, reflecting the red from the rim of her glasses and appearing more sunken that usual, due to her prominent cheekbones and the lighting. *Gads*, she looked rather scary.

She settled herself into her chair. Vee jumped up, placed her small white paws on Elda's thighs, and licked her hand.

"Mommy needs to make a call, Vee." Elda scratched Vee on her head while dialing a number on the secure hotline.

***

"You're going *where?*" Dawn shrieked at Elda.

Elda braced herself against Dawn's angry tirade and assured her, "Just to DC, honey. Ed needs me to consult on something."

Dawn shook her fist at Elda. "Damn it, Elda. You told me you were retiring. I never get time to do things with you. I feel as if I am all alone in this relationship." Dawn's lower lip started to quiver.

Elda took a deep breath to calm herself and avoid escalating the discussion into an argument. "I know I said I was retiring, honey. I am *really* trying to do that."

Dawn snarled, "Don't you 'honey' me, Elda. You *always* say you're going to retire, but you never really do. You promise me again and again, but then Ed calls and *off* you go again. You just got back from vacation, too!"

9

Voices raised, Elda and Dawn faced off at opposite ends of the kitchen table. Dawn, still in her PJs, had her hands on her hips and scowled at Elda. Elda, freshly showered and dressed in a button-down shirt and jeans, just stared at the ceiling, as if to find her answer for Dawn there. Vee lay on a small rug under the table, her head on her paws, watching the well-known routine with soulful brown eyes.

"You *were* on vacation, weren't you?"

Elda opened her mouth to speak, shut it, glanced briefly at Dawn and then at the floor. Pain shot up her jaw and into her skull as she clenched her teeth to keep from retorting something she'd later regret.

"Oh *no*, don't tell me you weren't! What did you *really* do in Italy?"

Elda grimaced. "You know I can't tell you that, honey."

Dawn tensely shook her finger at Elda. She glared and breathed heavily. She slammed her foot down, spun to leave, and then turned back, her face reddened and blotched. She pointed at Elda and yelled, "Damn it, no! Don't tell me. I don't want to know." Dawn stormed out of the kitchen and up the stairs.

Elda sadly watched her go, took a deep breath and then a sip of her now lukewarm coffee to wash down the bile in her throat. Her head pounded and her stomach churned as her body fought the war inside. She weighed years of devotion and service to her job and country and being of aid to many others, even saving lives, against her own happiness and relationship. Her heart clenched. She sighed deeply and looked down at Vee. "Should I follow her or just let her cool down, Vee?"

Vee popped up, wagged her tail, and then ran off to get a toy to cheer her mummy up. Elda patted Vee on the head when Vee plopped a well-chewed ducky on top of her foot. "Okay, Vee. I'll play with you. I'll give her some space."

She shook off the pain and loneliness that had flooded her and watched Vee run after the toy. She wondered if all relationships were this complicated. Vee trotted back and plopped Ducky down again. "Good girl, Vee. Your other mommy will come around, right?"

Silence filled the room.

***

Toshchiy Chelovek held tightly onto the edges of his leather seat as the chopper spun out of control, careening toward the earth. *Govno. Shit. This is it. This is how it all ends*, he thought. Sweat beaded up on his forehead, but his face showed no sign of distress.

Silent and focused on his instruments, the pilot tried to start the engine, which responded by sputtering and dying again. The chopper yawed, pitched, and rolled as plummeted downward. Tosh could feel his heart in his throat. He concentrated on his breathing, willing himself to stay calm. Checking the radar screen, he tried to see where the airplane that shot them down had gone. The screen didn't tell him much, but Tosh knew the enemy would return to ensure they had killed everyone. The pilot's hands flew over the instruments. The blades caught. And then stopped. Started. Died. The chopper bucked up and down. Gasoline vapors permeated the cockpit.

Suddenly the engine coughed back to life. The blades reengaged, and the craft stabilized and rose upward. The pilot fought with the controls to level the helicopter and get more altitude. He grazed the tops of the trees, battling to reach an opening in the sea of trees below. The chopper bucked and the engine sputtered, but the blades whirled and caught the air. The pilot brought the copter safely down with a jolt, barely missing the surrounding trees.

He cut the engine and turned to Tosh. "I apologize. I almost lost the craft." A strong smell of oil lingered in the air, and whisps of dark smoke seeped from the engine.

Tosh grabbed his handkerchief and patted his brow. His fingers were still white from gripping the seat so hard. But his voice was steady. "No, no need to apologize. You saved our lives. I owe you one. Now, quick, let's remove the portable radio, survival gear, and torch the craft so it appears as though we crashed."

Tosh grabbed the survival kit and the pilot hefted out the portable radio. They both jumped out of the chopper. Tosh leaned back in and threw everything flammable in a pile on the pilot's seat. The pilot added some dry kindling he had gathered and then threw a lit flare from the survival kit onto the pile. The pyre went up with a whoosh.

The two men jogged a short distance on unsteady legs and threw themselves onto the ground in the woods. Behind them, the helicopter ignited in a ball of fire, and thick black smoke spiraled upwards through the air.

Tosh ordered the pilot, "Erase our footprints and burrow down into the forest floor. We will cover ourselves with leaves and hide until that plane passes by and reports our demise. Then, we will hop on our lift home." He took a shovel from the emergency kit and dug a hole to hide the portable radio. Meanwhile, the pilot had smoothed the ground where their feet had disturbed it and returned to Tosh's side. Tosh handed the shovel to the pilot, who dug himself a shallow ditch and then crawled into it, covering himself with dirt and leaves with Tosh's assistance.

Breathing deeply, Tosh savored another chance at life, then went to work digging out a grave-like trench of his own. He had barely crawled in when the buzz of an approaching low flying aircraft filled his ears. Tosh lay there, breathing in the musty scent of leaves, for what seemed like an interminable time. The plane made two passes over the site before wheeling around and heading back to its home base. Tosh popped up, yelled an all clear to the pilot, and, using his bare hands, dug the radio out. "Hurry! We don't have much time. They will send a search party to go through the wreckage. We need to be gone by then."

Tosh powered up the radio, spun the dial to a frequency only Tosh and his support team knew and started broadcasting. "Mayday! This is Toshchiy Chelovek. My helicopter is down. We need immediate pickup."

Static filled the air—a voice answered. "Do you have your coordinates?"

The pilot grabbed the microphone and stated the coordinates. The voice on the other end repeated them and added, "We will be there in one half hour."

Tosh took out his black, semi-automatic SR-1 Vector pistol, popped out the cartridge and counted the rounds of body-armor-piercing ammunition that he had for it. The Vector was so perfectly proportioned, like a solidly built athlete, with the tapered line leading out from the grip to the barrel. After relishing the familiar heft of his gun, his hand hugging the ribbed grip, he slipped it back into his side holster. He then dug into the survival kit and found a rectangular, semi-automatic PYa pistol with two additional magazines of ammunition and handed them to the pilot. "I assume you know how to shoot?"

"Yes, sir."

"Good. Save the last bullet for yourself. Know that if you falter, I will be saving *two* bullets."

The pilot nodded and hefted the gun, checking the sights. He and Tosh stood behind a small grove of trees watching the chopper burn in the glade. After twenty-five minutes, they heard sounds in the distance—an enemy recovery team bushwhacking their way through the dense undergrowth.

Tosh turned and pointed his gun toward the noise. "I calculate we only have a few minutes before they get within range."

"*Ser?*"

"Yes?"

"If it comes to a choice, I will cover your escape."

"I will keep that in mind, but I have *never* left a man behind."

Overhead, they heard an unmistakable *whoop-whoop*. In seconds, a black helicopter swooped over them and dropped the end of a rope ladder into the clearing. "*Run!*" Tosh yelled as he fired a blast of warning shots behind him. "*Go!*"

Tosh and the pilot sprinted across the clearing. Bullets sprayed from the woods. They both leapt onto the ladder and were lifted up into the air as their pursuers emerged from the woods and sprayed bullets at them. The two men scrambled up the ladder to reach the floor of the helicopter.

Once inside, the pilot collapsed. Tosh tore open the pilot's jacket, only to see blood spurting from his chest. A round had torn through his back and left a gaping hole in his torso. The pilot smiled weakly at Tosh. "I did well, didn't I, sir?"

Tosh paused briefly to ensure his voice was steady. "Yes, you did. Go in peace now. We will take good care of your wife and son."

The pilot breathed deeply and gurgled. Blood gushed out of his mouth and his eyes rolled in his head. Tosh reached out and gently shut the man's eyelids.

***

The next morning, Tosh jerked awake. He had kicked off his covers and was clenching his pillow. He took a moment to orientate himself to his bedroom and looked over at his partner sleeping peacefully on the other side of their bed. Quietly he snuck out, taking care not to jiggle the mattress. He stood up and felt his muscles complain about yesterday's activities. A sharp pain shot through his neck, which seized as he turned to grab his black and white checkered robe from the back of a nearby chair. He massaged his neck and slipped his robe over his plain black pajamas. His hands smoothed down the sides, feeling the cozy softness of the material. Well-made utilitarian clothes were a weakness of his. He did consider the pattern to be a bit garish, but it was a Christmas present last year, which meant he needed to wear it or fess up that he didn't much like the design. Wearing it was much easier than any discussion. Tosh was a man of few words, and he chose those few carefully.

He ran his hands through his short cropped gray hair and shook his head, attempting to clear the physical sensation of spinning out of control toward death. He lifted his laptop from the bedside table. He plodded barefoot over the linoleum floor to the kitchen, to make himself a cup of tea and read any messages that may have come in during the night. He glanced at his Apple watch while walking, noting that it was 06:00 and the time he would normally rise.

He sipped his tea while rocking back and forth in a straight back wooden chair at a small metal table in the kitchen. He thought that he really should get new chairs. This one was rather wobbly.

He held his hand to the pulse in his throat and registered that it was rather rapid. Breathing deeply to lower his respiration rate and blood pressure, he opened his Toshiba computer and logged in to his secure network. One message was flagged as urgent.

He felt his pulse quicken with anxiety. Wondering how long the message had been sitting there, he checked the header and saw that it was sent on that morning, 2 March, and sighed from relief that he hadn't missed it. "*Govno. I have to call the Kremlin and see what's up*," he muttered to himself.

He recognized that it was unlike him to swear anymore. It seemed that the near crash had him more upset than he realized. He strode over to the brown-and-white tiled linoleum and down the hall to his study. There he reached across his wooden desk, picked up the secure line, and dialed a private extension.

***

Tosh arrived punctually at 07:30 at Alexei Alexeev's office in the Kremlin. The musty smell of the anteroom assaulted his nostrils. Alexei's secretary, who appeared sunk in her chair for eons, lethargically waved him on. Tosh strode forward and opened the inner door to Alexei's office. The smell of stale sweat and old coffee floated past Tosh's nose.

Alexei pulled his six-foot two-inch frame from behind his large, highly polished, wooden desk and lumbered over the aged oriental rug to shake Tosh's hand. Tosh noticed that Alexei had sucked in his paunchy gut as he stood.

"Prevet, Tosh. Pozhaluysta sidet'." Alexei motioned to the rigid wooden Mission style guest chair and settled his large body behind his desk into his high-back leather office chair. He smoothed the top of his greying hair and adjusted his horn-rimmed glasses. "We have a need for you and your team. Are they ready?"

"Yes sir, they are," Tosh replied confidently.

Alexei narrowed his eyes and inquired, "Who are you planning to use?"

Having been told that Alexei liked to let his subordinates know he was in charge and micromanage operations, Tosh informed him, "I think you are familiar with them. Anatoly Petrov, Snezhana Chelovek, and Yuri Kuznetsov."

Alexei nodded. "Anatoly is a good choice. I understand that he is KGB and GRU trained and an excellent assassin?"

Suppressing his impatience at the waste of time taken to fill this man in, Tosh flatly replied, "Yes sir. He is an expert at many weapons, accomplished at assassination with his bare hands, and overall is a killing machine."

Alexei smiled a thin smile. He continued probing, "Good. And Yuri was on your last operation, wasn't he? Didn't he used to work with the Americans?"

His grey eyes steely, Tosh continued the game, "Yes sir. He has had an assortment of training by the Mafia, KGB and GRU, but is not of the right temperament to be an assassin. He is a master of logistics and was very useful to the Mafia in their drug running business."

"Interesting choice …Chelovek… That wouldn't be a relative of yours, would it?"

Tosh willed his jaw muscles to relax enough to speak without clenching his teeth. "Yes sir. She is my sister's daughter's child. She has inherited my photographic memory and has an interest in the business. I am giving her a limited trial, since she is smart, trainable, and may be useful with her ability to manipulate others, especially men."

Alexei snorted.

Tosh ignored Alexei's disdain and responded, "I believe, that with Anatoly, Snezhana, and Yuri, I can win at anything. We are ready."

Chapter Two

Nigel Davies squinted into the bright light beaming into his eyes and reflecting off of the metal table. The chains that bound him clanked when he moved. He narrowed his eyes in an attempt to identify the tall black silhouette of an interrogator outlined behind the light. The room stank of Nigel's stale sweat and pee.

Perspiration poured down Nigel's face and dripped off his chin making small reflective pools on the table. "I turned my father. What more do you want?" His voice cracked, his mouth parched from lack of water.

"*Nyet*. We turned your father, not you, Nigel. You were only the leverage that we needed for him to obey us. Now we're upping the ante, but he has refused. It's time you called him. We must have him agree to be more active for us in his position at MI6."

"You won't kill me. You need me still." Nigel spat in the man's direction.

"If we decide to keep you alive, we don't have to keep your body parts intact." The tall Russian stepped up to loom over Nigel.

Terrified and angry, Nigel strained at the cuffs that chained him to the table. "I've had enough of this. I won't do it," he defiantly postured.

The Russian slapped Nigel across his face hard enough to whip his head to one side. A red mark instantly appeared on Nigel's cheek. He tried to reach his cheek, but couldn't. He blinked to ward off the pain and straightened himself up. "He's my father. I may not like him, but I have my principles."

The Russian's fist hit him squarely on his nose. His head snapped backwards, and his chair reared up on its back legs and then ratcheted forward from the pull of the chains, slamming Nigel's body into the edge of the table. Blood poured from his nose and Nigel struggled to catch his breath.

"You really *are* dispensable, you know?" The click of the hammer being pulled back and the cold metallic muzzle pressed against the side of his head was enough to convince Nigel to give in.

Nigel swallowed to avoid throwing up whatever remained in his stomach and shouted, "Don't shoot me! Okay! Okay! I'll call him! What do you want me to say?"

The Russian handed him a face cloth and loosened the chain slightly so Nigel could reach his nose to staunch the flow of blood.

"I thought you'd see it our way. Here is your script."

A sheet of paper dropped onto the table in front of Nigel. He stuck the end of the towel into his bleeding nostril and struggled to reach the paper. Finally picking it up with his chained together hands, he shook his head to plant his glasses more firmly on his slightly crooked, and now swollen, nose and read the typed words.

"Blimey!"

***

Nigel sat slouched on the comfy leather couch in Aurelio's apartment, holding an ice pack to his face and dejectedly smoking a bong with his new friend. Smoke whirled around their heads. He whistled slightly as the air moved through the gap between his two front teeth, and stated, "I don't know why I married her, Aurelio. My life has been a living hell ever since."

Aurelio tittered and replied, "Of course you know why, man. Nothing like banging a whore." He laughed again and grabbed his crotch to make the point. Aurelio kept it to himself that his own wife had left him and his abilities in that area had failed for many years now.

"I'm in trouble Aurelio. Like big trouble. I fucked up big time. At first it was so good. Like lots of money. And I was getting back at my father. He's a rigid establishment

23

prick who was never there for me. I hated him. But now it's deep trouble. I'm scared shitless, man."

"Wow man, that's bad. Are they after you too? I'm being spied upon by the CIA and many others. My double-crossing brother and half-sister have colluded with them against me." Aurelio took a giant slug of scotch from his crystal glass and offered the glass to Nigel. Nigel held up his hand and shook his head.

"I can't tell you what I have done. They'll kill me. I fucked up. I am in so deep."

Aurelio had dressed in pants in honor of his new friend's visit but was not wearing a shirt. He scratched at the white hairs on his flabby chest. He pointed at a lengthy ragged scar on his side. "See this? They already tried to murder me and didn't succeed! They sent a burly man after me. He stabbed me. But I didn't die. And my ex-wife tried to kill me many times herself. She also failed. Stick with me, man. I cannot die." He giggled and continued chortling, spewing spit drops of scotch onto the glass tabletop.

Nigel looked warily at his new friend and inched slightly away from him on the couch.

Aurelio continued manically, "Yes, we should celebrate our good fortune. Let me call Stanislav and Yevgeni, two friends I made while staying at an exclusive resort. I helped set them up here in Moscow." He cackled. "We can get some coke and go out on the town." He then turned to Nigel with a serious look on his face. "You need leverage man. Get yourself some leverage. Leverage. That's a cool word. Lever-age. Le-verage." He took another hit on the bong and laughed and continued. "Leh… lever…age… Old levers!"

Nigel carefully stood up and slowly backed his way to the door. He bowed and stated formally, "Thank you, Aurelio, that is a wonderful offer. I really must get home to my wife before she notifies someone that I have been gone too long."

Aurelio had already lost his train of thought and returned to the bong. Exhaling a plume of smoke, he waved goodbye and said, "Be careful, man, it's dangerous out there. They are watching."

"I know."

***

Nigel marched back and forth in his study, muttering to himself, "Aurelio may be nuts, but his fixation on leverage was smart. I need leverage. Who do I know? I need a Russian connection. I have to protect myself. I thought that setting up Doug's father would protect me after they had turned my father. But once they get all the information from Doug's father, they will no longer need me." He looked down at the worn carpet where years of pacing had worn down a strip on the Oriental carpet. He wiped the sweat from his forehead. It would not do to have his wife see him this way. He stopped and sat behind his wooden desk to think things through more calmly.

Nigel's roommate at Oxford, Doug Clark, hated his own father, John, and looked down on John's traditional career and distanced himself as much as possible, which is why he ended up overseas at Oxford. Nigel and Doug had bonded over their mutual anger at their fathers.

Doug had told him about his grandfather, Robert Clark. The family grapevine implied that Robert had run into some trouble during a business trip to Russia. He was very close mouthed about it, but his behavior changed after that trip. He took more frequent trips and seemed to have more money available than his job at Boeing would have paid him. And his son, John, a poor scholar, and not a sports player, was easily admitted into the military academy at West Point. Although he had had a lackluster academic performance and a non-inspiring military stint, the son's career had rocketed, and he was now an esteemed senator and sat on the United States Senate Select Committee on Intelligence.

When he was about to be eliminated after betraying his father, Henry, Nigel had passed the information on to his handlers that he, and only he, had leverage that could be used on a United States Senator. This had bought him time.

He had relaxed after that incident, thinking he was in the clear, until they sent someone to teach him who was in control. His face throbbed when he thought about that lesson. Apparently both his father and the senator were balking at their assigned tasks for Russia. He had agreed to pressure his father again and pass an ultimatum on to the senator.

Nigel was sick of being used and sick of his wife watching him. He wanted this done with. But in order to have that happen he needed to get control back. If he could intercept the information and perhaps get ahead of it, then he might still be valuable to the Russians. He just needed to use Doug as his patsy.

Nigel picked up his phone and then thought better of it. His wife was an ex-prostitute, who was still run by the Russian government. She kept close tabs on Nigel for Russia and the government probably had taps on his phone, and, he surmised, also in his house.

***

It was almost time. Nigel sat despondently in his study staring at his phone. As ordered, he had read the script to Doug's father and had been released from interrogation. Today he was to make a follow-up call to his father. He drummed his fingers on his desk, dancing them around a ray of sunlight that had settled there.

27

With a few minutes to spare, he sat back and reviewed what he had done the day before during his walk. He had kept his conversation with Doug short, and at the end of their conversation, he had wiped down the payphone. He felt confident that he had done it all without being observed. No one could know about Doug's existence.

In his conversation, he had gathered some data he could use, but he needed to find someone to trace down some more information. He swore to himself. He needed to be careful and limit his walks. No need to make his wife suspicious.

He glanced at his watch, reached for the phone, hesitated, and withdrew his hand. A knock at his study door caused him to jump up and tip over his chair. He set the chair upright and opened the door. He regarded his gorgeous wife standing there with a drink in either hand. She handed him one of the drinks and inquired, "Have you made the call yet or do I need to make one?"

"Dear, I was just reaching for the phone when you knocked. I'll make it momentarily."

She perched on the side of his desk, crossed her legs to show more thigh and sipped her drink. "I'll wait while you call."

He sighed, returned to his seat, picked up the phone and dialed. He spoke briefly into the phone, listened to the response, and hung up. He turned to his wife. "It is done. He is in." He walked around the desk.

His wife put down her drink, sank to her knees on the carpet in front of him, and unzipped his pants. "Good boy. And now you get your reward."

He placed his drink down on the glass covering the wooden desktop and leaned back against his desk and let her take control of him.

I sold my soul for this…

Chapter Three

The sunrise peeked through the brown sheer curtains in a small London flat. Dappled light danced off the flowered wallpaper and onto two people entwined in a double bed. Oliver Evans and Sophia Brown lay back sweaty and panting, their bodies tangled in the white down duvet. They were making up for having been apart for two months.

Oliver rolled over onto his arm and gently played with her firm breasts. "Shall we have another go?"

"Give me a moment to catch my breath … Oh my, you are ready."

He moved her blond hair away from her face and nibbled at her ear. She turned her face toward him, and their lips met. Just then their secure landline rang.

"Bloody hell! Who is calling us at six a.m. on a Saturday?" Oliver reached out flailing his hand on the small wooden bedside table. He connected with and answered the phone before it stopped ringing. He listened for a while and then hung up. "Bollocks. We need to report to MI6 now."

"Crap. Some days I wish we had different jobs," Sophia pouted, as she jumped out of bed and bent over to pick through the scattered clothing on the floor to find her clothes from the previous night. Oliver grinned broadly, enjoying the view of her tight ass and long legs. Sophia caught him looking at her, and she giggled, dropped her clothes, picked up his jeans, and threw them at his head. "Get up, lazy bones. Our masters have called."

She leered suggestively at him. He swung his legs over the side of the bed, slipping into his jeans as he stood up.

"What?" Oliver asked Sophia teasingly, wanting her to say the answer.

"You know I never get tired of looking at you," she leered.

"This old thing?" Oliver assumed a campy pose with one hand behind his head and his other hand on his hip.

"Oh, come off it. And stop primping. You are a catch, and you know it." Sophia gazed lustily at Oliver. He was tall and strikingly handsome with dark-brown hair and eyes, high cheekbones, and an endearing dimple on his cheek. He had the lean body of a runner, with clearly defined muscles in his legs, strong but slender arms, and a rock-hard flat abdomen. "You drive me wild when you smile. And your body…"

"Do tell…," Oliver said, striking an athletic pose.

Sophia opened her mouth and licked her lips. "Oh yes, I could lick you all over."

Oliver pirouetted and, as he spun around on one leg, swept her clothing up off the hardwood floor and tossed them her way.

Sophia's eyes teared up with her laughter, "Those ballet lessons were *so useful.*"

Oliver stuck his tongue out at Sophia in response.

"Bring that over here, dear…," she requested coyly.

Oliver checked his watch and said with an exaggerated sad tone, "Humm, I wish I could, Sophia, but we *must* dash."

"Oh, fine…If we must." Sophia walked over to her white ash bureau and pulled open the drawers, seemingly randomly selecting clean clothes. She drew on a pair of elasticized tight-fitting black pants and a white man's-styled shirt, cinched at the waist with a wide black belt, and slipped her feet into a pair of black loafers.

"Oh yes, a woman must accessorize." She reached inside the wooden bedside tabletop drawer and pulled out her weapon. Checking to ensure it was loaded, she inserted it into a holster that she clipped inside her belt and pants at the bottom of her back. She slipped an extra ammunition clip into a zippered compartment on the belt, then ran a brush through her short blond hair, added a line of green eyeshadow to accent her green eyes, and rolled on pale-pink lip gloss.

Oliver tugged a T-shirt over his head and then picked up another shirt off the hardwood floor, sniffed it, and threw it back down. He grabbed a newly laundered and pressed shirt out of the closet. He buttoned up his shirt, snatched his gun out of his bedside table, and jammed it into his concealed belt holster. He licked his fingers and ran them through his hair to stick the few strays back in place.

He glanced at Sophia, who rolled her eyes at his actions. He shrugged and gave her a boyish grin. "Right. Let's go."

***

Snezhana Chelovek woke from a dreamless sleep to her phone beeping. She snatched it off the nightstand and silenced it. Through her pounding headache, she struggled to remember what day it was. *Pushing* the time button on her pink sports watch she noted it was 3 March 2019—06:30. *Khorosho.* She had not lost any time.

Glancing at the person on the other side of the bed, she struggled to remember his name. Ah yes. He was Olaf, an aide from the Norwegian embassy. She considered him a safe sex toy since he was due to be transferred next week,

33

and there would be no romantic entanglement to clear up. Her uncle had warned her against forming any close relationships, but she was bored and had a high sex drive. Formal exercise bored her.

Wandering through the clothing that lay strewn across the beige rug on the bedroom floor, she picked up her items and silently tiptoed out of the room. Pausing briefly in the hallway, she slid on a blue top that mirrored her eyes and pulled up form-fitting leather black slacks over her long, slender legs, slipping her feet into a practical pair of black flats, as she tied her shoulder-length brown hair with a hair tie. Pulling the metal apartment door shut behind her she stepped out to face the day.

The bright light assailed her eyeballs. Mentally berating herself for drinking so much, she pulled on her sunglasses. Her uncle would be furious if he found out and would consider her a security risk. She had to find a different way to amuse herself while waiting for her next assignment. Hobbies seemed so boring, and her raging hormones were demanding satisfaction.

Snezhana checked her messages as she walked back to her apartment. Her long legs covered the distance in a short time. Spying an indicator on her encrypted messages app, she quickly opened it up. It was a demand to report immediately to her *dyadya* Tosh's office. Snezhana felt her heart skip a beat as she wondered if her uncle had discovered how she had been behaving, but she dismissed the idea. "I have been discrete," she told herself. "I hope…"

She sprinted up the stairs and into her apartment. Running across the linoleum-tiled hallway floor, she dashed into her bedroom. Stripping and tossing the clothes she was wearing onto the bedroom rug, she grabbed a clean set of clothes from her small, but well-organized closet. Rushing into the walk-in shower, she changed into a pink, pastel-colored, tailored shirt and black business slacks, to be more acceptable for her uncle and the office, and darted out for the short walk to the Kremlin.

Snezhana felt a surge of excitement as she jogged across Red Square and sped toward Tosh's office in the Kremlin. Although unsure that she wanted this career, the adrenal rush of being a spy was so much better than sex. She hoped this was a meaty mission. Throwing open the door to Tosh's building, she skidded to a halt as she nearly ran into Tosh, who was standing inside the entryway.

Stepping forward with open arms, Snezhana stopped short, abruptly dropping her arms. Tosh's steely gaze bore through her as if reading her very thoughts. "*Dyadya.*"

"Sir will do, Snezhana," corrected Tosh sternly.

"*Da, ser.*"

Tosh was a slender man who didn't warrant a second glance, but Snezhana knew he was a lethal assassin and, despite his age, a capable operative. As if he understood he was being evaluated against his age, Tosh stood straighter. "We will wait here for the others," he told her.

She nodded, turned, and joined him in silently watching out the door.

***

Awaking early, Yaromir Kozlov had an unusual sense of unease. He threw on his workout clothes and jogged towards the gym. Yaromir was a large and brutish man, usually given assignments that required physical force. He was pleased that, despite his error in an earlier assignment, Tosh was promising him a promotion to his "A" team. He hoped that he would be called for a mission soon. Until then, it was important to keep in shape.

A car came out of nowhere and broadsided Yaromir, speeding away into the blackness of the early morning. In Yaromir's pocket, his phone chirped, signifying an incoming message. Tosh's summon would remain unread.

***

Jogging across the cobblestones of Red Square, Anatoly Petrov saw Yuri Kuznetsov approaching from the other direction. Anatoly straightened his shoulders back to expand his chest to increase his oxygen intake. Proudly not out of breath, he stopped inches away from Yuri.

Anatoly was glad to see Yuri again. His piercing bright blue eyes studied Yuri. It had been months since they had last worked together. Knowing it irritated Yuri, he rubbed Yuri's fuzz of his military buzz cut, and inquired, *"Privet, Yuri. Kak dela?"*

Yuri slapped Anatoly's hand away. "I'm good, Anatoly. You must be raring to go."

"I am. It's been weeks since my last assignment. I would love to crack a neck this time. I love seeing that shock in someone's eyes just before they die. Or perhaps I'll get a chance to use my sniper rifle and peg someone right between the eyes. I haven't shot someone in a long time. *Yes*, that would be good."

"You're a strange man, Anatoly. I'm glad you're my friend."

"Who said we are friends?"

Anatoly chortled at the look on Yuri's face and gave him a friendly slam on the back. A smaller man would have fallen over from receiving Anatoly's enthusiasm.

They fell easily into step with each other and continued over the grey cobblestones toward St. Basil's Cathedral and the Kremlin, where Tosh's office was located. Anatoly knew that he and Yuri were often mistaken for brothers. However, a closer inspection would disclose that Anatoly was slightly taller, somewhat bigger overall, and harder, both on the inside and outside. Running into him would be like hitting a concrete wall.

Nearing the white stone-faced building, Anatoly immediately spotted Tosh and Snezhana, waiting for them. Tosh held his finger up to his lips and led the team to a secure operations room down the hall. Anatoly saw Yuri's jaw drop as he looked around in awe at the dark, windowless room lit only with the blue and red glow of equipment. Once his eyes adjusted, he spied the shiny communication gear with tiny blinking red and green lights, a large wooden oval conference table with microphones strategically placed around it, a set of black leather conference room chairs on rollers, and several sixty-inch monitors mounted on the walls of each end of the room. The cool air smelled cleanly metallic mixed with the odor of a newly installed carpet.

"*Kak dela bratishka?*" Anatoly asked Yuri, slapping him on his back.

"*Klassno*! I have never been in here before!"

"Well, button your seatbelt then. This means it will be a *big* mission."

***

The large screen at the end of the room burned brightly with the two words: Russian, *Ozhidaniye*, and English, *Stand By*. Tosh motioned for the team members to sit down at one end of the table and adjusted the microphones, so each person had one nearby. The silence hung heavily in the air. Yuri twitched slightly at each click of a microphone being dropped gently into position. Anatoly clenched his fists in anticipation of action. Snezhana nervously played with the ends of her hair.

"Has anyone seen Yaromir this morning?"

Heads were shaken in response.

"We will start without him." Tosh quickly strode to one end of the table, typed a few commands into the keyboard, and the microphones sprang to life by showing a green light on each. His team members sat tensely in their mesh-backed conference room seats. Tosh then turned to his operatives who had puzzled looks on their faces and answered their unspoken question.

"I don't have all the details yet, but this is an extremely important joint operation that we will be doing with the Americans and the British. My boss, Alexei Alexeev, will be listening in from his office."

"While we're waiting, Tosh, were you serious when you offered me an AK-103 assault rifle? I'd love to have that rifle to add to my collection. I am quite fond of my Vintorez. It's silent and uses armor-piercing ammo. Just a solid sniper rifle. But the AK looks poised to kill, with its sleek lines, curved magazine, and pistol grip. It looks ready to pounce on its prey. With the addition of Picatinny rails, I could bolt on add-ons such as the night vision, telescopic scope, and even add a grenade launcher to it."

Tosh's grey eyes crinkled in appreciation of Anatoly's love of weaponry. "We'll requisition it for you today."

"Thanks, Tosh. I do hope this is a good job. That mission you sent me on in January was all right. But the one before it was a nightmare. I did enjoy Amsterdam, though."

"You're unusually garrulous, Anatoly," Snezhana observed.

"I have been home too long."

Snezhana surveyed him and added, "You look armed and dangerous."

"Be careful or you'll learn the hard way that I am," Anatoly growled.

Snezhana clapped her hands. "That's my Anatoly back!"

Tosh raised an eyebrow and cleared his throat to get their attention. He looked at each one of them, sitting forward in their chairs to catch each word as it came out of his mouth.

Anatoly had his large hands on the top of the table, and his chair was pushed slightly back from the table, so he could leap up quickly if needed. He reminded Tosh of a panther ready to strike. Yuri was studiously sitting ramrod straight in his chair with his arms grasping the chair arms. He was wide-eyed, but more from curiosity rather than from fear.

Snezhana was swiveling in her chair, scanning the room and taking in all the details. She had her hair tied back into a short ponytail that swung slightly from side to side when she moved her head. Now that Snezhana was going to be an active agent, Tosh made a mental note to talk to her after the meeting about needing to cut her hair shorter. Long hair was a professional liability, a fact that she had already learned the hard way.

Out loud Tosh said, "Please, partake of the coffee, tea, and pastries. We are waiting for the others to gather and then we'll all be briefed at once." He pointed to a small table against the wall where coffee, tea, water, and pastries were laid out.

Anatoly was the first to jump up and reach the pastry table. He grinned as he spotted the sweet cheese-filled sochniki pastries in the mix. "*Spasibo*, Tosh." He snatched two off the platter, rolled them into a napkin, and returned to the table.

"You did leave some pastries for the rest of us?" Yuri teased, knowing how much Anatoly loved his sochniki. Anatoly opened his mouth and showed Yuri the half-chewed dough on his tongue.

"Gads! Men! You two are like children," Snezhana said in mock disgust, as she poured herself a cup of tea.

"*Sidet'*!" Tosh's barked command brought them back to the table. "I'm glad to see everyone getting along so well. The team training from last month seems to be paying off. However, I have yet to see how it translates into a well-coordinated killing squad. *Focus.* This mission has many players involved and promises to be intense."

Tosh responded with irritation to a knock on the conference room door. "Yuri, answer that, but in the corridor – we cannot be interrupted once this starts."

Yuri strode out of the room and promptly returned, a concerned look on his face.

"What?"

"Sir, it seems as if Yaromir has been hit by a car and is in critical condition in the hospital."

A flicker in Tosh's eyes showed his concern. "Perhaps this operation has already begun…"

Chapter Four

Elda sat locked alone in her farmhouse secure communications room that she had built off the spare bedroom. It was a small cluttered room with no windows, a wooden desk with drawers and a file cabinet, a large monitor with quality speakers, and a battery backup to ensure the room always had power and connectivity. There was a small set of humming servers and a few monitors off to one side. A weapons cache was also hidden behind a floor-to-ceiling case. Patiently staring at the monitor in front of her, Elda found her mind wandering. After checking she was on mute, she mused out loud. "How many years have I sat in this cramped space, alone, ready to receive my instructions? I wish Dawn could understand the world I operate in, but unless you have lived it, you cannot fully know what it's like. I used to be terrified. Now I feel dead inside. I probably have burnt out my adrenal glands by now." She glanced at the conference call and seeing nothing was happening yet, continued with her thoughts. "How much of the real me have I traded in doing the work I've done? Have I made the difference that I hope to make? Can I stop doing this, when it's all I know, and this is my community?"

Movement on the screen drew her attention back fully to the meeting. She could see the other meeting attendees in their respective locations, sitting down and focusing their attention to their monitors. Her display was split into four windows of unequal sizes. In one small portion the Russian team's conference room was shown and subtitled *Moscow*. At the bottom of Elda's segment there was a label, *USA*. Her boss, Ed, was in a third portion, also labeled *USA*. Ed was adjusting his glasses over his dark brown eyes, squinting at the screen and trying to flatten his cowlicked hair, when the monitor flashed on. He was alone in a windowless room that appeared to be the size of a closet. In the last portion of the screen, an operations room, similar to the Russian one, had three people sitting at the table, who Elda would soon find out were, Oliver, Sophia and James Richardson, a senior MI6 agent. Their screen had the title, *London*.

Aha, you sneaks! You are *operatives!* Elda sat back smiling as she recognized the amorous couple from her last operation in St. Petersburg. *There* was *something off about you two. But you* almost *fooled me!*

Elda's speaker crackled to life. A tall, distinguished looking man with salt-and-pepper hair, stood, turned toward the camera, tapped on his microphone, and spoke in a highbrow British accent. "I'm glad to see you all. I'm sure you are wondering what this is all about. Allow me to introduce myself. I am James Richardson, and I am a senior MI6 handler/operative here in London. Let me also introduce the team members to each other. Sitting with me here in London are John and Sonia, both MI6 agents. In the USA we have Elaine and Tom. And in Moscow we have Ted with his team—Tony, Jim, Sue.

Tosh interrupted, "Yes, we have met, and I would suspect have files on each person, in fact, Elda Ainsworth and I met many years ago when she was a lieutenant in the United States Navy. Perhaps we could skip the pseudo names and get real here. We are going to be working closely with each other and that requires we be able to trust that each is telling the truth."

Elda added, "Thank you Tosh. It's a pleasure to see you again, Yuri. You may not recall, James, that Yuri has worked for me in the past."

Unembarrassed James went on, "Ah yes. Well then, Oliver and Sophia are sitting here with me. Tosh, Anatoly, and Yuri are in Moscow. Elda and Ed are in the US. I did forget that many of you have met previously."

Anatoly grunted. Snezhana reached up behind her neck to touch her ponytail. Elda squinted and nodded.

James took a deep breath. "Now for why you are here: There is chatter on the dark web about a team of elite assassins being put together to eliminate major heads of state. The prime minister of England, the president of the United States, and the Russian president are the three that have definitely been identified as their targets. Their mission is apparently a long-term play, where the assassins have chosen the 2021 G20 Summit, which is planned to be held in Italy, tentatively, in the town of Bari, perhaps though, in Rome. According to our research, the three leaders will be there for an extended period of time, and it is a hard location to secure properly. This locale has a number of areas that afford possibilities for taking all three of them out at once, or if need be, one at a time. Their team also has ample time to place assassins unnoticed within the community. Therefore, we need to take this chatter seriously."

Tosh interrupted and asked, "But why all three leaders?"

"Excellent question, Tosh. We suspect that it is potentially a play by China to take world dominance. It could be North Korea too, but the MO seems to point more at China.

Elda broke in, "But could this be a ruse by Russia to disrupt our security systems and continue sowing chaos in the US and other Western nations?"

"We would normally suspect Russia too, but they have asked for our help and are seated at this table. I'm postulating that, with the three countries, who have been most strongly opposed to China's activities in Hong Kong and around Japan, made leaderless, those countries will be thrown into turmoil and China will be free to expand their influence further."

He paused to let this information sink in. Elda leaned forward with her hand holding her chin. She observed how the others were taking in the briefing. Tosh's face was calm. His grey eyes were scanning the room. Yuri sat wide eyed and open mouthed. Anatoly scratched his head. Snezhana looked like she would bounce off her chair in delight. Ed nodded sagely, as if he had expected something like this. Sophia had reached out and was now holding Oliver's hand under the table.

Ed inquired, "What do you have as an modus operandi? I would suspect Russia first, since they have been working to disrupt the United States for many years now. China has also been working to capture the US corporation intellectual property and trade secrets, as well as quietly disrupt their elections. But I can't see either country as being rash enough to take out those three leaders."

James nervously cleared his throat. "The electronic signatures point to China. However, it could very well be Russia."

Tosh disagreed, "History has shown us that all three of these aforementioned countries use digital footprints to point at each other. However, I do know that I and my team are here in good faith to help stop whatever is threatening our nations. It is not Russia."

Scratching his head and shifting his weight to one side, James answered, "Frankly, we just don't know enough, but we MUST get ahead of these assassins, if, as the messages imply, they are deploying now." James coughed, adjusted his tie, and consulted his notes before continuing. "We have assembled this joint team from the United States, the United Kingdom, and Russia to find and remove these assassins before they can do any harm. You are looking at the team members now, with the exception of an additional resource from the United States and one more from Russia. These people will be identified and introduced as soon as we have them. MI6 will help set up your communication equipment and electronic *toys*, and they will help continue the search on the dark web and any social networking sites for more clues."

Elda brightened at the mention of MI6's electronics and noticed Anatoly's eyes lit up too. James carried on. "It is *crucial* that this team find and eliminate the killers before the Summit, the sooner the better, in case they decide to accelerate the plans and target the 2020 Summit in Riyadh, Saudi Arabia. However, we have no concrete information at this time about who the killers are except for the one code name: *Operation Bittman."*

Elda made a mental note to follow up with Ed, since he had cocked his head and frowned at the mention of the code name. Right now, Ed was typing rapidly on his phone. Elda's phone beeped with an incoming message. She glanced down at a text directed at herself and at another analyst, David. *I have heard that codename before. I want to find and analyze the data we have about anything named Bittman, in preparation for our own team meeting. Also, get me all available information on the 2019, 2020 and 2021 G20 Summits, on the town of Bari in Italy, on Riyadh in Saudi Arabia, and full bios and habits of the Prime Minister of England, the Russian president, and our president. Oh, and any and all information that you have on the UK and Russian teams. Put everyone available on this. Get me the information as you find it. Don't wait for it to be complete.*

James went on, "We do know that at some time during this year, these killers are being brought in from all across the world to train together in a remote area around Florence, Italy, possibly Montepulciano or San Gimignano. They then will split up to continue various aspects of their training in different parts of Italy and potentially, in another country, to train for the Saudi Arabian contingency."

Most of the operatives frowned at the vagueness of the information. Elda broke in, "James what do you have that is real data that we can move forward on?"

James responded, "We are working hard to get you all some actionable intel. In the meantime, we need to set up the joint operations and command post, so that this team can start training together."

He looked pointedly at Elda, Anatoly, and Tosh. "One word of warning. Whatever went on between you folks during the last operation you were on as foes, is over. You will check any unfinished business at the door for the duration of this exercise. We are now one team. You will support each other. Understand?"

Anatoly's eyes narrowed as he looked at Elda, but he nodded in agreement. Elda was disgruntled and uncomfortable with the operation, but reluctantly nodded. Tosh sighed and acknowledged the command, "*Da. Ya ponimayu.*"

James took a deep breath, squared his shoulders, and asked, "Any questions?"

The meeting participants sat mute in their various locations. The enormity of the operation and the scant amount of information had floored them.

The pregnant silence hung heavy over the virtual room. Finally, Elda cleared her throat and asked, "Decision by committee is never effective. If this is a joint operation, who is the ultimate decision-maker?"

"Good question," James answered. "We will have a remote command center in London, with Ed, myself, and Tosh's boss, Alexei. I will speak for this committee of three, and any decision will be a consensus from us. If there is no consensus, I will make the final decision. In the field, since he is an experienced handler, Tosh will pull the operatives together in a command center nearer the action, and run the agents: Oliver, Sophia, Anatoly, Yuri, Snezhana, and the new agents joining the team. Elda will be the senior operative in the field. Both Elda and Tosh bring valuable skills to the table, and they will speak with one voice. If there is a conflict and no time to escalate, since Russia has more agents in the field, Elda will decide, to ensure fairness and balance."

"We need a codename for ourselves," Snezhana mentioned.

Anatoly growled at the thought. "Codenames. How cute. What are we, schoolchildren?"

Sophia spoke up, "It's a good idea."

Snezhana sneered at her, "Oh, you took your eyes off Oliver long enough to attend to what's being said."

Elda clapped her hands for attention. "I think we should be called the Terriers. We are barking and posturing and nipping at each other's heels."

James decided, "The Terriers it is."

Anatoly growled, "You won't catch me using a codename. *Bezumnyy*!"

In frustration, Sophia threw a wadded-up napkin at her screen.

Tosh inquired, "So are we going to Italy?"

Elda chided him, "You just want to see your lady again."

"Don't you?"

Elda paused a beat before replying, "I'd love to."

James took control again. "We may have to go to Italy. I want us to gather more actionable intel before we do that. We will get together and train while waiting for the information. Are there any other *serious* questions?"

"When do we expect new data?" Yuri inquired.

James shifted on his feet and scratched his head, as he replied, "We have no idea. Our researchers are diligently scanning the web for anything that may give us another clue."

"*Der'mo*. So, we really know nothing actionable?" Anatoly slammed his fist on the table in disgust.

"I expect we will all conduct ourselves in a professional manner," James primly reprimanded Anatoly. "We know that something is in the work. We know assassins are being deployed, perhaps as we speak. We know we have to stop them. We just need the who and the where. Get ready to deploy in a moment's notice."

Anatoly shook his head in response and snorted.

James deflected the conversation by asking, "Do we have the rest of the team members identified yet, Tosh and Ed?"

Tosh looked up from his phone and spoke up. "I've identified the other agent from Russia. He'll help set up all of the equipment and will monitor the dark web."

A fifth box opened up on the screen. Elda noted Anatoly's approval nod when the pale slender face of a young man appeared on the screen.

Elda inquired of Anatoly, "You know this man, Anatoly?"

Anatoly smiled as he answered, "*Da*, Elda. He is a hacker I know from apartment 804 in Moscow. Well done, Tosh, a good choice."

James directed the new arrival, "Please unmute and introduce yourself."

"*Dobroye utro*. Ah, good morning. I am Stas Garin. My specialty is digital information. I'm honored to be part of this team."

Tosh continued speaking. "Stas will be located with Elda and myself. We'll start working with him immediately to set up the communication network for this team."

Tosh's cell phone beeped. Diverted he merely said, "I'm done. Over."

Ed had been distractedly looking at his computer. He turned and volunteered, "James, we have also located the last member of our team."

A sixth box opened up on the screen and in it was a pleasant looking man in his mid-thirties who could have passed for a corporate executive or a schoolteacher. He had short brown hair and glasses framing a square face with a dimpled chin. His brown eyes sparkled with intelligence and a sense of humor. His Oxford-cut blue shirt was open at the neck, and he wore a dark-blue blazer, which emphasized his large shoulders.

"Hello all, I'm David Miller. I'm associated with the CIA and on loan to your task force. My background is in logistics and analysis, financial trading, and manipulation."

Ed spoke again. "David can be useful in helping trace the money financing this operation, as well as helping to analyze their next steps. He has also done some field work and is a capable operative. He can pair with Snezhana in the field to plan and analyze day by day movements."

Elda sensed the energy from each attendee perk up at the addition of the new team members. She noticed Snezhana smiling suggestively at David and Tosh frowning at Snezhana. She also took note that when Snezhana caught Tosh's look, she immediately dropped her smile and sat straighter in her chair.

"May I have your attention again," James said.

All eyes turned back to their screens.

"Now that we are all gathered, the next step is to ensure we can work together as a team. You will collect what you need and meet here at MI6 in London, in three days, for additional training and tools from MI6 at their facilities in London. You will then travel to the RAF Northolt base, near London, where you will have more intensive training. I expect that you will act as a SWAT team and deploy the necessary resources when we find out the locations."

"Will it be possible to bring my own weapons?"

Tosh acknowledged Anatoly's question. "Yes, Anatoly, and you will be able to keep any new ones too."

Elda's eyes lit up. "Do we have free rein in MI6's *toy room*?"

"Within limits, yes."

"Yes!" Elda smiled and pumped her fist.

"If there are no further questions, I will see you all in three days." With that, James terminated the connection. The screens in all locations went dark.

***

Alexei slowly turned off his computer. Glancing at his watch, he decided to see how his recruits were doing. He reached into his bottom drawer and pulled out his service revolver and placed it into a shoulder holster under a black business suit jacket. He left his office with surprising speed.

***

Elda stared at the black screen for a moment and then powered off her computer. She sat in the stillness of the room and cursed that she had promised Dawn that there would be no more trips, no more fieldwork. She hated the thought of yet another argument over Elda's missions. She recognized that she was risking their relationship. Why had Dawn become so insistent that Elda retire, when for years she was happy to enjoy the benefits of Elda's work, and claimed she enjoyed her alone time while Elda was traveling? Elda had worked hard to save for their home here in Maine. And it was all in Dawn's name. Of course, that was for safety's sake. It wouldn't do to have Elda's name on anything not connected to her career. She went by Dawn's last name in the small town they were next to. She

56

shook her head. It wouldn't be solved by perseverating on it. It was time to go and face the music.

"What do you think, Vee? Can you take good care of your other mommy while I'm gone?" Vee wagged her tail, licked Elda's face, and jumped off her lap.

"I'll take that as a yes."

Elda took a deep breath, squared her shoulders, opened the door, and marched behind Vee up the wide wooden stairs into the bedroom. She stood looking lovingly at Dawn peacefully sleeping in their bed. Suddenly Dawn rolled over and groggily asked, "When do you leave?"

Elda was always amazed at Dawn's ability to intuit what was going on with her, even when half asleep. She braced herself for the upcoming fight and answered, "I have to be in London in three days."

Dawn sighed heavily. "Come back to bed and get some sleep. We'll talk in the morning." Elda gratefully climbed back between the cotton sheets and under the down comforter and wrapped her arms around Dawn. Vee lobbied for bed real estate by wiggling her little body between them.

***

After the video conference Snezhana sat silently, her hands clenched in her lap. *Elda.* Her mind floated back to when she had first met Elda. She had been sent by her uncle to follow her. She had been very careful but somehow Elda had detected her. As she searched for Elda in a store dressing room, Elda had reached out and grabbed her by her ponytail and yanked her into the room. She pressed a knife against her throat and whispered into Snezhana's ear, "One more shriek like that and I'll cut your throat. Who are you? And why are you following me?"

"I will tell you nothing." Snezhana had felt so confident that she could resist interrogation.

But then Elda increased the pressure of the knife on her throat. Blood welled up at the cut and trickled down Snezhana's neck. Elda touched the blood, showed it to Snezhana, and smeared it on Snezhana's cheek. Elda had demanded, "I ask you again. Who are you?"

Snezhana had defiantly answered, "I am Snezhana Chelovek. You will get nothing more from me. I doubt that you will kill me."

"Do not doubt me, young pup. Hmm… Chelovek. You are related to Tosh then? I thought you reminded me of him. Now tell me why I shouldn't kill you."

Snezhana blurted out, "He is my uncle." She felt so ashamed at having caved so easily. She could still hear Elda's laugh as she removed the knife from her neck and swiftly cut off Snezhana's ponytail.

Elda put her trophy into her shopping bag saying, "*Tam*. I have relieved you of a liability and saved your life. You owe me one. Go back to Moscow and tell your *dyadya* what happened."

Elda…

***

Tosh turned from the blank screen and powered down the video equipment. He unplugged the internet just to be sure that the connection was gone. He commanded, "You will pack the essentials and come back here by lunchtime."

Yuri inquired, "Will you supply lunch?"

Tosh barked, "Focus! We have little time left for the four of you to learn to operate as a well-oiled machine. You three have been training together, but now we also have Stas. We will work together to gather as much preliminary information as we can and will memorize completely the profiles of your new teammates. We will not embarrass Mother Russia at all in this joint operation. Understand?"

The team parroted back, "*Da, Ser.*"

"*Idti!*"

Chairs smoothly rolled back. The three operatives stood to leave.

"*Snezhana*. Stay."

"*Da, dyadya* Tosh… I mean *sudar'* … *Akh*, Tosh … sir." Snezhana stammered. The door closed behind her, leaving her no escape.

Tosh ignored her attempt to correct her mistake of calling him uncle at the office and continued: "Cut your hair immediately. We are going after top notch assassins, and, as you have already experienced, they will use that long hair to catch you or to drag you. It is a liability in a hand-to-hand fight. That is an order. If you do not, I *will* replace you on the team."

Snezhana reached back and protectively held her hair that had slipped out of the topknot on her way over to Tosh's office. She swiftly tied it up into a short ponytail and answered, "*Da.* I will."

"*Khorosho*. The next thing I wish to discuss is your nocturnal activities."

Snezhana's eyes widened in surprise.

"You must stop picking up strangers. You can too easily be set up. There are plenty of safe companions for you."

Tosh stood tall and shook his finger at Snezhana. "You will apply yourself. You will work hard to learn a lot in a short amount of time. I selected you for this team to help glue it together. Anatoly and Yuri are good at in their own areas, but they are used to working alone. Your knowledge of computers will help bridge and translate Anatoly's lack of knowledge with Stas' deep skills. You will help Anatoly control his temper and you will help Yuri use his logistics to move the team forward. I am taking a risk on you. For the duration of this mission, I am not your uncle and, should you fail, I will remove you from the team and bar you from this profession. Do you clearly understand the stakes here?"

"*Da, ser.*"

"Now go back to your apartment and pack. Here's a card for a hairdresser on the way back here. He is extremely good and also a bit light on his feet, which will avoid the other issue, since there will be no temptation for you to return to his apartment."

Snezhana stared at the card.

"*Idti!*"

She grabbed the card and ran out the door.

***

How did he know about the men she'd slept with? It was amazing what he could find out. Snezhana walked quickly home. She checked the tell she had left on her door before entering her apartment. Good. No one else had entered while she was away. Once in her apartment, she immediately dialed the number that Tosh had given her and made an appointment for her haircut. She hung up and looked at her image in the mirror. She would miss her long hair. She'd been growing it out again after the incident with Elda.

She grabbed her camouflage-colored kit from her closet and set it on her bed and quickly filled it with black and dull colored clothing, a small stiletto knife with thigh holder, and different passports with an assortment of various pictures, names and countries, and money of different currencies and in various denominations. A well-worn rectangular barreled, nine mm PYa pistol with slide action and concealed hammer completed her packing.

Snezhana scanned the apartment one last time, then picked up her go-bag, wallet, cell phone, and keys and left for the hairdresser. She would make her uncle proud of her.

***

Yuri Kuznetsov glanced around his apartment trying to figure out what he should pack for this mission. He thought of the good time he had on his last mission in London, with the two girls. Sasha nibbled at his ear and her hair tickled his cheek while Dasha pressed against his side, trying to get under his t-shirt. He so missed having dogs.

The phone rang sharply. Yuri fumbled to grab his phone on the small bedside table. "*Chert!*" He swore as the phone fell onto and bounced on the brown linoleum covered floor. He tripped in his lunge to grab the phone and fell on top of it. *I really need to vacuum under the bed. Perhaps it's time to get a house cleaner,* he thought as he lay there. By the time he reached his phone and unlocked it, the call had gone to his messages.

He sat on the floor, rubbing his hand on his buzz cut brown hair. He rubbed his baby blue eyes and shook his head to focus his attention. He entered his passcode and checked his messages. It was from Tosh, sending a generic list of items to remember to pack, since Yuri was not seasoned as a spy yet. Yuri forced himself to pick up the pace. His superior logistical skills in helping others somehow hadn't translated to his personal life.

Checking his list from Tosh, Yuri moved quickly to gather items for the mission.

I must be missing something…

He checked the list and saw he had covered all the categories. He shrugged and exited his small, sparsely furnished apartment, taking the inside stairs two at a time down to the street. He started to jog toward the Kremlin.

***

"You're back early."

"I know Tosh, but I haven't worked with you as long as Anatoly has, and I haven't known you as long as Snezhana has. I wanted to talk more about the mission before the entire group is here and you move us forward on your already planned agenda."

"Why? Didn't you hear everything that I said?" Tosh demanded.

"Yes, but what else have *you* concluded so far, Tosh?"

"These things are never what they appear to be, Yuri. You must be suspicious of anyone you meet. Is this an attempt by MI6 and/or the United States government to get more information on how we operate? Is one of those countries behind this all or could it be China, or North Korea, or both together, or even Russia? I would never admit in front of those from the US and UK that it could be Russia, but I don't trust Alexei. He has obtained his position by compromising others and climbing over people while he stabs them in the back. He is not very skilled at the business, but he does play politics well. And I don't trust our new companions. Do they really want our help or are they hoping to weaken us and take the advantage? Are the messages so far even real or a smokescreen for some other reason? Perhaps it is to get our team out of the way so another operation can be pulled off without interference?"

Yuri nodded.

Tosh continued, "We don't know the real answers yet, but we must have theories. We must be ready for any of these situations to happen, or even something we haven't thought about yet. Trust no one and question all that you see, hear, or read. We need to take it one day at a time and sift through all the grains of information to see if we have enough to make a cohesive pattern. We need to look at each piece of information from many angles."

"What do you expect of me, Tosh?"

"I fear you will not be able to see what Elda is up to clearly because you like her. If she was pointing a gun at you, could you kill her?"

Yuri's eyes grew big. He shook his head and replied, "*Ya ne znayu.*" He grimaced and implored, "Would I have to?"

"Decide. You may well have to."

***

Elda sat at her old farmhouse kitchen table, idly stroking the well-worn wooden top and sipping her coffee. Across from her, two sets of eyes, one dark brown and one baby blue, stared at her reproachfully. Elda opened her mouth to speak, but Dawn held up her finger and shushed her.

65

"I know, dear. I've heard it all before. When you get back, we'll need to find a way to resolve this issue, though. I feel unimportant in your life and sad that you're leaving again. But that's not new and we won't solve that now. I know there is nothing I can say to change your mind. You have told me that you will be gone for only one to two weeks. It can wait that long. It's been going on for years."

Vee wagged her tail in agreement. Elda stayed silent and looked down at the table.

Dawn sadly shook her head, slowly stood up, stepped around the table, and firmly hugged Elda. "It would be easier if I didn't love you and our life together so much."

Elda sighed and asked, "Perhaps we should try counseling again?"

"Perhaps," Dawn responded flatly, "But you would have to *really* want to go this time. It can't just be a checkbox to please me. For now, why don't we call Korinna and Egor and have them and the troodles over for dinner tonight? We can relax and have some fun before you have to leave. I know your go-bag is already packed and you're just waiting to hear from Ed the arrangements to get to the UK."

Elda blinked rapidly to hold back her emotions. "I love you, Dawn."

"I know." Dawn turned and strode over and picked up her phone to call Korinna and Egor.

67

Chapter Five

"Attention on deck!"

The trainees in the metal and concrete hanger snapped to attention, heels clicking as one.

"At ease."

With precision the group shifted position. A tall middle-aged portly man in a business suit marched up in front of the assembly. "You are all here on behalf of Mother Russia. Your miserable little lives were saved from the hellhole prisons you were rotting in on death's row or life imprisonment. Succeed in this mission and you will reclaim your freedom. Die for this mission and your families will be well taken care of for the rest of their lives. Fail and you will learn what serving hard time is all about. And if you thought it was miserable before, just wait—it can, and it will, get worse. Resist and the price is death. Understand?"

The recruits yelled, "Yes, sir!"

The man ran his hand over his hair and continued. "Your initial military indoctrination training is over. You will now undergo intensive specialized training. You are all accomplished killers, but we are going to turn you into trained assassins. The best may potentially have a job with this service in the future. You will follow orders without question. Understand?”

“*Da, ser*!” they yelled.

“Our mission is to distract, delay and eliminate enemy teams. The top squad will have the job of assassinating our primary target. Work hard and that could be one of you in that squad. Our mission will severely weaken our enemy and potentially spark a civil war within their nation.” He pointed at each one of them in the front row. “Look to your left. Now look to your right. That man will not survive the training. We only keep the best. Understand?”

They shouted in unison, “*Da!*”

“Who is this for?”

“For Mother Russia!”

“Louder!”

The retort echoed loudly off the metal walls, “For Mother Russia!”

“Instructors, they are now yours.”

The man pivoted on his heel and toe and marched out of the room, the sound of his footsteps lingering behind.

***

A man wearing a Vietnam War–era army uniform stood screaming by the fence in front of the White House. He pulled out a revolver and began shooting into the air. Tourists scattered. The Secret Service ran down with their weapons drawn.

The man held his weapon to his head. "Don't come any closer or I will kill myself."

The lead Secret Service agent quickly called for a negotiator.

Behind the White House, a small team carefully skulked from tree to tree, and then slithered across the grass, making their way to the entrance, without setting off the alarms. Dressed in business suits, they split up and confidently walked through the halls.

In advance of them, sprinted a soldier in camouflage uniform. He kicked open a door, only to be faced by two of their prey. Before they could react, he cut them down with two silenced rapid bursts from his submachine gun. He then wheeled around and sprinted deeper into the building. One of the businessmen walked calmly along behind him, stopping only to check that the two were dead.

Turning a corner, the soldier almost ran down another target and easily shot him on his way by. The man that followed rolled the body casually to one side and continued on. The soldier kicked in a second door and was immediately riddled with bullets.

"Stop!" The lights went on and the simulated White House disappeared.

"*Nyet*. Not quick enough. You have failed. You will start again from the beginning."

The instructor stalked out of the building and over to an adjacent one.

"Start."

The set darkened and a 3-D map of Montreal rotated in the air. Below the city the map sunk down into a second view of the underground city and tunnels.

"Memorize it. Every street, every tunnel. Go."

***

A small team of soldiers walked along the streets of Washington, DC, in the woods northwest of Moscow. Passing groups of tourists they wandered along the National Mall, heading in the direction of the Lincoln Memorial. When they reached the halfway point they fanned out into the streets. One man stood on his own, checking the street sign against his map and turning in circles.

A disembodied voice called out from above. "Vladimir, where are you?"

"I am not sure. There is no street sign."

"Halt! Vladimir, leave the group immediately and report back to me. The rest continue."

Vladimir dejectedly stepped off of the curb at 14th Street SW into the mud and leaves. He swung onto the gravel trail and marched to the small hut at the end. He took a deep breath and opened the door. Stepping inside, he was surrounded by large screen monitors and microphones. Instructors in black and white camouflage uniforms were monitoring different groups in various mock scenes. He reluctantly marched up and stood in front of his instructor.

"Reporting as ordered, *ser*."

His instructor scowled at him. "There is no room for failure, Vladimir."

"*Da, ser*."

"You know what to do. Your family will be well taken care of."

Vladimir nodded, took a deep breath, and bit down hard. He crumpled to the dirty wooden floor. A white foam bubbled from his mouth. The instructor snapped his fingers.

“Dispose of him.”

***

They stood at attention on the cracked concrete runway. They were wearing camouflage uniforms without any insignia, their black Corfam shoes shining in the sunlight.

“At ease!”

As if one, they shifted into position.

“Your training is completed. You all have your orders and your new identification. You have been preassigned group numbers. When I call your group number you will assemble next to the runway for your plane. The planes will start to arrive here in fifteen minutes. You have never been here. You have never seen this place. Understand?”

A chorus of affirmation followed: “*Da, ser.*”

“Excellent. Operation Bittman has commenced. Now go over by your bags and wait for your group to be called.”

A swarm of black and gray, peppered by green, white, and brown, flowed off the runway over to the nearby grassy field. Two remained.

“Your operatives are in place?”

"Yes, we have already removed one of the Russian team and are receiving information from within MI6."

"And we are sure there is only this one small group to dispose of?"

"Yes, we should have no problems. We have the advantage of numbers and of knowing who and where they are. Even if they dispatch more operatives in addition to these, our inside mole will let us know their identities. We will divide and eliminate each team as they spin up."

"Do it. We must accomplish our mission of sowing chaos to degrade democracy. Pick them off as they deploy. Put suspicion on their allies."

"Yes sir."

***

A de Havilland Canada DHC-3 Otter single-engine, high-wing, propeller-driven, short take-off and landing (STOL) plane bumped across a remote field northwest of Montreal. It jarred to a stop in the middle of the field, near a waiting van that had its side windows covered over. A squad of soldiers, dressed in black and white camouflage, jumped out and ran across the field to the black Mercedes Sprinter van. One man hopped into the passenger seat and the rest smoothly filled the seats in the back, sliding the side door closed after the last one. The driver started the van and in a cloud of dust accelerated southeast.

"You're clear to land."

An Antonov An-32 Russian turboprop, twin-engine Military Transport plane came in fast for a landing at Pulkovo Airport in St. Petersburg, Russia. It skidded to a stop at the end of the runway where two black Lada XRAY SUVs were waiting.

Boots hit the ground as a small squad of black and white camouflage attired soldiers sprinted off the plane and leapt into the cars. The vehicles immediately took off leaving dark black skid marks on the tarmac. They exited the airport at a high speed and convoyed north.

***

A de Havilland Otter float plane skimmed the top of the water and landed off the coast of South Carolina. Two men in civilian clothes swung off the plane and into a small dingy and rowed over to a waiting white, thirty-four foot, bullet-shaped Azimut Atlantis yacht. Once the men were on board, the yacht took off in a beeline for the coast. The plane sped off, flying low to avoid detection.

***

Off the eastern coast of Delaware in the United States, a grey, blue striped, United States Air Force surplus, large, twin–engine amphibious seaplane, the Grumman HU-16

Albatross Flying Boat, flew under the radar, dangerously close to the water. A few minutes after it landed, a squad of soldiers in green, white, and brown camouflage jumped off into the water and swam to a waiting Lazzara 80 foot Alchemist yacht. The yacht and plane quickly took off in different directions.

***

His phone vibrated in his jacket pocket. He quickly left the others and walked outside to hide around the corner of the building and answer it in private.

"*Privet.*"

He listened carefully.

"They are in place? Good. I will leave here at a suitable moment to assume command."

He frowned and shook his head.

"*Nyet, nyet.* Do not wait for me. I will get there when I can leave here. Keep on schedule. Remember the mission is to derail them from their original plans, lure them away from the real target and to kill as many of them as possible. We will pick off each team as they deploy."

He held the phone tightly to his ear to catch every word.

"Correct. It's a go. Start now."

Chapter Six

A pile of go-bags was stacked against the bookcase on one side of the large operations room. Metal file cabinets flanked the bags on both sides. The overhead florescent lights threw a harsh white glow onto the occupants of the windowless room. A whiteboard filled one side wall of the room. A dark blue couch and a wooden side table that had seen better days were placed next to a small refrigerator at the back of the room. A coffee pot and cups graced the top of the refrigerator. Paper lunch bags were lined up along the top of the table. A slim pile of brown folders was stacked at each seat around the conference room table.

"What is this, Tosh?" asked Yuri, sitting down in front of one of the piles.

Tosh walked around the table, pointing at each pile. "We will eat and work while waiting for transport. In front of each of you is a stack of folders. There is a folder on Elda, Ed, James, Sophia, and Oliver. Stacked underneath these are folders on myself, Snezhana, Anatoly, and Yuri. Stas does not yet have a folder, but do include him in this exercise. Read through these folders and rank them from most dangerous to least. We will discuss your reasoning after you rank them all. I have done my own ranking. Now read while I enjoy my cup of tea." He sat down at the head of the table, put his feet up on another chair and slowly sipped his tea, carefully observing each team member. "Start!"

Anatoly snarled, "*Der'mo*. I thought I was done with pop quizzes after I graduated."

"You graduated?" Yuri gave Anatoly an engaging smile.

Snezhana snapped, "Shush, Yuri, I'm trying to think."

Anatoly whopped Yuri on top of his head with a folder. After a stern look from Tosh, they all grabbed a lunch bag and settled down to their assigned task, while munching on their sandwiches. Quickly finishing, Snezhana doublechecked her answers and flipped her paper to signify she was done.

After ten minutes, Tosh checked in to see if they were ready: "*Sdelano*?"

"*Da.*"

Tosh singled out Stas. "Stas, you're up first. Who's your most dangerous?"

Stas stood up to answer. Tosh barked, "Sit!"

Stas fell back in his chair and stuttered, "Definitely Anatoly is the most dangerous."

"*Pochemu*?" demanded Tosh.

Wide eyed, Stas threw his arms out, exclaiming "Just look at him!"

Everybody laughed and Anatoly scowled his meanest.

Tosh acknowledged Stas' selections and continued grilling him, "Okay. Who is the least dangerous?"

Stas grinned and pointed his hands at his chest, replying, "Myself of course."

Tosh said sharply, "And, again, why?"

"Just look at me!" Stas got up and stood next to Anatoly, who rose out of his chair and flexed his muscles. Anatoly's bicep was bigger than Stas' thigh.

Undeterred, Tosh continued to grill Stas, "And where would you put Elda?"

Stas waved the thought of Elda being a threat away and replied, "Easy, she's a woman and she's old. I would put her just above me."

"*Interesnyy...*" Tosh's face showed no emotion. Yuri's body was shaking as he stifled a laugh. Anatoly shook his head. Snezhana raised her hand to go next.

Tosh pointed at Snezhana and commanded, "Your most and least?"

"Most, Elda. She beat you, Anatoly, and me in the last operation. She is unpredictable and deceptively strong. She's also a master at disguises."

Tosh acknowledged her answer with a nod. "And least?"

"Stas. He has no training. His computer knowledge is worth a lot, but he is completely unskilled at the spy game."

Tosh nodded again and quizzed the rest of the team. When done, he wrote a synopsis of the replies on the white board. "Look at just these two responses." He paused to let the team absorb what was on the whiteboard, then continued. "There are *many* different ways to define dangerous. Stas went by the physical attributes and those that we normally attribute to gender. However, we've learned *not* to discount Elda because she's an older female."

Pointedly staring at Snezhana, Tosh continued, "As Snezhana pointed out, Elda is unexpectedly strong, and fast, but *most of all*, clever. She's kept up to date on new techniques, but she is also well versed in those methods that we learned during the Cold War. And this combination allows her to run circles around agents half her age."

Stas frowned and then hung his head. Yuri gave him a comforting swat that knocked Stas' glasses off.

"*Khorosho*." Tosh stood in front of the room and glared at his team. "Remember: We will learn more about each person while working with them, including those who are sitting around this table. Learn from each other and from our new teammates, but do *not* let your guard down. Don't trust any of these new people. Just as we are trying to grow our folders on them, they will be adding particulars on us, as they glean it, to theirs. At the end of this mission these folders on our opponents need to be doubled in size. Keep in mind that in the end, these people are not our friends, they are our enemies. *Ponimayu?*"

"*Ya ponimayu.*"

"*Da.*"

"*Da, ser.*"

"*Da.*"

"And what did we learn about Sophia and Oliver?"

Snezhana snorted, "Those two?!"

"Yes, *those two*, Snezhana. Assess them."

"Sophia is in MI-6 operations but has not had an extensive amount of field experience. She met Oliver on a mission, and they fell in love and are newlyweds. Oliver went rogue in his last mission and was injured. I think because of their involvement with each other and youth that they are potentially weak links in this operation."

"Well done, Snezhana. You can see how personal involvement can endanger a mission."

Snezhana blushed. Tosh had made his point.

"Take note, however, of Sophia's marksmanship and grades on her tests when in training. She is very clever and analytical. That can be an asset. I agree that Oliver can be a loose cannon."

Tosh erased the whiteboard and turned to dismiss his team. Just then his phone vibrated. He consulted the message and typed one in return. "Unfortunately, our transportation is delayed until tomorrow morning. I'll arranged for you all to stay here at the barracks. Go get some shut eye. We'll reconvene in the morning. Anatoly, take Yuri to the shooting range and help him improve his skills there." Yuri's head jerked up. "Yuri, your shooting abilities are good, but for this mission I want them to be great. Anatoly can help you there."

Anatoly leered at Yuri, who returned a wary look.

Tosh continued to give orders, "Snezhana, you are already an ace shot, and Stas won't be able to learn enough about shooting in this short time. Instead, you will work with Stas on making fake IDs and the art of disguising oneself. You did extremely well at that in GRU school and I think Stas will excel at that. I will see you all at breakfast."

"Where are you staying, Tosh?" inquired Yuri.

"This couch and I are old friends. I want to analyze this operation further. I don't trust the other agents, nor do I trust the totality of the data we've been fed. There's information out there that we don't know yet."

The group lingered.

"*Idti!*"

They pushed back their chairs and rushed out the door.

***

Anatoly sat on the black and white checkered linoleum floor of the barracks and inspected the contents of his weapons bag. He emptied the black leather bag, placed it on the floor next to him and started re-filling it. He selected his favorite pistol, the black break-open MP-412 REX .357 Magnum revolver. It was a limited-edition prototype from the 1990's and had an automatic ejector. He loved the feel of the polymer grip and the look of the shorter fat muzzle. To him it was like a dangerous biting dog, squat and muscular.

He next picked up his silver MSS Vul silent pistol that had a grip wider and longer than the snub nose muzzle and nearly disappeared in his hand. He selected the cartridge ammunition that went with the gun and placed both within his bag.

He caressed the matt black NRS-2 survival kit that combined a knife with a single shot noiseless pistol. Pressed the opening lever, he rotated out the barrel to ensure there was a cartridge in place. After reinserting the barrel into the knife, he placed the blade into its black metal sheath and into his bag.

He admired the polished wooden stock of his VSS Vintorez silent sniper rifle. He checked the optic sight that was seated on top and ran along one-third of the rifle. He carefully stored his old friend and then lovingly stroked his new toy, the AK-103 assault rifle. It was sleek, black, and lightweight, due to addition of plastic parts. It had corrugated metal Pic rails around the front to mount more components. The forward curve of the magazine enhanced the lethal look of the weapon.

He assembled, checked, and disassembled the rifles and placed them with the pistols in the center of the bag. Each pistol had a holster attached to the side of the center compartment so they wouldn't rattle around. He inserted into a pocket next to them his small zipped brown leather case containing a collection of poisons and tools for administering them. He checked the pocket next to that for the more mundane tools of a pair of needle nose pliers, a larger pair of regular pliers, a small wrecking bar, and a Philips Head screwdriver that had multiple types of other heads secreted in the handle. In an outside pocket he stowed a blue and a red tie and a wire slip noose.

In a separate inside pocket, he positioned a few knives, complete with a switchblade and one that he could release quickly from a firing mechanism that strapped on the inside of his wrist. He felt satisfaction remembering the last time he had used it on Aurelio. *It is a shame that weakling lived.*

He inserted various passports, identification papers, and paper bills from many countries, including a large amount of American dollars and Euros into an exterior pocket of the bag. *All good.* He then dropped into another outside pocket a selection of hair dyes and added a plastic case with contacts that turned his eyes from their normal blue, to green or brown. He cleaned and put in a thick pair of horn-rimmed glasses with clear glass lenses. Finally, he picked up and placed with the other electronics a small monitoring device and a scrambler. *I am ready.*

Chapter Seven

Stas reached to lift his black converted computer bag and nearly fell over. Yuri reached out to help him when Anatoly snatched the bag to carry it to the airplane. "*Der'mo*! Stas! What on earth do you have in this bag?" he asked, surprised at the heft.

Stas rattled off, "A MacBook Pro, a T-Platforms rugged laptop machine containing the Elbrus-8S chip and running the ultra-secure Astra Linux Operating System, a 2T rugged backup drive, a portable firewall, a cell phone jamming device, a WIFI jammer, various cables, an external mouse, and a folding external keyboard. Also, a few thumb drives, a voice scrambler, a GPS and GPS jammer, a RF sweeper and signal detector, and a small EMP device, a small robot, a drone with camera and microphone, and a few tiny electronic audio and camera bugs."

Anatoly snorted, "*Stoy komp'yuternaya yerunda*. It's all gibberish to me anyway. Did you remember clothes, money and your passport, just in case?"

Stas frowned at him. "Of course I did. I have one t-shirt, a pair of socks, and underwear in the bag, money and my passport in my front jeans pocket and my cell phone in my back pocket."

Snezhana dramatically held her nose. "I think we may be throwing Stas and his clothes into a shower periodically."

The team snickered, grabbed their bags and jogged out to the bus that was waiting to take them to the Moscow airport.

***

Elda marched into the windowless, well-lit, MI6 briefing room. She held a brown paper wrapped package under her left arm and had another package, also wrapped in a brown paper bag, sticking out of her back pocket. She spotted Yuri sitting at one end of the large wooden conference room table. She smiled broadly and went over to see him. Yuri rolled back his chair, ran over and hugged her.

"How are the troodles?" Yuri inquired.

"I thought you might ask. Here." Elda handed him a small packet of pictures from the inside pocket of her brown leather jacket.

'*Spasibo*!" Yuri bounced back to his chair and immediately started to look at the pictures. His smile nearly split his face in two.

Elda moved around the table to Tosh, who pushed back his chair, stood, and hugged her.

Glancing at her jacket, Elda inquired, "Do I now need to scan my clothing for trackers?"

"Perhaps," Tosh responded with a shrug.

"*Vot.*" Elda, handed Tosh the small package from her back pocket. Tosh's gray eyes lit up and he reached inside his jacket and handed Elda a slightly larger package, also wrapped in a brown paper bag.

Tosh observed, "I see we have similar tastes in packaging."

"It took me hours to wrap," quipped Elda in return. She broke the tape holding the bag closed and reached inside and pulled out a small rectangular white box. She opened the box and inside was a man's wallet made out of alligator skin. She threw back her head and laughed. She took out of her pocket a portable scanner and located the tracking device. Removing her jacket, she located that tracker and threw both devices away.

Tosh carefully peeled back the tape on his bag and opened it to find a smaller rectangular box. Opening it he found a micro-transmitter similar to the one that he had placed on Elda's collar last year when they were in Florence together. His mouth twitched and he raised an eyebrow.

Elda explained, "I thought you might have had trouble retrieving your micro-transmitter, but seeing my new wallet, perhaps not."

"*Touché*. You won that round, Elda. Beware, you will not be so lucky next time," tosh warned.

Elda looked at Anatoly, who was sitting on the same side of the table as Tosh, and walked over and placed the large package in front of him.

"*Vot*, Anatoly."

Anatoly's smile did not reach his eyes.

"*Spasibo*, Elda. *Vot*." He handed her a large white unwrapped rectangular box.

"*Spasibo*, Anatoly." Elda went to the other side of the table and sat down next to Ed and started to open the box. She paused and inquired of Anatoly, "It won't attack me, will it?"

Anatoly remained silent. Elda ripped off the tape and lifted the cover. Inside was a white kimono with a black belt. As she lifted the kimono to take it out of the box, she noted that one side was weighted down by something in the right-hand side pocket. She took a box from the pocket and smiled at the shape and heft of it. With anticipation she opened it to find a M&P 380 SHIELD EZ pistol. Running her fingers over the raised design on the polymer grip she picked it up. She appreciated the thin design and lightness of it, at just over eighteen ounces. Noting it felt heavier than that, she popped out the clip, which was loaded. She placed the clip and the gun in front of her on the table. "Oh how wonderful. I have wanted one of these for a while. *Spasibo,* Anatoly." She held the kimono up to her. It was the right size. She thanked Anatoly, "Well done."

Anatoly shrugged again and shook his box which was wrapped in a large paper bag.

Elda warned, "You may not want to shake that."

Anatoly looked sharply at Elda and saw that she was grinning. He snorted and returned to his task. He ripped off the paper and opened the box to see a camouflaged life jacket staring up at him with smaller packages inserted into the straps. He shook his head and snarled, "Thanks," Elda grinned back at him.

"I have taken swimming lessons since we last met," he growled and then started to unwrap the individual packages. "*Aga! Eto ochen' khorosho!*" He held up a push dagger, and then a scalpel, followed by a combat knife, a throwing knife and a Karambit knife. He lovingly stroked each one. "These are fine instruments." He looked up to see Elda field stripping her pistol. Anatoly threw one of his knives and it landed point down, planted firmly in the table in front of Elda. He observed, "Nice, I like it. *Spasibo,* Elda."

Elda pulled the knife out of the table, hefted it and flipped it back to Anatoly, where it embedded itself point down in the table, next to Anatoly's hand.

Her eyes steely, Elda responded, "Yes, very nice, Anatoly. Thanks for letting me try it out."

It appeared there might be some residual feelings from when they had tried to kill each other in St Petersburg and again in Amsterdam.

"OK. Stop wrecking the furniture." Ed ran his hand over his errant hair and groaned theatrically, "What a fine lot you all are. You guys are going to be difficult to manage."

Just then James walked in with Alexei, Sophia and Oliver. James looked around the room and asked. "Where are Stas, Snezhana, and David?"

Elda answered, "They are in the MI6 computer room looking over the information that has come in to date. I'll text them now."

Once the group was assembled, James passed a piece of printer paper out to each one, and remarked, "This is your schedule for our training here."

Anatoly looked at his paper and groaned. "School?! *Der'mo*!"

Elda read the schedule out loud: "09:00: Weapons Training. Really, James and Ed?"

James frowned, but answered her, "Yes, *really*, Elda. We have many new weapons here at MI6 that we would like for you to be proficient at, and, we will be analyzing each person for any weaknesses in their weapon handling. No matter how good you all are, there is *always* room for improvement."

"*Khorosho!*" Anatoly pointed his finger at Elda, holding his hand like a gun.

"10:00: Cyber Security."

"*Da!*" Stas clapped. Anatoly scowled.

"11:00: Wiretapping."

Stas smiled broadly. Anatoly and David gave two thumbs up.

"12:00: Lunch."

"*Da!*" Anatoly and Yuri did a high five. Snezhana looked up and shook her head in pretended irritation.

David leaned over and said in a low voice to Snezhana and Stas, "We can check the intel during lunch too." Both gave him a sign of approval and returned their attention to

Elda. Sophia and Oliver were playing footsie with each other. James glared at them and they stopped for a moment.

"Here you go, Anatoly," said Elda, "13:00: Hand to Hand Combat. James, is there a pool, or better yet, a canal, nearby?"

Anatoly threw an empty cardboard coffee cup at Elda, who batted it down with her hand, and wiped the coffee drops off the table with a nearby napkin. Tosh got up to get a pastry from the side table and dropped it in her lap on his way back to his seat. He sat there licking his fingers. Elda picked the powdered confection up out of her lap and pointedly ripped a piece off with her teeth. James knitted his brow and shook his head in puzzlement. Ed groaned. Elda continued calmly: "14:00: Successful Tracking. That sounds interesting. I can't wait to hear more."

"Any alligators involved?" asked Tosh.

"Was it an alligator or a croc?" replied Elda.

James turned to Ed with his brows knitted. "What on earth are they on about?"

Ed replied, "Long story. These two sparred a lot on their last mission."

Elda continued on, "15:00: Losing a Tail."

"Do they also have finding one?"

"Is Eeyore teaching it?"

Elda shook her head and kept reading, "Here's another one for you, Anatoly. 16:00: Close Quarter fighting and sniper evasion."

"*Oy khorosho*! I brought my sniper rifle. Would you like to play target?"

James strode over to Elda and grabbed the schedule from her and took over reading it. They all sat at attention, with their hands folded, like schoolchildren.

"Let's get on with this and then take a break to check the chatter on the internet. On *Day Two* you will have the following sessions: Security around the three leaders, geography and layout of the major Italian locations, G20 information, Riyadh, Rome and Bari's geographies, lunch, more hand to hand combat, techniques for silently killing prey..." That one got a round of excited aha and hums. "...continuing on," said James in a school teacher's stern voice, "leadership and team work, and the pistol range. We will all have a group supper and briefing each evening and will depart on the third day for additional training at the RAF base."

Chairs were rolled back in anticipation of leaving the conference room.

"One more thing," added James. "Leave your computers here. I will direct my communications manager,

Henry, to have his team here at MI6 install special communications software for us."

***

The team reconvened in the conference room.

Elda was now sporting a hairdo that was buzz cut short on the sides with some of her curls left on top and front. They glistened in the florescent lights. Ed walked over and whispered in her ear. "Special gel?"

Elda winked and nodded. Both Ed and Elda had read in the thin file they had on Tosh that some of his suspected victims had tufts of hair torn from their heads.

The instructor clapped his hands for their attention. "Now in this session I have hidden a number of wiretaps in rooms throughout this part of the base. You will each be given a map and on that map, you will notate the location of each wiretap you have detected. You will do two passes at this. For the first pass you will not have any electronic detection equipment. You will be timed."

The group rushed to the door, each holding their map and a pencil.

Tosh and Elda came back first, with Elda beating Tosh by just two seconds. They compared their papers as they handed them to the instructor. From a glance they looked almost identical.

95

The instructor asked, "How did you two find so many without any equipment?"

They looked at the instructor as if he were crazy and answered in unison, adding to each other's sentences, "You couldn't rely on equipment when we were first in the field. …We had to be attentive to minute changes. …Did we find them all? …Who won?"

"I won't tell you until each team member is back. Now pick up a bug detector and take a new map from that table over there. You'll soon see how good you were."

The group reassembled after both passes.

***

The metal table shook back and forth. Anatoly and Yuri were arm wrestling while waiting for the hand to hand combat session to start at 13:00. Elda walked into the conference room, tapped Yuri out and sat across from Anatoly, her arm bent at the elbow and hand up and open. Anatoly sneered and put his right arm up in the start position. Elda's hand met his and within minutes Anatoly's arm was over on its side. Anatoly's eyes were wide open and his mouth kept moving but no words were coming out. Finally he blurted, "How on earth did you do that?"

"It's all in the leverage, Anatoly. Rather like hip checking someone over a railing into a canal."

"*Der'mo*. You cheat." He slammed his hand down on the table and stomped to stand by the door, knocking over his chair on the way. Elda picked up the chair and put it and the table against the wall.

James strolled in with a stopwatch to officiate the exercises, proclaiming, "We will start with Elda and Tosh."

James cleared his throat and addressed each team member. "We need all you healthy for this mission. You may not use any weapons except your bare hands. You will keep the combat confined to the mats. If your opponent gives in, you will stop *immediately* and help him or her up off the mat, and shake hands. You will go until your opponent concedes, or the time runs out, or we stop the match. Understand?" Eyeballs rolled in response.

James sternly reinforced his message: "The rules are as follows: *Do not permanently injure, maim or kill your opponent*." A chorus of dismayed groans and swears followed his announcement.

***

Elda and Tosh faced each other warily, standing at opposite ends of the large black square rubber mat. Elda realized she needed to rely on her speed and agility, and adjust her positioning to avoid his longer reach, to be able to beat Tosh. Tosh winked at Elda as if he had read her thoughts.

97

One moment Tosh seemed far away and the next he had his hands around Elda's neck. Elda quickly responded by spinning and breaking his hold by bringing her right arm over and down across his arms. She finished her turn by bending low and bringing her elbow up into Tosh's gut. Tosh grunted but kept on his feet.

Before she could move out of range, Tosh had grabbed her arm and spun her back into a choke hold. Elda brought her right leg back between Tosh's legs and hooked it around his leg to kick his right leg out from under him, causing them both to fall backwards and Tosh to lose his grip. Lying on the mat, they both twirled away from each other and slowly got up to face each other again.

The two old warriors carefully circled each other while coming closer together. Tosh made the first move and pounced to grab Elda. She bent low and rolled under him, knocking his legs out from under him and he came down to the mat with a thud. Elda finished rolling and jumped up. Tosh had already arisen and ran over to her with his head down and butted her to the ground. His forward momentum threw him onto the mat on top of her. Elda grunted and quickly rotated away, rolling him off of her. They both got up and sneered at the other.

They circled each other again and Tosh threw a punch that connected with Elda's shoulder and nearly knocked her down. She responded by grabbing his arm, stepping into him and knocking his legs out from under him again.

As he fell he grabbed Elda and pulled her down on top of him. She landed on him with a thud causing him to lose his breath for a moment. He grabbed at Elda's hair and his fingers slipped right off.

"*Chert*! You cheat!" He frowned at his glistening hand.

The whistle blew. Elda and Tosh rolled on their backs panting and looked at each other.

"It was good for me, and you?"

"Oh yes, I wish I had a cigarette to top it off with."

The two old warriors stood up to await the verdict.

James, Alexei, Ed and Stas were deep in conversation. Finally James stepped forward, raised one of each of the combatant's arms and declared the match a draw. The others in the room clapped. Elda and Tosh bowed to each other and then shook hands.

***

The winners and losers reassembled in the MI6 conference room to continue their seminars.

Snezhana walked over to Elda and asked, "What did you put in your hair?"

Elda grinned. "Good observation, Snezhana. It's a special non-greasy, but slippery, hair gel. If you want some, MI6 has it in their lab."

"*Spasibo*."

"If you don't mind a bit of advice, Snezhana, you might want to look at how you show and act on your feelings. I noticed that you lead with your emotions. In the hand-to-hand combat sessions, you allowed yourself to get angry and rush at your opponent. It's time to let that reaction go. There is no room for emotions in our profession. Shape up quickly if you want to stay on the team."

Chapter Eight

Elda leaped up, grabbed Yuri's chair and yanked it out from under him. He fell to the floor with a thump and a snort. *"Chert!"* The sound of loud snoring was now quieted.

Anatoly and Snezhana clapped. Sophia spoke, "Thanks for stopping the racket, Elda."

Elda picked up Yuri's glasses. "I wondered why you were wearing these." Behind each lens was posted a picture of an eyeball, allowing Yuri to sleep through the lecture. "You're awake now, Yuri. Your penance is to stand for the rest of the morning. It's an old trick I learned in Navy training." Elda pointed to the back of the room.

"What if I want to take notes?"

Elda handed him a pen and pad of paper from the table and pointed again.

"Govno." Yuri rubbed his rump and scowled, but obediently wandered to the back of the room and stood.

"You do have some unusual talents, Yuri," Elda observed with a chuckle.

"Spasibo, Elda."

***

Snezhana, David and Stas quickly disappeared back to the computer room to check the traffic. The rest of the crew reconvened in the conference room and discussed where to have dinner, with Anatoly lobbying for Italian food.

Elda teased him, "We're in England, Anatoly! Let's go for fish and chips, or steak and kidney pie!"

Anatoly put a finger in his mouth and pantomimed throwing up.

When the three returned from the computer room, Snezhana was definitely no longer pouting over her hand to hand combat defeat. She had a bounce in her step and was smiling. Stas was skipping in delight.

Stas said excitedly, "We have a lead to track down! There's an unmasked IP address. I will work on this more with the MI6 computer team."

David added, "But I'm getting the run around on trying to trace the root of this mission. There are a number of financial transactions happening between China and black ops operatives, but when I get to a certain point, it all disappears. I've never seen anything like this before." Snezhana chimed in, "I can help you David, if you'd like. Cyber was a strength of mine in school."

"Thanks Snez. I'd like that," replied David.

Tosh's eyes narrowed.

James nodded. "Good work. We will all meet here for the bus ride to the RAF base after breakfast tomorrow. Have anything essential packed in your go-bags. Understood?"

A flurry of answers overlapped each other in response to his school teacher stare:

"*Ya ponimayu.*"

"*Da.*"

"Yes."

"I understand."

"OK."

"*Khorosho.*"

"Certainly."

"*Da.*"

James shook his head at the assembled group of trained spies and killers. "I worry about the tensions between the members of this group."

Elda touched James' arm to get his attention. "It appears to be a motley crew but we are all working together, James. There will naturally be some tension. We are after all, trained to be suspicious, and, some of us are each other's sworn enemies."

"I agree, Elda, but I worry, if circumstances allowed, that you would readily kill each other."

"Oh, that's a given, James. Our loyalties will always be to our home countries."

Elda saluted James and watched for his reaction. He automatically snapped to attention and returned her salute, confirming her suspicion that he was ex-military. She enjoyed gathering little bits of information about the people she worked with. As a trained therapist she was constantly analyzing others. She glanced around and saw Tosh looking at her. She mentally bet he was playing the same game. Tosh smiled and nodded. For a brief moment she thought he *had* read her mind. His ability to see through to the roots of people's actions rivaled her own and that was scary to see in an adversary. She vowed to learn as much as she could about him while they were on the same side.

Elda had studied all that she could find on Tosh. She had first met him many years ago in Moscow where he had posed as a student at the university and offered her a ride. Elda had assumed the identity of a mathematics instructor and had managed to not give him any information during their extended ride together.

They had next met last year in Florence as rivals. During their two days there, Elda had learned that Tosh also was a lover of the arts and admired much of the same artwork that Elda liked. She intuited that he was deeply patriotic and intelligent, but he was so skilled at the art of illusion and appearing insignificant and almost invisible, that it was hard to get a handle on who he really was. She knew one thing: he was not to be underestimated. It was clear that she could not let down her guard around him.

Chapter Nine

"No!"

All eyes turned to Elda. The group was milling around, impatiently waiting, having reassembled in the conference room for their transport to jump school. Elda pointed at David's pile of luggage and stated firmly, "David, you need to leave most of that crap here. Either repack it yourself or we'll do it for you. Don't worry, we'll send it back to MI6 headquarters where you can pick it up on your return."

Complaining each time he had to leave an item behind, David, under Elda's watchful eyes, sorted through his multiple bags to condense his belongings into one small carryon. At the last minute he added a book to read and his harmonica into his go-bag.

Stas rushed in late, looking as if he had not slept all night. His normally pale face was almost white except for the dark circles under his eyes.

Anatoly shook his head. *"Khakeram…* They are all alike."

Snezhana chastised Stas, "Stas, you need to take better care of yourself!" She handed Stas a paper napkin with a pastry folded in it and pointed him over to the pot of coffee and hot water for tea. "Eat and get some caffeine." On the way past Anatoly, she hit him in the arm. "We need to watch out for all of the team members."

Anatoly shrugged. He had little empathy for others. Tosh raised an eyebrow and glared at Anatoly. Anatoly acknowledged the unspoken reprimand. "*Da*, Tosh. I will attend to the team members. I always follow your orders."

Stas poured himself a cup of coffee with a splash of cream and took a bite of pastry. Washing it down with coffee, he talked around the food in his mouth. "Snezhana, David and I have analyzed the data and we think that one of the assassins may be in Canada. But we will need an hour to trace him to his exact location." He ran back to the computer room.

"Good work from Stas," said James. "We'll hold the bus and will arrange to have a flight to Canada. Tosh and Elda, whom would you like to send on this mission?"

Tosh proclaimed, "Oliver and Sophia, you will be the team that goes to Canada."

Elda cocked her head at Tosh's selection and signaled to Tosh that she would like a word with him outside.

Oliver and Sophia eyes showed their excitement at being the first team selected. Anatoly gave a black look and Snezhana's bottom lip stuck out in a pout. Yuri rolled his eyes in relief. David looked studious, as always.

***

Elda and Tosh faced off in the parking lot outside the building.

With her arms folded across her chest, Elda snapped, "You're sending a married couple into the field together?"

Fists clenched, Tosh responded, "Yes. I am."

Jaw set Elda inquired, "Please explain *that* one."

"Certainly. They are both British and both used to working with each other. Their skills are complementary. They will either do an amazing job out there or really mess up."

Elda shook her head. "I don't see the reasoning."

Tosh held his hands out palms up and answered her, "Look, those two are newlyweds and have to drop their obsession with each other and perform or they will be no good to us in this operation. We need to find out early on before one of us gets killed because of their carelessness."

Elda relaxed and asked, "So sacrifice one, or perhaps two, for the good of the entire team?"

Tosh nodded and replied, "*Da.*"

***

"*U nas eto yest*! We have it!" A clearly recovered Stas ran into the chow hall, excitedly pointing at his laptop.

Snezhana gently pulled him into a chair and handed him a plate of food. "Eat while you tell us. *Ty slishkom khudoy.* Gain weight. We need you to survive."

Stas spoke around the food he was shoveling into his mouth. "Montreal. The assassin is in Montreal."

"Oliver and Sophia. Grab your bags and get to the airfield," Tosh commanded.

Oliver whined, "*Now*? Can't we eat first?"

"Now!" Elda snapped and pointed to their bags and the door. "We have to catch them before they go on the move again. You can eat and sleep on the plane."

"Blimey. All right." Oliver snatched a sandwich off his plate and held it in his teeth, picked up his bag, handed Sophia's bag to her and the two of them trudged out the door.

The rest of the team sat impatiently waiting for their transportation. In a short time, a battered gray-blue military bus pulled up at the door of the building.

"Line up and board the bus. Remember to come back alive," James said magnanimously with a flourish toward the bus.

Anatoly spat out, *"Chert," and marched to the bus.*

Tosh said, "Spasibo, James."

***

In the front of the bus David took out his harmonica and was attempting to play a tune on it.

Anatoly grimaced, *"Bozhe moy*, David! That sounds terrible."

Elda asked, "What on earth are you trying to play, David?"

"Moscow Nights," he responded, petulantly.

Elda put a finger in each of her ears and pronounced, "Oh, please stop! Play a cowboy tune on that thing. 'Moscow Nights' is beautifully haunting, but it *must* be played on a violin!"

With that, Yuri started to hum "Moscow Nights." Elda closed her eyes and joined him. Tosh and Snezhana joined in. They all swayed to the haunting tune.

David laughed. "Okay, okay, I get it!"

He started to play "Lonesome Cowboy," followed by "Home on the Range." After finishing his second song, he loped to the back of the bus to sit next to Snezhana.

"*Dobryy den'*, Snezhana. We haven't had a chance to talk much and we are going to be working closely together. Why so glum?"

Snezhana breathed in deeply and took a moment before answering David. His warm brown eyes were looking at her so seriously behind his glasses. She briefly rubbed the left side of her chest before answering, "It is nothing, David."

David squinted his eyes and shook his head at her. He asked, "Ah you can't fool a spy, you know? Is it because you lost at the hand to hand combat matches?"

Snezhana sighed. "It is not only that, David, although I do wish I were better at hand-to-hand combat and I am going to train until I can easily beat you." David's smile lit up his eyes, and his mouth was invitingly curled up. Snezhana paused and caught her breath. She automatically leaned in toward him, and said sincerely, "I have always been very, very, good at everything I have done. I received top marks in school. I have been born into this job and have studied my uncle for years. But now that it is time for me to really do my job, I find that I'm not really sure I want to be a spy."

"I'll tell you what, Snezhana, since it is important that my partner know what she is doing without thinking, you and I will spend our lunches together and I will teach you different moves."

Snezhana started to respond and stopped. Her eyes roamed his handsome face and across his chest. She stifled the reply she wanted to say and instead simply stated, "Thank you, David. I would be most appreciative."

"*Pozhaluysta*, Snezhana."

Snezhana admired David's butt in his tight jeans as he ambled back to his seat and his harmonica. Soon notes from "Red River Valley" floated back toward Snezhana.

***

Elda had been sitting sideways in her seat, observing the interaction. Her eyes caught Tosh's. She cocked her head and raised an eyebrow. Tosh nodded.

112

Chapter Ten

The mud oozed under her shirt and gathered at her armpits. It encroached into her nostrils and splattered her glasses. Wondering why she hadn't listened to Dawn and retired early, Elda crawled face first through the mud and dove down under the barbed wire. She wiped the mud off her mouth and sputtered to the mud-covered apparition to her left, "There are some experiences better left behind in our youth."

A pair of gray eyes glared back at her from the muddy face of the person crawling next to her. Tosh's look said so much. Elda pushed herself to try and beat him to the end of this part of the obstacle course. Tosh sensed her picking up the pace and accelerated. As Tosh and Elda passed by a large struggling lump of mud, she noticed that Yuri was caught on the barbed wire. She stopped and untangled his t-shirt from the barb that had snagged it.

"*Spasibo*, Elda."

"*Pozhaluysta*, Yuri."

Tosh slowed down and waited for Elda to catch back up and then the two of them struggled to pass each other, ending again in a draw. They chuckled with self-satisfaction as they stood up, dripping mud.

"What are you laughing at, you green slime? Get your lard filled arses up the wall!"

The drill sergeant pointed at a 15-foot tall wooden wall, where Snezhana had just lost her grip on Anatoly's hand and was sliding back down into the mud below. Anatoly was hanging on to the top of the wall by his feet and was assisting the others.

"I've never seen such a sorry lot of poofters! Move it! Move it! Move it!"

With the screams of the drill sergeant ringing in their ears, Tosh positioned himself at the bottom of the wall. Elda climbed up him and stood on his shoulders and grabbed Anatoly's wrists. Tosh then used Elda's body and clothing to climb up her, ensuring he stepped solidly on her head on his way up. He continued on over Anatoly to the top. Once there, he helped Anatoly pull Elda up and onto the summit of the wall.

Yuri reached the wall, where Snezhana was still struggling. He reached down and cupped his hands for her to put her foot in and boosted her up so she could reach Anatoly's hands.

"Grab my wrists, not my hands," instructed Anatoly. Elda and Tosh both hung down on either side of Anatoly to help grab Snezhana and pull her up.

Elda moved over next to Tosh. Yuri waited for Stas to crawl out from under the wire and he boosted him up. When Tosh was distracted by looking down at the action, Elda reached over behind him, grabbed his collar and toppled him backwards into a large mud puddle below.

"*Chert*, Elda."

"Oops, sorry Tosh!"

Yuri walked back from the wall and then ran forward and took a huge running leap up but missed reaching Anatoly's hands by almost three feet. Anatoly lowered Stas down by his ankles. Yuri grabbed onto Stas' wrists and crawled over him, using Stas' clothing and belt as handholds. Anatoly brought Stas back up. The team all slid down the other side of the wall joining Tosh in the mud puddle.

"*Chert*!"

"Bollocks!"

"*Der'mo*!"

"Crap!"

The instructor yelled above their complaints, "Attention! Get on your feet you disgusting excuses for fighting men! Grab a pack and double-time it back to the barracks! Go, go, go! Now! Move it!"

They all scrambled out of the mud and ran to pick up a 40-pound pack each, then started running the two miles back to the barracks. Elda and Tosh fell easily into step with each other. Snezhana struggled to keep up with David.

Yuri and Anatoly loped along like two large bears, chatting as they ran. Stas half ran, half walked in a feeble attempt to keep up with them, and after ¼ mile he sat down with the Drill instructor circling him and shouting, trying in vain to encourage him to get up and continue. Finally the drill instructor stopped yelling, shook his finger at the underfed, pasty geek and relieved him of his pack.

In a normal tone of voice the instructor said, "You ninny civi. Now march your arse back to the base."

Stas sighed in relief and slowly started the trek back to the base.

The rest of the crew staggered into the barracks and threw themselves down on their bunks in relief. The drill sergeant marched in and yelled, "You sneaky beakies. Shower, and be ready to march to the mess hall in 15 minutes."

A collective groan arose from the prone bodies. Elda's Navy training kicked in and she rolled off her bunk and rushed to get ready, dragging her muddy bedspread behind her to clean it in the shower at the same time.

"Hey? Who's going to clean the floor?"

"Don't worry, Anatoly. I'll get it on the way back."

They were all barely dressed and presentable when the sergeant bellowed from outside, "Now, you lizards. Hit the deck!"

They raggedly lined up two by two ready to march to get chow.

"Right, left, right – stay in step! Move it, move it, move it!"

The drill instructor put them in a long line for food and then went and got his own food through a short line reserved for staff.

***

"Hurry you secret squirrels. Line up!"

The team jogged by the trash cans and tray return area, shoving the food they had just received into their mouths and dumping their trays. The drill instructor marched them over to a bus where they were transported to RAF Brize

117

Norton and then put on an Airbus A400M Atlas craft for parachute practice. They each strapped themselves into the pulldown seats along the perimeter of the large empty cargo area. Elda put her hand over her stomach and swallowed hard as the plane took off. Her fear of heights was kicking in. She glanced over at Tosh and thought he looked a little green too. She unbuckled the straps holding her in, slid into a seat next to him and whispered, "Tosh, I need a favor."

Tosh narrowed his eyes and cocked his head, "What Elda?"

Elda looked Tosh directly in the eyes and stated, "If I freeze I want you to shove me out the door."

Tosh, raising his eyebrows, asked, "With or without a chute?"

Elda scowled, sighed, and said, "I'm serious. It's important we set an example."

Tosh frowned and asked, "Have you jumped before?"

"Yes, twice, and I *hate* it," Elda answered.

Tosh relaxed and nodded, saying, "*Khorosho*. How about if we jump together? I'm not fond of jumping out of a perfectly good plane either. It brings back memories of near crashes."

Wrinkling her forehead, Elda probed, "Can I trust you?"

"As much as I can trust you," Tosh answered, smiling.

"That's fair."

The two warriors shook on their pact.

The instructor shouted over the plane's noise, "Come on you muppets. Hook up. Over here. We're sending you out the side door instead of the rear." They stood up and clipped their lines to the anchor cable inside the aircraft. The rush of air streaming along the sides of the plane pulled at them.

The jump instructor pointed to Stas. "Get ready, little one. You're first."

Stas curled into a ball on the floor and refused to move. The instructor looked at the others for help. "OK. We're at the jump zone. Let's get moving. Who can get this guy going?"

From his position of second to jump, Anatoly walked over to Stas and picked him up and threw him out the door.

"I hope he had his chute on," he mused flatly.

The group looked at Anatoly in horror.

"Relax. He did." Anatoly threw himself out the door into a nose dive to catch up with Stas.

Elda and Tosh strode hand in hand to the open door of the craft and jumped out together.

"Geronimo!"

"*Umeret' khorosho!*"

Snezhana froze in the doorway looking down at the ground rushing by so far below.

David walked up next to he and suggested, "Let's go together too." Before she could respond, he put his arm around Snezhana and threw the two of them out the door.

The instructor looked expectantly at Yuri.

"*Chert.*" He jumped out.

*****

Stas was sobbing and curled into a ball on the grassy ground.

Anatoly patted him on the back, saying, "*Khorosho.* Take it easy man. I'll send a truck back for you."

Anatoly marked their position, removed the harness from Stas, wrapped the parachute around him to keep the shivering, crying lump warm, and set off in a run for the base.

Chapter Eleven

Nigel sat next to Aurelio on the brown leather couch in Aurelio's apartment. "How good are your connections, Aurelio?"

Aurelio, contrasting Nigel's white Oxford shirt and pressed pants with his outfit of stained t-shirt and baggy grey sweatpants, inhaled deeply from his bong before replying, "I am a great man, Nigel. I know everyone. What do you need?"

Nigel paused as if reconsidering telling Aurelio, and then quickly spoke, "I need to find records of a man who entered Russia on business in the late 1970's. I've got his name."

"Whew, man, that's a hard one." Aurelio took a hit on his bong and then laid out and snorted a line of coke. He pushed the mirror across the glass topped coffee table over to Nigel. "Here man, have some."

Nigel held up his hand. "I can't. My wife would kill me. And then she'd freeze me out, if you know what I mean." Aurelio cackled his agreement and snatched the mirror back, sucking down a second line. Nigel looked at him beseechingly and pleaded, "Please Aurelio. You're the only one I know that knows a lot of people. Really man, I need this!."

Aurelio, swaying back and forth to an internal tune, nodded. "I can call someone. However, the people he sends you to will probably want a lot of money." He bounced his rear on the couch and pointed at his bong, then the crystal scotch glass, then the mirror, humming, "One, two, three. Which is next for me?" Deciding, he reached for the bong.

Nigel waved his hand dismissively at Aurelio's implication of excessive cost. "That isn't an issue for me. My dad has been sending me money for years. I haven't spent any of it, because I felt it was dirty, but I did invest it wisely."

Aurelio put down his bong and dialed a number on his phone.

"*Da*, Aurelio?"

"Yuri, man, I need your help here."

"I'm not your keeper anymore, Aurelio."

Aurelio rapidly said, "I know, I know, but please hear me out. I don't have many friends since you and Natasha left St. Petersburg. My new friend, Nigel, has people out to kill him…"

Yuri's laughter came through the phone. "Aurelio, you're always making these stories up. Not everyone has black trucks following them and people out to kill them. Are you high?"

"No, no, I am not making it up. Yes, I am trashed, but only somewhat. *Please* he is my new friend. Just hear him out. Please?" Aurelio pleaded.

"Fine. Have him call me." Click. The line went dead.

Aurelio put down his phone with a satisfied smile. "He will hear you out, but you will need to use a burner phone. Here is the number for you to call." Aurelio jotted the number down on a piece of paper and passed it to Nigel. "So, my young friend. Your problems are solved by yours truly. I am amazingly clever, aren't I?"

"Oh yes, you are, Aurelio."

"Good, let's get stoned." Aurelio relit the bong and inhaled deeply.

Nigel stood to go. "Another time Aurelio. I've got to go shopping for that burner phone."

Aurelio looked at him in confusion. "What phone?"

"Never mind. Thank you," Nigel said backing towards the door.

Aurelio rubbed his chin and blinked rapidly. He asked, "For what?"

Nigel quickly reassured him, "Never mind. No worries."

"Never a care. I am great though, aren't I." Aurelio took a large hit off the bong, sat back on his couch and started laughing.

Nigel let himself out.

***

In the small café, Nigel warily looked at the large Russian who was wearing a gold choker, a tight dark blue sweater and a black leather jacket and sitting across the table from him. He hoped that he wasn't being set up, and that he could trust this man to bring him the information he needed for leverage.

Without prelude Yuri snapped, "How much money do you have?"

Nigel put an envelope on the table, and stated, "I have brought 50,000 US dollars with me."

Yuri snatched and pocketed the money. "*Khorosho.* We can work with you. The final price will depend on what you need."

"I need proof that this man got his position with help from Russia." Nigel slid a piece of paper across the metal topped table.

Without looking at it, the Russian picked it up and folded the paper slipping it into his inside jacket pocket, alongside the money. "What nationality is he?"

"American," stated Nigel.

Yuri frowned and grunted, "50K may not be enough."

"I will get you more if needed. I must have this information. Please help me," Nigel beseeched.

"We will let you know."

***

Nigel called to his wife, "I'm going out for a walk, would you like to come?" He held his breath as he waited for her answer. She hated exercise but she also disliked it when he was roaming around unwatched.

She walked into the hallway where he was standing and demanded, "Where are you going?"

Nigel smiled at her and replied, "Just going to take a long brisk walk. I'm getting a bit paunchy around the middle, you know? I'm going to start taking longer walks and try to work it off."

She reached out and poked him in his middle, "Yes, go do that. You know I like my men to be fit."

Nigel laughed with her and then turned quickly to leave, hiding the relief that spread across his face.

It was a short walk to the café where the large Russian was sitting. Nigel slid in the chair across from him. "Do you have anything for me?"

Yuri slid a piece of paper with a name and an address on it across the table to Nigel. "Memorize this."

Nigel looked at the paper. There was a woman's name on it and the name and address of an elderly community. Confused, he looked up at Yuri, asking, "Is this a joke?"

Yuri growled, "I assure you. No joke. She will help you." He stood and held his hand out for the piece of paper.

Nigel studied the information and then, having committed it to memory, handed it back to Yuri who much to Nigel's surprise, put it in his mouth, chewed and swallowed it. Yuri smiled at Nigel's shocked face and turned and walked away.

***

An old woman sat in her chair in the old folks home peering at Nigel through rheumy, cataract clouded eyes. A multi-colored crocheted throw covered her lap. "Come closer son, I can't see you," she croaked in a quivery voice.

Nigel stepped to her side and gestured to the wooden high back chair next to her. "May I sit and join you?"

"Oh, a gentleman and a Brit. I like that. Please do, young man. It's been a while since I have had male company."

Nigel held out his hands palms up and gave her a tentative smile. He stated, "I am hoping that you can help me."

"Of course you are." She put out her wrinkled, age spotted hand and Nigel took it in both of his. She closed her eyes, breathed deeply, and then coughed from the effort of breathing. "Ah the touch of human contact. I never thought that I would miss that so much. I had quite a bit of skin to skin contact in my youth. Do tell me your story. I enjoy a good tale."

Nigel leaned in close so she could hear him and spoke to her of Robert's story and his own quest to get more facts. She closed her eyes again and nodded as he spun the tale. He stopped. She opened her eyes and waved her hand in a motion for him to go on. "Ah yes, but you are leaving much out. You haven't told me your story and why you are seeking this information. These old ears have heard a lot of stories. Yours is missing parts. Do please fill me in."

Nigel patted her hand. It was obvious that he was enjoying her company. The old prostitute hadn't lost her skill with men. "It is so nice to have a conversation with a woman again. My own wife acts as if she hates me. She probably does. She's stuck with me and I'm no prize. Admittedly I am kind, but she could do so much better. She is so gorgeous. I would love to be able to let her go and to go back to England. But I am in too deep and I involved my father. Now I fear that there's no way out for any of us. But I thought if I had more knowledge, I might be able to get some leverage and turn this situation around." Nigel took a long breath after spilling out his tale at a fast pace.

The old woman nodded and encouraged Nigel, "Go on dear."

Nigel continued and told her his entire predicament, from the day he came to Russia and was entrapped, until now.

The woman looked at Nigel sagely, "What a familiar story. How much money do you have dear?"

Nigel grabbed his wallet, held it out to her and stated anxiously, "I have 20,000 US dollars on me right now."

She shook her head in mock dismay. "You are not experienced at this at all, are you, dear? I will help you. Please give me the money."

Nigel reached into his wallet and handed her a wad of dollars. She snatched it, tucked it down her bodice, and rearranged her lace edged shawl around her shoulders. "Not much there any more to hold things, but it will do for temporary storage." She removed her hand and opened it to display a key. "Please unlock that file cabinet over there."

Nigel looked around. "I only see a table with a brightly colored throw on it and a beautiful bouquet of flowers on that."

The woman smiled with dead eyes and then replied in a monotone, "They are fake. There is no one alive who would send me flowers anymore." She sighed, stared at her hands and whispered, "I do miss that." Her voice stronger, she commanded, "Lift up the throw and you will see the cabinet under the table. Unlock it, and take out a file marked *R 1978*. Remove it, photograph the contents and put it back where you found it."

Nigel did what he was told. Before he could lock the cabinet, she added, "I like you young man. I don't have many visitors anymore and these files should benefit someone. I know the father of the man who is running your case. Also, pull the file *B 1990*." Nigel lifted out the folder, photographed the contents, and, after replacing both folders he locked the cabinet. He smoothed the throw and ensured it covered the cabinet from view. He walked over to the woman, who was starting to nod off, and gently placed the key in her hand and kissed her cheek. A tear formed in the corner of her eye and started its journey down her face. He carefully lifted it off with his finger, patted her hand and walked away.

Chapter Twelve

The plane jarred to a stop on the tarmac at CFB Trenton. Oliver and Sophia grabbed their bags, exited quickly, and ran to the waiting car. Once settled in the back seat, Sophia turned to Oliver and stated seriously, "Now remember, Oliver. No playing the hero this time. I want you in one piece."

"Despite how you treated my parts during training?" Oliver looked hurt and held his crotch.

Sophia looked pointedly at his protective hand, "I *especially* want to keep *those* pieces."

"Humm, I know of a romantic little place where we can grab a bite to eat after checking into the hotel. Then perhaps we can ensure our bedroom is secure while we wait for further instructions?" Oliver smiled his most charming crooked grin and winked at Sophia.

Sophia rolled her eyes. "You know I can't resist you when you smile at me like that. But please stop deflecting this conversation. I'm serious, dear. We *have* to stick together on this mission. You could have been killed last time."

Oliver squinted his eyes and grimaced. He sighed and replied, "You do know I still need to prove myself as an agent, my love. Right? I'm not as skilled as you are."

"I know Oliver. But just remember that getting yourself killed will not prove a thing."

The car sped onwards.

***

"Why don't you want to have children?"

Sophia's food dropped from her fork as she looked at Oliver in surprise. "Where did *that one* come from?"

It was Oliver's turn to be serious. He frowned at her across the Bistro's small copper topped table. "Each time I bring it up, you change the subject. We're on a dangerous mission together. It's *time* we had some of these discussions."

A rainbow of emotions played across Sophia's face. She took a deep breath and blurted out quickly, the words almost running together in her haste to tell Oliver the truth. "You're right, I have been avoiding this conversation. But you deserve the answer. I love you. We would make beautiful babies and god knows I enjoy the lovemaking, but I have my entire career ahead of me. I don't want to take the mommy track at work. And the thought of bloating up and having this thing growing inside me just *doesn't* appeal. You would be a great father, but I'm not sure about me being a good mother. However, I *am* an excellent spy. And I thoroughly enjoy my work. It is my advocation."

Oliver regarded Sophia with love and understanding, and, narrowing missing the candle in the middle of the table, reached across to take her hand in his. "You are much more professional, dedicated and accomplished than I am. My accident during that mission got me thinking about our future. When we were dating, we talked about having a family someday. I think we should do it. I would love to be a stay at home father. And my dad left me a heap of dosh when he passed last year." He ended with a happy frivolity, "So you wouldn't have to carry it. We can afford get a surrogate to bear our child!" He sat there grinning at her.

Sophia yanked her hand out of Oliver's grasp and stared at him wide-eyed, her energy coiled, ready to strike. "You're stinking rich? Bloody hell. Why didn't you tell me this *before* we got married?"

Oliver gently and cautiously put his hand on hers and responded evenly. "Careful dear, we're in a restaurant and I know the damage you can do. I didn't say anything because you had a number of suitors: a doctor, a barrister, and that rich playboy. I wanted you to love me for me and not be influenced pro or con by the fact that I was a bit flush."

Sophia angrily pushed back her chair. "You bastard. Do you *really* think I am that bloody shallow?"

Oliver looked at her with pleading eyes and held his arms out in surrender. He beseechingly asked, "Will you forgive me? My bad. I was stupid not to tell you. Please help me out of this hole I keep digging."

Sophia's phone binged. "Saved by the bell?" inquired Oliver, coyly.

Sophia curtly responded, "We have a picture of the assassin, as well as his last known location."

Oliver stood up, walked over to Sophia and gave her a passionate kiss. Sophia stiffened at first but then relaxed into her love for Oliver and melted her body into his. Oliver held her tightly and then let go. "It's time to move. Just think on it dear."

"Don't get killed and *perhaps* I will."

***

Elda groggily peered at the black monitors set up around the conference room, turned temporary command center. The lack of windows in the interior room made it difficult to determine whether it was day or night. The florescent lights above, and the glow from the monitors, made Elda look worn and haggard. "When are we going to have comms?" she wearily asked Stas.

Stas was hunched over his keyboard, typing frantically. "I'm working as quickly as I can. I am having difficulty setting up the link. There seems to be some sort of interference."

Tosh, standing on the other side of Stas, had bags under his eyes and his short straight hair was sticking up at odd angles. He frowned, tapped his earpiece and shook his head. A loud sharp crackling sound suddenly came through the earpiece, causing Tosh to flinch.

"There I have sound," said Stas as he patched the sound into the speakers located around the room.

Elda shook her head. "Something doesn't seem right, Tosh," she commented.

"What makes you say that, Elda?" snapped Tosh, glaring at her, crossing his arms over his chest.

Elda squinted and shrugged. She remarked, "I don't know. Something isn't adding up in my head yet." She held her hands, palms up, out to Tosh.

"That observation doesn't help a lot, you know? Talk to me when you can say something meaningful." Tosh turned his back on Elda and tapped Stas on the shoulder, asking in a rough tone, "Do we have any visual yet with Oliver and Sophia?"

"*Nyet.* We will soon." Stas rechecked all of his cables and continued to type furiously.

"You knotty-pated nincompoop!" Sophia's voice came through with a slight echo and muffled, as if she was underwater.

Elda leaned in close to the main microphone, inquiring, "Sophia is that you?" Her voice cracked as the last word stuck in her throat. She grabbed a bottle of water and slugged down half of it.

Sophia's voice came through clearly. "Yes. He bloody went and did it again. He had to play the hero. Wanker."

Tosh snapped, "Did what? What's going on?"

Elda added, "We are trying to establish visuals but may not be able to in time."

Sophia answered, "We saw the hit man and Oliver ran down into the underground city after him. I told him we should be cautious and track him at a distance, but he was off and running."

Elda moved her shoulders and neck to release the tension. She nodded her acknowledgment of the situation and then probed for more information, asking, "Where are you?"

Sophia's voice came through the speakers and headsets, "I am following from above ground, hoping to head them off at the next entrance."

Elda rubbed the bridge of her nose. Her voice was soft as she spoke, "Be careful, Sophia. It feels off. "

***

Dashing through the well-lit tunnel, Oliver saw his target ahead of him and spurred himself on to run faster over the bricks. He careened around tourists sauntering through the tunnels to the shopping areas. His footsteps echoed off the hard floor.

The tunnel opened up into a large bright two-story area with a fountain in the middle. The assassin glanced back at Oliver and fired a shot into the air. People screamed and scattered, hiding under tables and escaping into the tunnels. Oliver lunged to reach the agent, who vaulted over a table, knocking chairs over. Oliver crashed into the table with his hip.

"Bollocks!"

The previously full area was now deserted except for islands of people huddled under tables and the two men barreling through. Oliver swerved as a stool came flying his way, cracking as it hit the marble floor. Oliver hesitated drawing his weapon due to the remaining people. He ran faster, slipped on the water by the fountain, skidded, and somersaulted back up to his feet. The assassin karate-kicked a garbage can, which rolled in front of Oliver, knocking his legs out from underneath him. He landed face first with a thud and felt his nose snap.

"Bugger."

Bleeding from his nose, Oliver leapt to his feet to see his target disappear into a tunnel. He dashed after him, knocking people aside as he went. He tapped his comm device in his ear.

Nothing but static.

***

In the street above the tunnel Sophia knelt behind a car, surveying three masked men with S&T Motiv K12 machine guns positioning themselves at the entrance to the subway. One man was lying on the ground with the machine gun's bipod unfolded to steady and support the barrel and he was positioning the ammunition strip to feed into the weapon. Wanting to scream but aware that she needed to not draw attention to herself, Sophia spoke in a low voice into her comms. "Oliver. Can you hear me? Get down. Do *not* exit the tunnel. It's a trap….Oliver?"

Knowing that there was nothing she could do faced with that firepower, she started filming the assailants with her cell phone.

Sophia whispered sadly into her microphone, "Oliver. Where are you?"

***

Oliver ran at full speed through the tunnel on the way to the subway. He reached into his back pocket and retrieved a wad of Kleenex and shoved it up his nose to staunch the bleeding. He hip checked a man out of his way and winced at the pain that shot down his leg. He wheeled around a person who stumbled and fell and screamed at him. He knocked a man down and leapt over a fallen tourist, who must have been bowled over by the escaping assassin. It was hard to get a clear unobstructed view up the tunnel, but occasionally he could catch glimpses of the man ahead of him.

Viewing his quarry veer up the stairs to the streets, Oliver spun around a frozen in place bystander and took the stairs up two at a time. Over the crackling in his headphones he could start to hear Sophia's voice, but he couldn't make out the words. He appeared above ground in the street and was jolted by the impact and pain of bullets ripping into his body. He desperately threw himself in the direction of a parked car to get shelter.

His world went black.

***

Sounds of machine gun fire filled the command center. Elda started biting the sides of her fingers. Tosh was scowling, bent over the communication setup. He vainly repeated again and again, "Oliver, Sophia, come in," only to be met with silence.

A black plastic and metal chair flew across the conference room and thudded into the front wall. It missed the whiteboard and bounced harmlessly off the concrete bricks.

"*Der'mo!*" Anatoly had his fist bunched up and was ready to explode. He reached for a second chair.

"Stop that now, Anatoly," commanded Elda sharply.

"*Stoy!*" shouted Tosh. His voice cut through the emotions and his steely gaze brought everyone to a dead stop.

Anatoly looked at Elda and Tosh, breathing heavily through his nose.

Elda spoke softly, "Yuri and Anatoly get your sneakers on and go to the gym. Anatoly, Yuri can hold the punching bag for you. If you break it, it's okay, we'll pay for it."

Snezhana was rocking back and forth in her chair, pounding her thigh. David was pacing.

Elda gently addressed them, "Snezhana and David, go for a run. Tosh and I will handle this here."

Stas was crying. Elda handed him a box of Kleenex and said kindly, "Go to the communication room and see if you can get us any more information, okay? If there is none, spend some time playing a video game."

Yuri reached over to motion Anatoly on to the gym. Anatoly slapped away Yuri's hand and stomped out of the room. Yuri jogged out after him. David reached out his hand. Snezhana ignored it, rising to go for a run. The two of them left with David talking softly to Snezhana.

Tosh turned to Elda. "Well, that didn't go so well, did it?" he said angrily.

Elda responded in a monotone voice, "I'll contact the British Embassy in Montreal to get MI6 involved. Can you contact the Russian Embassy? I'll also talk to the Canadian Security Intelligence Agency and brief them."

Tosh's jaw muscles were clenched as he stated n a carefully controlled tone, "We need to retrieve the bodies."

Elda winced and replied tersely, "Yes."

Chapter Thirteen

James paced back and forth in front of the group in the conference room. A sob escaped from Sophia, who had flown back from Canada.

James stopped, sighed, and pushed his fingers from front to back through his hair. He adjusted his glasses and addressed the group, "Let's put together what we know so far. First of all, it will be touch and go, but Oliver is strong and should pull through. But he's definitely out of action for the rest of this operation. His injuries are severe and he will be in hospital and then rehab for a while. As soon as he is stable enough, we will medivac him to the UK."

James indicated Sophia, who was slumped in a chair. Snezhana was patting her on the back. Sophia shook her off and sat up at attention. "Sophia has asked to continue on the mission with us. The information we were following led us into a trap. The assassin was killed by the spray of bullets that cut down Oliver. We retrieved his body and he is of Eastern European origin. His weapons, clothing and haircut indicate he is most probably Ukrainian, but perhaps he is Russian."

All eyes turned to Alexei and Tosh. Alexei stated firmly, "He may have been of Russian ethnicity, but it wasn't the Russians. I will return to the Kremlin where I can access more resources to track this down. With Tosh and Elda, I am not value added anyway."

James stood still and pointedly asked Alexei, "Are you sure, Alexei, that this joint operation is not a way to sabotage our efforts?"

"Let's not start accusing each other," interrupted Elda. "Russia's stake in this operation is as high as ours. Let's take a step back and analyze the situation and see what we can find out. Let's frame it, as we look at the facts, that perhaps the assassin was a decoy, in an attempt to flush us out, and to cause discord among us."

James spun around and snapped, "Don't you use that new age babble on me, Elda."

Tosh stopped James with a glance and snapped, "James, Elda is right. They have succeeded in pruning our team by one, perhaps two, if they were behind Yaromir's accident, as I suspect. Their goal may be to plant seeds of distrust between us. Let's not buy into their plan." Tosh hooked Sophia's cell phone up to an overhead projector. "Let's review the footage we have. Please dim the lights, Anatoly."

Tosh played the scene twice. The sounds of Sophia blowing her nose added to the sadness and shock of watching Oliver be riddled with bullets. Tosh turned off the projector and demanded, "What did you see?"

Yuri started by ponying up, "They were definitely there to kill the assassin and anyone following him."

"*Khorosho*. What else?" asked Tosh curtly.

Elda sat silent. She had formulated a lot of the answers to Tosh's anticipated questions but she wanted the team to observe and learn.

Snezhana volunteered, "The men with the machine guns have trained together. They were coordinated and each knew his position and role."

Tosh barked, "Very good. What else?"

Anatoly offered, "They are not Russian. I know how Russian military, KGB and GRU operatives are trained. Their movements are different."

Snezhana added, "Their body dimensions suggest they may be Asian. Perhaps Chinese."

Elda waited to ensure all had spoken and then chimed in: "Those machine guns are not Russian. They are used by the Koreans."

Tosh nodded at the team's correct answers and summarized, "Exactly."

***

Elda faced Tosh and looked directly at him, her brown eyes boring into his grey ones. She asked, "Can we trust Stas, Tosh?"

Elda and Tosh were alone in the conference room, having dismissed the team.

Tosh replied without hesitation, "*Da*. He is a civilian but he is a loner, has no family, and is not motivated by money. There's really nothing that others can leverage to get to him."

"Fine." Elda accepted his assessment without question.

They turned to leave and Tosh asked. "Tell me Elda. What made you think this operation was off?"

"I don't know, Tosh," Elda replied with a shrug. "I sometimes without thinking gather bits of information in the background and piece them together until they bubble up to my conscious stream of thinking. I've always had that, shall we say, sixth sense about things."

Tosh rolled his eyes, but then squinted and leaned in towards Elda. "And, what does that *sixth sense* of yours tell you now, Elda?" he queried.

Elda scratched her head and responded, "There's definitely something not right here. Let's discretely run background checks on each team member again. I don't think we have a mole on our core team, but I am suspicious that we may have a leak somewhere else. They *knew* we were in Montreal. There are too many people involved with all the base personnel, and MI6 and their communication personnel. I would like to pare this team down to the essentials. With Alexei heading back to the Kremlin, I think we should get away from James and Ed too. We need to establish our own headquarters away from London and run this ourselves."

Tosh rubbed his chin, paused, and then agreed, "*Khorosho*. We need to be lean and able to strike when we want to, without layers of bureaucratic overhead. *You* tell our bosses."

***

The team shuffled dejectedly to the chow hall for breakfast. Stas, having run to the computer center to see if he could get any more leads, was not with the group.

Anatoly slammed his fist on the table. "*Der'mo*, Tosh and Elda. Send me out next. I will bring back bodies."

Elda said calmly, "It's not bodies we need Anatoly. We need prisoners and actionable information. We'll send you when we have the right lead for you."

147

Anatoly balled his hands up and looked around for something to take his frustration out on. Tosh cleared his throat. Anatoly took a deep breath and unclenched his fists.

Just then Stas rejoined the group. Snezhana looked closely at him and said, "You need to get more sleep and eat more, Stas."

Stas shook his head, "*Nyet*, not yet."

Tosh spoke up, "Stas! Snezhana is right. Listen!."

Elda chimed in, "Well then, Stas, before you go nap, do you have any information?"

"*Nyet*, not really. We do have some chatter about a cell of Russians being trained in Maine on Mt. Desert Island, but I don't know if it's related to this."

"Tosh and I will go check it out. We need to stretch our legs a bit."

"We do?" asked Tosh skeptically, turning to stare into Elda's eyes.

"Of course we do, Tosh," said Elda pointedly, opening her eyes wide and setting her mouth in a stern line.

Tosh nodded.

Chapter Fourteen

Tosh stood in the parking lot, with his hands on his hips, glaring at Elda, and demanded, "What are you doing? I'm in charge here."

"I know. Hop in." Elda threw Tosh's *go-bag* at him and tossed her bag in the back seat of a Jeep. She jumped into the driver's side and started the borrowed vehicle.

Tosh stood still. "*No*, Elda. *First*, you tell me what this is all about."

"We're going to the airport. You will spin off, change into a disguise and hop on a flight to Italy where you will rent us a villa near Montepulciano. It's near Florence, so I expect you may be able to squeeze in a few extra hours and see our favorite statue. *Now* will you get in?"

Tosh angrily popped into the passenger's seat and dropped his bag between his feet. Elda put the truck into gear and bounced across the field to the road leading to the base gate. "And what will *you* be doing, Elda?" Tosh inquired with a note of sarcasm.

"I will head up to Maine, as we have told the team we are doing, and flush out the cell, if there even is one. If possible, I'll capture a prisoner and send him or her to DC for Ed to interrogate. I have a rented camper waiting for me at the airport, and I have also arranged for a stand-in for you. Although you *are* hard to replicate."

Tosh, not amused at Elda's attempt at humor, said dryly, "I'm sure the stand-in won't be as interesting as I would be. So I get to view artwork and you get to fight the bad guys? What the fuck, Elda."

"We can't all have fun, you know?" Noticing that Tosh was not at all receptive to levity, Elda dropped the attempt at humor and glanced seriously at Tosh. "Really, Tosh, I'd switch destinations with you in a heartbeat, but this way makes the most sense. It's Italy, Tosh. They will rent to a male without questions. And we need a cover in order to get our new base secretly set up. This mission provides a way to get prepared without the mole discovering what we are doing, but *only* if we split up. This Maine cell may be nothing and I'm using it as a smokescreen, so you can do the important work for our future survival. But, the main point is that we can't just sit on our butts and send our people into danger when we're not willing to do it ourselves. We need to set an example and be leaders here."

Tosh was still frowning. "You cannot make decisions without me. I am in charge. Do you understand, Elda??"

Elda smiled, agreeing, "You're right Tosh. I'm sorry. I should have asked you. It's definitely an example of how I have been working by myself my whole career and also need to learn how to be a better teammate. I'll try to improve in the future. Please do point it out to me when I screw up again."

Tosh visibly relaxed. "Oh, I'll point it out, but you may not appreciate how I do that," he replied, with a slight hint of a smile in his eyes. "You win, Elda. I'll go to Italy. It'll serve my purpose well. I have contacts there and I may dig out some more leads, since it was the first place mentioned in our original briefing."

***

A slender elderly man huddled over a cane, wearing a gray houndstooth jacket with leather patches on the elbows and a blue handkerchief in his upper pocket, tottered into Heathrow Airport. He shuffled his way to the British Airway counter. His face was lined and sagged with age. He had a scraggly mustache and a hint of a beard. His hat shaded his eyes from view. With trembling hands he pushed his passport and ticket onto the counter and hung onto the counter's edge for support.

"May I help you sir?" A British Airways representative picked up his ID.

In a thin cracking voice the man replied, "Yes, my name is Edward Tolinsky and I am flying to Pisa today."

The representative opened and checked the passport. Her fingers then flew over her keyboard as she accessed his reservation. "Ah yes, Mister Tolinsky. We have you booked in first class. May I get you a wheelchair?"

"Yes, please." Tosh slowly looked around and scanned the area. He had noted the location of the security cameras on the way in, but knew there were more hidden in the ceiling and pole supports. He hated being exposed in airports. No matter how good his disguise, the prolonged waits made for a higher probability that his cover could be blown. He needed to go to Italy and back undetected, in order for their plan to set up a secret base for the team to work.

***

Elda's heart leapt in her chest. She looked out the window of the single engine plane, viewing the green of the pine, spruce and fir trees, contrasted against the brown rocks and blue water of Maine's coastline. She was so close to home and Dawn and Vee.

The plane caught a pocket of air and jostled her, catching her off guard. She grabbed the arm of her chair and tightened her seatbelt. She was reassured by watching the propellers on the engine move and by the knowledge that there were two of them. Her father, an airline pilot, had always advised flying in planes that had more than one engine, so if one went you could still land the plane. She missed her long talks with her father and his sage advice. He had died far too young. Elda fatalistically believed that she would, like him, also die young. It was probably partly why she threw herself into dangerous situations.

The puddle jumper bounced down the concrete runway as it landed. Once the engines were cut, Elda grabbed her bag from the overhead, climbed down the stairs, and crossed to the terminal at the Hancock County Bar Harbor Airport. Waiting for her in the terminal was a gaunt scruffy gray-haired man, holding a set of keys.

"Welcome to Maine, Elder."

Elda took a set of keys from his hand and awkwardly hugged him. "Thanks, Jim. Did you get me the RV?"

He returned the hug and patted her on the back. "Ah-yup, Ah did. 'Tis rahight outside. All gassed up. In the first row of cahs. Ah rented it with the names you told me to use."

Elda stepped back and smiled at him. She stated, "'Preciate it, Jim. We'll all have to get together when I get back home. Do me one more favor?"

Jim brightened and nodded. "Ah-yup."

"Pop by and see Dawn and let her know I'm okay?" Elda asked, fighting down the urge to tear up.

He briefly touched her shoulder and said, "Ah-yup. Will do."

Elda looked down at the ground so Jim wouldn't see the tears in her eyes. She blinked rapidly and then uttered, "Thanks much."

Elda watched wistfully as her friend hobbled away. He and she had known each other for many years. He was a crusty New Englander, who had been wounded in Vietnam, but still loved to serve his country and often did small jobs for her. The two of them shared their commitment to duty and the loss of their mutual friend, Fred Perry, who had committed suicide a few years after coming home from Vietnam. She stood there for a moment and let a wave of sadness move through her, then shook it off and walked outside to see what he had rented for her.

She walked around the 24-foot Coachmen Galleria Class B Motorhome, admiring Jim's selection, while checking the tires for road worthiness. She moved inside, located and opened a box full of the materials she had requested. She gave silent thanks to Jim for his attention to detail. Everything she had asked for was there.

She extracted a small collection of equipment and planted inside the RV hidden video cameras and microphones, and then did the same on the outside. There was a bike rack and two bikes mounted on the back of the RV, as she had requested, and a realistic mannequin lying on the rear couch. Elda pulled down the blinds and sat the mannequin upright and set a baseball cap on his head. She turned on the television, adjusted the volume, then turned it back off. She adjusted a reading lamp near the dummy, so his shadow could be displayed, once the light was turned on. She then attached the light and TV to a Bluetooth remote control that sync'd with her iPhone. She added another similar light and timer to the kitchen area.

Satisfied that everything she set up was good to go, Elda jumped up into the driver's seat, carefully backed out, and started the journey down to the Mount Desert Island Campground on the coast of Maine, where she had reserved a waterfront site. As she turned south instead of north she softly murmured, "I'm sorry, Dawn."

***

An old man, leaning heavily on his cane, doddered his way into the bathroom in the Milan Malpensa airport. A few minutes later, Tosh, dressed in a sporty cap and a black leather jacket, exited the men's room. Tanned, with brown hair and a goatee, he jauntily walked with a bag over his shoulder and traversed the short walk from the baggage claim area to the train out of the airport.

He hopped off the train at Milano Centrale and checked the departure board. He noted that there was a train leaving in 10 minutes for Florence. He jogged over to the designated platform, jumped through the door onto the train and plopped himself down into a seat, holding his bag on his lap. Out of breath, he admonished himself to slow down. His energy level was not what it had been in his hay day.

Tosh found himself lulled to sleep by the rhythmic sounds of the train speeding along on its way to Florence via Bologna. Waking, he shook his head and went to the bathroom to splash water on his face. He then traipsed over to the dining car to get a cup of coffee with a double shot of expresso added to it. He was fully awake by the time the train arrived at the Santa Maria Novella train station in Florence.

After taking a few minutes to orientate himself, Tosh took off for the Museum Santa Maria Novella. Tosh loved Florence and had been there many times, most recently the previous year for a meeting with Elda. He enjoyed the cat and mouse game they played to try to outwit and get more information on the other. He knew her to be a formidable opponent. But aside from that, it was pleasant to share a mutual love of Florence and the arts. He always found it remarkable the bonding that could come from being strangers together in the land of spies and how much he could like someone he might later kill.

***

At dusk, Elda pulled the red bike off the bike rack. She jumped on it and biked away down the dirt road. Once out of sight of the RV, she stopped and pushed a button on her cell phone to turn on the presets inside the camper. Further down the path, she stopped again and let the air out of one of her tires, then walked the bike over to a family camping nearby. Thankfully they did not have a bike pump, since that would have ruined her plan.

She negotiated with one of the parents to have their oldest child take her bike back to her camper and leave it on the side away from the road, so she could continue on her way on foot. The money she offered was enough to persuade them to help, but not too much to cast suspicion on her request. The child grabbed her bike and trotted off with it.

Satisfied that the bait had been set, she threw her backpack over one shoulder and loped away.

***

The lone man put down his binoculars and nervously adjusted the string around his thick neck. The woman had just left on her bike. He would now need to wait until she came back. He leaned in against a fir tree and stared out over the water, while stretching out a cramp in his calf. He noticed the rocky cliffs and wondered if he should throw her over the cliff when she returned. To check the feasibility of that plan, he got up and stared down the cliffs and decided to keep it as a backup option. Killing them both inside the trailer would be his first preference.

He walked back to his tree. Just then a child walked by. Going in the other direction, a muddy, short, bearded fisherman, wearing a yellow slicker, and carrying a fishing rod, passed the boy. The man ground his teeth at frustration at the sudden foot traffic.

Then he noticed that the light had turned on in the trailer and he could see faintly the outline of a man, who appeared to be sitting and watching TV. He decided to crawl around the camper and set some plastic explosives while the man inside was distracted by the TV.

Once he was around the other side of the camper, he saw the red bike with a flat, propped up against the side of the camper. He wondered when she had returned, but decided it didn't matter. It was a sign to take them both out now. He carefully placed his first piece of plastic explosive on the side of the RV.

***

Tosh stood quietly admiring the wooden statue of Mary Magdalene. She stood penitent but proud. Her struggles through the years were etched into her face. Her clothing was tattered but covered her like a fine gown as a tribute to what she had been through. Her body was gaunt but powerful. Her bare feet gripped the ground with the practiced stance of one who had never worn shoes. Her hands were held as if she may be about to pray, but hesitant, as if she may not be worthy of the effort. The raw emotions from hunger and poverty surrounded her. And yet, she stood tall with a hint of hope in her eyes.

A young man in a dress suit walked up beside Tosh, knelt to tie his shoe and stood again. He asked, *"Bellissima non e vero?"*

"Si. Adoro questa statua," answered Tosh.

"Yes, I also love it." The man looked down and exclaimed, "Aha! Is this your notebook down at your feet here, *signore*?"

Tosh glanced at the notebook, proclaiming, *"Grazie.* Yes it is. I placed it there when I arrived and forgot about it."

The man nodded and walked away. Tosh put on a pair of black leather driving gloves, bent and picked up the small thick notebook. He took one last fond look at the statue and strode away. As he wove through the streets of Florence back toward the train station to meet an agent at the Precious Villas rental agency, he took a peek inside the notebook. In the middle there was a section cut out of the pages and a thumb drive was inserted there. He removed and pocketed the thumb drive and threw the notebook away in the next trash can he went by.

Tosh soon arrived at the rental agency and strolled in. A friendly looking stout bodied woman, with thick dark black hair pulled back into a bun, walked up to him.

"*Ciao*. How can I help you, *signore*?" she asked cheerily.

Tosh responded, "I am interested in renting a villa near Montepulciano for myself and a number of other friends."

Her smile widened as she informed him, "You've come to the right place. We have a number of places available. When would you be wanting to rent it and for how long?"

"Immediately, if possible. Probably for a number of months too," Tosh estimated, returning the woman's smile.

She rubbed her hands and queried, "How many people will be staying there?"

"Seven," Tosh stated.

The woman's smile threatened to cut her face in two. Her eyes sparkled. She quickly asked, "Do you have a price range in mind?"

Tosh waved his hand at her and shook his head to dismiss that absurd possibility. She broke into a full grin. "*Eccellente, signore*. I can show you some wonderful places right now, if you have the time."

Tosh gestured towards the door and said, "Lead the way."

The agent grabbed a slightly wrinkled tan linen jacket from the back of her chair and a set of keys from a small rack on their way out. She briskly led Tosh to the car park. "While we're driving you can tell me more about what you're looking for."

Settling back into the leather passenger seat, Tosh explained, "We have been working extraordinarily hard and my company has rewarded us with a combination vacation/remote work opportunity. I adore Italy, so I requested that I bring my team here. Since we will be working, we will need a quiet and remote location."

The agent expertly wove around cars at a high speed, driving with one hand on the wheel and gesturing with the other. She briefly threw both hands in the air and replied delightedly, "Ah yes, I have just the place in mind." Her right hand returned to the wheel.

Tosh stared out the window, as they sped by the rolling grassy fields, punctuated by spikes of green cypress trees and bushy olive groves. For the first time in weeks he felt a calmness and had to remind himself to stay alert and focus on the mission. He assumed that at any moment the enemy could attack. For all he knew, she could be one. He sized her up out of the corner of his eyes.

They careened off the strade locali onto a hardpacked dirt road. They bumped along in a cloud of dust, the woman telling Tosh about the history of the area. She waved her arm at the rolling expanse in front of them. *"Bella vero?"*

"Sì."

She suddenly pulled off the dirt road into a gravel driveway in front of a large yellow terracotta brick and stone villa topped by a red-orange clay tile roof. She parked in the middle of the driveway and selected a set of keys from a pile in the car's center console. Tosh walked around the outside of the villa first, noting that it was surrounded by open space, so it would be hard to approach from any direction without detection. Entering, he admired the number of windows and the good visibility they had of the road and the countryside. The agent patiently let him finish his inspection.

She pointed out, "There are five bedrooms, a pullout bed and a large couch."

Tosh acknowledged her statement, "Excellent." He looked around again. The open concept kitchen/living room/dining room was bright and painted a cheery yellow. There was a large fireplace against one wall surrounded by comfy looking chairs with a sizeable oval coffee table in the middle and, opposite that, a leather couch. It was perfect for a conference area. "I'll take it."

The agent's eyes lit up. *"Eccellente, signore.* Let's go back to the office and fill out the paperwork."

***

Elda, disguised as a slightly built fisherman, watched from behind a large tree as the solidly built man set the plastic explosives under the RV and headed to the door of the camper. Elda leapt out, tackled the man, bringing him down with a thump flat on his face. The man groaned and slowly attempted to rise. The metal tip of her fisherman's work boot caught the trespasser solidly in his jaw and he fell backwards, hitting his head on a rock. The man lay there temporarily stunned.

The fisherman jumped on top of the interloper and held a knife to his throat, increasing the pressure, until blood started to seep out where the knife was cutting into skin. In a daze, the man moaned and instead of trying to remove the knife, gently adjusted his jaw with one hand. His other hand was pinned under Elda's knee. He made no attempt to remove it.

"I think you broke it," he weakly mumbled, his eyes tearing up from the pain.

Elda snarled, "I'll break more if you don't talk. Who sent you?"

"I don't know," he whispered.

Elda barked back at him, "Bull shit." She demanded, "What was your mission and how did you receive it?" The knife cut in deeper.

The strength returned to his voice, as he desperately tried to reason with her. He started to babble quickly. "Wait! Wait! I really don't know. I have done work for a man, whose name I don't know. He calls me occasionally and I do small jobs for him, no questions asked. He called a couple of days ago, gave me a list of names and said one, or all of these people, would be in this area and I would be paid well to take them out. The box of explosives was delivered to my door." He stopped, overcome by the pain of talking.

Elda backed off the knife slightly. "How did you find this RV?"

He reached up and touched the knife blade where it pressed against his throat and then held his hand up to his eyes and turned it, staring at the blood on his fingers. He answered flatly, "I had a watch on all the car, RV, hotel, inn, and campground rental places. Two of the people on the list, Tosh and Elda rented this RV. I followed it here."

Elda continued to pump him for information, "What other information were you given?"

"None. Just these names." He looked at her directly as he answered.

"Why should I believe you?" she queried.

He answered softly, "Because I have nothing left to lose."

Elda drilled him, "What were you instructed to do with these people?"

He answered succinctly, "Kill them."

Elda pressed the knife in again. Blood seeped from around the blade. "Be truthful. Have you ever met this man?"

Struck with the seriousness of his no-win situation, the man started crying. He spit out between sobs, "No, he has a Russian accent and he pays me by direct transfer into my account."

Elda cajoled, "Give me the account number and we will pay you more to work for us."

The man's eyes went dark with hopelessness. "You don't understand. You might as well kill me now. I have no way out of this now. He is much too powerful. He has a long reach, and has killed others for far less. I have failed him in this mission, so he will have me killed."

"We will protect you," she promised, relaxing in her certainty that he would accept her offer.

"No you can't. I told you, I am a dead man." With that said, he grabbed Elda's wrist and jabbed the knife further in, severing his carotid artery. Blood pumped out to the beat of his heart, spurting from his neck onto Elda's sleeve.

Elda watched dispassionately, as the blood and life drained from him. She was relieved it was quick. And quiet. She glanced down at the blood that had splashed on her and was thankful that it had landed on her raincoat. She quickly looked around and saw that they were both fully hidden from the camp road by the RV. She wiped the knife on his clothing and rolled him over the cliff. She confirmed that he had splashed down into the deeper water and the tide was going out. The unweighted body would soon pop up, but it would stay submerged until the gases formed, which would give her enough time to get far away. She rushed to unhook the water from the RV and thoroughly washed off her coat and the surrounding area, before coiling the hose and stowing it. She then disconnected the sewer line and electrical, put the bike back on the rack, removed the blocks of C4 from the undercarriage and carefully stashed them into a storage compartment. Pulling herself up and into the driver's seat, she slowly drove away.

Her phone pinged as she exited the campground. Looking down she saw that Tosh had sent her a picture of the Penitent Magdalene statue by her favorite sculptor, Donatello. She assumed Tosh had completed his mission.

***

Stamp. The immigration officer let Tosh through without a second glance. He had returned to Heathrow just prior to Elda. He had no need to assume his disguise since the two of them had been traveling to the US. Tosh had placed a counterfeit entry to the USA on the passport he was using to return to the UK.

While waiting for Elda, he popped into the business center located in the Queens Building between terminals 1 and 2. He inserted the thumb drive into a computer there and scrolled through its contents.

OPERATION BITTMAN… DISINFORMATION… MI6… USA… ASSASSINATION… KREMLIN… UNIT 74455 OF THE RUSSIAN MAIN INTELLIGENCE DIRECTORATE (GRU)…

The words streaming by on the screen confirmed his suspicions that Russia was actively working on disinformation campaign to stir up opposing factions in the Western world and in particular to derail the political structure of the United States. Their end goal was to throw the USA into a Civil War and eliminate it as a rival super power. Tosh was glad he had chosen Stas to work with them and not anyone from the Kremlin's cyber team. There was mention of an Operation Bittman and a mole in MI6, but no mention of who that was, or even a codename to follow. There also was no reference to who in the Kremlin was running this operation. He scrolled onward.

TOSH… ELDA… ELIMINATE TEAMS…

Just then he realized he had not heard from Elda since they parted ways at Heathrow.

Chapter Fifteen

Elda and Tosh strolled into the situation room in London's MI6 offices. Ed left the side of James and stalked up to them and stared them both in the eyes.

"Did you have any difficulty?" Ed asked in a stern voice.

"None at all," answered Tosh without blinking. "Everything went smoothly. My mission was accomplished."

Ed glared at Elda. "Was that your experience also, Elda?" he interrogated.

Elda smiled at Ed with dead eyes and said dully, "Just a minor complication. But it all went smoothly for both of us." Her eyes flitted over to James to signify to Ed that *now* was *not* the time to discuss it.

Missing the signal, Ed continued, "And was the complication by any chance a dead body that recently washed up off the coast of Maine with his throat slit?"

"Oh my, in Maine? It's such a beautiful place too. I do hope that it isn't becoming a high crime area. That will ruin tourism." Elda glared at Ed, pointedly squinting her eyes and frowning.

Ed backed off, "Ah. All right. I see."

Tosh raised his eyebrows and turned to Elda. "A dead body, hey?"

Elda shrugged. "There's not much to say about it." She started to turn away to end the conversation.

Ed reached out and stopped her, "Do you remember the day you joined the military?"

Elda turned back. "Vividly. I remember parking my car outside of the Officer Candidate barracks and feeling as if a large steel door was clanging shut behind me and that I would never be again who I was before."

Ed persisted, "When I joined, I also had that strong sense of transition into a new life. In the military, however, I learned to compartmentalize: to shut the bad away. I'm not sure that it's the right way, but it is all we know to do to handle our emotions around the horrific things we see and do."

Elda exhaled loudly and nodded. This time, there was a hint of life in her eyes. "You are so correct, Ed.

She left Ed's side and moved over to Tosh, asking in a low voice, "And how was Italy?"

Tosh rubbed the back of his neck and responded in a subdued voice, "You'll like the villa. It's perfect for our needs."

Elda cocked her head and rubbed her chin. "Thank you for the picture. How is Mary?"

Tosh broke eye contact and blinked before replying, "As beautiful as always."

Having her suspicion confirmed that Tosh went willingly to Italy, since he had other business to attend to in Florence, Elda simply said, "I am envious you got to see her."

Tosh nodded in response and stated, "I know."

Before Elda could ask another question of Tosh, Stas ran excitedly into the situation room. "We have another lead. Chatter has it that an assassin is being activated in St. Petersburg."

"How good is this information, Stas?" Elda inquired.

"*Ya ne znayu*, Elda. I'm sorry. I really don't know."

Just then David and Snezhana popped into the room. Tosh snapped at them, "What do we know? We have already walked into one trap. How do we know this isn't another?"

David answered, "The funding trail also leads to St. Petersburg. It stems from Korea. That information could also be planted, but it does help legitimize the lead."

Snezhana added, "And even if they are trying to entrap us, knowing that gives us the upper hand, right? So we turn the tables on them."

Tosh smirked at Elda, who looked surprised at Snezhana's correct analysis. Tosh clapped his hands sharply, "Snezhana! Identify the source of the data. You, David, and Stas continue to dig for ways to turn this around. Move on this *now*. Stas, go find everyone and return here with them. We need them back here immediately. I will also text them." Tosh texted Anatoly and Yuri to find Sophia and to reconvene in the conference room. Within minutes, the team was assembled again with Stas in the rear herding them in like a border collie.

Elda took charge. "All right. Listen up. Anatoly and Yuri, you two are to head to St. Petersburg and wait for further instructions. Be aware that this could be another set-up. Be hypervigilant. Do not take unnecessary risks. We're looking for information. For prisoners, not more dead bodies."

The group looked at Elda and Tosh expectantly.

Tosh clapped his hands. *"Idti! Seychas!"*

Anatoly and Yuri grabbed their go-bags and jogged out to catch their plane.

"The rest of us are going to double down on our training here, while Tosh and I work on setting up a new command post. You are dismissed."

The remaining team members lingered, anxious for action, for something to do that would directly impact the mission.

" *Idti, idti, idti*!" yelled Tosh, clapping his hands to help move them along.

The room emptied.

Tosh turned to Elda and quietly muttered, "I am going to Moscow for a day."

Elda narrowed her eyes. "Did you find Florence just full of interesting objects?"

"Yes. They just can't be appreciated electronically. It really does take a face to face to appreciate all the hidden nuances."

Elda lowered her voice and covered her mouth from any watching cameras, pantomiming a sneeze, "And you don't want Alexei to know?"

Tosh gave an almost imperceptible nod.

"Right. Got it." Elda simultaneously blew her nose for effect, masking the sound of her voice and hiding her mouth under the trailing tissue. She left in search of James and Ed.

***

Snezhana could feel the sweat dripping off her chin and pooling in her cleavage. She warily circled David, watching his hands for signs of his next move. She wondered how those hands would feel on her body. Her mind wandered.

Snezhana stared up at David, and at the steel beams that crossed the ceiling, from the black padded mat in the small gym. David's face stared down at her with a look of concern. "You have to pay attention, Snezhana," he stated, "This is the third time I've easily thrown you today. Are you feeling all right?"

She cursed herself in her head as she lay there, looking into his soulful brown eyes, then answered, "*Da*. I think I should go for a run before we continue. Perhaps it will clear my head."

David reached out a hand and helped pull Snezhana to her feet. They were inches away from each other. The closeness of him made it hard for her to move.

"Okay Snez, but you're taking a lot of runs lately. Be careful not to over train."

Snezhana stared at his glistening bare chest. His concern for her added to his sexiness.

***

The sound of their breathing and footsteps filled the concrete and metal stairwell as Anatoly and Yuri jogged up the hotel stairs in the Radisson Royal Hotel in St. Petersburg. They paused at a landing to listen to ensure no one was behind or in front of them. Satisfied they bounded up the stairs again.

"They have elevators in this hotel, you know?" Yuri remarked.

Anatoly chuckled, "Whimp. *Slabovol'nyy chelovek.* This is good for you, Yuri. Anyway, it's too easy to get trapped in an elevator."

"Do you have a plan, Anatoly?" Yuri accelerated and passed Anatoly and then waited for him to catch up. They continued upwards side by side.

Anatoly shared his plan, "We will set up audio and visual to monitor the room and who visits us. You did ask your contact to reserve an extra room, connecting to the room we reserved under our real names?"

"*Da.* It is all set. I have two keys. Here is one for you. Logistics is my specialty. Drugs, planes, rooms,

174

whatever…" Yuri slipped the key into Anatoly's waiting hand.

They stopped on the landing and cracked open the door to peek out into the hallway. After ensuring the hallway was clear, they exited the stairwell. The hallway door closed behind them with a soft click. The two of them ran lightly, and quickly slipped into the second room. They put down their bags and padded across the soft brightly colored patterned carpet. Anatoly listened at the connecting door, retrieved his bag, and used a master key to silently pop open the lock. Yuri hung back while Anatoly expertly searched the room, finding two bugs. Leaving the bugs in place, he secreted a tiny surveillance camera and his own listening device. He swiftly returned to Yuri, closing and locking the door between the two rooms.

Anatoly commented, "Now we wait."

***

"I *must* be in charge of MI6's assets." James shook his fist at Ed.

"Elda's right. This mission is too top heavy." Ed balled his hands into fists at his side, stood up tall and squared his shoulders.

"You Americans just want to be in charge of everything. Who brought you the intel that started this joint op in the first place?" James' voice cracked as he raised the

175

volume. The two men stood facing each other, their eyes throwing daggers

Elda interrupted the peacock display. "Just shut up and listen, Ed and James."

Shocked at being bossed around, the two of them turned from glaring at each other and looked wide-eyed at Elda. The three were standing in the close quarters of James' temporary office at the base.

Having obtained their attention, Elda continued, "James, you are partially correct. We do need MI6 and we need all the help that we can get. But we also need to shut down the leaks and go dark."

"But you actively need our involvement," James argued, taking a step toward Elda. Elda stood her ground and shook her head at Ed who had moved to intercept James.

Elda retorted firmly, "Not when it's doing more harm than good. You know my track record and you know Tosh's. You need to back off, but support us *when we ask for help*. There will be no more situation room level ops. Stas has all the access he needs. You, James, will ensure Stas is given all the electronic equipment that he requests. The two of you can best serve this mission by going back to your offices in the US and UK, respectively, and, as

Alexei is doing in Moscow, work your trusted contacts to back channel us intel."

"We can back out and leave you Americans on your own," belligerently shouted James, towering over Elda.

Elda stepped in closer to James and eyeballed him. James inched backwards. Elda took another step forward, forcing him to move back again. She stated icily and firmly, "But you won't, James, because the British Prime Minister's life is on the line *too*. And *you* need our help. So *this* is how it will go: Tosh and I will take the team to an undisclosed location. Don't try to follow us, or find us, or wheedle the information from Ed, since he won't know where we are either. Ed will be my point of contact, if and when we need anything, or if we have information we feel you need."

"You think you're that good?" James growled.

Unable to contain himself any longer, Ed jumped in. He hissed, "Oh quit the bullshit, James. You know Elda is that good, as is Tosh. Let's try this and see how it goes."

Elda gratefully declared, "Thank you, Ed."

Ed snapped at Elda, shaking his finger at her, "You screw up and I'll have your ass."

Elda snapped to attention and responded, "Yes sir."

***

A slender man with brown hair and dark brown eyes sat at a back-corner table, surveying the other diners in the library room at Café Pushkin. His slightly hooked nose wrinkled in disgust at the dust that had collected on the books, telescopes, ancient globes and other artifacts that were scattered about in an attempt to make the room look like a library. He glanced at his watch. The time had come. *Where was he?* Just then, an older man in a Russian Army uniform marched in and peered around the room. Tosh stood up and waved him over to the table. The two men hugged and sat down.

"Leonid, my good friend. I am so glad you could come," Tosh said with a smile.

Leonid shook his head and stated, "I wouldn't have recognized you, Tosh."

Tosh stated emphatically, "It can't be known that I was here."

Leonid placed his hand palm down on the table, and looked directly at Tosh. He vowed, "You have no worries. Your secret is safe with me."

Tosh nodded, responding, "You have shown that you are trustworthy in the past." He leaned forward and lowered his voice to almost a whisper, stating, "I need your assistance, general. Your loyalty must be with me. Do I have your word on that?"

The general placed the palm of his right hand on his left chest. "You know I'm in your debt. *Anything* you want. I would do it for you even if I didn't owe you," he pledged.

"I know. That's why I called you." Tosh gave the general a faint smile and then frowned. He lowered his voice even more and continued. "I think that I have been sent on a suicide mission. And I am angry that my team is being used in this way. I can't use the usual channels for information. Nor can I call on others who work for me, since the Kremlin will be watching for that. However, there may be times when I might need backup or a clean-up crew or some other work done, without anyone else knowing."

Leonid thumped his chest with his fist and stated, "I am your man. I will supply reliable resources when you need them. They will not be associated with the Kremlin. Why are they targeting your team?"

Tosh responded, "As you know, I and my team have been very successful in accomplishing our missions. That success threatens Alexie and he would love to replace me. However, I am well connected and he can't do that directly. My theory is that they need a fall guy to ensure no one suspects the Russians. If the Russian agents are killed as part of this operation, that helps strengthen the story."

Leonid raised his eyebrows and then nodded. He reminded Tosh, "Alexie has always been ambitious and is not above removing any impediment to his further promotion."

Tosh, pleased that Leonid was making the connections so quickly, agreed, "Exactly. And if he manages to set up top teams from the US and UK as well, then his job is made even easier."

Leonid sat back for a moment. He scowled and scratched his head and then leaned back into the conversation, inquiring, "May I ask what this operation is? That information may be helpful for me as I deploy folks to aid you."

Tosh nodded and answered, "We have been told there is chatter about an operation called Bitmann, where assassins are being deployed to kill world leaders."

Leonid knitted his brows together and rubbed his chin. "Why not let them?"

"I wish it were so easy, Leonid," Tosh responded, "However, one of the world leaders is our president."

Leonid raised an eyebrow. Tosh cocked his head slightly.

Tosh wisely changed the subject, "Despite that story line, my team is in danger, and I want to get rid of the assassins before they dispose of us. Can I use our old codes to communicate with you?"

Tosh and Leonid made plans for lines of secure communication between the two of them and then ordered lunch. Half-way through their meal, Tosh noticed that a number of men, whom he knew to be assassins, were gathered by the exit.

"Were you followed, Leonid?" he demanded.

Leonid looked at Tosh blankly, "I am always followed, Tosh. Why?"

Tosh whispered through clenched teeth, "Don't look around but there are three suspicious men at a table near the exit." He moved his head to loosen the tenseness in his neck.

Leonid looked penitent and apologized, "I'm sorry, Tosh. Someone must have figured out that you and I are connected. I doubt that they are out to get me. I am too powerful still."

Tosh slowly moved his chair backwards, stating, "If you don't mind then, I will leave you with the check."

Leonid waved him on, "Not to worry. You'll owe me a dinner next time we meet."

"*Spasibo*." Tosh stood up, used his chair to break the window next to the table and jumped out.

***

The general watched as the assassins leapt out of their chairs and rushed out the door of the restaurant. He looked out the broken window and saw Tosh hurl himself onto the back bed of a slow-moving farm truck.

A waiter ran over to the general's table. "Are you all right, sir?"

The general nodded and held up both hands palms forward. He reassured the waiter, "Yes, I am. My friend had to rush out, but I think we were done eating. Can you please bring me the check and include the price of the damage in it? I will cover it."

"Certainly, sir."

The general turned and glanced out the window at the now quiet street. He whispered, "Be safe, my friend."

***

Tosh looked out the back of the truck he was riding in and spotted the three assassins running full bore up the road after him. He fretted at the slow pace of the truck. He had selected the restaurant since he intimately knew this neighborhood. He just needed to ride for a few more blocks and then he would be able to corner the assassins in a dead-end alleyway. He watched the road pavement go by and counted. Calculating the truck's rate of speed and their running speed in his head, he decided that, despite the truck's seemingly glacial pace, he would beat them to his destination.

Tosh looked around the truck bed for anything that could be used as a weapon. The smell of fertilizer was overpowering. He took out his knife and slashed into one of the bags.

He glanced back at the men racing down the street and redid his calculations. It would be close.

Chapter Sixteen

The medical inspector stepped over the first body in an alleyway in Moscow to examine the second one.

"*Interesnyy*. There is no obvious sign of why these three died. The first one does have a clump of hair pulled out and a gash on his forehead, but that would not have been fatal. This one obviously has a broken leg, but we know *that* didn't kill him. Let me examine the third one."

A young enlisted man in an army uniform stated, "He is going to want answers."

"Tell him I can't give them to him yet," the inspector commanded.

"I cannot do that!" stuttered the young man.

The inspector grimaced and said, "Well then *I* will tell him. I'll have to take them to the morgue at the Kremlin and do autopsies and hope I can find out something that way. I am suspicious of poisoning since they all have blue fingernails. And there are traces of what might be dirt around their mouths."

The enlisted man shook his head and declared, "Dirt? I don't understand."

The medical inspector confessed, "Neither do I at this point in time. Again, I will need to autopsy them. Whoever did this is a highly skilled professional. There are few signs of a fight and there are absolutely no clues left behind of who did this, or how many people did this."

The army man raised his hand and then quickly lowered it. "Yes?" asked the inspector with a small grin.

The young man said in a rush, "I have heard stories about one man who could have done this on his own, but he is in England."

The medical inspector unbuttoned the shirt of the third corpse. He ran his gloved hands through the body's hair looking for bumps or cuts. He turned the dead man over and lifted his shirt, inspecting the man's back. "This third one doesn't have a mark on him," the medical inspector concluded.

Eyes wide and bouncing slightly on his toes, the army man declared, "We will check with England."

***

Tosh sprinted into Elda's room. "I never left."

Elda looked at his messed hair and ripped shirt. And then she noticed a bandage peeking out from the end of his shirt sleeve. "Got it. We do have to stop meeting like this." She reached out for his arm, declaring, "And, while you're here, let me look at that wound."

Tosh batted her hand away. "It's nothing. I cleaned and bandaged the injury. It will hold."

Elda put an opened bottle of water in Tosh's good hand. "Drink this," she commanded. "Do you need stitches?"

Tosh looked away from her and then wincing, waved his bandaged hand at her. "No. I'm good." He turned away from her.

Elda persisted, "When was your last tetanus shot?"

"I'm not due yet," Tosh responded tersely.

Sighing, Elda gave up, "Okay tough guy. I'll let you be. But tuck that bandage in more or buy a shirt with longer sleeves."

Tosh's cell buzzed. He looked down and frowned. "It's Alexei." He pressed a button and answered. "*Da*?" He held out his phone to Elda. "He wishes to speak with you." His gray eyes bored into her brown ones. She nodded her understanding and took the phone from Tosh.

Smiling to lighten her voice, Elda pressed SPEAKER and then spoke into the phone. "Hi Alexei."

An angry voice came out of the speaker. "Where is Tosh?"

Elda glanced over at Tosh, replying, "Tosh? He's been with me these past few days. Why?"

Silence. Then Alexei responded, "Nothing."

Elda said cheerily, "No worries. We are sticking closely together. Would you like to speak with him?"

"*Nyet.*" The phone went dead.

She hung up the phone and handed it back to Tosh. "No worries."

"*Spasibo.*" Tosh pocketed his phone.

Elda held her nose and scowled at Tosh, "You stink of fertilizer. Were you farming?"

"I was helping some folks with their diet," Tosh said dryly.

Suppressing a smile, Elda responded matter-of-factly, "I'm sure that went down well. I'm glad you're all right. It's time you got showered and changed before someone else notices your new aftershave."

"*Da. Spasibo.*" Tosh started to turn away.

Elda reached out to stop him. She inquired, "Before you run off. Did you achieve your objectives?"

"Yes."

***

Stas excitedly dashed into the situation room, holding tightly to his laptop, bringing a waft of unwashed male scent with him. A better smelling Tosh followed Stas into the room.

"Stas, after you give us the information, please go shower and change your clothes." Elda noticed the deep bags under his eyes and added, "And get something good to eat, plus take a nap." She turned to Tosh, "Welcome Tosh. The group hasn't seen much of you lately."

"Yes." He swiveled away from Elda and snapped at Stas, "Do we have any more information on the assassin in St. Petersburg yet?"

"Nothing on St. Petersburg. But I think we have a lead on a third assassin," Stas offered.

"Where's this one?" demanded Tosh.

Stas sniffed his armpit and grimaced before responding, "Seattle."

188

Elda made a quick decision and ordered, "Okay, Snezhana and David, this one is yours."

David seized the handles of both Snezhana's and his go-bags, politely handing Snezhana her bag as they rushed out the door.

Tosh raised his eyebrows and shook his head. He caught Elda staring at him.

"She's your asset, Tosh. Do you have her under control or have you been blinded by the fact that she's your niece?"

Tosh stiffened and glared at Elda. "It's none of your concern, Elda."

Elda acknowledged that truth with a nod and commented, "You did tell me that you would remove her if she got out of line."

Shoving his hands in his pockets, Tosh took a step backwards, apologizing, "She can't help it. Her upbringing was less than optimal."

Elda stared at Tosh, folded her arms and asked, "How does that excuse her behavior, Tosh?"

Tosh held up a hand and pleaded, "Let me *finish*. Snez never felt treated as a true daughter and I think the anger my brother had for his son came out on her. He did beat her. He said it was to make her *bukskirovka linii*, ah, what you would say as, *tow the line*. He wanted her to go into a nunnery, but I knew it would kill her soul and persuaded him to let me use my influence and bring her into my fold. Because of my nephew abandoning her and my brother's strictness, Snez resented men and used and discarded them. This trait, along with her beauty and natural sexuality, adds to her usefulness as a spy."

"Yes, I can see that she has great potential," Elda said dryly, "*if* she doesn't get herself or someone else killed in the process. She better keep her pants on. We don't need David to try and protect her."

***

"How long has it been?" growled Anatoly.

"Only an hour, Anatoly. This could take days," replied Yuri calmly.

"*Der'mo*!" Anatoly hit his thigh with his fist.

Yuri and Anatoly were sitting side by side at the small wooden desk in the hotel room. They were playing Durak with a deck of cards Yuri had brought, while watching the display on the laptop that Anatoly had carried in his gadget bag.

Yuri started asking Anatoly questions to quell Anatoly's frustration from the lack of action. "How did you get here, Anatoly?"

Without looking up from his cards, Anatoly quipped, "By plane."

Yuri sighed dramatically. "You *know* what I mean."

Anatoly rolled his eyes in defeat and settled into Yuri's questioning. "I really had no choice. I guess I was born for this. I was recruited at a young age because of my strength and lack of empathy."

Yuri inquired, "Have you ever failed on a mission?"

Anatoly winced at that question. "According to the official records never, but yes, I failed to kill Elda. Although I can kill in many different ways with many implements, I love the feeling of the death struggles of a person being strangled. It's the most intimate relationship ever. I would enjoy killing Elda even more now that I know her better. Killing's all that really brings me pleasure."

"Except for sochniki," winked Yuri.

"Ah yes, there is nothing like a good sochniki. We should find a place to buy some before leaving." Anatoly patted his firm stomach.

"Is there *any* one person that you care for?" Yuri sat back after asking that question.

Anatoly scratched his head and contemplated the question a while before answering, "Tosh is like a father to me. I would do anything for him. I will *never* let him down." He frowned and shook his head. "Enough about me. I don't really care about your answer, but since we're passing time, how did *you* get here, Yuri?"

"My parents died when I was just a boy so I grew up without any role models. Because of my size I also got recruited young, but I failed to make it into the assassin program. Their assessment was that, despite the fact that I had a shaky morale compass and therefore would stray over the letter of the law to perform tasks that others might call illegal, I had too much heart and was too kind to others. I cannot kill an animal, never mind another human being. Tosh recommended that I still receive training, since my affinity for people and relationships and shall we say, different, ethical rules, would make me useful in gathering information."

Anatoly nodded. It fit with what he knew already. "But you worked for Elda at one point in time, didn't you?"

"I worked for anyone who would pay me, the Russian Mafia, the GRU, the SVR, the CIA, other cartels. I felt useful and it was thrilling, until the last gig that I had babysitting expats. Of course that assignment had a lovely side benefit." Yuri grinned lecherously and continued, "But Tosh made me pick a side. So here I am."

Anatoly had been closely watching the screen while Yuri talked. "Aga!" He held up his hand to silence Yuri.

They intently watched the screen as the other room's doorknob slowly turned and the barrel of a Makorov PM was thrust through the opening door. This was soon followed by a large combat boot and camouflaged leg. A man with a black facemask and black and white camouflaged fatigues entered, and quickly and efficiently checked the room, bathroom and closet. He then spoke into his watch in heavily accented English, "No one has been here." His hand went up to his ear and he pressed the earpiece to better hear the response. "Tak. I understand." With one last look around, he marched out of the room, pulling the door shut behind him.

***

The wide-angle view of Seattle was dizzying. Snezhana clutched at David's shirt. David and Snezhana stared down from the observation tower of the Space Needle at the tiny city below. David placed one arm around Snezhana, who leaned into him. They were sharing a map, each holding one side of it. David pointed his finger toward the skyline. "Look over there. I think that's a ghostly image of Mt. Rainer as it attempts to peak out of the clouds and haze."

"I think that's Elliot Bay over there. I get turned around at this height. I've never liked heights." Snezhana pressed herself closer into David. David tightened his arm reassuringly around Snezhana.

"You're well protected here, Snez," he declared. "Now let's get familiar with this area, so we can instinctively move around it without needing the map. Look at your map and the landmarks below. How would you get from here to the piers? What would you pass along the way? Where would be potential areas for ambushes?"

They silently compared their map of Seattle to the landmarks they could see below, enjoying the feel of their bodies touching. Just then their phones simultaneously vibrated and each of them received a picture of the potential assassin. They stared at the clean-cut face. David's phone rang.

"Can you talk?" Elda inquired over the phone.

David answered her, "Let us call you back from the street. Less chance of being overheard there."

David and Snezhana reluctantly separated and walked briskly to the elevators. They took the long elevator ride down and exited the Space Needle. After ensuring no one was near, David called Elda back, putting his phone on speaker, so Snezhana could overhear the conversation.

A tinny version of Elda's voice came through the speaker, "We are worried that this may be another decoy, but have nothing to base that on. Intel on this assassin has him as an American Navy veteran from Seattle."

"Where is he?" asked Snezhana.

Elda answered, "We don't know yet but we will send you the rest of the information as soon as we get it. All we have right now is that single picture. We did get some info that he has been known to hang out at the Starbucks near Pike's Place. Check that out."

"Shall we engage?" queried David, frowning. Snezhana looked on hopefully.

"Yes. Track and capture, if possible," Elda ordered, and then added quietly, "Be careful." She hung up.

David pocketed his phone and spun Snezhana around twice. "Now Snez, open your eyes. Which direction do we head in for Pike's Place?" Snezhana took a minute to orientate herself and then pointed southwest. "Well done. Let's go and see if we can find this guy. Ready to jog?"

David and Snezhana ran side by side at a medium pace, dodging tourists along the way, heading down Broad Street to Western Avenue, slowing to a walk as they approached the more congested area nearing the Pikes Place Metro stop.

"Snez, Starbucks will be up a short distance on your left. I will wait outside. Those places usually have only one entrance and exit, so you go in and flush him out. If you see him, hit my number on speed dial. If my phone goes off, I will immediately move in."

Snezhana nodded and tensely moved into the shop.

The assassin barreled out of Starbucks, knocking people to the side, with Snezhana on his heels. A tourist jumped back and tangled with David, impeding his start. After disentangling himself, David took off after the assassin down the street and into the Farmers Market, where shoppers clogged the narrow corridor and vendors wares were displayed on either side.

The assassin picked up jars of jam and honey as he ran, throwing them back at David, making a sticky, slippery mess. David reached into his pocket and threw money back at the screaming vendors while chasing at full speed. People were bumped sideways and crashed into different boothes, scattering carefully displayed rows of earrings and sending hand crafted pottery crashing to the floor.

The two men came out into a wider area near the fish market. A salmon flew over their heads. The assassin reached over to the iced display of fish and hurtled one back at David, hitting him square in the face. He slipped on the wet floor and fell backwards. The people watching the show clapped, thinking it was all part of the fish market theatrics.

Snezhana took the outside and followed the noise of the chase, entering the market near the fish mongers. She grabbed a fish out of the fish monger's hands and whipped it at the assassin, cutting his legs out from under him. A loud round of clapping followed her actions. The assassin summersaulted as he fell forward and rolled up and back onto his feet and threw a large sockeye salmon into Snezhana's face. As David closed in on him, the assassin pirouetted around a tourist and shoved that person into Snez and David, and took off up Pike Street hill.

One of the fish mongers was in David's face yelling at him about the mess. Snezhana ran after the assassin but missed catching him when he jumped into a cab. She quickly scanned for a taxi to grab to follow him, but none were around.

"Blyad'."

Chapter Seventeen

Aurelio Ainsworth staggered into the brick building housing the Mickey & Monkeys club in St. Petersburg, Russia, to meet his friend Olav, for a weekend of drugs and women. His eyes nearly popped out of his head when he spied Yuri sitting at a table near the middle of the room, talking to a man who had his back to Aurelio.

Aurelio yelled across the room, "Yuri, man, it is fantastic to see you."

He trotted over to Yuri, who had quickly risen from his chair to intercept him. The other man turned and Aurelio screamed, "It is the man with the black truck! Don't hurt me."

Aurelio started backing up, tripped over a chair, and fell flat on his back. He stared up at the wooden beams. From the floor he asked, "Yuri, where am I? Am I on a ship?"

"Shhh, *tikhiy*, Aurelio. *Tam, tam.* It's okay. This man will not hurt you, but it isn't safe for you here. You need to leave." Yuri lifted Aurelio up onto his feet.

Aurelio warily squinted at Anatoly and asked Yuri, "Yuri, what do you have? I really could use some drugs. Pot? Bath salts? Coke?"

Yuri responded, "I don't do that anymore, Aurelio."

Anatoly slowly rose and faced Aurelio. Aurelio let out a squeak, and tip-toed away from Anatoly.

Yuri touched Aurelio's arm to get his attention. "You have to leave now, Aurelio. But before you go, does my key to your apartment still work?"

"S-s-s-sure Yuri," stammered Aurelio. "I never ch-ch-changed the locks after Natasha left and you moved away. P-p-p-pop b-b-by any time."

"Good. I will come by soon. Wipe your nose, man. It's running down your face," yuri commanded, handing Aurelio a tissue.

Aurelio held the Kleenex up to his nose and mince-stepped out of the restaurant, latching on to a man just walking in. "Olav!" Aurelio squeaked, "We're leaving. It's not safe here."

Yuri sat down with a sigh. Anatoly looked at him with a cocked head and raised eyebrows.

Yuri explained, "He's an expat. I baby sat him for close to three years. You remember that he's Elda's half brother?"

"*Da*. What was that about the drugs though?"

"I used to score drugs for him. It kept him complacent and pliable. It appears that he's still in bad shape, even after his stint in the, … what's the English for, *durdom*?" Yuri asked.

Anatoly laughed, "*On bly v psikhiatricheskaya bol'nitsa*? - The nuthouse. It doesn't appear that the treatment was successful. He better stay out of my way. I don't want to stab him accidently again."

***

David wrinkled his nose and said theatrically, "Whew, Snezhana, you smell fishy. I think a shower is in your future."

Snezhana playfully slapped David's arm and flirted, "You're not a bed of roses yourself, David. You may have to join me in that shower."

Turning serious, David inquired, "Did you get the number of the cab he took, Snez?"

"Yes." She handed him her phone open to where she had jotted down the number.

David looked at the number, nodded, and handed her phone back. He stated, "Okay, let's call Elda and see if Stas can trace it through the traffic cameras."

David had a short conversation and then pocketed his phone. "Elda says we should stand down until they get more information. We have drawn enough attention to ourselves back at the fish market."

Snezhana sighed and inquired, "Do we have any idea how long that will be?"

"No, she didn't say. Meanwhile, let's go back to the hotel to clean off the fish slime. We can pick up some markers and a flip chart along the way, so we can also debrief on what happened at Starbucks and this chase through the market and correct any errors for the future," David directed.

"Can we also pick up some food, David?" inquired Snezhana.

"Sure," David readily agreed, "any preferences?"

Snezhana wrinkled her nose and said, "Anything but fish would suit me for a meal."

David agreed whole heartedly and they took off at a jog to the hotel, carefully examining each taxi that drove by.

***

The noise was deafening. Staying close to each other, Tosh and Elda jogged around the base. The roar of planes taking off and landing ensured their conversation would not be overheard.

Tosh shook his finger at Elda. "We need to talk about who runs this operation, Elda."

Elda frowned and squinted in confusion. "Why?"

"I am running this operation right now. I have more years of experience than you do, Elda, and I am also an experienced handler," Tosh shouted over a plane revving its engines.

Elda stopped and performed a military pivot to face Tosh. "I'll be sure to tap into that experience, Tosh, but I have to be able to make my own decisions."

Tosh emphatically shook his head in disagreement. "I don't agree with that Elda."

Elda adopted a conciliatory but firm tone. "Who bested you in the last operation where we faced off? In fact, who bested you the first time we met?"

"*Chert tebya poderi*, Elda," barked Tosh.

Elda kept her voice neutral. "Okay, damn you too, Tosh. I know it's hard for us to work together, and I know that each of us is gathering information to use against the other in the future, but for *now* we are a team. I get that this team has *one* and *only* one leader, and, *right now*, that leader is you. But I need to be empowered to make decisions without you when you're not around. Are we clear?"

Tosh's eyes narrowed and he replied through gritted teeth, "*Ochen'.*"

***

Anatoly and Yuri carefully poked their heads out of the hotel stairwell. They saw another masked man disappear into their registered hotel room. Anatoly muttered, "*Der'mo.*"

Yuri grabbed Anatoly's arm and whispered, "Someone is onto us, Anatoly. We need to disappear. I have safe contacts here, but first we need to get out of this hotel and off the streets."

Anatoly shook Yuri's hand off and declared in a soft voice, "I can take him down."

"*Nyet,*" stated Yuri firmly, still whispering, "Elda ordered us to disengage and return. We had a false lead with Montreal. This is probably another. And we know how Montreal turned out…"

"So what is *your* plan, Yuri?"

203

"Do you have any American dollars, Anatoly? I forgot to add them to my bag when I left my apartment. I knew I had forgotten something."

"*Da.* How much do you need?" Anatoly reached into his pocket and pulled out a large wad of American dollars.

"That should do," said Yuri grabbing the money.

"*Podozhdite*! That's $10,000!" Anatoly tried to snatch the money back, but Yuri quickly stowed it away.

"We'll need it all, and perhaps even more. It will not be cheap getting us out of here. If we can even get out alive." Yuri turned and started back down the stairs. "First we need to get disguises, Anatoly. I know someone who can help us."

Only the sound of his own footsteps in the stairwell answered him.

"Anatoly?!"

***

Snezhana rolled away from David onto her back. She fluffed up the feather pillow under her head and stretched luxuriously.

David sighed, "Damn. We should not have done that."

"Why? Wasn't it good, David?" Snezhana said huskily.

He turned on his side and traced the outline of her naked body with his forefinger. He then pulled the sheet up over her to help him resist further temptation. "You know that's *not* what I mean."

"I know." Snezhana stretched again, letting the sheet fall off one shoulder. David reached out, hesitated, and then replaced it over her shoulder.

David explained, "For one, your uncle will have my hide. And he's not someone I want to cross. And, secondly, we should not be mixing business with pleasure. It can cloud our thinking."

"But we have nothing to do but wait and this is probably the only opportunity we'll get," Snezhana pouted. "The next time we meet after this operation we may be on opposite sides. And I would hate to have to kill you." She stuck a long inviting leg out from under the sheet.

"That's exactly what I mean," David said hoarsely.

Snezhana gave a throaty and sensual laugh and rolled over, reaching for David.

Just then their cell phones simultaneously buzzed. David groaned and punched in his password. Snezhana sighed with disappointment and then perked up when David announced, "We have an address."

***

Listening at the door connecting the two rooms, Anatoly heard someone rustling around in the adjourning room. Silently he unlocked the door and slipped quickly inside. He spied a man bent down over the side table in the living room. That man was dressed in black and gray camouflage with a black ski mask over his face. The intruder straightened up, turned, and startled seeing Anatoly in the room. Before he could finish reaching for his weapon from his shoulder holster, Anatoly had knocked him flat on his back.

Anatoly jumped on top of the man, put a knee on his chest and pummeled his face with his fists. The man reached a knife in a leather sheath on his belt and drew it, slashing out at Anatoly, who quickly rolled off to avoid the knife, and sprung to his feet.

The masked man rolled to one side and came to his feet in an attack stance. The two men warily circled each other like two large wild animals sizing the other up. Anatoly flipped a knife out of his sleeve. Noting that the man appeared to be right-handed, Anatoly attacked from the left and sliced open the man's arm and jumped back again. Blood poured from the cut.

Ignoring his wound, the man lunged at Anatoly, who reached out and caught the blade in his fist. Blood dripped from Anatoly's hand. While the man repeatedly hit him in his stomach with his free hand, Anatoly bent the man's captured wrist backwards until it snapped, causing the man to drop the knife. Anatoly twirled and kicked the man in his knee with his steel capped boot and heard a satisfying crack. The man fell face forward onto the carpet.

Anatoly rolled him over, put a knee on his chest and dug his fingers into the cut he had made in the man's arm. "Who sent you?" He repeated, "*Kto tebya poslal?*"

The man screamed in pain and responded, "*Vy ne mozhete vyigrat'.*"

"Oh but we *will* win," Anatoly responded, digging his fingers in deeper. "*Kto tebya poslal?*"

"*Ty Proigal. Dlya materi Rossii!*" the man responded.

The man snapped his teeth down hard and instantly his eyes rolled back and his body went limp. Anatoly stood as Yuri entered the room.

Yuri stood stock still, staring at the body with white froth along its mouth, sprawled out on the floor, "*Chert.* What have you done here?"

Anatoly snapped, "Don't touch him. That's probably poison. We'll have Tosh send someone to clean it all up, but we have to leave quickly before they miss him."

"What did he mean by 'You lose'?" Yuri asked, backing up slightly.

Staring at the limp body, Anatoly explained, "He said we cannot win. So I told him we will win. *You lose* was his response. I guess in a way we did. We won't get any information from him now."

"His last words were, 'For mother Russia,'" Yuri observed, standing still with his hands by his sides.

Anatoly nodded and agreed, "Yes, that helps confirm the suspicion that the Kremlin may be behind all of this, but he also could be a mercenary."

Yuri turned from the body and looked at Anatoly, "You're bleeding!"

"It's nothing." Anatoly took a face cloth and a hand towel from the bathroom, wadded the face cloth up to apply pressure to the cut in his hand and wrapped the hand towel around it.

"You'll need stitches," Yuri pointed out.

"Add that to the things you need to arrange to get us out of here," Anatoly remarked, wrapping an elastic from the desk around his makeshift bandage.

Chapter Eighteen

Snezhana was sobbing uncontrollably. Standing across from where she was seated on a metal chair in the situation room, Tosh and Elda looked at her dispassionately.

"Let's go through the details again. You got the address we sent you. *Then* what happened?" demanded Elda. Tosh stood gritting his teeth, his eyes almost black from anger.

Snezhana blew her nose and answered through her tears. "We drove there from the hotel. It was around midnight and dark out, but there was a good amount of light from the streetlamps and the moon. We wanted to sneak up on him, so we parked the rental car around the block from the address you sent and walked the rest of the way. David told me to stay back, cover him, and be able to catch the suspect if he got away from David. I stayed slightly behind to cover the front of the house.

"Continue," barked Elda. Tosh paced back and forth angrily.

"David snuck around the back of the house and I hid behind the bushes in the side yard. The back light suddenly flashed on, illuminating David. I drew my weapon. A man inside the house called out David's name and said he wished to negotiate. David told him to come out with his hands up." Snezhana started sobbing again.

Elda snapped, "Oh straighten up, Snezhana. You are a disgrace to your profession and to our gender. He's dead. You can't change that. It's time you stopped sniffling and got your head on straight. And *then* what happened?"

Tosh hit the table with his fist. Elda continued on with the debriefing, rapidly firing questions at Snezhana, "Think! What happened?"

"My phone buzzed, but I didn't pick up. The man fired at David. David's gun went off almost simultaneously. I fired my weapon and shot the man in his head."

Tosh snatched Snezhana's phone from the table and started scrolling through her messages. "Chert! There's a text here telling Snezhana that they had her covered and she needed to stand down or David would get killed." Tosh threw the phone back down onto the table in disgust.

Elda held up her hand to silence him. "Was there a sound? Voices? Put yourself back there now."

"I heard the man talk to David, just before he fired his pistol," Snezhana disclosed.

"What did he say?" demanded Elda.

Snezhana shifted in her chair and mumbled, "Step inside, David. You can choose who dies today, you or your girlfriend."

"*Blyad'*!" Tosh kicked the metal wastebasket across the room.

"Tosh, we have a leak," Elda noted.

"*Razve? Der'mo*!" Tosh sarcastically replied.

Snezhana started wailing.

"Let's walk, Elda." Tosh stalked out of the room without waiting for Elda to agree. Once outside he turned to her. His grey eyes were serious and worried. "You were right, Elda. We have to get out of here now. We need to work together on this and shut out the rest." He continued walking.

Elda walked in step with Tosh. "I don't have a clear picture yet. I was hoping to get more information before we left."

"*Nyet*. We can't afford to stay here any longer. Have Ed retrieve the bodies. We are leaving *now*," Tosh barked.

"What do you think is going on here, Tosh?" Elda inquired, stopping to look directly at him.

Tosh stopped briefly, looked at Elda and then continued walking. Elda kept in step with him.

"I'm also not sure, Elda, but I *am* sure that someone is out to kill all of us. And that there is such a swirl of disinformation and misdirection that we may not know who is behind this for a while. Right now our goal needs to be to survive long enough to find that out," Tosh postulated. He stopped again and looked at Elda..

"Okay. I'll handle Ed and James, if you will inform Alexei," Elda suggested.

"*Da*." Tosh turned to head back inside.

"Wait." Elda put her hand on Tosh's arm to stop him and asked. "Tosh, do you trust Alexei?"

Tosh turned back to answer. He shrugged and then uttered. "I once thought I could, but this operation has me doubtful. Do you trust Ed and James?"

Elda scratched her head and responded, "I don't know James well, so no, not yet, but I have no concrete reason to mistrust him." Elda turned to go back in. This time it was Tosh who put his hand out to stop her. He asked, "And Ed?"

Elda summed up her feelings for Ed by saying, "I would trust him with my life."

"You better be right in that, Elda."

***

Elda walked at a face pace around the building. Suddenly she stopped short and leaned against the wall. An overwhelming wave of sadness and loneliness engulfed her. She shook her head angrily to rid herself of these feelings. "I cannot do this. Not here. Not now." She had to be able to trust Ed. Ed was the most ethical man she knew plus he was her lifeline; the one person who really got why she did this job and was always there for her. Only another person in this industry could understand her struggles, her pain, her victories. Although he was her handler and boss, she also thought of him as a friend. Other spies, even Tosh, got her on a level that no civilian could, especially Dawn, who believed in the goodness of mankind. "Everyone has his or her price," she muttered to herself. "But not Ed," she added hopefully, "Not Ed," she said again, hoping to rid herself of any doubt.

Elda set her jaw and continued lecturing herself, "This is why I don't want to continue therapy with Dawn! These awakened feelings weaken and distract me. I *cannot* have them during a mission. I need to not trust anyone. To even be suspicious of Ed right now. To be strong and to bury whatever is going on for me. Feelings are a liability." She took a deep breath and reached inside for the deadness. Squaring her shoulders she marched around the corner to re-enter the building and nearly stumbled over Tosh sitting on the steps, staring off into space. Tapping him on the shoulder, she ordered, "Let's go. We have business to attend to." She watched as Tosh's eyes refocused and went hard.

They both were ready.

Chapter Nineteen

"*No!*" Elda stood with her arms crossed, facing down Ed and James in their small cramped storage room, turned temporary office. She added more calmly, "No, I will not tell you where we are going. I have recalled Anatoly and Yuri from St. Petersburg. Seattle was another trap."

Ed responded, glaring at and chastising James. "It makes sense. There's a communication leak somewhere. It could be a tap on the lines from MI6. James can you please have them scanned?"

"Why MI6? It could be you Yanks or the Russians," snarled James.

Elda rolled her eyes. "True, James, but let's not go into *that* again. We have to start somewhere and everything goes through MI6 communication channels as a choke point."

James shook his fist at Elda. "I think you should check out your own team first, before pointing fingers at us. Our British security is impeccable, which is more than I can say for you Yanks. Look at how the Russians so easily hacked your elections and other critical systems of yours. *My* bet is on an American leak."

"I'll take that bet," challenged Ed.

James wheeled to face Ed. "1,000 US dollars?" countered James.

"You're on," growled Ed.

They glowered at each other. The air was electrified by their anger.

Elda held up her hand and said in a calming voice, "Boys, let's not fight. It may be someone on this base too. Someone had to observe what was going on between Snezhana and David. It was obvious enough. Speaking of which, Ed, we'll need a replacement for David. Hopefully Snezhana has learned her lesson here, but just in case, please do not make him young and handsome."

Ed nodded. "Will do. How do I let you know that I have someone?"

"I'll contact you in a couple of days to see who you have located," Elda responded.

"And how will you get where you are going?" James asked sarcastically.

Elda replied evenly, "Oh yes, we will need your assistance in that matter. Thanks James. We'll just need transportation back into London. We'll take it from there. You can drop us back at MI6 headquarters."

James snorted and stomped out of the office.

Ed held up his hand to stop Elda from leaving and warned, "Okay, Elda. We'll back off, but at the first sign that this operation is going south, we will come in guns blaring."

***

The aged military bus swayed and jostled its occupants on the way to London. Tosh handed a dark green folder labeled TOP SECRET to Elda. Raising his voice just enough to be heard over the rattling noise of the bus and the sputtering engine, he summarized the folder's contents. "The DNA matches our records for the American veteran. The other remains found in the blast match with David. There are no other identifiable body parts."

"Congratulations on smuggling this out. I'll have to keep a closer eye on you, sticky fingers." Elda scanned the report. "Apparently they were blown to smithereens. Ugh. There's not much information on this dude. After he left the service he got mixed up in some fringe pro-Russian groups in eastern Washington State." Elda handed the folder back to Tosh.

"*Spasibo*." He placed the folder into his backpack and summarized, "So we have a dead American assassin and a dead Russian assassin."

"Two dead American assassins," Elda corrected. "However, the second one in Maine was definitely being run by a Russian. This really does start to smell like a Russian operation." Elda tilted her head, raised her eyebrows and looked quizzically at Tosh.

Tosh, commented dryly, "*Interestnyy*," emphasizing that he understood her implication that he might be part of the Russian operation. "So that was the dead body in Maine… But how do you know it's not the Americans trying to pin this on the Russians? You know there's no love lost on either side. And your president is not ethical."

Elda waved a hand in the air to acknowledge that statement. "True, but I don't believe that he is smart enough to pull off that type of operation. *If* he is behind it then they are running him. The Russians do run rings around us, since our intelligence arms have been crippled and our relationships with our allies so damaged."

"It still could be the Chinese," disputed Tosh halfheartedly.

"*Tosh*, you *know* that it doesn't feel like one of their ops."

"But we don't know for sure if these were both plants to distract us from the real assassins," countered Tosh again.

"Right now we don't know what is real or whom to trust," Elda said pointedly.

Ignoring her insinuation, Tosh relied, "Let's ask Alexei, Ed, and James to see what else they can find through their networks. It will be instructive if we find they are giving us different information. Then at least if two of the sources line up and the third doesn't, we will have a hint of who is lying to us."

"True, but we also need information from a trustworthy source. We could use Stas," suggested Elda.

"I have other plans for him."

***

"I'd like to select my own protection team," whispered Oliver weakly from his hospital bed. "And what on earth is *that*?"

James maneuvered around the monitors and tubing to set down a huge wicker basket of cellophane wrapped fruit on the table next to Oliver's bed.

"I don't know. It's tradition to bring fruit or flowers, and you don't seem like the flowers type to me. So I asked my secretary to order a basket a fruit for me to bring you."

Oliver shifted in his bed and grimaced. "Ugh. I'd rather a pint." He groaned. "Please drop that rubbish off at the nurses station. I'm sure they'd love it. So, may I select my guards?"

James frowned, but quickly changed to a look of concern. He reassuringly patted Oliver on the shoulder. "Certainly. No worries. Give me the names and I'll ensure you have a handpicked team to protect you."

Oliver winced and smiled thinly. "Thank you. I'd like to get out of here alive."

***

"*Eccellente*! Here it comes now." A man in an Italian military uniform put down his binoculars and jogged to his waiting white Opel Vivaro minibus. He spun it around and positioned it, with the side door slid open toward the runway, to swiftly board his passengers.

On the runway at the Peretola airport near Florence, the dark grey Italian C-27J Spartan military cargo plane landed gently, belying its stout appearance. It had barely stopped its taxi when a squad of black and white camouflaged soldiers darted off the plane. They disappeared as if sucked into the van.

The van driver accelerated out of the airport and turned southward, deeper into Tuscany.

Chapter Twenty

Alexei sat dejectedly on a bench in Gorky Park near the skating rink, nervously tapping his foot, waiting for his Russian superior to arrive. *He is late.* Suddenly he spied him striding down the walkway and brought his bulk up to attention.

His boss hissed, "Sit down you fool. You don't want others to notice us."

Alexei plunked himself back onto the bench and waited.

"Report."

Alexei eagerly offered, "It is going well, sir. They have fallen for our bait. We have killed one agent and disabled a second one. And I expect to hear another positive report shortly from our team in St. Petersburg. At this rate we should soon have the entire team out of action in no time." He sat back and put one arm on the back of the bench.

The man from the Kremlin smiled, "Excellent. I was right to think of you as my successor. There will be a promotion waiting for you after the success of this operation."

"No one could fill your shoes sir, and I wish you a long career. One detail I'd like guidance on from you, however. After eliminating the operatives, should we also eliminate their handlers?" Alexei eagerly awaited the answer.

"*Nyet*. There will be no need to. They will be disgraced after such a total failure and removed from their positions. We don't need to worry about them."

Disappointed that he was robbed of a way to easily rid himself of Tosh, he hid his feelings, replying, "Very good, sir. Thank you." He brightened, thinking, *At least he could spin the operation as a failure and sideline Tosh.*

"Do not fail me. Disgrace and demotion after failure applies here too," his boss reminded him.

Alexei reassured him, "Yes sir. You have no worries, sir. Consider the team good as gone."

The senior man rose and strode away, his bodyguards falling in step behind him.

Alexei's phone vibrated. Answering it, he heard, "Our man in St. Petersburg is dead."

He yelled into his phone, "What? When? This is unacceptable. I *just* told him all is fine. Do not tell anyone else. Send the cleaners for the body immediately. Find them and eliminate them on sight."

He stood up and started pacing while listening to his agent ask about guidelines and barked back, "Yes, of course collateral damage is acceptable. Do NOT let them leave Russia."

He hung up and collapsed back down on the bench and put his head in his hands. He ran his fingers through his hair muttering, *think, think.* Raising his head he looked skyward in search of his next move. He gnashed his teeth and breathed heavily. *Think!* Then he brightened, took out his phone and dialed a number. "Get here immediately. The next flight out. No excuses." He hung up before the man on the other end could say a word.

***

Henry strode past the columns of the main entrance into Gorky Park. He was angry at having been summoned to Moscow and impatient to be back in London before his absence was noted. Arriving at the fountains, he paced back and forth, anxious for this meeting to be over with. He was keenly aware that he was in a tight spot, trying to please James in London and keep his position at MI6, as well as obey his Russian handlers. He turned and spotted a large man, flanked by two bodyguards, ambling in his direction. Henry stopped pacing and waited.

Stopping a few feet away from Henry, Alexie started without preamble. "This operation is a mess. I will not tolerate failure."

Henry blanched and stuttered, "Bbbuttt, …"

Alexei held up his hand and crossed the distance between them and growled, "I just had to clean up a mess in Saint Petersburg. I called you here to impress upon you the seriousness of your situation." The two men with Alexei also moved closer and opened their jackets so Henry could see the weapons they carried.

Henry stammered, "I will do anything. What do you want?"

Alexei tersely commanded, "It's time to get rid of them all. Actively engage wherever you find them. No survivors." He turned and left with his entourage.

Henry stood and watched them leave. His feet felt heavy and his head was pounding. His stomach churned. He gave a deep breath and willed himself to move forward.

***

Wearing a workman's outfit and carrying a heavy bag with *Ralph's Appliance and Air Conditioning* stamped on it, Yuri clumped into Aurelio's apartment. He dumped his bag down with a thud inside the door on the marble entryway. Aurelio jumped up to greet him.

"Yuri, you came! Did you bring me drugs?"

"*Da*, Aurelio." Yuri tossed Aurelio a small, square, tin foil wrapped object. "You will want to smoke some of this now. But perhaps you would like to put some clothes on?"

Aurelio glanced down at his pudgy belly sticking out over his dingy briefs and replied, "I'm good."

Yuri sighed and stood by the door, while Aurelio unwrapped his present grinning broadly in delight, displaying his yellowing and coffee stained teeth.

"Hash! Fantastic. Let me get my bong." Aurelio tiptoed off to his bedroom.

Just then there was a short rap on the door. Yuri opened the door and Anatoly quickly slipped in, carrying in one hand plumbing equipment in a tool bag labeled, *Clog King*. His other hand was almost hidden, wrapped in a large bandage.

Aurelio pranced back into the living room with his bong, focused on lighting up. Anatoly cleared his throat. Aurelio screamed and dropped the bong onto the white pile carpet.

"*Lisus*, Aurelio. You've pissed yourself. Come with me," Yuri ordered.

Yuri picked up the bong and guided a shaking Aurelio by his arm to clean him up. Returning, he plunked Aurelio firmly down on the leather couch and passed him a lit bong.

Aurelio inhaled deeply while warily keeping an eye on Anatoly.

"You should let me kill him, Yuri. It would be better for him," stated Anatoly.

"*Nyet,* Anatoly. Aurelio give me your phone. I need to make a phone call." Yuri held out his hand for the phone.

Frozen in place and still staring at Anatoly, Aurelio pointed at his iPhone on the glass and marble table and sucked hard on the bong.

"Is this Petersburg Construction Company? Yes, this is Aurelio Ainsworth. I have a plumbing and an electrical issue here, but I will also need some wall repair. Can you please send someone?" Yuri listened to the affirmative answer and then responded, "*Da.* That would be perfect. *Spasibo.*"

He hung up and then addressed Aurelio. "Aurelio, I'm going to steal some of your American dollars. I will pay you back."

Aurelio nodded and returned his attention to the bong, peering at Anatoly as he sucked the smoke in. Anatoly stared back at Aurelio in disgust, and asked Yuri, "Can you get us out of here?"

Yuri shrugged and remarked, "I hope so. If we have enough money for them to come and extract us."

***

The bus's brakes squealed with a loud hiss as it stopped outside of MI6. The team, having memorized their next meeting place, popped down the steps and split up, each taking off in different directions.

Tosh and Elda hopped on a bus for a 20-minute ride to Superdrug located nearby on Butterfly Walk.

Snezhana made a phone call and then ran to catch a train to Gatwick airport.

Sophia also made a quick phone call and jogged off to see a friend living nearby.

Stas sat down on a bench and typed furiously for a few minutes. He then closed his computer and strolled the short distance to Mail Boxes Etc.

***

A hunched over old lady wearing a gray shawl and using a folding cane, followed by a frail old man with a battered brown fedora on his head and pushing a rollator, left the Superdrug store together. She tottered along and stopped to urge the old man forward, "Come on dear, we have a flight to catch." Her voice cracked with the effort of speaking.

The bent over old man coughed and spit on the ground. "Stop nagging me, Bertha. You've been nagging me for sixty years now." He pushed the walker slowly in front of him.

"Fifty-nine years, Frederick. Now come along, dear. The bus will be here soon."

They wheeled and hobbled their way down the sidewalk to the bus stop, to start their journey to Heathrow airport.

***

Already at Gatwick airport, Snezhana, wearing tight shiny black leather pants and a bright red silk blouse, stood outside the terminal hugging a handsome man in a black suit and dark blue tie. "I am delighted I could catch a ride with you, Lorenzo."

"*Certamente*, my lovely Snez. The pleasure is all mine. I remember fondly the one night we had together in Moscow."

"Well, we have two hours together now."

They walked hand in hand to a shiny white private jet sitting on the runway.

***

229

"Now boarding First Class passengers to Milan, Italy."

A slender, pale faced man, dressed in a jaunty fedora, suit coat, t-shirt and jeans, carrying a worn backpack, retrieved his fake passport and sauntered up to join the line of first-class passengers.

"Welcome aboard, Mr. Torvalds. Seat 2B."

"Thank you."

***

Sophia sat back against the cloth of the passenger seat in the white 2-door Fiat as they entered the train for the 35-minute ride through the tunnel to France. "Now remember, Emily. You never saw me."

"No worries, Sophia. My lips are sealed," Emily replied, making a zipping motion with her thumb and forefinger across her lips.

"Remember my name is Sally. Sally White," Sophia instructed.

"Sally White? How inventive!" Emily's lips were quivering.

Sophia glared at Emily who quickly reframed her statement, "Ah yes, Sally. Sally White. Excellent name. Got it."

Sophia nodded, the official business was now over. "Good. Now let's catch up on gossip," Sophia eagerly said with a grin.

"So, *Sally,* are you happy you married Ollie? I know you had at least a dozen suitors!" Emily probed.

Sophia relaxed in her seat, smiling at her memories. "Ha! Not that many, but it was a fun time. Yes, I am. I needed someone I could trust and not have to hide secrets from. I also just adore that man. He is funny, smart, a great cook, and amazing in bed."

Emily flinched and held her hands over her ears. "TMI, *Sally*, remember he's one of my best friends."

"Sorry, Emily. But I worry about him in this line of business. He's too nice for it. And he's trying to prove himself to me, and to his father. I think he wants to show how masculine he is, when he has such a wonderful feminine side of him."

Emily chuckled, "Yes, I remember him asking his parents for ballet lessons and the uproar that caused. They finally gave in. His father *so* wanted him to play football instead."

"Really? Football! That is so not Oliver!" Sophia declared in between laughs.

They both giggled at the thought of Oliver trying to play a sport.

Sophia turned serious and declared, "I really don't care what he is now, Emily. He is the other half of my heart and soul. Through him I have a reason to want to come home. He is the love of my life."

Emily turned in her seat towards Sophia and inquired, "Would you ever throw in the towel and do something else to spend more time with him?"

Shaking her head, Sophia responded, "As much as I love him, that would feel as if I have given part of me away. This job makes me feel important. And I'm good at it. I want to stay alive long enough to be a legend like Elda and Tosh are."

Emily probed further, "Does Ollie know that?"

Sophia frowned while answering, "I think he does on some level, but it's a conversation we need to have when we're home for a breather after this operation. That is, if we both come home." Sophia looked down at her iPhone. "Good, we're on track to make it there in time to get a nap and a shower." She stared out the window to hide the tears that were silently streaming down her face.

***

An old woman on a cane, assisted by the driver, backed down the stairs of the rental car shuttle at the Milan airport. Once the driver was sure the woman was able to stand on the sidewalk by herself, he went back in to assist an old man on a rolling walker, wearing a raggedly backpack.

The old man slapped at the driver's hand and exclaimed in a crackly voice, "I may be old, young whippersnapper, but I'm not feeble."

"Sorry sir." The driver stepped back, but kept close, watching the walker precariously sway with each step.

The old woman called out from the sidewalk, "Oh hush, Frederick. The nice young man was just trying to help you."

"I can do it myself, Bertha."

Frederick slowly pushed the walker until he was by Bertha's side. Bertha thanked the driver and slipped him a pound note. "There young man. You did well. Thank you." The driver smiled wryly and pocketed the bill.

Frederick and Bertha shuffled and rolled their way into the rental car building where they each entered the rest rooms. A blond, with spiked hair, pranced out of the ladies' room, wearing jeans, a white shirt, a leather jacket and jaunty cap. Her good looks were marred by cheeks that were a tad too full and a nose that looked as if it had once been broken. A spectacled Tosh paraded out of the men's room, looking dapper in his blue and white Cuban collar shirt, leather flat cap, leather jacket and jeans. The handsomeness of his face was diminished by old scars left from chicken pox. As they met up Elda exclaimed, "Whew, it's so good to be able to stride normally again. That shuffle was so slow."

"I rather enjoyed my new wheels," declared Tosh, with a bounce falling in step beside Elda.

Elda chuckled and suggested, "Well, let's get a bit of an upgrade to your wheels. Perhaps a van or a SUV that will fit us all? Then we should head to the hotel and wait for everyone to show up. Sophia's driving so she should be the last one."

No longer jovial, Tosh declared, "Let's hope they all make it."

Chapter Twenty-One

Emily glanced in her rearview mirror with a worried look on her face.

Apprehensive, Sophia inquired, "What's up, Em? That's the third time you've looked behind us."

Swiveling he head to keep her focus split between in back of and in front of the car, Emily replied cautiously, "I'm concerned that we may have picked up a tail in Calais. There's this beige car that is staying a fixed distance behind us. It could be on cruise control as I am, but…"

Sophia took out her makeup mirror and scanned the road behind them. "Vary your speed and see what happens."

Emily pressed the accelerator and slowly picked up speed. The car behind them mirrored her actions.

Sophia nodded her agreement. "Looks like you're right, Em. Good eye. We'll make an agent out of you yet. Now let's test your driving skills. Take the next right onto D77, but wait until you're almost past it and veer off," she directed Emily.

"Righto."

The wheels squealed as Emily whipped the car off the highway onto the exit. They heard the skidding and saw dust fly, as the other car nearly missed the exit and went off the road and veered back on.

Emily shouted, "Bollocks. He's still behind us."

"Go left, *now!*" commanded Sophia.

Emily spun the car to catch the exit, that they had almost passed, onto D341 south. The sound of horns bleating and brakes slamming confirmed their tail was still there.

Sophia spat out directions, "Now left, right, left. Merge!'

Emily smoothly brought the car at high speeds back onto E15 south. Behind them they heard a semi-trailer horn blow loudly and metal crumpling and tearing.

"He was a bit slow making it back onto the highway," Emily declared.

Sophia reached over and patted Emily's shoulder, "Well done, Emily. From the looks of it, I doubt the driver survived. Nice driving."

"This is fun." Emily giggled in a high pitch.

Sophia frowned and looked closely at Emily. "That's either your adrenaline speaking or you need a life, Emily. Are you sure you're okay? This is the first time you've been operational in the field."

Emily sighed deeply and her hands started to quiver. "Enjoyable as that was, I am hoping we make it to Milan in one piece. How about we switch and you drive for a while? I seem to be shaking a bit."

Sophia patted Emily's arm reassuringly, "Sure, let's pull over at the next layby. I'll switch out your plates there too."

***

Exhausted, Sophia walked into the lobby of the hotel in Milan and popped into the restaurant to grab a cup of coffee. Elda, Tosh, Snezhana and Stas were sitting eating breakfast.

"About time you showed up, Sophia. Everyone's here now. Let's get a move on."

"I've been traveling for 16 hours. I would love a nosh and a shower."

"No time for that." Elda put butter and jam on two slices of toast and handed them to Sophia. She poured a cup of coffee into a cardboard cup. "Cream and sugar?"

"Yes, please," Sophia said in a dull tone.

Elda squinted her eyes and probed, "Why are you so late?"

Sophia wiped her eye with her fingers and shook her head to try for a greater state of alertness. She responded slowly, "We had a problem, but we dealt with it."

Elda cocked her head. "Do we need to worry?" She asked.

Sophia shook her head, replying, "Not about that one. He's dead, but they were watching the port."

Elda jumped up and addressed the team, "Time to move out."

Tosh spurred them on, "*Shag! Idti!*"

***

"Paul has failed to report in."

The voice of his remote teams leader came in clearly over his phone. He shifted his bulk in his office chair and snapped, "Where was he stationed?"

The leader answered, "He was at the port of Calais watching for cars exiting the Chunnel."

He barked, "Assume they are in Europe. Find them!" He slammed the phone down.

Where are they?

Alexei ran his fingers through his salt and pepper hair while pondering the map of the world that covered one wall of his office. He stepped forward and stuck a pin in Calais, France. Holding his thumb on the bridge of his glasses and his forefinger to his forehead he mentally calculated the distance they may have traveled since the last sighting. A shrill ringing interrupted his mathematics. He sat down, swiveled his desk chair, and reached to answer his private line.

As soon as it connected he heard, "We have a location."

"Where are they?" Alexei demanded, receiving the answer, "They are at a hotel in Milan, Italy."

Alexie instructed, "Send a team up there."

***

"Elda, give them the plan." Tosh pulled the Fiat Doblò into a parking spot near the Piazzale Michelangelo and cut the engine.

Elda turned and addressed the crew in the back, "Okay, here's the plan….no Stas, I have forbidden you to work in the car. You do not need to be carsick again. Do not turn on your computer until we reach the villa. We are taking you with us. You need the fresh air. Tosh, Stas, and I will go pick up the keys to the villa. The rest of you are going to go grocery shopping."

Sophia leaned forward and asked, "Elda, may I come with you too? I have never seen the Duomo."

"*Der'mo*. It's just a big building, Sophia." Anatoly groused.

"You have no couth, Anatoly," Sophia said, slapping him on his arm.

Elda shook her head and rolled her eyes, then replied, "Yes, Sophia, you may come with us. We will meet back here in three hours. The rest of you stay out of trouble."

***

Snezhana stopped suddenly and pointed across the street. "There! That's the grocery store – Conad's. We just walked past it."

Anatoly dismissed her observation by waving her on and continuing to walk. "I know Snezhana, but I thought perhaps we could wander around the neighborhood a bit to find a decent pastry shop."

Snezhana rolled her eyes at Anatoly. "We only have slightly over two and a half hours left. They will have pastry in the grocery store, you know?"

"Ah, but not like these. I think the place was called Café Neri. They had these things called a Schiacciata all Fiorentina and a Chantilly Cream pastry that was fantastic! It's around here somewhere." Anatoly smiled and patted his trim stomach.

Across the street, a short Italian man, stopped in his tracks, pointed, and shouted, "*You*! You stole my Vespa last year!"

"Der'mo! What's the odds of that?" Anatoly growled and took off at a run, leaving Yuri and Snezhana looking puzzled.

Anatoly ran full bore past the Pitti Palace where a he spied a policeman. He whipped right onto the Via Santa Maria, and took another right at the end of the street. His breath was ragged and sweat was obscuring his vision. He spun left onto the Via della Chiesa and was a blur running by the old nunnery. He glanced behind him. He was alone. Just to make sure, Anatoly took a left at the end of the street, another left, and again a left, and then a right, to find himself back on the Via della Chiesa. "*Der'mo!*"

***

Snezhana watched Anatoly disappear around the corner and sighed. "Let me handle this." She sauntered up to the Italian man, making sure she exaggerated the roll of her hips in her black leather pants.

"*Mi scusi, signore*. That is my younger brother. He is not quite right in the head. *È pazzo*." She held her index finger near her head and circled it around.

The man surveyed Snezhana appreciatively with his eyes and waving his hands excitedly explained, "Last year, I swear it was that man who threw me from my Vespa and stole it. She was later found in the parking lot at the Piazzale Michelangelo, out of gas and *dented*." With a dismayed look on his face he waved at the ground showing the invisible wounded Vespa lying there.

"I am so sorry that happened to you." Snezhana leaned in closer to him and put her hand on his arm. "My demented brother does have a passion for motorcycles, but I doubt it was him. He rarely is allowed out by himself. However, if you are free for dinner tonight, I would love to hear more of your story."

The Italian's face lit up and his eyebrows nearly jumped off his forehead. "*Certamente, bella donna*," he said with insinuating undertones. He quickly wrote his address on a piece of paper. "I apologize for accusing your brother. Time has probably blurred my memory. It is fortunate, though, since I ran into you. I look forward to our dinner. Shall we say 20:00 tonight?"

Snezhana smiled charmingly at him and winked. "*Certamente.*" She pocketed the paper he had handed her.

***

Lost, Anatoly stood consulting the map application on his phone when Snezhana, chatting and laughing with her new Italian friend and Yuri, strolled around the corner. Anatoly's eyes narrowed.

Snezhana walked up to Anatoly and slapped him on the head. "*Cosa sie pazzo?*" A stream of angry Italian followed. Snezhana slapped him on the head again. "*Sie pazzo!*" Anatoly smiled and nodded.

Snezhana blinked her long brown lashes and gave the Italian a soulful look, "I must handle this family matter, but I will see you later tonight." The man patted his brow with his handkerchief and jauntily strutted away.

"*Spasibo*, Snezhana," Anatoly said. "I am grateful."

Snezhana smiled at Anatoly, saying, "You're welcome, Anatoly. Now let's buy groceries and get out of here before you get arrested for some other past crime."

***

A small group of soldiers, dressed in Italian uniforms, marched into the Sheraton Milan Malpensa Airport Hotel & Conference Centre. The clerk at the front desk snapped to attention. "How can I help you, *signori*?"

One of the soldiers held his phone out with a picture of Anatoly on it. "Have you seen this man?"

The clerk frowned and shook his head, "No. But today is my first hour on duty here."

The soldier swiped left to a picture of Yuri. "This one?"

"No, mi dispiace."

The soldier showed the clerk pictures of Tosh, Elda, Sophia and Snezhana, and received the same no answer to each picture and query.

"May we see your security footage?"

"Si, certamente." The hotel clerk quickly led them into the office where they reviewed the footage from the last few days. They stopped at the footage of Elda and Tosh walking in together. The lead soldier pounded the table and exclaimed, "There! We need to review your check-ins from this time."

The now nervous clerk's fingers stumbled on his keyboard as he searched for those records. Finding the check-ins for that time, he pointed to the room number. The squad leader circled his hand and pointed a finger upward. The soldiers set off, dragging along the desk clerk with his pass key.

The squad lined up in the hallway on either side of the room's door. The clerk passed the key over the reader and jumped backwards. The door clicked open. The squad stormed into the room.

"*Blyad'.*"

The room was empty.

Chapter Twenty-Two

Elda looked inside one of the grocery bags. "What is all this junk food? That's the *last* time you three go shopping on your own. Tosh look at this crap!"

Tosh rummaged around and located a bag of Milka XL chocolate chip cookies and ripped it open. He stuffed one in his mouth letting the crumbs spill out. Spitting as he spoke, he mumbled, "I see nothing wrong with their shopping skills."

Elda noticed that Snezhana didn't laugh or roll her eyes as she usually did at Tosh's antics. In fact she, Anatoly and Yuri all looked rather subdued and tired.

"Okay, spill it. What happened?" Elda demanded.

Yuri shrugged, Snezhana looked down at her feet, and Anatoly defiantly said, "It was all your fault, Elda."

Elda's head jerked up. "What? Mine? I wasn't even with you. What happened?" she exclaimed.

"Apparently Anatoly is an international Vespa thief," snorted Yuri, unable to keep a straight face.

Elda looked at Anatoly and asked, "Oh my. From last year?"

Anatoly pointed his finger at her and nodded, saying, "*Da. See*, it *is* all your fault. But Snezhana charmed us out of that spot. There will be one disappointed Italian, however, when she doesn't show up."

Snezhana playfully slapped Anatoly lightly on his head. "*Il mio fratello è pazzo.*"

"I can't help it big sister. I just love to ride Vespas." Anatoly cupped his hands around his chin and batted his eyes at Snezhana.

Tosh and Elda shook their heads. Elda gestured resignedly to Tosh, "They are all yours, you know."

Tosh playfully answered, "Yes, but they obviously have your genes."

Elda shook her head and chuckled. She noticed that Sophia had not joined in but was staring out across at Florence with the sun shining off the Duomo. "Are you with us, Sophia?" asked Elda.

Sophia turned around and had tears in her eyes. "Yes, yes… it was all so beautiful. And the wooden sculpture of Mary Magdalene… I am just speechless," she declared.

"You took her to see that old bag you guys love so much?" Anatoly asked, with a smile.

Sophia hit Anatoly on the other side of his head.

Anatoly put his hands up on both sides of his head. "Ouch! I need to protect my amazing brains!"

Yuri and Snezhana rolled their eyes at that comment.

Elda motioned with both hands to herd the team forward. "Okay, gang. In the car. We have to get to the villa and settle in."

Tosh and Elda stood for one last moment side by side breathing in the scenery.

Elda observed, "That may have been our last visit to see her, Tosh. I don't feel right about this mission and I fear it may be my last one."

Chapter Twenty-Three

The team gathered in the large living room of the villa in Montepulciano, Italy. Despite the warm and sunny day outside, the stone floors and walls kept the room so cool, that Tosh had made a small fire in the fireplace.

Elda sat by the fire in a leather chair, sipping a cup of tea. She commented,

"It's good to have you back, Anatoly and Yuri. Now that we are settled, we'll need to debrief you further on your mission."

"Yuri did a good job planning and executing our extraction," Anatoly declared while he slapped Yuri on the back, causing him to spit out coffee. "How did you all arrive here?" Anatoly inquired.

Elda took a sip of tea and explained, "We all took a military bus to London and then scattered, in case we were followed. We reconvened in Milan. Tosh and I caught a flight from Heathrow to Milan at Gatwick from a friend who owed me one. Snezhana asked an old flame to transport her to Milan in his private jet. Sophia grabbed a lift with a friend and drove all the way. Stas hacked into a few systems, created a fake ID and put himself into first class for the trip. Well done by the way, Stas."

"*Spasibo*, Elda." A beaming Stas sat up a bit straighter.

Tosh raised an eyebrow and asked, "I forgot to ask you, Elda, what did you do for that friend? He was quite the looker."

Elda rolled her eyes at Tosh's probe for more personal information about her and answered curtly, "I saved his son's life. Luckily they have a good father son relationship, so I could cash in on the favor."

"*Interesnyy*… I would love to hear more of that story," Tosh murmured. He winked at Elda.

"In your dreams, Tosh. How is your hand, Anatoly?" Elda inquired.

Anatoly lifted his bandaged hand for all to see. "My hand is healing nicely, Elda. Luckily Yuri also had *friends* that had a lot of experience sewing up wounds in their drug smuggling business."

Unconvinced, Elda quizzed Anatoly further about his injury, "Let me see you move your fingers, Anatoly."

Anatoly held his thumb to his nose and wiggled his fingers at Elda.

"Ah yes, all looks normal there," Elda remarked caustically. She turned to Tosh. "So the hotel room had been completely cleaned by the time Leonid got his people there, Tosh?"

Tosh nodded while rubbing his chin and answered, "*Da.* They were experts. Not a trace of blood, nor any fingerprints."

Elda continued to probe for information. She turned back to Anatoly and asked, "But we think the man was Russian, Anatoly?"

Anatoly nodded, and replied, "Yes, he spoke Russian fluently. His accent implied he was probably from Moscow. And the last thing he said was 'For Mother Russia,' and then he bit down on the suicide pill."

Elda acknowledged his analysis and addressed Yuri next. "Yuri, I'm merely curious. Is there really a Saint Petersburg Construction Company?"

Yuri smiled broadly. "Yes, there is, but they had some new workers for a while. They arrived with a van and transported us past those who were watching your half brother's apartment. It helped to have drug running connections with private planes. Oh, and I owe Anatoly $10,000. Can the operation pay him back?"

"Certainly, Yuri." agreed Elda.

"And I borrowed another $10,000 from Aurelio," added Yuri, with his most beguiling smile.

Elda made a face. "We will pay him back too, but I'm sure he won't have missed it."

Yuri looked at Elda with big blue puppy sad eyes and added, "And…I have no American cash. Can the operation give me some too?"

Elda chuckled. "Sure, Yuri. Only no more buying hash for Aurelio," she reprimanded.

Turning to the group at large, Tosh commanded, "Snezhana, you are now teamed up with Sophia. Stas, you will take one of the bedrooms and turn it into command central. Let us know if you need any equipment and we will arrange to smuggle it over to here. Elda has contacted Ed and we should soon be joined by a new member of our team to replace David as our analyst. That person will stay here and work with Stas to trace the money behind this operation."

"*Da.*" Stas moved toward the bedrooms with a spring in his step. The rest of the team scattered to claim their beds. Elda and Tosh remained.

Elda stood up. "Tosh, let's go for a jog and check out the area."

Tosh frowned and responded, "Now, Elda? In this temperature?"

"What? You can't handle the heat?" Elda taunted.

Tosh held up his hand with his middle finger extended from his fist and snapped, "Fuck you, Elda. You're on. I'll meet you back here in five minutes."

***

Elda and Tosh stopped at a rise and admired the view across the green rolling hills, with windy roads lined by spikes of cypress trees and gnarled olive trees. The powerful smells of the trees, combined with the sweetness of rosemary, pungent aroma of sage, floral scent of lavender, mixed with the dust of the dirt roads, was almost overwhelming as they each attempted to catch their breath from their competitive run up the hill.

"I can see why so many great artists came from this area," said Elda as she coughed, trying to regulate her breathing.

"You didn't drag me up here for the scenery, though, did you?" wheezed Tosh, leaning forward with his hands on his thighs.

"No Tosh, I didn't. I'm curious. Why, with all of GRU's counter-intelligence and hacking resources at your disposal, did you instead reach out for Stas? Who don't you trust in your organization?" Elda interrogated.

The sound of their breathing filled the silence. Tosh turned away from Elda in pretense of admiring the vista. "You're right, Elda. It is beautiful here."

"Here's my thinking, Tosh. It never made sense that we were spun up now for something that will happen in 2020," Elda continued.

Tosh glanced over his shoulder at Elda. "So, what do *you* think, Elda?"

"Our mission is a scam, a smoke screen, to cover up what Russia is really trying to do. By focusing our resources on the 2020 and 2021 G20 Summits and pointing fingers toward China or North Korea, or even the Ukraine, they are keeping us out of the way so they can move forward on their real operation. Since misdirection is often based loosely on the truth, they may be trying to eliminate the United States president. This way they can increase the chaos they have sown in the United States, perhaps even sparking a Civil War."

Silence. Tosh stared out across the olive trees.

Elda continued doggedly, speaking to his back, "The question is: Is that the real goal? Where and when, and perhaps even, what and why? I think that is why you brought in Stas, as an attempt to get around the obfuscation and to get at the truth. You are a loyal Russian, but you are also ethical in your own way. You dislike being manipulated and used, especially by your own government. We may be on opposite sides of the fence most of the time, but we are alike in this."

Tosh shrugged and nodded slightly. His eyes sparkled, acknowledging Elda's truths.

Elda continued, "The other question is: once you have the information, what will you do with it?"

"No, Elda," Tosh countered. "The real question is, if *you* had the information, what would *you* do with it?"

They both turned toward each other and stared, brown eyes boring into gray, neither blinking. Elda broke the silent tension between them.

"As much as I abhor the corrupt con man who is currently in office in the United States, I took an oath to serve my country. I may not agree with him, or even like him, but I will protect him from assassination. However, you took no such oath. And it would now benefit *your* country if he were removed. I need to know if you are working with me or against me in this."

Tosh sighed and visibly relaxed into the conversation. "True, Elda. You have analyzed the situation well. However, what you *don't* know is that there is a network of hackers throughout the world who are dedicated to ensure your president does not get re-elected and to ensuring that the authorities get enough information at the end of his term, so that he can be brought to justice and imprisoned. He will be thoroughly discredited and without protection. It would be easy enough to kill him then and still pit the internal forces against each other in the United States."

Elda frowned and shook her head. "So why kill him now?"

Tosh continued sharing his information, "The issue now is that there are forces on high within the Kremlin who are impatient and don't want to wait for that to happen, and are afraid that he may leak information harmful to them, so those forces are accelerating his removal. Also, killing him now and blaming it on the UK or Canada, or even France, will further split the Allies. And the best part of killing him now while he is in office is that it will cause chaos in the United States, with warring factions fighting each other, splitting the country in two. I had no knowledge of all this prior to starting our mission, but I collected some information while in Italy. Now I have had Stas gathering as much data as he can, without tipping his hand. That is why Stas was unavailable to chase down the DNA from the assassins."

Still trying to put all the pieces together, Elda asked, "Did you get in trouble for selecting Stas instead of using someone from the GRU unit?"

"Alexei was rather surprised and buzzed me right after I announced Stas. I explained to him that there shouldn't be much heavy lifting on this mission that would require the caliber of the GRU team and also, their work has been traced, so I wanted to go to someone completely unknown."

Elda put a hand up to her head and squinted at Tosh. She probed, "And he bought that?"

Tosh nodded and explained, "Yes. Alexie didn't get to where he is by being clever, but by deceit and brute strength."

Elda looked suspiciously at Tosh. "Why would you go against the direction the Kremlin wants?"

Tosh looked her in the eyes and declared, "The objective will be done in the end. America is already heading toward a civil war and the end of democracy. There are other ways to accomplish accelerating it without killing my team and other innocents."

Elda held his gaze and queried, "So you agree that we should continue to pool our resources and stay of the grid while we determine the facts?"

Tosh held out both hands palms up and stated, "Anatoly is like a son to me. Snezhana is my niece. Some day they may die with honor on a mission for the Motherland. This is not that mission."

Her suspicion allayed, but needing Tosh's confirmation, Elda pushed the point. "So we work together?"

"*Da*," he said.

Elda and Tosh shook hands as equals. Elda suggested, "Let's revisit our list of all the venues that the US president will be at, for the rest of 2019, and look for anywhere he may be more vulnerable to an attack."

Tosh smiled and revealed, "I already have Stas working on that. Some locations are secret and some trips are not yet fully planned, but he is analyzing all potential future meetings, summits and conferences for security vulnerabilities. We'll go from there."

Just then Elda's burner phone rang. The only person who had that number was Ed.

"It's Ed," she noted. "I have to take this."

"I will saunter off and admire the landscape."

A tinny version of Ed's voice came through the cheap burner phone's speaker, "Are you alone?"

"Yes, Ed. Tosh has just wandered off. What's up?"

"This is all a sham, Elda."

"We know. Tosh and I have been talking about it. How did you discover that?"

"I'll tell you when I see you. I will meet you in Montepulciano at the Osteria del Conte. I will be in disguise. Do come alone."

Chapter Twenty-Four

"What if this is another trap?"

"Ed requested that I come alone," she stated emphatically. Elda stood confronting Tosh in the living room of the villa.

"You're not known to be that obedient. This could end like the other missions. Don't go alone. Take Anatoly with you. He can stay outside and report back to us with valuable information, in the event that you do not survive."

Elda frowned, but agreed, "Okay. He stays in the parking lot and out of sight. If they take me, he does not attempt to save me, but he rejoins you to escape with the team. If I don't return, you must leave Italy immediately and find a safe locale to work from."

"*Da. Khorosho.*"

Satisfied, Tosh walked away from Elda in search of Anatoly. Elda grabbed the keys to the Fiat Doblò panel van and sprinted outside. Tosh returned with Anatoly to the sound of wheels whirling on gravel, as Elda sped away.

***

Elda spun the Fiat into the parking lot near the imposing stone Porta al Prato gate and slammed it into park. She walked through the arches leading to the old town and strode across the wide cobblestones, past beautiful stone houses with beautiful flower boxes, green shutters and laundry hung out to dry. She wove her way by memory to the Osteria del Conte restaurant. She carefully scanned the area for anyone who might be observing her, but saw no one suspicious. Entering the restaurant, she stood for a moment admiring the thick beams on the ceiling and bright yellow walls, as she surveyed the restaurant for Ed. She spotted him sitting at a wooden table near the back of the restaurant. He was in disguise with a scruffy beard and mustache, wearing dirty workman clothes, sitting with another man, who had his back to Elda.

Elda sauntered over and sat with her back against the wall, facing the door, on the same side of the table as Ed. She said softly, "You know, it's a good disguise, Ed, but you still would fail facial recognition. You need to change the shape of your face more. Put on glasses too." While speaking to Ed, she observed the man sitting opposite him.

"I'll take that under advisement for my exit from the country. Elda, this is Jackson Taylor, an analyst that I'd like you to add to your team."

Elda leaned in toward Jackson to greet him. "Hello Jackson. And what's your background?" Elda asked, while analyzing his facial expressions, body language and calculating his approximate age. She figured from his greying hair that he was around fifty years old, with a pitted face from childhood acne, which probably resulted to a touch of insecurity. She also noticed his hooked nose, which caused him to wheeze slightly when he breathed. She detected no nervousness, however, and his body language was open.

Jackson removed, cleaned and replaced his glasses before replying. He spoke with a hint of a British accent. "I'm ex-MI6 and CIA, but I left intelligence to teach at Harvard University."

Elda rapid fire peppered him with questions. "You're from the Blackpool area originally?"

"You have a good ear. Kirkham, actually."

"Ah, Kirkham. My great aunt's cousin lived in Kirkham. She loved when I visited. She would insist that I drive her to Blackpool for the best fish and chips."

"That had to be at *The Cottage.* Best chippy around. I love their tartar sauce. And they serve the take out in newspapers, as it should be."

Elda continued rapidly firing questions at Jackson, "Is it still there?"

"Oh yes. I go there whenever I'm near that area."

"A foodie, I see?"

"I've been known to travel on my stomach."

"Do you like burgers?"

"Mr. Bartley's still has the best burgers around."

"There were rumors that they were going to close. I was heartbroken."

"Oh no; they are still open. It's *The Out of Town News Kiosk* that finally closed, much to my dismay."

"In Harvard Yard, right?"

"No, no, Harvard Square. Harvard Yard is part of the university campus. But you know all this already, *don't you*?"

Elda nodded with satisfaction and sat back in her chair. "Yes, I do. I was just checking to see if you are who you say you are. So why are you here?"

"Ed reached out to me after David passed away. When I studied at the Program for the Study of Disinformation at Boston University, my professor was Ladislav Bittman, or as he was then known, Professor Lawrence Martin."

Elda looked up and to the left and then back at Jackson. "Oh! Now the penny drops. Bittman wrote a couple of books on Soviet disinformation."

"Yes, he did. Under the direction of the Soviet Secret police, Bittman was deputy chief of the disinformation division for Czech intelligence, called the Department for Active Measures and Disinformation. He wrote a book about the KGB's use of disinformation and information warfare during the Soviet Union period. The book includes case studies of joint disinformation campaigns by the Soviet Union and Czech intelligence and their repercussions."

Ed leaned in to interject. "Elda, I think you can use Jackson's help to determine if the information that Stas uncovers is real or a trap. It could save you time and save your team too. David and I, and now Jackson and I, have researched all available information from our mission so far. *Operation Bittman* appears to be a series of Soviet bait and switch and misinformation operations pitting others against the United States, while Russia achieves its objectives."

"Okay Jackson, you're on the team." Elda reached across the table to shake his hand. She looked at Ed to see if he had anything else to add.

"One more thing. I was never here."

"Yes, Ed. Are you heading back to DC?"

"Yes. You'll be able to contact me through our channels. I think that Tosh is in the dark about Russia's goals too, but you cannot be sure. Trust no one."

"Can I trust you, Ed?"

"Trust no one, Elda."

***

"Stas, shut down any equipment now!"

"*Chto?*"

"*Seychas!*"

A few minutes later, Stas ran into the living room from the back bedroom to stand by Tosh, who was hiding to one side behind the long drapes while looking, with the aid of binoculars, out the living room window of the villa.

"Everything is shut down and unplugged."

"*Khorosho.* Quick, go pack it all up and get ready to leave. Snezhana!"

"*Da, sudar'?*"

"Stoke up the fire in the fireplace. Everyone lie down in front of it – pile up! I want to minimize the separate heat signatures coming from here. Chert! Where is Elda with our vehicle?"

265

Tosh watched as a van, with antennas on top, moved slowly down the hill toward the villa, leaving a trail of dust behind it. Tosh grabbed his camera and took pictures as he crouched, backing up away from the window, as the van drove slowly by. The van's passenger took pictures of the villa with a Zenit Leica M Type 240 camera sporting a zoom lens. The van disappeared up the dirt road in a cloud of dust.

"It's no longer safe here. We have to leave."

***

The villa was engulfed in flames and billowing black smoke, surrounded by rescue vehicles. Elda drove by slowly and saw no one from her team milling about. The building was a complete loss. She continued past it and once she was out of sight around a bend in the road, pulled the van over.

"Was that your villa?"

"Yes, Jackson. But our team is not in sight. Either they are all dead or they managed to get away. If I were Tosh, what would I do?"

Elda got out of the Fiat with a pair of binoculars in her hand. She scanned the countryside in all directions. She jumped back in behind the wheel. "Hang on! This may get a bit rough." She turned off of the main dirt road onto an ungraded dirt track formed by farmers' tractors and

266

bounced along heading to a villa about two miles away. She stopped suddenly near a grove of chestnut trees. She got out and called softly: "Olly olly oxen free."

A pair of gray eyes peered at her from between two branches. "About time you returned with our van. And, *who* is this?"

"This is Jackson. I'll fill you in on the way. Get in. We need to put some distance between us and whomever did that to the villa."

Tosh crawled out from behind the brush under the trees, followed by the rest of the team. "You do realize, Elda, that this van only sits seven people, and now we have eight," he said tersely and motioned to indicate the group behind him.

"*Yes, Tosh*, I do. Put the luggage between the back two seats and have our smallest person sit on it."

Tosh took command, "Stas, you're the skinniest. You get to ride there. I have shotgun. Anatoly, you will sit in the middle seats next to the door, in case we need a quick exit or to open it for shooting. Put the rest of the luggage on your laps or in the top carrier. Elda, you are not allowed to pick up any more strays."

The team efficiently crammed into the van and Elda took off over the dirt track again heading away from the villa.

"So where now?"

"I have a place in mind."

***

A bullet smashed the Fiat's back window. Glass shattered and shards sprayed over Jackson, Stas and Yuri who were ducked down in their seats. Elda looked in the rear window and spied a helmeted man. in black and white camouflage on a black Aprilla RSV4 racing motorcycle approaching their rear at a high speed.

Elda shouted, "Get ready, Anatoly. We can't out run him. That bike is too fast. You'll only get one chance. Hang on! Buckle up!"

Anatoly, slammed a cartridge full of 9mm armor piercing bullets into his Vityaz-SN submachine gun, then threw back the side door panel and braced himself. He positioned the butt of the short lightweight weapon against his shoulder and pointed its snub-nosed barrel out the door. Elda took her foot off the accelerator and stomped on the brakes, causing everyone to fly forward against their seat belts. Stas flew off the luggage. Yuri flung his arm out to slow Stas's forward motion. Elda rotated the wheel to the right and accelerated sharply. The Fiat spun around in a cloud of dust, wobbling and threatening to overturn. When they were at a ninety-degree angle to the road, Elda slammed on the brakes again and Anatoly started firing.

268

Snezhana and Sophia were at the ready, with their guns drawn behind him. Anatoly hit the bike with his first and third blasts, and the driver with his second.

The driver was flung off the bike. The bike exploded into a ball of fire and skidded on its side directly toward the van.

"*Idti, idti, idti!*"

Elda had already pressed the accelerator to the floor, while yanking the wheel back to the left. The van whipped around and tottered and Elda struggled with the steering to keep the van upright and going forward. The tires, looking for traction, threw up gravel and a whirling cloud of dust. Anatoly pulled the door shut.

"Well there goes that security deposit," grumbled Elda, as she glanced at the rear view mirror. "Is everyone unharmed?"

"Can someone help me back up?" mumbled Stas from the floor of the backseat. Yuri gently picked him up and deposited him on top of the pile of luggage.

"Hang on. Tosh, we need to find a different mode of transportation and way out of here. For now let's get some distance between us and the villa." They sped off down the road leaving the wreckage behind them.

*****

Five men in Italian firemen uniforms spread out in a line to sort through the smoking rubble. Their leader shouted, "*Toropit'sya*! We don't have much time before the Italian police arrive."

With military precision they swiftly and carefully crisscrossed the area and picked through the charred remains of the villa, filtering the ashes with their gloved hands. They removed any traces of the weaponry that had destroyed it and poured a cup of gasoline on the fireplace. They convened at the end of area and had a short discussion.

Done, they hurtled into the idling white Opel Vivaro van, and, with a spray of gravel, sped away. One man picked up his phone and punched in a number. When he was connected he spoke: "There are no bones."

***

Tosh straightened his military cap, started the Iveco LMV-stretch variant camolflauged military armored vehicle and drove off the Forze Armate Esercito base. From her position on the front floor between Tosh's and Anatoly's legs, Elda asked, "How on earth did you manage to get these uniforms and this vehicle, Tosh?"

"Some secrets are better off kept to oneself."

Anatoly jumped up on his seat and stuck his head out the roof hatch. "*Fantasticheskiy*! I can pop out the roof and shoot."

"I hope you don't need to, but taking out the motorcycle and the driver in just three shots was excellent shooting, Anatoly. For now you may want to come down inside with the rest of us."

"Thank you, Elda, but I should have been able to do it in two shots," growled Anatoly as he smoothly slid back down into a seated position in the front passenger's seat, without disturbing either Tosh or Elda.

Elda turned around as far as she could to yell over the truck noise. "How's everyone back there?"

"Why do I always get the floor?"

"Couldn't you find a larger vehicle?"

"My left leg is numb."

"I can't straighten up."

"Okay, Tosh, sounds like status quo. Let's get out of Italy."

"On it, Elda."

Elda took off her cap and squinted at the map unfolded in front of her. "They are making maps smaller. Let's head to Darby Military Base to drop this vehicle off. I'd love to catch a plane from Pisa, but they will be watching the airports for us. I think getting a train to Barcelona will be better. We can catch one out of Livorno Centrale. These uniforms should keep us disguised."

"Oh Barcelona is lovely," opined Jackson wistfully from the back.

Elda and Tosh smashed Jackson's daydream, "Don't get attached, Jackson," reprimanded Elda. "We'll only be passing through," added Tosh.

Elda yelled over her shoulder, "Yuri, you are sure you have people who can help us get from Spain to the United States?"

"*Da*, Elda. It won't be first class travel, of course."

"Can we at least have a bigger car? I can't use my laptop!"

"Oh hush, Stas. You're lucky to be alive. Tosh, here's E35. Go north. We'll cut around Florence from the south and head out to the coast."

"*Khorosho*." Tosh smoothly joined E35N.

"Tosh, how much of a leeway do we have before they discover we *borrowed* this vehicle?"

"Probably not long."

***

The truck backfired when Tosh slowed and stopped outside the entrance of Darby Military base. "*Chert*! I hope this truck has enough gas in it to slide into a parking space!"

"Didn't you check that when you stole it?"

Tosh fixed Elda a steely gaze. "*Blyad'*, Elda. All – get out! Wait for me here. If I'm not back in fifteen minutes, run like hell."

The team spilled out, like clowns from a VW bug, stumbling over each other as they willed cramped legs to stand. Tosh dove off in the sputtering truck. Elda wandered over to the designated smoking area, where one young soldier was standing smoking a cigarette. After accepting the light for the cigarette she had bummed from him, she asked, "So where are you going, soldier?"

"Livorne Centrale and then to Pisa for a flight back home to the Sates."

"Is there a bus that goes to Livorne Centrale or are you waiting for a cab? And where are you from in the States?"

"You'll need a taxi, probably two for that lot. I can call back and ask them to send two more if you'd like. And I'm from Newport, RI."

"Thank you. Yes. Could you please get us two cabs? Isn't Newport an old Navy town? You're in the wrong uniform soldier."

The soldier guffawed and called for the additional cabs.

Tosh came marching out of the main gate and joined Elda.

"Well?"

"It's returned. It may take them a while to figure out where it came from."

"So much the better. Where did you leave it?"

"In the admiral's parking space. The guy at the gate was chatty and told me the admiral only visited once a month and had just left."

"Gads. Let's get out of here."

***

A rumpled and tired looking crew staggered off the train in Barcelona after the fifteen-hour train ride.

"*Der'mo*! Yuri, next time send us first class. Those seats were not big enough."

"I should know, Anatoly. You fell asleep on me," Stas commented, rubbing his sore shoulder.

"*Mne zhal'* Stas."

Elda clapped her hands to get their attention. "Okay, listen up everyone. Now we need to change out of these uniforms into new disguises. Let's pick up maps of the city from over there and reconvene here in an hour. Okay? And Anatoly, can you please take Stas and help him out??"

"*Da*, Elda."

"Oh Elda?"

"Yes, Stas?"

"I did some searching while being buried by Anatoly's largeness and there's chatter about someone from MI6 looking for us."

***

The blast of a train whistle filled the air. A slender Hassidic Jew wandered past the waiting travelers to a small mustached man, who was wearing a flat cap and matching brown vest and slacks.

"*Isvinite menya.* Do you know someone called Elda?"

"*Nyet*, Tosh, but my associate over there may," Elda replied, pointing at a large brown-haired man with brown eyes wearing a bowler hat, black slacks with suspenders, and holding a leather bag. Anatoly waved back at Elda and then threw her a figa. "And should I ask where you got those wonderful payots, Tosh? Is someone else now bald?"

"It's better you don't know the details."

Standing on the train platform next to Anatoly was Yuri, wearing a black and white Newcastle United shirt, jeans, and a backwards Red Sox baseball cap. He was holding hands with Sophia who had on a baggy t-shirt, jeans, and a matching baseball cap. They were talking with Stas who looked much the same as he always did and was attired in khaki painters pants, a blue t-shirt and a multi-colored headband. All three had well-worn backpacks.

Standing stiffly to one side was Snezhana with severely slicked back black hair, green eyes, a black business suit and a large gray computer bag.

Jackson was near her, wearing horn-rimmed glasses, a business suit, a fedora hat, black leather shoes, and his go-bag by his side.

"Well I recognize that one. Where did you find him, Elda?"

"He was a present from Ed."

"Can we send him back?"

Yuri walked over to Tosh and Elda.

"I see that you are a supporter of The Magpies, Yuri."

"Huh?"

"Your shirt. It's from the Newcastle United Football Club and their nickname is *The Magpies*. You should know that."

"*Spasibo*, Elda. I will remember that."

"What have you arranged with the smugglers?"

"We need to get to El Prat de Llobregat Aeropuerto. It's about a 50-minute ride. We will be flown out of there."

"Thanks for handling the logistics, Yuri. Okay, let's go!"

"*Idti!*"

***

Elda flinched as each nail was hammered into the wood of the top of the crate she was lying in. She closed her eyes in the darkness and slowed her breath to help lengthen the time the small oxygen tank would last. Trying to envision large open fields and views of a wide expanse of beach and the rolling waves of the ocean, she felt her breath come in slowly and fully through her nose. She could taste the plastic and metal smell of the hose and connector.

I apologize again, Korinna for the days you had to spend in that container on the ride to Hamburg.

A voice whispered in her earpiece. "So you *do* have a soft side, Elda?"

"Damn it Tosh – those were my own thoughts! Did I speak them?"

"I heard your mouth move, Tosh joked."

"I wouldn't put it past you."

The conversation got cut off as the crates were jostled and loaded onto the plane to Connecticut.

Chapter Twenty-Five

James stormed into the command center and fired up the large screen communication system, connecting to Ed in DC. "Where are they, Ed?" he yelled at the face on the screen.

Ed was sitting at his desk in his office receiving the call on his computer there. "I don't know James."

James paced back and forth in front of the room, running his hand in frustration through his hair and then shaking his finger at Ed. "I tracked them to Italy. The villa they had rented there has burned to the ground. There is no trace of them leaving the country."

Ed put his chin in his hand and his elbow on the desk and sighed heavily. "Why were you looking for them, James?"

"One of my operatives is with them and has gone dark," blasted James.

Ed rolled his eyes. "Yes, that's the plan. They were to go dark until they needed us."

James retorted, "Wouldn't you say having their villa burn to the ground *might* be a cry for help?"

James stood so close to the camera that his face filled Ed's screen. Ed sat back with a disgusted look on his face. "You never answered my question, really. *Why* were you looking for them?"

"I don't trust you, Ed, nor do I trust Tosh and Elda. This operation is too big to have rouge agents running around. You seem to have conveniently forgotten that it's not just the American and Russian presidents' lives that are at stake, it's the British Prime Minister's too."

"And you seem to have conveniently forgotten that we both have one dead agent and another in the hospital. We can only be successful if we protect our team."

Ed and James glared at each other's image with their nostrils flared and their fists clenched.

Just then James' and Ed's phones beeped. Each opened their messages to see a picture of a white van with antennas on it and a license plate clearly visible. A brief text accompanied it: *Find this van. Last seen near the villa outside of Montepulciano. James stop looking for us. You only endanger us. Love and kisses, Tosh and Elda.*

Ed doubled over in laughter. James stared at his phone in disbelief.

Chapter Twenty-Six

The aide ambled over to the nurses station with his hand on his cheek. "Blimey, I think I broke a tooth!" He held out his hand with a dented metal shard in it.

Two nurses peered at the object. One inquired, "What on *earth* were you eating?"

The aide pointed at the wicker basket at the end of the counter. "An apple from that fruit basket over there. It looks like some joker inserted a metal toy in it."

The senior nurse commanded, "Throw it all out. It was delivered by that sneaky looking MI6 chap. I don't trust any of them."

The second nurse stamped over to the basket, picked it up, and, with a flourish, threw it into a nearby trash receptacle. "There. Problem solved. It'll get picked up this afternoon."

***

As a man and a woman passed each other in the MI6 hallway, the woman dropped a handful of papers onto the gleaming linoleum floor. Heads close together, they both bent to pick the papers up. The woman whispered to the man, "There's no signal from the basket."

"Did you turn on the device?"

She answered stiffly through clenched teeth, "Of course I did. We need another plan, in case Sophia contacts Oliver."

"He's too well protected. He's demanded his own guards by name. I can't even get one of my men in to guard him."

"Well, think of something quickly. Time is counting down."

***

While driving the lead car, Elda pinged Anatoly on Facetime.

"*Privet*, Elda. You do know it's illegal to use your cell phone as a hand held device while driving in Massachusetts?"

"Oh cram it, Anatoly. If you're going to be such a boy scout then hand your phone to Snezhana." Anatoly snickered. Elda continued with her reason for calling, "When we get to Newburyport, we'll stop at Market Basket and get enough food to last us a while. I am really stiff from driving all this way from the Connecticut airfield. I'd like to get a run in, so perhaps I can leave you guys to do the shopping? We will need more than just pastries, however, so don't listen to Anatoly."

"I'll join you Elda."

"I'd appreciate the company, Tosh, but who will be the adult for the shopping spree? It would be good to get some clothes too. Marshalls is in the same plaza."

Jackson spoke up from the back seat, "Give me the list, Elda and I'll run the operation."

"Thanks, Jackson."

Yuri's face popped up on the screen of Elda's phone. "Hey, Elda, don't forget that I was the one who got Anatoly and me out of Russia and all of us flown back to the United States from Barcelona," he said petulantly.

"True, Yuri. You have always been good at logistics and arrangements. You had to be babysitting all those feeble ex-Pats. I didn't mean to overlook you."

"*Spasibo*." Satisfied, Yuri relaxed back into the backseat.

Elda caught sight of Stas sitting next to Yuri. He was hunched over his computer and typing. "Stas, turn off your computer, now! I asked that you rest your eyes and stomach while riding in the car. You will help hunt and gather. I'll give Anatoly directions. Tosh and I will get out at Scotland Road. We'll run to Parker Street and the rail trail to High Street, where you guys can pick us up again. That will give us time to clear our heads and you guys time to shop."

"Everyone have American dollars?" queried Tosh. "You better have, after all the amounts we gave out after the St. Petersburg mission."

"*Da*," answered Anatoly and Yuri in unison.

"OK. Operation Food Shopping is a go."

***

Deep in the bowels of MI6, a slender pale-faced woman looked up from her equipment and admitted, "I lost them," to the man who had just entered the closet-sized room.

"Where were they?" he asked standing over her with his arms crossed over his chest.

She pointed at the data on her screen. "Without being able to triangulate the signal, it's hard to pinpoint."

He leaned in and took a look at her computer and asked, "What's your best guess?"

She pointed out areas of the map. "Somewhere north of Boston, Massachusetts in the USA. Perhaps closer to Georgetown, Newburyport or even Amesbury. The signal was live for a while, and then cut off, so they are probably stopped somewhere."

"Do we have anyone in that area of the United States?"

"I know someone we can activate."

***

"I understand. Send me the pictures. I will start by searching the exits from Georgetown to Amesbury."

The woman put down the phone, shook her short brown hair into place, took her gun out of a lock box, grabbed ammo and a packet of money and passports, which she shoved into a handbag, and left the old farmhouse.

***

Elda and Tosh ran by quaint New England homes, surrounded by stone walls and set back from the road. The sun was shining and the traffic was light, keeping the exhaust fumes down. They ran in step with an easy gate like two old friends, pulling in to single file when cars passed them.

"It's nice to get out jogging again. Fleeing from country to country is bad for maintaining an exercise program."

"*Da*. It's good to be moving again. Do you jog every day, Elda?"

285

"I try."

"Do you have a regular jogging route that you like near your house?"

"Yes."

"Is it hilly or are you at sea level?"

"Probing again, Tosh?"

Tosh looked back at Elda, winked and picked up the pace.

A blue and white mud splattered mini passed them slowly. Elda noticed that the driver was looking down at her cell phone.

"Tosh, be alert. We may have a situation here."

The car pulled over on the dirt shoulder by the side of the road. The driver exited the car, leaving the car running and the driver's side door partially open, and popped open the hood. She bent over the side of the car and peered at the engine, shaking her short brown hair out of her eyes.

Having pulled into a single file formation for the passing traffic, Tosh was still jogging slightly in front of Elda. "*Chert.* I wish we had brought our weapons."

As Tosh passed the front of the car, the driver straightened up and, pivoting quickly, backhanded him with a tire iron, adding to his forward momentum, sending him off into a ditch. She swung back around with the iron raised to clobber Elda. Elda caught the tire iron with her hand and with her other hand, grabbed the woman by her hair and slammed her face into the car.

The woman showed no sign of pain and ripped away from Elda, leaving strands of hair in Elda's fist. She reached with her free hand to grab her gun from her back waistband, only to find it missing.

"Looking for this?" asked a mud-encrusted Tosh, pointing her gun at her. She flung herself into Elda, knocking her on her back, and leapt into the car, before Tosh could get a clean shot off. The car peeled away, splattering mud on both Tosh and the fallen Elda.

"*Chert.*" Tosh wiped his hand across his face, managing only to smear the mud more. Clearly enraged, he looked around for a way to chase her.

Elda touched his arm and spoke in a calming voice, "Let her go Tosh. She's too far away to shoot and we have no way to catch her. We must scurry to get out of here before others come this way."

"Who was she?"

Elda shook gravel and leaves out of her hair before answering. "I don't know. I managed to snap a picture of the license plate number, and, of her, when I was lying on the ground. It's a bit blurry but perhaps Ed can run it through our systems and see if there is a match. I'll send it to him now. She'll ditch the car as soon as she can, of course, but perhaps they can lift some information from it when they locate it. She was wearing gloves so there won't be any fingerprints on this tire iron except mine. I'll toss it further up the road where there are no skid marks to draw attention to the area."

"*Chert.*" Tosh grimaced and touched his right arm.

"You okay?" Elda asked sincerely.

"Of course."

"That little bitch was pretty strong. Let's get jogging and off this road."

"If she's part of all of this, why didn't she kill us?"

"I don't know."

***

A man paced back and forth in a small windowless room, holding a cell phone up to his ear. "You are sure it was them?"

He listened to the answer.

"So go search for them. We need to capture them to find the rest."

288

He listened again.

"What do you mean you can't?"

He heard his own voice rise up in pitch and level and cleared his throat. He held his phone in one hand and nervously scratched his head with his other. He listened to her answer and then nodded.

"Fine, fine… I see why you can't stay in that area. Well, we can have another assignment for you. Are you up to it?" Through his phone he felt the dangerous chill in her answer. He quickly responded back,

"No, no, no. I am not making any implications about your abilities. I know you're the best. Yes, *of course* we will pay you for today. And, as you wish, I will rescind the capture and do not kill order. Handle the situation as you see fit. How well do you know New York City?"

Chapter Twenty-Seven

The sun sparkled on the tips of the swaying blades of grass and reflected like diamonds off the pools of water. A blue heron stalked its prey in the marsh.

"*Chert*! What is that bird? It looks like a dinosaur!" Yuri turned from the living room bay window with a look of amazement on his face.

Laughing, Elda pointed over the two cars in the driveway into the marsh, showing Yuri the two blue herons and the six great white egrets that were bobbing up and down, hunting for their dinner. A Coopers hawk soared and circled overhead and a seagull oversaw everything from his perch on a nearby telephone pole.

"There's a whole bird city out there." Yuri remarked in awe. "What are they hunting?"

"The egrets are fishing and the hawk probably is after mice or voles. The seagull is an opportunist and will go for the remains."

"By the way, Yuri, well done getting us smuggled into the United States," remarked Tosh from the couch in the living room.

"Not a problem Tosh, It's pretty easy when you have enough money to flash around, and especially, drug running acquaintances,"

Elda turned and strode over the ash floor to join Tosh. She sat next to him on the down stuffed couch. "I was impressed. All that money spent on building a wall and we just walked underground. That was one scary tunnel though. It did not look like it passed any building codes with the dirt leaking through the ceiling. Hopefully when we need to leave the United States we can find another way out of the country."

"At the end of this I am flying back First Class," stated Anatoly.

"How did you know about this place, Elda? How safe is it?" queried Tosh.

"We should be pretty well hidden. At least for a while, Tosh. There are no ties to the government or directly to me. I call this my Aunt Helen's house, but it really belongs to someone unrelated to me – just a friend." A shadow briefly passed across Elda's expression. Tosh raised an eyebrow. Elda ignored him and continued, "I used to spend quite a few summers here, but I haven't been here for many years. They would have to dig very deeply to connect me to this location. We shouldn't show our faces in town, though."

"Where did Snezhana and Sophia disappear to?"

"They're downstairs using the equipment in the home gym. It's a pretty decent one with a treadmill and a rowing machine. Aunt Helen used to like to keep in shape, but she was Yankee to the core and refused to pay for gym memberships."

Tosh stood up and strode over to Jackson and Stas who were working in the adjourning office area. "We need some leads here, Jackson and Stas," he demanded. "Do you have anything? We have to keep moving. We've already lost four days traveling here."

Stas answered as he continued typing simultaneously on two computers, "We've found satellite imagery of the attack on the villa. It looks like they used a portable rocket-propelled grenade launcher, most likely the RPG-7V2, probably armed with a fuel-air explosive."

"That points directly to the Russians, although those weapons are obtainable on the black market," surmised Jackson, as he squinted, adjusted his glasses and zoomed in on an image.

Elda postulated, "Maybe they are sending a clear warning to anyone who follows us. Ed and James put an article in the paper that listed DNA remains from seven bodies were found in the rubble. They also sent a lightly encrypted message to Alexei with condolences for the loss of Tosh, Snezhana, Yuri and Anatoly. That should buy us some time."

"Perhaps not though, Elda. Someone found us today."

"True, Tosh. I wonder how…"

Just then Sophia and Snezhana bounded up the basement stairs and into the living room. They were dripping in sweat and had been working out in their underwear.

"*Chert*! Snezhana! Get dressed!" grumbled Tosh.

"*Da dyadya*. But what did we miss??"

"Come back when you're dressed and I'll tell you," growled Tosh.

Snezhana and Sophia returned to the living room more suitably clad in their new clothes from Target. Tosh continued to speak. "We will split up once we get leads. We can have Stas and Jackson be the home base. Snezhana and Sophia can be one team. Yuri and Anatoly another. And you and I, Elda, can make up the third team."

"I agree, Tosh," pronounced Elda. "Do you have anything, Stas?"

"I do, Elda, but I am not sure it's credible. We have ruled out any leads that we know are definitely fake. This one is just a brief mention of commemoration activities in New York to mark the seventy-fifth anniversary of the signing of the United Nation's Charter."

"Thanks Stas. What do you think, Jackson?"

"The American president is obsessed with the cost of United Nations. I would speculate that he will be making a speech there."

Elda continued to dig into the credibility of the new information. "What's the probability?"

"50-60%. You know how whimsical he can be."

"Anything else?"

"We also caught chatter around the United Nations Special Committee on Peacekeeping Operations. Those sessions are also held in New York. The United States, Russia and the United Kingdom are all members of that committee. There's no indication however that the heads of state will be attending any of the sessions. I've analyzed the messages and they appear to be genuine."

"So, both of those leads point to New York City. Anatoly and Yuri can go since they will not stand out as much there as they do in this small New England town. Do you agree, Tosh?"

"Not entirely. We *could* send them to New York to see what they can ferret out. They do stand out like sore fingers in this town."

"Sore thumbs."

Tosh held up his fist with his thumb thrust in between the first and second finger. Elda flashed back an upright middle finger.

"You have mud behind your left ear, Tosh."

Tosh lifted his hand to check and then saw the smile in Elda's eyes and, fighting a grin, dropped his hand. "However, as I was saying… we *could* send them to New York,… but I don't think that's the threat. I think we are being misdirected again."

"True. That could very well be, Tosh. Why would Russia choose to attack their president? And the British Prime Minister is still a good foil for them. I think that they only want to eliminate the American president."

"Exactly, Elda."

"But if they attack all three, succeed in only eliminating the one, and pin it on a fourth country, they will succeed in their mission and obscure who really did it. Look at how they concealed their attack on the 2018 Olympics. Russia's GRU Unit 74455 is expert at leaving trails that point to other countries. This is Operation Bittman, after all. So it will be steeped in dead-end leads and other misdirection. Long story short, we need to go to where the data points."

"I hate it when you may be right, Elda."

“We need to do something, Tosh. We can’t just sit here until they find us again.”

“*Khorosho. But* let’s first discover how they found us in Italy.”

“Good point, Tosh. Also who was that woman on Scotland Road? How did she find us? Stas, scour all of our electronics. We *have* to find how they are tracking us.”

***

Sitting in his home office, Ed stared in disbelief at the screen in front of him. It was a match. He took out his burner phone to call Elda and once connected, put her on speaker, so he could still type on his computer. “You won’t believe this, Elda. We think the woman who attacked you is Angelina Rodin.”

“The infamous international free-lance assassin? What on earth was she doing in Massachusetts, Ed?

Ed scrolled down a page. “Apparently living in a farmhouse in Rowley. We found she had been living there for the past 10 years. Clever. Who would think of looking for her in quaint old New England?”

Elda responded, “I have heard of some pretty major criminals hiding out in New Hampshire. Tales say they were model citizens. She’s Russian, isn’t she?”

Ed informed Elda, "Or at least of Russian descent. I think with enough money her loyalties can be changed. Her car was dumped at the train station and she had left her old credentials in it. Pure arrogance. She's long gone. The world has looked all over for her, but no one has captured her yet. I'm not surprised she managed to shake you two. What surprises me is that she didn't kill you outright."

"I doubt we would be that lucky a second time," Elda mused.

Ed nodded. "Yes, exactly. Be careful. Whoever is behind this has an eclectic and dispersed network."

***

Tosh and Elda were sitting in the front seat of a dark blue rental car in a parking spot on the side of the Bird Watcher's Supply & Gift store in Newburyport, Massachusetts, just on the other side of the train station parking lot. Elda was behind the wheel, and Anatoly and Yuri were in the back seat. Tosh was sporting a gray mustache and a baby blue baseball cap. Elda was in the new jogging clothes that Yuri had picked up for her in Target. She had a white sports cap on her head and a face mask covering the lower part of her face. Both Elda and Tosh had mirrored sunglasses on to hide their eyes.

"Okay, the train to Boston is in a few minutes. I'm going to pull out of here and drive to the train station lot. I will circle around the parking lot once, and, if all looks clear, park the car in a spot near the platform. Anatoly and Yuri, you two will hop out and catch the train. Tosh and I will follow you onto the platform and sit where we can keep an eye on the car. Good so far?"

Anatoly and Yuri responded in unison, *"Khorosho."*

Elda started the car and carefully pulled out onto route 1A. While driving she continued to brief the team, "If Stas is correct, all of our computers had a hidden program on them. This program ran continuously. Whenever or computers were powered up it sent out our location information." Elda continued, speculating, "The only place that the software could have been placed on all of our computers was when MI6 took the computers to install the communication software. That further confirms that MI6 has a mole and we cannot trust them. "

"Damn Brits," Tosh exclaimed, throwing a finger.

Elda held up her hand and cautioned, "Careful Tosh, those are our allies in this operation. It's the Russians we should curse."

Tosh chuckled and agreed, *"Chert. Da. Proklyatyye russkiye!"*

Elda put on her directional signal to make the right hand turn to the train station. She finished giving the background information to the team, "We left the program running on one computer. I will stash that computer in a backpack in the front seat of the car. We're guessing someone will be following our electronic signal. Tosh and I should be disguised enough so that we won't be recognized. The rest of our equipment has been reformatted and restored by Stas. Therefore, unless the tracking is hardware based, they should no longer be able to find us via our computers."

Elda cruised into the train station parking lot. Before she had even put the car in park, Anatoly and Yuri were off running to catch the train. Tosh and Elda followed at a slower pace. They each settled down on the platform, on separate benches facing the parking lot.

Elda sighed. This operation had so many players. She wondered, *What next? Now we wait.*

***

Elda peeked over the top of her book surveying two men crossing the parking lot from different directions. The men were looking down at their cell phones as they slowly converged paths and approached the dark blue rental car. She watched as one of them swiftly inserted a wedge at the top of the door and then snaked a metal rod down to pop the lock, while the other was the lookout. The B&E man was inside in seconds. He reached down to the backpack on the passenger seat floor and checked its contents. Satisfied, he put it back and then took a small package from

299

the other man. He bent down out of view for a few minutes and then left the car, relocking the door. He gave his partner a thumbs up and they both jogged off to a car that had pulled up nearby.

Elda walked over to a seat on the bench that backed up to Tosh's and spoke softly through the metal mesh between them.

"I think they just put plastic explosive in the car," she said in a low voice.

"Obviously, Elda," Tosh rejoined. "Do you have your walking shoes on?"

Elda automatically looked down at her feet, answering, "I have my jogging shoes on. But we don't want someone else to get hurt by that bomb."

"Don't be a soft hearted fool. It'll take days before they contact Enterprise to pick up the rental, so we have plenty of time to call the threat in. We accomplished our mission here. We now know for sure that the computers were rigged. Let's get back to the house on the island, round the rest of the team up and get out of here," Tosh hissed.

Elda bit back her retort, sighed heavily and responded calmly, "Fine. You go first. Walk down the platform, cross the street and follow the rail trail a short way to the sign for Haley's Ice Cream. Cut through their parking lot and across Route One and up Hill Street. Take a right at the end and head a couple of blocks to CVS. Call a cab from there. I'll follow in around 5 minutes."

"*Da.*" Tosh stood up and lightly jogged away down the platform.

Elda watched as one man got into the car and the other waved them on. He patted his side pocket and headed up toward the platform. *So that's where your gun is. Good to know.* The car drove slowly through the parking lot to the exit as the passenger looked carefully at the parked cars. The man on the platform stopped and typed quickly into his cell phone.

I better get out of here.

Elda checked her watch, put her book in her bag and slowly started sauntering down the concrete platform, away from the train station. Her pulse was thudding in her neck as she sensed the other man coming up behind her. Elda took a small compact make-up case out of her pocket and opened it up, rubbing one finger along her eyelid as she checked the rear view. She saw the man pull out his gun and start to advance quicker toward her.

*****

The man stopped in the hallway at MI6, ensured no one was near and answered his buzzing cell phone. His contact in the United States informed him, "We may have located them at the Newburyport Train Station.

"Are we sure?" he inquired, while leaning against the wall and polishing his shoe on his pant leg.

The contact answered, "No, but there was a slender man with a woman on the platform and we have one man in pursuit."

The MI6 employee ordered, "Kill them anyway. Where are the others?"

The reply came, "We are still searching the area. Their car is at the train station. We have placed a bomb in it, in case they return."

The man switched legs and started polishing his other shoe and asked, "Is New York City all set?" Hearing the affirmative response, "Yes," he straightened up to his full height and impeccable posture. He checked the crease in his trousers and ran his hand through his greying hair, then ordered, "Excellent. Kill whomever shows up. We are no longer taking prisoners."

***

Elda took off in a run, barely missing being hit by cars as she dashed across Parker Street. She zigged and zagged along the rail trail. Thankfully there was no one else traveling along that section. A bullet hit the wooden arch over the rail trail, sending a shower of splinters down. A second bullet reverberated as it ricocheted off the metal sculpture of two doves. Elda accelerated even more and took the right to Haley's. She ran along the short trail to the parking lot, and, once there, veered left to skid sharply to a stop at the front of an abandoned warehouse. She took out her gun. Within minutes her pursuer ran by her location and stopped suddenly, confused, unable to see where she had gone. She took a shot and smashed his knee. He fell to the ground, dropping his military issue Luger Glock 17 handgun. Elda ran up to him and kicked it out of his reach.

"Who sent you?" demanded Elda.

He sneered at her and bit down hard. Soon a froth appeared at his lips and his eyes rolled back into his head.

"Damn!" Elda took a picture of him, pocketed her gun, picked up his, and then dragged his body over behind a pile of dirt and rocks. Satisfied that the body was out of view, she took off across Route 1 and over to Hill Street, arriving at CVS breathless, just as a cab pulled up for Tosh. She hopped into the back with him. She ordered the driver, "Please drop us off at Bobs' Lobster on the Turnpike." She wiped the sweat from her eyes. "I'll have to call Ed and have him clean up this mess."

Tosh glanced at Elda who dropped into his lap her phone with the picture of the dead man on it. He swore, "*Chert*. I was right. We need to get out of here immediately."

Elda agreed, "Yes. Even if the tracking software is gone, we are no longer safe here."

***

Elda stood gazing unseeingly at the marsh through the bay window of *Aunt Helen's* house. Tosh walked up behind her and put a hand on her shoulder and said with uncharacteristic kindness, "We have to go now Elda. The rest are in the car."

Elda sighed and without turning asked, "Do you ever want to just chuck it all, Tosh? Run away where you can never be found again? Start anew?"

Tosh gave a sad chuckle in return, "We don't have that option, Elda. The end for us is death."

Elda sighed again. "I know," she said, her shoulders slumping. She turned, their eyes met acknowledging their common fate, and they both exited the house, the door closing behind them with a finality.

***

"We need a second car," said Stas from the floor of the backseat.

"We'll pick one up in Boston," Elda consoled Stas.

304

Route 1 was blocked off by a fire engine and two police cars. More blue lights were flashing from Haley's parking lot. They drove down Parker Street to Scotland Road to pick up Route 95 South.

Smiling, Elda observed, "Well it looks like Ed called the bomb squad for the car and also reported the body."

"Where are we going?" inquired Tosh, checking the rearview mirror.

Elda shrugged her shoulders and replied, "After Boston? I don't have a clue, Tosh. Any ideas?"

"Yes," responded Tosh, "We will send Sophia and Snezhana to London to try and find the mole in MI6 and the four of us will head to DC. That's where the president currently is. I think they will drop the obscuration and accelerate their plans to focus on the real target. We don't have much time."

"The assassin in Newburyport had this gun, a Glock 17," said Elda pointing at the black, square nosed weapon on the floor next to Tosh. "That indicates the Ukrainian special forces. I feel like we are deep in a murky swirl of misdirection."

"The assassin was Asian," added Jackson from the backseat. "Potentially Korean, but possibly Japanese. If we reach out to Ed, we could narrow that down."

"No, Ed himself said trust no one," Elda said sharply. "I'm convinced *he's* trustworthy, but we've already involved him a lot, and we don't know who around Ed may be compromised. We've already leaked our last location by needing him to clean up the wreckage we left behind. He'll automatically check facial recognition and DNA. But does that matter anyway? We know that Russia is most likely behind all this."

Tosh looked in the mirror again. "Elda, we have a tail. See the gray car keeping three cars in back of us?"

"Crap, Tosh. How could that be?" Elda pounded her fist into the steering wheel. Without turning she addressed the backseat. "Stas are you sure everything is clean? Everyone power down your equipment now. That means cell phones too."

A meek voice piped up from the back, "Elda…"

"Yes Stas?" Elda responded.

More strongly Stas asserted, "The car has a GPS in it. They could have obtained our rental records and be tracking us that way."

"Damn it. Hold on." Elda accelerated to 80 mph and the car behind kept pace. She floored the accelerator and soon was at 95 mph. The car was still behind her and catching up. "What the hell type of engine do they have in that car?"

"Perhaps we have too much weight in ours? We could jettison Stas," Sophia said dryly.

Stas bleeped indistinguishably in distress and held on tight to Jackson's ankles. The car swayed as Elda cut in and out of traffic, trying to lose the car that was following them. Sophia tightened her seatbelt. Jackson was buffeted on both sides, as Sophia and Snezhana banged into him with the swaying of the car. Finally he put an arm around each woman so they all swayed together without battering each other.

Just as Elda was about to pass exit 54, she turned the wheel sharply and skidded off onto Route 133 heading west. She spun the car into a sharp right onto Carleton Drive, pulled the car over to the side of the road, behind a stand of trees, and cut the motor. They sat silently in the car with their guns drawn, and waited.

"Elda…," said a small voice from the backseat floor.

Elda sighed. Bad news certainly accompanied that voice. "Yes, Stas?"

Stas hesitated and then brought forth, "If they have the GPS, that means they will be able to hack the car's systems and take control. You can't turn it back on."

"Damn it!" Elda took a deep breath to calm herself.

"Where's the nearest train station, Elda?" inquired Tosh.

"It's about 7 miles away in Rowley, Tosh. Stas won't be able to walk that far. And we can't call an Uber or a Taxi, because they will probably check those and find out where we went. *Damn.* We're stuck." Elda frowned and shook her head in frustration.

"Perhaps not," said Tosh, eying the cars in the nearby parking lot. "Snezhana, how charming can you be?"

***

"Thank you so very much." Snezhana smiled broadly at the elderly man in the Silver Volvo, holding his trembling hand, while the group tumbled out of the sides and back of the car. "Are you sure we can't pay you anything for gas?"

"Oh no, my pleasure." The man was almost falling out the window in his admiration of Snezhana's svelte figure.

"Daughter dear, we must go," Elda stated, in a sweet voice.

"Here I come, mummy dearest," replied Snezhana in a singsong voice.

Snezhana ran toward Elda, who was glowering at her. When Snezhana came close, Elda muttered between her clenched teeth, "Mummy dearest, *really*?"

Snezhana smiled, and declared, "I have such love for you and papa and Uncle Jackson. And here is my wonderful little geeky brother." Snezhana pinched Stas's cheek.

"Ouch! That hurt!" Stas slapped at Snezhana's hand.

"We can stop role playing now," commanded Tosh with a scowl that conflicted with the turned-up corners of his mouth. "Well done though, Snezhana. You were quick at making up a cover for this group and aptly persuaded that man to give us all a ride. Good spy work."

Snezhana was bouncing with happiness and pride at being praised by her uncle.

The group paraded across the small parking lot to the train departing for Boston. Sophia and Jackson boarded, shortly followed by Snezhana and Stas. Tosh and Elda boarded at the last minute, to ensure no one had followed them onto the train. They sat opposite each other at the back of the car, in order to view anyone coming in either direction through the car.

Stas dejectedly stared out the window as the train sped by the brown, but greening, marshes.

Elda consoled Stas, "Don't worry, Stas. Tosh will get you more equipment."

A distraught Stas declared, "I can't believe we had to leave it all behind, Snezhana. It was mostly my equipment that I had brought with me too! I wiped everything clean and ripped out the hard drives and threw them into a dumpster near that company, but what a waste. And my computer was so high powered. I had configured it exactly for me."

Elda shut Stas down, "We couldn't trust *any* of it. MI6 had placed one program on it that went unidentified for quite a while. What if there were more that you just hadn't found yet? Who knows what else they added. There's definitely at least one mole at MI6."

Chapter Twenty-Eight

The neon lights illuminated the area as if it were daylight. A shout disappeared into the rest of the surrounding hubbub.

"*Der'mo*! Get your grubby hands off of me!" Holding the man by one wrist, Anatoly reached back to throw a punch at the man he had caught trying to pick his pocket. As he did his arm was held back from swinging forward. He let go and turned snarling to confront his new attacker. The pickpocket took the opportunity to dash away empty-handed.

"*Eto ya* –It's me! Yuri! Don't hit me." Yuri held his arms off to ward off a blow.

Anatoly snarled at Yuri, but dropped his hands. "Damn pickpocket."

Yuri chided Anatoly, "We are supposed to keep a low profile, Anatoly."

"I hope I broke his wrist," Anatoly growled, looking around for someone else to challenge.

Yuri tugged at Anatoly's arm, redirecting him, and said, "I would imagine you did. So let's buy our new phones and a laptop and then see if Stas and Jackson have any news for us. We need to find a hotel to hole up in under new identities too. Elda said there was a Hampton Inn over at 51st and 8th with a free breakfast, WIFI and a gym. Let's go there."

Yuri tightened his grip on his backpack as they strode through Times Square, jostled by tourists wandering aimlessly, lit up by lights and billboards flashing all around them.

"I would welcome some action right now," growled Anatoly with a menacing stare at an unfortunate tourist who bumped into him.

Yuri admonished, "Be careful what you wish for, Anatoly."

***

Henry ran his hands through his graying hair and looked out the window at the Houses of Parliament, sipping a pint of Amstel. The fish fingers and tartar sauce he had ordered sat untouched in front of him. He cleared his throat and spoke softly. "They obviously disabled the software on their computers. We have no way of locating them."

Henry's Russian handler hissed, "You do know that what we have on you will destroy your reputation and land you in jail for the rest of your life. Not to mention what will happen to your only son."

"I'm doing the best I can." Henry tapped his fingers nervously on his glass.

The handler reprimanded Henry, "You have to do better. They *cannot* stop this operation."

Henry took a sip from his glass. The beer stuck in the back of his throat. He coughed. He explained while gasping for air, "The last information we sent out pointed them to New York City. After the shootout in Newburyport, their car was found in Rowley, which indicates they were heading south. I would imagine they continued on to New York."

"Find them. We must get rid of them," the Russian demanded.

Henry's heart was beating rapidly. He worked to catch his breath before replying, "New York City is a pretty large place. I don't have that many people left to be able to conduct a search for them."

The other man snarled, "Then send them information that leads them to us. You know how to do that. You did it in Montreal and you did it again in Seattle. It worked then. It should work now. *Handle it*." He pushed his chair back, snagged a fish finger from Henry's plate, took a bite, threw the rest back, and marched away without paying for his own drink.

Henry ran his fingers through his hair again and sullenly stared at the half eaten fish stick on his plate. *Bastard.*

***

"Yes, yes, yes, you can buy anything you need. Just hurry up, we have a long way to go," Elda remarked, shooing Stas and Jackson toward the checkout. Stas excitedly ran to the checkout with a cart filled with electronic equipment. Elda rolled her eyes and loudly exclaimed, "Children."

Tosh shook his head and addressed her, "I told you dear, we should have stopped after the two girls."

A nearby shopper chuckled as she rolled her cart past Tosh and Elda.

"Can we leave soon?" Jackson stood holding two large Best Buy bags filled to the brim.

Elda smiled and observed, "You just want to free up a hand so you can start playing with the equipment you bought."

"Of course!" Jackson acknowledged, moving quickly outside.

314

Stas was unwrapping his new computer even before they reached the rental car. Elda bent and picked up a stray piece of cardboard. "Don't litter, Stas."

Stas, failing at an attempt to look apologetic, replied, "*Mne zhal'*, Elda. I had the checkout guy sell me his portable charger since it was fully charged. I can be setting this up and using it in the car."

***

"Some more intel on the New York United Nations possibilities just came through. It seems that a number of attendees are staying at the Crowne Plaza Time Square Hotel. It could be a dead end but it seems worth checking out," Tosh advised the team.

Huddled together over a laptop in their New York City hotel room, Anatoly and Yuri looked at Tosh's face on the secure network that Stas had managed to set up while in transit. They asked, "Do you think this is another trap?"

"Oh very probably so," chimed in Jackson cheerily from the backseat of the car. "The message was found posted in an anonymous chat room known to be frequented by, shall we say, shady characters from all over the world. We traced the message as far as we could, but it had a masked IP address and had been bounced through a number of servers to obscure its origin. The encryption keys used point to the Chinese, but the language structure used is similar to that of a North Korean message. However, the message header had some strange metadata embedded in it which is similar to that of other messages that we have eventually linked to Russia's GRU Unit 74455 in Khimki, Moscow. So I would say this message most probably was posted by the Russians."

Anatoly's sarcasm came clearly over the line, "Zzzzzz… *Der'mo*, Jackson, so all that, how do you say …*tarabarshchina*, you just said sums up to the Russians are behind this message?"

"Yes, Anatoly. And the word is gibberish," stated Jackson primly.

Elda chimed in from the driver's seat, "If we can somehow prevent the next assassin from chopping down on a suicide pill, we may get some actionable information that will lead us somewhere."

Yuri inquired, "Do you have any other information to help us narrow it down?"

Jackson hesitated, and then slowly responded, "We have a name, *John Smith*."

"*Razve? John Smith?*" Yuri chortled. Anatoly snorted.

"*Da, ya znayu.* Crazy, hey? Look for *Jane Doe* too," Jackson added.

Yuri spit out in between laughs, "Now you *are* kidding us!"

Jackson gave the sobering response, "No."

The connection ended. Yuri shut down the laptop and asked, "So what's your plan, Anatoly?"

Anatoly shrugged and replied, "The best defense is a good offense. I think we should march in and see if they are registered at the hotel. With names like that, a background search will come up with too many matches, and I have had great luck in the past getting information from desk clerks."

"They are going to be expecting us," Yuri stated, his confusion showing on his face.

Anatoly explained, "Yes, Yuri. All the better. We know that, so that gives us an edge. Plus they have never met *me* before. I am going to call them out."

"Oh like Clint Eastwood!" Yuri made the gesture of pulling two guns from imaginary side hosters.

Anatoly deadpanned, "Ask yourself, Yuri. Do you feel lucky?"

Yuri looked at Anatoly incredulously, "Wow. *You* have seen a movie?"

Anatoly growled at Yuri.

***

The raindrops slid down the apartment window. Outside was gray and gloomy, mirroring the atmosphere indoors. Sophia turned sideways in her chair and put her legs over the oversized arm. Snezhana sat with the wooden desk chair turned backwards, her arms crossed on the back of the chair and her chin resting on her arms. She looked tired and discouraged.

Sophia decided it was a good time to distract Snezhana from her thoughts, and, as a side benefit she could find out more about Snezhana's background. "How did you decide to become a spy, Snezhana?"

Snezhana sat up straighter and scratched her head. She responded, "I don't think I ever *decided*. There never really was another profession for me. From the time I was a toddler I adored my uncle Tosh. I loved it when he would breeze in from faraway places with exotic presents for me. And he would teach me these neat judo and karate tricks. When I got older I saw how astute and smart he was. I wanted to be *exactly* like him. And I *was* like him in so many ways. I have his photographic memory and his ability to slip silently in and out of a room."

Truly interested in Snezhana's unfolding story, Sophia inquired, "What did your parents think?"

Snezhana grimaced. "I was never that close to my parents. My father was, how do you say, *zhestkiy*, in English? Ah, …harsh. He also loved uncle Tosh, but did not want me to follow in his footsteps. My parents were disappointed when I was chosen to train with the GRU."

"Any regrets?" Sophia asked, swinging her legs back and sitting in the chair to face Snezhana.

Snezhana paused before answering, "Yes." Silence. And then she began again, "I'm not sure I'm cut out to be a spy. And I don't feel *adekvatnyy*…ah…adequate. I wish I had completed my training before coming on a mission. I want to be as good as my uncle, if not better. I want him to be proud of me."

Sophia nodded and smiled. Her thoughts of wanting to grill Snezhana for personal information and turned to wanting to support and encourage her. "Yes, I can see that, with more experience, you will be, and I think he will be proud."

Snezhana answered with pride, "Thank you, Sophia. So, how on earth are we to find the mole?"

Sophia stood up, ready for action. She laid out her plan. "I think, Snezhana, that we need to let the mole find us. I'll pop over to *The Rose* around 11:00 am, when the lunch crowd starts to arrive. It's a popular watering hole for MI6 folks. It's also got a great view of the Houses of Parliament and a good menu."

"*Khorosho*, Sophia. And don't worry, I will have your back," Snezhana reassured her.

Sophia stared, with a steely gaze, directly into Snezhana's eyes and declared, "You better."

***

Anatoly jumped off the end of the escalator, briskly crossed the white tiled floor of the Crowne Plaza Time Square hotel lobby, and marched up to the wood paneled front desk. Yuri followed behind, scanning the lobby for potential threats. A clerk appeared, backlit by the neon lights and bright depictions of New York.

Anatoly flagged him down. "Excuse me, do you have a Mr. John Smith and Ms. Jane Doe staying here?"

"Ah, yes sir," responded the clerk in a high brow tone. "They said that they would be expecting a few people. Are you Anatoly?"

Yuri raised an eyebrow. Anatoly answered, without changing his expression, "Yes. Where would I find them?" His voice had taken on a similar tone as the clerk's.

The clerk informed Anatoly, "They left to take a dip in the pool and asked that you gentlemen join them there."

320

"And how do we get to the pool?" Anatoly inquired, with extreme politeness.

The clerk pointed down the hall, "The elevators are over there on the right. The pool is on the 15th floor in the New York Sports Club. The Club is only open until 9pm but we often allow guests to stay there longer. You will need a card key to enter it. I took the liberty of making one up for you in anticipation of your arrival." The clerk handed Anatoly a card key.

Anatoly checked his Rolex and saw that it was 22:00, an hour past closing. "Are you sure they will still be there?"

"Most certainly sir," the clerk replied primly.

"Thank you my good man," Anatoly said, turning to head in the direction of the pool.

The desk clerk waited until they walked out of hearing range and dialed a number. "They are on their way to the Sports Club pool. There are two of them."

***

Elda pulled the latest rental car into the parking lot of the Comfort Inn in Bordertown, N.J. She cut the car engine and shook out her hands and wrists. "We got such a late start after dropping Sophia and Snezhana off at the airport and I'm exhausted. I can't think any more. I need to crash."

Tosh, sitting in the passenger seat, was rubbing his eyes. He looked haggard. "I join you in that way of thinking, Elda."

"*Spasibo*, Tosh." Running her hands over her face, Elda suggested, "Let's just grab a couple of rooms and get at least a few hours' sleep."

"I hope we don't get bedbugs," Jackson chimed in from the back seat.

Elda hit the steering wheel with her fist. "Crap, Jackson. You *would* have to say that! Tosh, I know you're a good driver and would drive without a license, but you're as tired as I am. Is anyone else awake enough to drive us into DC and the horrific traffic?"

"*Nyet*," Stas stated.

"Not me." Jackson added, "I don't even have a license. Plus you didn't add us to the rental agreement, *Mrs. Jones*."

Elda snapped, "Now you worry about legalities, Jackson? Crap."

Tosh admonished Elda, "Language, Elda, language."

"Oh, cram it, Tosh." Elda held her head in her hand. "Sorry. I have to get some rest. Okay, command decision everyone: we crash here and go over what we know in the morning. Stas, did you ever do those background checks on the extended team?"

Stas let Elda know, "I checked each of our team members, Elda and they all came out clear. I will run a check on Jackson, Ed, James, and Alexei in the morning."

"Hey! On me?" Jackson exclaimed.

Elda explained, "We're all fair game, Jackson. Any one of us could be a traitor."

***

"It's dark in here," Yuri remarked.

Anatoly led Yuri through the darkened empty gym, following the signs for the pool. "If people were really here, there would be lights on, Yuri. I think we are walking into a trap."

"*Otlichnyy*," replied Yuri sarcastically. "So what's the plan *now*, Anatoly?"

"You go into the pool area in front of me. I will cover you," Anatoly replied without turning around.

"I'm not sure I like that idea," Yuri groused.

"Got another?" Anatoly inquired, continuing to lead the way.

Yuri stopped for a few seconds, scratched his head and then stated, "No." He jogged a few steps to catch up with Anatoly.

Anatoly strode on. "Okay. Let's go."

***

"Sophia! How good to see you! Where have you been? And where is Ollie? I heard through the grapevine that he had been horribly injured while on a mission!" Emily stood smiling next to Sophia's table at the Rose in London.

Sophia looked up from her fish fingers and chips. "Hello, Emily. Long time no see." She smiled at the loudly chatty woman, whose pleasant face was framed by an old-fashioned bob of dark hair. "Are you still working over at the cookie factory?"

Emily exclaimed, "Yes, Sophia, I am still working at the shop. I've missed seeing you. You've been gone for a while. I thought you might have also gone on a mission. Is Ollie all right?"

Sophia grimaced. She explained, "He's getting there. He did get badly injured and is out of the game for a while. He is healing well, but it *will* be a long rehabilitation stint for him."

Emily gushed, "Oh I'm so glad to hear that he is on the mend. Are you around for a while? Are you still living in

324

that same flat over at Keybridge Apartments?" Emily bounced from foot to foot.

Sophia stared at Emily and made a gesture with her hand patting the air. Emily stopped moving back and forth. Sophia commented, "You have a good memory, Emily. Yes, we are still there at Keybridge. Although rather small, it's just so convenient to the office. I haven't been in to the office because I needed to take a bit of leave after what happened to Oliver, but I hope to be back soon."

"I can understand that. When will you return?" Emily inquired loudly.

"I don't know. It does all depend on how fast Oliver recovers." Sophia pointed at the other diners who were listening to the high-volume conversation. "We are disturbing their lunches. Would you like to sit and join me?"

Emily lowered her voice, conspiratorially, "Oh no, I'm meeting a dreadfully boring chap from accounting for lunch before we go over this month's numbers, but we *must* go out for a drink some time and catch up."

"Oh, yes, definitely," Sophia agreed.

Emily turned as if to leave and then swung back, asking, "Are you coming into the office at all today?"

"Not today," replied Sophia, "but *do* say hi to James for me."

"I *certainly* will," Emily responded.

Sophia watched as Emily bounced away to her table. *Well the hook has been baited. Let's see who bites.*

***

Silhouetted by the pool lights, Yuri entered the pool area and immediately he felt a gun pressed to his head. He stopped and raised his hands and then sidestepped, as Anatoly rushed in, grabbed the gun, and slid across the slippery deck into the water. A man jumped on top of Yuri and started beating him about his head. Through the blows Yuri heard another loud splash as a woman jumped into the pool after Anatoly. Yuri threw himself to the ground with the man still clinging to his back. He rolled and flipped the two of them into the pool. He felt himself dragged downwards by the weight of his clothes and the man's body on top of his. He fervently wished he had had Alpha group training and had learned how to swim. He felt his lungs struggling for air as water seeped into his mouth through his nose. He silently prayed, *Bozhe, pozhaluysta, ne day mne umeret' segodnya.*

***

Anatoly climbed up out of the pool with a small dark-haired woman clinging to his neck trying to strangle him.

He turned and repeatedly smashed her hard against the wall until she lost her grip. He whirled around and kicked her in the head with his steel-tipped boot, knocking her out. He flipped her over and threw a zip-tie around her wrists and then shoved a towel into her mouth, to keep her from gnashing her teeth together and activating a suicide pill. He looked over at the pool and saw that a man was on top of Yuri and holding Yuri's head under water. Yuri was feebly kicking and struggling and air bubbles were escaping from his lungs to the surface.

Anatoly jumped into the pool on top of the man and tightly squeezed his hands around the man's neck. He increased the pressure, not caring if the man lived or died. The man went limp, releasing Yuri who bobbed up to the surface face down, but didn't move. Anatoly dragged the man out of the water, shoved a towel into his mouth, rapidly bound him, and flew back in to get Yuri. There was no sign of life. He laid him flat on the deck and started CPR.

"*Der'mo*! Come on Yuri wake up!" Anatoly rapidly pumped Yuri's chest and scanned him for any positive signs of life. Just as Anatoly was beginning to worry that Yuri may not make it, Yuri started gagging, coughing, and throwing up pool water.

Anatoly rolled Yuri onto his side, to ensure he wouldn't choke on his own vomit, and returned to his two captives. He felt both their pulses. They were still alive. He flipped the man onto his back and, removing the gag, he placed a knife edge up between his front and back teeth, so that any sudden attempt by the man to clench his teeth down would be extremely painful.

Anatoly addressed the man, "I hate this part. I'd much rather have enjoyed strangling you. Much cleaner. I am an assassin, not a fucking dentist." The man's eyes grew wide with terror.

Anatoly reached into his bag for a pair of pliers and began extracting the man's back molars, one by one. Blood poured from the man's mouth. When the teeth were out, Anatoly laid the man on his side, to better drain the residual blood. Grabbing a pile of towels from the side of the pool, he jerked out the knife and rapidly stuffed a clean towel into the man's mouth. Pulling duct tape from his bag, he tore a strip off and slapped it on the attacker's mouth, while ensuring the man could breathe through his nose. The man had passed out during the procedure.

Anatoly nodded his head in satisfaction, "*Khorosho.* You will be happier that way and we don't need either of you to scream."

The woman had woken up and had been watching Anatoly pull her colleague's teeth out. Wide eyed with horror, she tried to loosen her wrists and started wiggling away.

"Oh no, *dragotsennyy*. You are much too precious to leave us now." Anatoly grabbed her by an ankle and dragged her back to him.

Yuri staggered to his feet.

"How are you feeling," asked a concerned Anatoly.

"*Kak der'mo*," replied Yuri, shaking his head.

Glad that Yuri was talking and moving, Anatoly turned back to his work at hand and commented, "You should. You were dead." He then instructed Yuri, "Contact Elda and Tosh. Let them know we need help here. We have to get these two prisoners extracted with us."

"I have contacts here from Russia," Yuri mentioned.

"Like the St. Petersburg ones?" inquired Anatoly, picking up his pliers.

Yuri informed him, "The very same organization."

"*Fantasticheskiy*! Contact them and tell them we need transport for us and two prisoners. And let them know we can't let anyone see us leave," Anatoly ordered.

Yuri turned and threw up more pool water before making his phone calls.

Anatoly knelt down holding the bloody pliers to address the woman's teeth.

***

Tosh's burner phone rang, waking both him and Elda up. He fumbled to turn on the bedside lamp in the seedy hotel room. He grabbed his phone off the table. Fully dressed, Elda slid out of bed and tiredly stumbled over to the bathroom sink to throw water on her face.

Tosh answered his phone, "*Da. Khoroshaya rabota*! Hold on." He addressed Elda, "Elda. First of all, you snore." Elda threw Tosh a finger, followed by a damp towel. "Secondly, Anatoly and Yuri have two prisoners. They want to know where they should bring them."

Elda thought a moment and then answered Tosh, "Wonderful. I have an idea. We should have Anatoly and Yuri take the prisoners in the opposite direction from where we are going and have Ed pick them up there. I know a place."

Tosh smirked and quipped, "You know a lot of places."

"It comes in handy, Tosh. Please hand me the phone and I'll let them know where to take their prisoners." She rapidly gave Yuri and Anatoly directions and tossed the phone back to Tosh. She then made a quick call to Ed on her own burner phone. After she hung up she noticed Tosh was frowning. "What?" she snipped.

Tosh asked with sincerity, "Do you trust Ed, Elda?"

Elda responded emphatically, "I do. As I said before, I am not sure of those around him. However, right now I have no choice."

Chapter Twenty-Nine

The aide marched into Alexei's office in the Kremlin and stood at attention. "We have a problem sir."

"Where?" Alexei barked.

Still standing at attention, the messenger informed Alexei, "New York City. Broya and Angelina did not report in and are assumed missing. We have dispatched a team to the hotel to investigate."

Alexei narrowed his eyes and demanded, "Did they achieve their objective?"

The aide stood taller, bracing himself as he replied, "*Ya yeshche ne znayu.*"

"You don't know yet?" Alexei's voice was icy and flat.

The man's knees shook as he answered, "*Nyet, ser.*"

Alexei placed his hand on the trigger of his desk gun. He breathed deeply. *Wait. This man has served you well to date. It isn't his fault that the others are screwing up. And it's hard to find and train a good assistant.* He slowly released the trigger and instructed his man, "Very well. If you value your life, do not report back until you have actionable intel. However, make that soon. Meanwhile, I will prepare another team in the United States to be ready to deal with them, once they have been located."

"*Da ser*!" The aide did a crisp about face and marched out of the office.

Alexei opened the bottom drawer of his desk and grabbed a candy bar to sooth his frustration.

Chapter Thirty

Emily walked into work humming. She stopped to admire the bronze statue of Sir Mansfield Cumming, who had set up the agency nearly a century ago. Although desiring more friends at work, and finding her job rather tedious, she never lost the thrill of walking into the ostentatious building that headquartered MI6. She would love to be an agent and longed to work with Sophia and Oliver.

Emily decided to go upstairs and find James before she went to her desk. Turning a corner she bumped into him and nearly knocked him down. She exclaimed, "James! Sorry about that. But how nice to see you. I was just talking about you. You never will guess who I ran into at the Rose."

James stiffened and smiled thinly. He grumbled, "You seem to be quite good at running into people, Emily. Whom did you run into at the Rose?"

"Sophia! She's back," Emily explained, with a broad smile.

"How wonderful," said James flatly. "I know she took Oliver's injuries hard and she needed time off, so I gave her an open ended leave. Did she say when she would be back in the office?"

"No she didn't, but she did say she was staying at her flat. It was so nice of you to give her leave," Emily said warmly.

James tersely replied, "Yes. Quite. I'll have to call on her and ensure she's doing well."

***

"*Der'mo*! Damn, Yuri, I will get you for this one," said a muffled voice from a canvas sided laundry cart.

"Shut up!" hissed the man pushing the cart.

Four men in white uniforms split off in different directions, pushing laundry carts through the hotel hallways. Converging at the loading dock, they pushed their carts into the back of an idling large white van with blue lettering on the side advertising their laundry service. Two men got into the back with the carts and the other two hopped into the front seat. The van moved slowly and steadily away from the dock and onto the main street.

The driver called into the back, "It's clear now."

Anatoly's head popped up through layers of towels. "*Der'mo*. My legs are cramped." He slowly pulled himself up and out of the cart and sat on the floor massaging his calves.

Yuri soon followed from his cart, tumbling over the side and onto the floor, tipping the cart on top of him.

One of the uniformed men reached over to the remaining two carts and uncovered the prisoner's heads. "God! What on earth did you do to these people?" he asked, viewing the bruised, swollen faces.

Anatoly held up a bloody towel and opened it, revealing a collection of extracted back teeth. "You wouldn't happen to have a plastic bag, would you?"

***

Elda and Tosh sat, in the breakfast area apart from the rest of the hotel residents, on metal chairs at a rectangular table. Elda was playing with her soupy oatmeal, repeatedly picking up a spoonful and letting the watery mess drip off the spoon back into the bowl.

"Jesus, Elda, just go get something else to eat!" Tosh complained, frowning.

Elda gestured to the table, "This food is disgusting. Breakfast is the most important meal of the day. What did you get, Tosh?"

Tosh was nibbling at a dry piece of toast. He held it out to Elda. She reached for it and he pulled it back. "Go get your own," he admonished.

"Crap." Elda jerked back her chair and stomped to the kitchen area to try and find something she could eat. She spied Jackson and Stas looking into the dining area. She waved them toward the table with Tosh. She returned to the table with a number of pieces of coffee cake to share, and a coffee for herself. After taking a sip of coffee and grimacing, she checked in with the team. "So the prisoners are with Ed in South Carolina, and Anatoly and Yuri are heading back north. They will meet us in DC," she summarized, inquiring further, "Jackson and Stas, do we have any new information?"

"I did the rest of the background checks," Stas offered.

"Thank you, Stas. And…?" Elda prompted.

Stas filled Elda and Tosh in, "Jackson and Ed check out. Alexei, as we know is a loyal Russian and there is nothing shady in his past. That alone, since this is a Russian operation, doesn't rule him out entirely. I need a higher access to get at the rest of James' files. The files on him that I can access check out, but there are some missing years. I'll need more time to get at that information. I've started looking into the MI6 communication team too."

"Good work, Stas," Elda acknowledged, continuing, "Please continue working on it and let us know if you pick up on any irregularities. What did it say about James' military service?"

"There was no mention of that," Stas stated.

Elda frowned. "Dig deeper. I am certain that he is ex-military. Anything else?"

Stas referred to his notes and then answered, "*Nyet.*"

"Thank you, Stas." Elda rose and addressed the team: "Okay guys, everyone into the car. Next stop DC, where we'll meet back up with Anatoly and Yuri. So, I'm the only one who can drive legally here? Jackson, you really don't have a license?"

"Nope! Never needed one in DC," Jackson replied cheerily.

Elda scowled. "Damn. I never thought I'd miss Anatoly and his international driver's license. Tosh, you're going to have one. We can forge one for you, once we're in the apartment. Buckle up then. DC beltway traffic here we come!"

Chapter Thirty-One

Standing by large glass doors leading to an outside deck, Ed stared out across the South Carolina marshes and spoke into his phone. "Yes, we have the prisoners, and they are still alive. The medic is attending to their injuries now. I am sending the teeth to the lab to find out what type of poison they use and hopefully we can also determine where it originated."

Elda's voice on the other end was asking about the next steps. Ed listened and responded, "I have a small handpicked team here. I will interrogate the prisoners myself and alone. We'll have to turn them in shortly, but our story is that their injuries were too severe to interrogate them. Hopefully that will buy you more time."

"If they survive," Elda observed.

Ed nodded at his phone, "Yes. We will see if they survive after we turn them in." He asked, "Have we any leads on the mole yet?"

Elda quipped, "Well we know it's definitely not you or me."

Ed laughed. "Yes, I am glad to hear it's not me. Good luck and stay alive."

Ed hung up, squared his shoulders and marched into the room where the prisoners were being held. He closed the door behind him. A few minutes later a scream echoed off the walls.

***

Snezhana and Sophia were in Snezhana's newly rented London flat, sitting closely together on the bare wooden living room floor, sharing a computer. Each had headphones on and was staring intently at the screen. Sophia & Oliver had secreted listening devices and cameras in each of their rooms in their London flat as part of their own security precautions. Sophia and Snezhana were using those feeds now to spy on the flat.

Sophia stretched her legs out in front of her. "I'm getting stiff. Do you think we can snag something to sit on? There's only one desk chair here."

"I saw some milk crates downstairs," Snezhana observed, adding, "We can stack them to make a second placed to sit at the desk. I'll pop out to get them, since no one knows who I am, but they will be looking for you, Sophia."

340

"Great idea. Thanks much, Snezhana. Anything would be better than this cold hard wood floor." Sophia massaged the small of her back with both hands.

"*Khorosho*, I'll be right back." Snezhana gracefully uncoiled her legs from the cross-legged position and smoothly rose to stand.

Sophia heard a slight click in her earphones. "Wait!" she ordered.

Snezhana twirled around and lowered herself down to the floor again, picking up the headphones she had dropped. They both watched the screen intently. The door opened and a man and a woman slipped in and started to methodically search Oliver and Sophia's apartment.

Sophia leaned forward and shook her finger at the computer. "You aresholes. Get your manky hands off of my stuff," she spitted out from between her clenched teeth.

Snezhana started to shush Sophia, then realized that the intruders couldn't hear Sophia and started giggling.

"My god, Snezhana, what is wrong with you? Straighten up!" Sophia glared at Snezhana.

Snezhana decided now was not the time to tell Sophia what she had been thinking and instead asked, "What do you think they are looking for?"

The two invaders reconvened at the front door. They spoke in accented English.

The first man stated, "I don't think she has been here at all." He picked up a boot from the rubber shoe man and replaced it.

The second man agreed, "This flat looks pretty sterile. I see no clues as to where she might be."

"But she was seen in London," the first remarked.

"Yes. I assume it was to see her husband," the second man postulated.

"Well, perhaps we can abduct her outside the hospital?" the first invader suggested, "He's too well guarded to get either him or her inside the hospital."

The other agreed, "OK. Wire the door so that we get alerted if she shows up here. I'll call and ask for a van for us to sit in to watch the hospital."

Sophia punched her fist into the air and yelled, "You dodgy aresholes! Now I can't even go visit Oliver!"

The second intruder reached into the shoulder bag he was carrying, pulled out and rapidly installed a tiny piece of electronic equipment, discretely attached to the door hinges. "This will do the trick," he declared.

"It better," warned number one. "He wants to know what she knows and where the rest of the team is, before we eliminate her."

They shut the door firmly behind them.

"Who is *he*, Sophia?" questioned Snezhana, putting a calming hand on Sophia's shoulder.

Sophia shook her head, stating sadly, "I wish I knew."

***

"OMG you nearly hit that guy's bumper!" Jackson yelled.

Elda admonished him, "Don't be a backseat driver, Jackson." She expertly changed lanes, weaving around a slower driver.

Tosh sassed, "You would do well as a Moscow driver, Elda. Perhaps you will become mine?"

"In your dreams, Tosh," Elda quipped.

A faint voice came from the back seat, "I may throw up."

Elda directed, "Someone hand Stas a paper bag to breathe into." She maneuvered the car through the four lanes of beltway traffic. She swerved around a car and smoothly exited onto the George Washington Memorial

Parkway. She wove her way in the direction of Arlington and cut across to Colonial Village West. Once through the turns, she commented, "We have a safe house, well, really a safe apartment here. Only Ed and I know about it."

"Speaking of Ed, did he get any information out of the two prisoners?" Tosh questioned.

Without taking her eyes off of the traffic in front of them and the mirrors for sides and back, Elda answered, "Partially, Tosh, but nothing from the woman. Ed termed her a *tough bitch*. Although that term can be overused, in this case I agree with him. She is the same woman who attacked us in Newburyport, so she probably doesn't have any information anyway. People like her are hired anonymously and work just for the money."

Tosh queried, "What about the man? Did he say anything?"

Elda put on her directional signal and Stas moaned in preparation for the turn. She informed Tosh, "We ran him through facial recognition and got a hit. Once we confronted him with it, he sang like a bird."

"Who is he?" Tosh wondered.

Elda revealed, "An MI6 operative."

***

344

Henry anxiously looked around. No-one was within earshot. Nevertheless, he kept his voice low, "Sophia is in London. We have her apartment staked out. And also the hospital, in case she goes to see Oliver."

The speaker ran his fingers nervously through his salt and pepper hair and swiveled his head right and left still checking that no one could overhear their conversation. The two men sat side by side on the wooden seat of a metal sided bench, feeding the pigeons, that were cooing, strolling and bobbing in front of them on the well-manicured pathway in Vauxhall Park.

Alexei hissed, "Settle down. You're not an amateur. If you love your freedom and your son you *must* do exactly as I say."

James put his hand out and stopped just shy of touching the Alexei's arm. "Please do not harm him," he entreated, drawing his hand back.

"Remember that wish and act accordingly. Get this team out of our way. Now!" Alexei commanded.

Henry flinched and whined, "I have limited staff for this operation here in London. I may need more."

Alexei sneered at Henry, telling him, "You will work with what you have. Forget capturing Sophia. The rest will surface, just as she has. Shoot to kill."

“Blimey. Really?” gasped Henry, wide eyed.

Alexei rolled his eyes. “Yes, you dolt. Really. I have a situation in America to clean up. You will handle the agents on this side of the pond and cover your tracks. Eliminate the team one by one if need be. We’re running out of time. Understand?”

Henry shrank back on the bench. He was way in over his head. His voice quivered as he answered, “I understand.”

Alexei stood and kicked his foot at the pigeons, sending them flapping away. He marched away without a backward glance at the bench.

Bastard.

***

Sophia sat across the table from Emily and stared at the view of the Houses of Parliament while framing in her mind the questions she wanted to ask.

Emily started the conversation, “I’m so glad you found the time to have lunch with me, Sophia. I know you must be terribly occupied with helping Ollie recuperate. How is he?”

Sophia surprised herself by genuinely laughing, “Ha! Only his childhood friends call him that, you know? He’s doing so much better, Emily. Thanks for asking. I just need to decompress before throwing myself back into the fray. How are *you*? Is there a new man in your life yet?"

"Unfortunately no. I'm just starting dating again since that last fiasco." Emily looked down at her place setting and absent mindedly played with her fork.

"It was rather weird, the two of us dating those twin brother doctors, wasn't it?" Sophia observed with a grin.

Emily threw her fork down in disgust. "Well at least your Jacob went on to become a surgeon, whereas mine dropped out of school to travel the world and *find himself*. How trite." She started twisting her serviette.

Sophia put a hand on Emily's to comfort her. "So have you been throwing yourself into work?"

"Oh that's so *dreadfully* boring." Emily rolled her eyes dramatically. "All we do is help protect members of Parliament. I *do* wish I could work with you on James' team."

"Speaking of James…did you get to tell him I'm back?" Sophia looked at Emily pointedly.

Emily perked up. "Oh yes. I took care of that for you. He said he would have to drop in on you some time."

Sophia acknowledged the information with a nod of her head and commented, "It would be delightful to see him. Did you speak with anyone else?"

Emily shook her head with such force that Sophia hoped she didn't hurt herself. Emily avowed, "No, no one, just as you instructed. Anyway, you and Ollie are the only friends I have on that floor."

Sophia smiled at Emily's sincerity and steadfast loyalty to Oliver. "Well, once he has more strength and they lighten the security around Oliver, you must see him. He would love to see his old friend, *Em*."

"Oh yes!," Emily gushed, "Please do let me know when Ollie is receiving visitors. I miss you both."

"I will," Sophia promised. Business done, Sophia picked up the menu. "Shall we order now?"

***

James sat on a park bench and scratched his head. He watched the pigeons pecking the ground and flapping away from people walking by. Sighing heavily, he picked up his burner phone and dialed a number. When it connected he asked, "What do you know?"

"They captured Angelina and Borya at the Crowne Plaza Hotel," said a disembodied, disguised voice on the other end of the line.

"Were they taken alive?" James probed.

The answer was not satisfying, "I don't know. The report says there was a lot of blood around."

James rubbed the back of his neck and breathed deeply. *Twit. Just give me the full answer.* "Where are they now?" he said through clenched jaw.

His contact replied, "I don't know."

Bloody moron. "What *do* you know?" James asked with a note of sarcasm.

"There is no sign of them leaving the hotel. I checked the cameras. Unfortunately, there was no camera in the pool area," his informant said, in a matter of fact tone.

"That is *very* unfortunate," James said, implying more.

"For *you* too…" countered the man on the other end of the phone.

James gulped and ran his hand through his graying hair. "Just give me *something*."

He could almost hear a shrug in the answer, "There's just no unusual activity for that day."

James sighed and clenched and unclenched his fists. *This is like pulling teeth...* "What about deliveries and pickups?"

"Same as always. No new vendors. As I said, nothing unusual."

The man sounded bored! James snarled, "This isn't enough. Get back on the comms and get me a lead." He cut off the call and sat cursing life and the pigeons.

***

Sophia was sitting cross-legged on the dark blue overstuffed chair. Snezhana was lying on the hardwood floor with her legs straight up against the wall.

"What on *earth* are you doing, Snez?" Sophia wondered.

Snezhana explained. "This is supposed to be good for circulating blood to your brain."

Sophia laughed, "You're daft. All you're going to get from that is a backache."

"So, Sophia, what did you find out from Emily? With whom did Emily speak?" Snezhana inquired. She wiggled her feet.

Sophia replied, "The only one she spoke to was James. How long do you have to stay in that position?"

"Not too long. A half-hour at most. Do you think he's the mole?" Snezhana asked.

Sophia jerked her head to stare wide-eyed at Snezhana. "My god – that would be horrific. He has been there for so many years and has such a high security clearance. It *can't* be James."

Snezhana agreed, "I certainly hope not, for MI6's sake. We should let Elda know about this immediately though."

"Let me grab a burner phone." Sophia pushed up off the arms of her chair and landed in a standing position. She reached over and grabbed her phone from the coffee table.

Snezhana swung her legs down, turned and sat in the Lotus position. "We don't have any information about anyone James may have talked to?"

"No we don't, Snezhana."

Sophia dialed and connected with Elda. "Elda, Snezhana is here with me. I'm putting you on speaker phone."

Elda's voice came clearly over the phone. "The mole has to be in MI-6. Sophia, can you vouch for Emily?"

"Yes, Elda, I am sure that Emily is not the mole. Oliver has known her and her family since Year 1 in Primary school. We did extensive background checks ourselves on all our friends when we joined the company, and MI6 also did the requisite checks before we joined."

Sophia held the phone out to ensure Snezhana could hear Elda as she directed the two of them to get rid of those who were watching the hospital.

Snezhana spoke up, "In any way possible?"

"Yes," said Elda, "Just please do not cause an international incident. Ensure it's not traced back to us."

"Righto!" Sophia agreed, and then disconnected from the call.

"So how are we to do that?" inquired Snezhana from her spot on the floor.

"You and I, Snezhana, are going to see if we can flush out those that are watching the hospital. I will go in first and you will cover me."

Just then the burner phone rang. Sophia picked it up, and after answering, handed it over to Snezhana. "It's Tosh for you."

Snezhana snapped up to attention.

Sophia watched as Snezhana's face increasingly reddened as she listened to her uncle. Snezhana finally said, "*Da, sudar'. Ya ponimayu.* It will not happen again."

Sophia waited until Snezhana had broken the connection. "What did he say?"

Snezhana took a deep breath and responded, "He reminded me of my errors in previous missions and said if I *isportit'*, …how do you say that in English, …ah, screw up… again, I am out of the service." She hung her head.

Sophia walked over to her and put two fingers under her chin and forced Snezhana to look her in the eyes. "If you screw this up, one or both of us will be dead. I expect you to have my back at all times." Sophia backed up and shook her finger at Snezhana.

"I will not let you down, Sophia," Snezhana promised.

Sophia cautioned her, "You better not, because if I live, you will have *me* to answer to, as well as your uncle, and you do *not* want that."

Chapter Thirty-Two

Elda, Tosh, Anatoly, Yuri, Stas, and Jackson had convened in a small, two-bedroom, safe house. Elda perched on a wooden bar stool from the kitchen area. Anatoly sprawled in the large living room chair. Jackson and Stas sat on the beige IKEA style cloth couch with Tosh sitting in front of them on the edge of the wood crate coffee table. And, next to the table, Yuri lay on the bland, deep pile, wall to wall carpet, with his head propped in his hands.

The presence of Anatoly and Yuri made the living room seem even tinier than it was. The two men related their New York City story, as well as reported on having successfully left the prisoners off in South Carolina.

At the end, Elda joshed, "Gee Anatoly, still need swimming lessons I see? Where's your life jacket. Perhaps I need to give one to Yuri too?"

"*Otvali*," snarled Anatoly.

"That's not nice, Anatoly." Elda reprimanded, "My apologies. It's too soon to joke. Although I tease you, I am actually relieved that you both made it back alive. You did an excellent job capturing the prisoners alive too. Immensely impressive. Yuri, how are you feeling?"

Yuri replied, "I'm fine Elda."

"Count backwards from ten for me," Elda requested.

Yuri did, in both English and Russian, "*Desyat'*, ten, *devyat'*, nine, *vosem'*, eight, *sem'*, seven, *shest'*, six, *pyat'*, five, *chetyre*, four, *tri*, three, *dva*, two, *odin*, one."

"What year is this?" grilled Elda.

"2019," he replied.

"What is your name?" she asked.

He answered, "Yuri Kuznetsov."

"Who is that?" Elda asked, pointing at Anatoly.

"My lord and savior," Yuri joked.

The team broke out laughing.

"I'd say his brain definitely improved from the lack of oxygen," said Anatoly.

Elda wanted to know, "How long was he deprived of oxygen, Anatoly?"

Anatoly paused briefly and then responded, "No more than a couple of minutes, I'd say."

Elda nodded. "Good, it was probably well under six minutes then. Still, I don't think we should send you out into the field just yet, Yuri." She turned to Tosh and checked, "Do you agree, Tosh?"

"I do, Elda," Tosh agreed, "I would be much more comfortable if we could get him cleared by a neurological exam. Is there anyone you trust? Perhaps a connection from your days as a therapist?" Tosh inquired.

Elda looked at Tosh in surprise. "My days as a therapist?"

Tosh admonished her, sneering, "Oh come on, Elda, it's obvious. You have at least trained as one."

In a professionally modulated voice, Elda quipped, "How long have you felt that way, Tosh? Are you also hearing voices?"

Tosh threw her a figa and Elda automatically returned a middle finger. She stated, "I will see who I can dig up. For now, Yuri, you will stay put with Jackson and Stas."

Tosh looked around the two bedroom apartment and wondered, "Where on earth are we supposed to put everyone?"

Elda smiled knowingly, "This place is deceptive. It may appear to be only a two-bedroom apartment, but we have a secret passageway built in, that can be used as an escape route, as well as a way to travel to another apartment." She jumped down from her stool, walked over to the kitchen and opened the pantry door. She flicked on the overhead light, walked to the back of the small space and pressed a hidden switch. The pantry back wall, complete with all its shelves of canned goods receded. Elda reached along the inside wall and flicked another switch, which illuminated the tunnel to the second apartment.

Anatoly stood up and walked over to join her. He peered into the small passageway and swore, "*Chert*! You do not expect that we will fit through there?"

Elda shrugged, "No, I don't. Anatoly and Yuri, you'll probably have a hard time fitting. You two will sleep in the spare bedroom in this apartment and Tosh will go with Jackson and Stas to the other. We have a couple of cans of Crisco stored here in the pantry in case we need to slick you up to get you through the tunnel in an emergency."

Elda glanced at Tosh, who was obviously trying to keep a straight face at the vision of a Crisco covered Anatoly being pushed through the tunnel. Tears were starting to form in his eyes from the effort to keep from laughing. Elda's lips quivered and her eyes crinkled up as she also fought back the urge to laugh. She took a deep breath, cleared her throat, and continued: "We hope it won't come to that. We also have the couch and a roll-out bed if we want to keep squashed in one apartment for now, but we'll have to spread out once Sophia and Snezhana join us."

Tosh interjected, "Where are Sophia and Snezhana, Elda? We haven't heard from them for a while."

***

The day was clear and warm. Sophia and Snezhana decided to do the one-mile walk along the Thames River to St Thomas Hospital. They walked in silence, each occupied with their own thoughts. Snezhana had assumed a disguise, but Sophia, being the bait, had not.

They stopped near the Lambeth Palace Library to make sure they were on the same page for the operation. They decided that Snezhana would take a head start and slip in through the side door, exit through the front, and then position herself near the front entrance. Sophia would enter the hospital at the main pedestrian entrance on Westminster Bridge Road. Snezhana sauntered off toward the hospital with an exaggerated wiggle to her hips that accentuated her form fitting leather pants.

***

Snezhana slumped against the outside wall of the hospital building, blowing her nose and chewing gum loudly. Her head was shaved on one side and the rest of her hair was dyed purple. Her mirrored sunglasses kept others from seeing her alert eyes scanning the area. She saw another woman standing across from the exit, smoking a cigarette.

Snezhana noticed that something seemed off about the woman: the cigarette seemed to be used as a prop, the woman wasn't inhaling, and she was checking her surroundings a bit too often. The woman turned and stared at her. Snezhana pantomimed bumming a cigarette. The woman shook her head and motioned back that she was all out. Snezhana shrugged and spit on the ground.

Just then Sophia came into view. Snezhana saw the woman tense up, throw the cigarette onto the ground and start toward Sophia. As the woman turned, Snezhana saw the bulge of a gun tucked into her slacks at the small of her back.

"Sophia look out! Gun!"

Hearing the alarm, the woman drew her gun, swiveled around and shot at Snezhana, hitting her in the leg. Snezhana, having drawn her weapon, fired back, as she crumpled to the ground. The shot ran true and the woman fell over backwards.

Sophia heard a rustle on her right and turned. A second woman emerged from the bushes and leapt from the concrete retaining wall onto Sophia's back. Alert and ready, Sophia countered by tumbling forward, rolling the woman over her back and under her. The attacker reached out a hand to gouge Sophia's neck with her nails, while attempting to reach for a weapon with her other hand.

Sophia pounded her forehead into the woman's face, while grabbing the woman's arms to keep her from reaching her gun or knife. Blood poured from the woman's broken nose. Sophia pounded it again. The woman stopped struggling.

Sophia felt for a pulse. There was none. "Bollocks," Sophia uttered in disappointment. She was hoping to have at least one hostage. She arose from the body, picked it up, slung it over her shoulders and tossed it back into the bushes. She ran over to where Snezhana was lying and looked at the woman near her, briefly admiring the hole between the woman's eyes.

"Nice shot, Snez."

She slung the second body over her shoulders and quickly deposited it with the first. Hurrying back, she pointed at Snezhana's leg. "We need to get you medical care and get out of here fast."

Sophia ran into the hospital and emerged in a doctor's coat pushing a gurney. She helped Snezhana onto the gurney, picked up the weapons, tucking them under the small pillow on the gurney, and vanished into the hospital.

***

The secure phone on James' desk rang. James noticed Ed's number on the caller ID. He sighed and picked up the receiver.

Ed's far too cheerful voice came over the line, "Good afternoon, James, I heard there was a dust up over at St. Thomas."

James resented Ed's delight at James' problems and responded in a tired, put upon tone, "Yes, Ed, a local bobbie responded to a call that someone heard shots. When he got there, there was blood on the ground and he found some shell casings that we've analyzed. They correspond to a P-96 9mm pistol and a SR-1 Vektor semi-automatic gun, both Russian, the latter indicating possible involvement by the GRU. Both weapons are missing."

"What do you make of it?" inquired Ed, his tone still light hearted.

James sighed and responded, "I'm not sure. I have people searching the grounds now. There is a lot of blood scattered about. We will send a forensic unit over."

Ed directed James, "Keep me posted."

"Of course," James replied sarcastically.

James reached for the interoffice phone and punched in a number. He spoke tersely, "Check to see if anyone has been admitted to St. Thomas or any surrounding hospital.

Look for patients with gunshot and possibly knife wounds."

James hung up and nervously ran his hands through his hair.

***

"When you called me I was hoping perhaps it was for something more romantic."

Sophia punched Dr. Jacob Williams in his arm. He startled and backed up, causing a pile of towels to fall off of the shelf behind him.

He complained, "Ouch. A surgeon needs all of his limb."

Sophia reached to steady him and started putting the towels back. She pleaded, "Will you help us?"

Dr. Williams assured her, "Of course I will help you, Sophia. But I cannot operate on her in a supply closet. We will need to move her to a room at least. And we'll need an anesthesiologist."

Sophia shook her head and informed Jacob, "No anesthesiologist. She's going to have to tough it out. No one can know we were here. I know who is guarding Oliver. They are trustworthy and won't tell the others we were here. Let's move her to that floor. The rooms are empty on that wing."

"One second, I'll need some supplies." Jacob pulled a surgery kit, a bag of saline, and bandages from one shelf and, after checking that the temporary bandage was holding on Snezhana's leg, put the supplies onto the gurney with her and covered everything with a blanket.

"Men, you don't think of accessories." Sophia grabbed a set of scrubs that appeared to be Snezhana's size and put them on top of the weapons under Snezhana' pillow. She turned to open the door.

Jacob stopped her with a gentle touch on her arm. "Do you ever regret marrying Oliver instead of me?"

Snezhana groaned. "Shit! Guys, don't start with the personal stuff now."

"She's right. We need to shelve that for now." Sophia listened at the door and then opened it a crack and glanced out of the supply closet. "All clear." She walked out into the hallway pulling the gurney. Jacob followed pushing it.

"Can you pick up the pace?" asked Snezhana.

"No," Sophia countered and ordered, "Hush. We must act normal and fit in to not arose suspicion. We don't yet know how many assassins there are."

The wheels of the gurney on the tile filled the ensuing silence. Then Jacob angrily spoke up, "For God's sake, Sophia. You neglected to mention we may still be in danger."

"Oops, sorry Jacob. We are," Sophia mentioned.

Chapter Thirty-Three

A large black SUV pulled up to the small shingled cottage in South Carolina. Two prisoners were escorted out, pushed into the back seat, and cuffed to each other. A guard sat next to them in back and the driver got into the front of the car. Ed leaned in the driver's side window and directed, "Take them to the Naval Hospital in Charleston and once they are patched up, over to the NWS Charleston Navy base in Goose Creek, where they can be held for interrogation."

The driver acknowledged the order, "Yes sir."

The SUV pulled away and headed out to the highway east and north. Ed picked up his phone and dialed James. When James picked up, Ed informed him, "The prisoners are on their way to the Naval Hospital in South Carolina. They have had a fair amount of blood loss and are pretty battered."

James' normally polished voice sounded scratchy and worried. He inquired, "Did you get any information from them?"

Ed replied, "No, I didn't interrogate them. I think their injuries should be attended to first. Then we should have a seasoned interrogator shake them out. Any news from the London incident?"

***

Frowning, Elda hung up the burner phone and sat back on the couch in their safe house apartment. Tosh, Jackson and Stas had joined the rest for breakfast together.

Elda informed the team, "They found two bodies in London, neither of which is Sophia nor Snezhana."

Tosh threw down his fork and exclaimed, "I'm going over there to see if I can find Snezhana."

Elda held up her hand and cautioned him, "Tosh, you are letting your emotions run you right now. We are understaffed as it is. Stas, have you found anything more on the background checks?"

Stas swallowed the mouthful of scrambled eggs he had just shoveled into his mouth and replied, "*Da*. We have a heavily redacted copy of those missing years for James. He was in a top-secret operation for the military."

"Where?" Elda demanded.

"Moscow," Stas replied, before biting off a chunk of his toast.

Elda raised her eyebrows and stated, "Really, Stas? Moscow? How convenient of him. Please find out more. Have you run the checks on the communication staff?"

Stas paused his fork on its trip to his mouth and informed Elda, "*Da*. There is one who doesn't quite check out, Arabella Johnson. She is supposedly from an orphanage in Birmingham England, but there is no record of her being adopted from the orphanage." He quickly shoved in some food before the next question arrived.

Elda waited until he had finished that mouthful and queried, "Anyone else?"

Stas took a sip of his orange juice and answered, "*Nyet*. But I'm not yet done with the communication staff."

"Widen the search. Look at MI6 operatives too," Elda commanded. She took a sip of her own coffee and smiled. "There is nothing like a decent cup of coffee in the morning," she opined.

Tosh interrupted. "I *am* going to London, Elda," he said firmly, his eyes closing down any further debate.

"Okay," agreed Elda resignedly. "I expected you'd want to personally look for Snezhana. I'll go with you, Tosh. We can see if we can finish the work of smoking out the mole while we search for Sophia and Snezhana. It's been too long since we have heard from either of them. I'm also worried."

"*Spasibo*, Elda. I am glad I don't have to fight you over this," Tosh remarked. He sat back and slowly drank his cup of tea.

Elda continued organizing the team, "Stas and Jackson, Ed will send over information when he has it on the bodies to this account. Stas, are you sure this line you've set up is untraceable?"

Stas nodded and assured her, "*Da*, Elda. It is."

Satisfied with Stas' work, Elda turned to Anatoly and told him, "*Khorosho*. Anatoly, you are to guard these three. If you go out, please go out in disguise."

Anatoly frowned and complained, "I'd like to go with you too, Tosh and Elda."

"No, Anatoly," reprimanded Tosh sternly, " Someone has to be the muscle for Yuri, Stas and Jackson."

Anatoly avowed, "I will guard them well."

Elda next turned to Yuri and asked, "Yuri, I have set up our old communication network and protocol in case you need to reach Tosh or me in the UK. Do you remember it?"

Yuri replied, "*Da. Ya ponimayu.*"

Elda continued, "Before Tosh and I go, let's review what we know so far. We have a lot of dead bodies, mostly

Russian. We managed to capture two alive. The freelance assassin had no information, but the MI6 operative who was stationed in New York City had some tidbits. He was activated remotely, but he doesn't know by whom. All he knows is that the codewords matched and he was sent pictures and names of our entire team and told to kill on contact. He was then sent the hotel address and told a woman would meet him there to assist him. So, we have nothing more from him, except confirmation that MI6 has *someone* pulling the strings behind this operation."

"So who is *pulling the strings*. Elda?" Tosh inquired.

Elda shrugged and answered, "I don't know yet, Tosh. I sure hope it's not James. Unfortunately so far he's the common denominator."

"Another reason to go to London," Tosh insisted, scowling with his arms across his chest.

Elda held up a hand to placate him and said gently, "I agree, Tosh, but I have a feeling we are being distracted from the real mission."

***

The black SUV, with the two prisoners in the back seat, was cruising at the speed limit on route 17, heading to Charleston, when a semi-tractor-trailer passing them lost control and started fishtailing. The SUV driver cranked the steering wheel sharply to the right to avoid a collision but the SUV got sideswiped by the end of the truck, damaging the front tire and wheelbase area. The truck continued on.

The driver managed to keep the SUV in a controlled skid off to the side of the road. The driver sat composing himself and turned off the ignition. Immediately another car, containing two men dressed in business suits, pulled in behind them. The guard, noticing that they had company, pulled his gun and kept it on his lap.

The men walked up to the driver's side of the SUV and simultaneously spoke:

"We saw it all. Anyone hurt? How can we help?"

"Should we notify the police? It was *obviously* the truck's fault."

The driver got out of the SUV to inspect the damage. The guard holstered his weapon and joined him. The driver waved off the other two. "Yes, we're fine. No need to notify the police. We'll take care of it."

One man walked up to the front of the vehicle and exclaimed, "Oh wow!" The guard and driver moved closer to look. The man stepped back to give them a better view of the damage and effectively blocked their view of the back of the SUV. He pointed at the front wheel. "Look there. Even if we pulled the fender off, this car isn't drivable. The tire has been sliced and you've driven on the rim. We don't have enough room for the four of you, but we can stay here with you while you wait for help to arrive, if you would like. Or perhaps we can take one of you to a service area?"

"No, *really*, it's all right," answered the driver. "You been especially kind but we can *definitely* take it from here. I'll call for assistance. *Please*, you two can leave. We'll be fine."

"If you insist. Good luck." The men got back in their car and drove away.

The driver pulled out his phone to call for a pickup. The guard got back in the car and jumped back out a couple of minutes later. "They're dead!" He was wide eyed and backing away from the car.

The driver put out a hand to steady him and looked at him in confusion, "What?"

"Look at them!" The guard pointed at the bodies in the back seat. The two prisoners were leaning on each other, appearing as if they had fallen into a deep sleep.

The driver looked into the back seat and commented, "They are just asleep."

The agitated guard insisted, "No, no. I checked him and there's no pulse, no breath."

"Damn it! What happened?" the driver wondered.

***

Sophia held her hand with a green hospital towel in it over Snezhana's mouth. "Bite down on the towel, Snezhana, or pass out if you want, but you *have* to keep quiet."

Snezhana had sweat dripping off her face, her hair matted on one side. Her eyes were bulging out as she struggled not to scream. Her body was strapped down to the gurney. Jacob was bent over her leg.

"I'm making as small of an incision as I can to get the bullet out," he said with concern, squinting to see in the dim light.

Sophia reassured him, "That's all right, Jacob. Do what you need to do."

A muffled, "*Blyad'*!" sounded from under the towel.

Jacob looked around. "Any chance of more light here?"

Sophia pointed to the overhead lights which were already on and responded, "Only if we bring the gurney more to the window."

Jacob motioned to Sophia to take one end of the gurney and ordered, "Then let's do that."

Sophia and Jacob repositioned the gurney and he started in again. Snezhana groaned and passed out.

373

Chapter Thirty-Four

Tosh and Elda were brainstorming in their room at the Holiday Inn Express near Vauxhall Park in London. The smell of coffee wafted from the hotel room coffee machine. Tosh poured two cups and handed one to Elda.

Elda skeptically eyed her cup and then addressed Tosh, "No poison, right?"

Tosh shrugged. "You never know…," he said in a flat tone.

Elda looked into his eyes and took a deep sip. "Thank you, Tosh. This operation is unlike any we have been on before, isn't it?"

"*Da*. Before it was clear. We had the good guys against bad guys, and a code for working together. It was more straightforward in those days. We knew our mission and got in and got out. Mostly we handled things on our own, and, as long as we didn't get in each other's way, we allowed the others to live. Now there's too many lies and collateral damage."

Elda took another sip of her coffee and leaned back in her chair. "That was a good summation of how I'm feeling too, Tosh. Tell me, though, I thought you once told me that your niece was like any other operative. Do you have any other reason for being here?"

Tosh looked directly at Elda and spoke sternly, "Elda, I am not getting soft in my old age. She is just another person on my team. But this mission is not for any of my team members to die on. I would do the same for *any* of them."

"For me?" Elda asked, struggling to keep a smile from her face.

Tosh turned away quickly, hiding his face from Elda, and replied, "While on this mission, *da*, for you also."

Elda quickly took a sip of coffee to hide her grin. "Okay. Then let's figure out how to find them, and when we do, how to get out of London alive."

***

A slightly built janitor with brown hair and brown eyes went through security and slipped down the stairs to the MI6 basement. Once there, he swapped his first badge for a second one that gave him access to the Records department. Out of sight of the security cameras, he put on a tie and reversed his white janitorial coat to a long dark gray jacket and placed a cap on his now gray hair and put a pair of horn rim glasses over piercing grey eyes. He casually sauntered into the Records department, handed over his work order and had his badge scanned. He then disappeared into the bowels of the Human Resources records department. He left Records ten minutes later.

He tapped a message into his phone. *Success. On my way upstairs. Will pass you outside.* On the way out, while in the camera dead spot, he took a wig out of the bag he was carrying and swapped the horn rim glasses for a pair of mirrored ones.

***

A man with long brown hair, wearing mirrored sunglasses, brushed by Elda as she bounded up the walkway to MI6. She smoothly pocketed the thumb drive he had passed to her, strode into MI6 and bounced up the stairs. Elda barged into James's office, slamming the door behind her.

He stood up behind his desk and stared at her in bewilderment. "What on *earth* are you doing here?"

Elda shrugged. "I'm not sure. It seemed like the logical next step. May I sit?"

"Certainly. Are you alone?" James settled back into his leather office chair.

"Yes. Where are Sophia and Snezhana?" Elda demanded, leaning in toward James and staring at him.

James pulled back defensively. "I wish I could tell you."

With one hand on the edge of his desk, Elda slapped a picture down on the desk in front of James. "Why was one of the captives in South Carolina a MI6 operative?" she demanded.

James winced, picked up the image and then dropped it again. He took a deep breath and countered, "I've never seen this man. And anyway, how do you know that? The captives were killed before they could be interrogated."

"Were they? Are you the mole, James?" She loudly slapped the side of his monitor.

James slammed his fist down onto his desktop. "What?! How dare you ask that?!" His eyes narrowed and his nostrils flared.

Elda flipped a sheet of paper at him. "There's a redacted part of your service record where it turns out you were in Moscow. What were you doing there?"

James picked the paper up with shaking hands. "How did you find that? That is beyond your level."

Elda chuckled, responding, "You have no idea what my level really is. And, if you don't want anyone to find it, then move it to a deeper security level."

"Bloody hell. I will immediately. I was in a deep cover in Russia during this op, where we turned some crucial double agents, who are still planted over there. This information could imperil their lives." He looked at the papers on his desk and scratched his head with his fingertips, his salt and pepper hair askew.

Elda spoke softly, "Are you sure they didn't turn you too?"

"Damn it, Elda! No, they didn't," James retorted, his voice turning upward into a whine.

Elda sat back. The tension in the room sharply released like air escaping out of a burst balloon. Elda questioned in a friendlier tone, "Then who here in MI6 would you suspect if you had to? Will you give us complete access to the records of each person involved in this case?"

James rolled back his chair and stood. "Certainly." He held up his hand. "Wait here and I will be back with that information for you."

Just then a young aide knocked and stepped into the office. "Sir…" He spotted Elda and hesitated.

"Yes? Speak. What is it?" James said curtly.

The aide cleared his throat, "Well sir, we've identified one of the bodies from the hospital incident."

"Well spit it out. Who are they?"

"One is potentially a Russian operative. We are still researching that one. The other…" he paused…

"Now!" James barked.

The aide grimaced and then said quickly, "…well, the other is one of ours, sir."

"What!?" James shouted.

The aide backed up toward the door and said faintly, "MI6, sir."

"Damn it!" James said to no-one in particular and pounded his fist on his desk.

***

The guard paced back and forth on the side of the road outside of the black SUV. The driver, sitting in the front seat, called in to his superiors to report the death of the two captives.

He rolled down the window to speak with the guard. "Okay, they will send someone out here from the base to help us out, but we'll have to wait for a while."

The guard shook his head and uttered, "I'm not sitting in back with those dead bodies."

"There's nothing for you to guard back there. Get in front with me," the driver offered.

The guard slid into the front seat of the SUV. The windows were down for fresh air. The sounds of the birds could be heard calling to each other in the nearby woods. A fly flew in and landed on the male corpse's face and crawled around.

The two in the front seat ignored the death in the back seat. The guard rummaged through the glove compartment to see if there was anything interesting in there. The driver was playing solitaire on his iPhone. A hand slipped between the seats and carefully removed the guard's gun from its holster.

The guard turned and reached back to see what had touched his hip. Suddenly the driver's head exploded, spraying blood, bone and brain, all over the dashboard and front window.

He opened his mouth to say, "What the…" The words were prematurely cut off. The guard's DNA soon mingled with the driver's, as the blood dripped down the inside of the window.

Angelina unclipped the guard's keychain from his belt and unlocked her hand cuffs. She searched both bodies and removed all the cash from their wallets and the spare ammunition from the guard's belt. She checked to ensure her clothing was blood free and then ran away from the car, disappearing into the dense woods of the Donnelley Wildlife Management Area.

***

A stooped over elderly custodian shuffled along the hospital hallway, pushing a trash cart in front of him across the shiny linoleum tiles. The guard in front of Oliver's door stopped him. "What are you doing here, old man?"

"I have to collect the trash on this floor," the janitor offered.

The guard held up his hand with the palm facing the old man and said, "I'll walk in with you."

Oliver was sitting up in bed, reading a book on baby names.

The custodian came aside the bed and peered up at him with his piecing gray eyes and whispered, "Do you know where they are?"

Oliver's eyes widened and then he called to the watching guard, "George, I know this custodian. It's fine. Can you be a saint and go get me a Coca Cola from the machine at the end of the hall."

"You sure?" George inquired.

381

Oliver nodded and stated, "Yes. I will never be safer than I am now."

George squinted at the man and then told Oliver, "Okay.. I'll be *right* back."

Oliver shook his head and stated, "Give us five."

George eyeballed the custodian but then said, "You got it, mate." George slipped out.

Smiling, Oliver asked, "Tosh! What are you doing here?"

Tosh held up his hand. "Shush, there's not much time. Do you know where they are?"

"Yes, Snezhana is in a room two doors down." Oliver pointed in that direction, then continued, "She got smuggled in. No one knows she is here. She was shot in the leg." Tosh's gray eyes narrowed. Oliver quickly added, "It's not serious – she'll recover."

Tosh gestured down the length of the hospital bed and nodded at the nearby wheelchair. "Are you mobile yet, Oliver?"

Oliver sighed and looked down at his legs under the hospital blanket before answering, "Not really. I can walk, but not any distance."

Tosh nodded and then probed, "Tell me about the guards. Is there any that we can trust not to tell MI6 if we slip in here?"

"Yes, the guard you just saw, George, is an old friend. He and I have served together. We are like brothers."

Tosh handed Oliver a phone and instructed him, "We will call you an hour before we arrive. Make sure George is on duty. We'll make sure he's not hurt when we extract you two. For now, say nothing."

Tosh emptied the trash into his cart and disappeared out the door as George walked back in.

***

The contact whistled and walked along the wide gravel path past the mole who was sitting on a green painted bench in Kennington Park, watching the wild parakeets. The whistler stopped, wadded up a paper lunch bag, and threw it into the nearby elevated wooden trash bin, then continued walking through the park. The mole rose, lifted the paper bag out of the trash and returned to his bench, opening it as if he were eating his lunch, and read the single piece of paper within.

The Pure Gym at London Oval at midnight tonight.

***

On her way out of MI6, Elda detoured to find Emily. She poked her head over the low wall of Emily's cubicle. "Sophia speaks highly of you."

Emily looked up and recognized Elda from Sophia's description. "You're Elda, right? Thank you. I just love her and Ollie. They are like family to me."

"Yes," Elda responded, "I'm Elda. Can you discreetly do me a favor?"

Emily raised her eyebrows, but kept her voice steady. "Certainly."

Elda stepped into Sophia's cubicle. She tore a piece of paper from Emily's notepad and wrote down a set of instructions and handed them to her along with two thumb drives.

Emily read the instructions, smiled excitedly, but calmly stated, "Sure I can do this. No problem."

"Good." Elda acknowledged curtly, and after a pause added, "Thank you. It's exceedingly important that they get the information as soon as possible. Memorize and destroy the instructions."

Elda turned and left the building. Although the lavender garden was not yet in bloom, she decided to cut through the scenic Vauxhall Park to get out of the hubbub of the city.

Just into the park by the drinking fountain, a man jumped out, pushed her, and threw her to the walkway. He kicked out and his boot grazed her head. She grabbed his leg and pulled it out from under him, causing him to crash onto the ground. Rising to a crouching position she sprung forward and leapt on top of him. He flailed out and hit her in the head. Elda put her forearm down on his neck and pressed while he continued to bash at her. Coughing and gagging, he stopped hitting her and instead tried to remove her arm from his neck.

Just shy of choking him, Elda released her hold and jumped to her feet. He came up to his elbows and knees, coughing and spitting. Elda kicked him solidly in the ribs, hearing a satisfying crack in return. He screamed and fell over. She sat on him and held a knife to his neck.

"Who are you?" Elda demanded.

He wheezed in return.

Elda reached in her pocket, took out her phone and dialed James. "James. Vauxhall Park. Now. I'm coming in with a prisoner. I may need backup."

Hanging up she addressed the man again, pressing the knife into his neck deeply enough to draw blood. "You will come peacefully with me or I will kill you. Understand?"

The man nodded. He screamed in pain as she helped him to his feet. Elda hissed at him. "Shut your mouth."

She grabbed his arm in a vice and firmly escorted him to
MI6.

Chapter Thirty-Five

"Jackson look at this," Stas shouted.

Jackson adjusted his glasses and strolled over to the couch where Stas was rapidly typing away on his laptop. "What do you have, Stas?" He sat and leaned in over Stas' shoulder and viewed the computer screen.

Stas stopped typing and pointed at one line. He explained, "The list on the left is the one that Elda sent us. The one on the right is what I have dug out. Both contain the names plus background information on the communication staff at MI6." Stas scrolled, stopped and pointed again. "There seems to be a number of discrepancies. Notice that the two lists do not match. The one Elda got from James is missing two names, Henry Davis and Arabella Johnson." Stas then popped up two windows and scrolled to display the associated background on each. "And, if you look at their backgrounds, there seems to be a lot of holes, especially in this person's." He pointed at Arabella's name.

"I see it." Jackson acknowledged, asking, "Can you trace the deletions to the source?"

Stas shrugged, replying, "*Ya ne znayu.* But I'll try."

Jackson took note of the two names and stated, "Good. I'll look deeper into each of their background information and see what I can piece together from other sources."

***

In the almost empty gym, the mole was lying on a weight bench, working out with hand weights. A man in sweats walked over to the mole, took the hand weights, and handed the mole a bar with heavier weights loaded on each end. "Here, try this. I'll spot you."

"Thank you." The mole looked around to ensure no one was using the other benches. He struggled to lift the weights. The man put both hands on the bar and assisted his lifts. While lifting, the mole grunted out: "I need additional help. We lost Broya and Angelina in the States and now our MI6 agent, Thomas, as well as the GRU agent that you assigned to the team here. Our network is decimated. And, they now have a prisoner who could lead them to me. We only have two of us left in MI6 and we are not field agents."

"I told you before I cannot help you. All resources are focused on the USA right now. The end is too close. If you cannot eliminate them, distract them and keep them here in the UK. Kill the prisoner before he talks. You know the price of failure."

The man let go and dropped the weighted bar on the mole's chest. He walked briskly away.

Henry coughed and struggled to remove the weight. *Bastard.*

***

Elda slumped in the hotel room desk chair holding chunks of ice wrapped in a bathroom hand towel to her head while she made her phone calls. Tosh walked over, lifted her hand and the towel, frowned at the large multi-colored lump, and put the ice pack gently back, replacing her hand on top of it. He observed, "You'll live."

Elda winced and responded, "Thanks Tosh. So good to know."

Tosh perched backwards in the room chair next to the desk. "Did you make the arrangements, Elda?"

"Yes. It's all set," she stated. Elda's burner phone rang. She gingerly reached for it and answered, "Hello? … let me put you on speaker James. Tosh is here too."

James' voice reverberated through the cheap phone speaker, "The man who attacked you is a custodian who cleans the floor that houses our communication department."

"So Elda beat up the *dvornik*?" Tosh's gray eyes sparkled with mirth. Elda threw the pad of paper from the desk at him. It bounced harmlessly off his arm.

James replied, "We think he is really a Russian agent. We have been interrogating him, but he so far is staying close mouthed."

Tosh chuckled. Elda waved a hand at him and responded to James, "Thanks James. Please do keep us posted."

Elda hung up and Tosh handed her the metal wastebasket from under the desk. "Perhaps you would like a present for your new friend?"

"Gads. And I have to work with *you*." Elda attempted to sneer at Tosh, but started laughing instead. "Okay, it is rather humorous. I'll give you that one. Now let's get to work. We have a lot of logistics to pull together."

***

Jackson ran into the living room and skidded to a stop in front of Stas. "Stas, we have to give Elda this information immediately. This is an amazingly deep and long operation." Jackson paced back and forth in front of the coffee table where Stas was working on his computer.

Stas looked up from his laptop. "So did you pull all the pieces together?"

"Yes," Jackson responded, "I think I have the full story here. It looks as if the Russians had this operative in place from childhood. Her parents adopted her from an orphanage in Russia, just after their other daughter died in a hit and run. They gave her the dead daughter's identity and brought her up as a British citizen."

Stas took his hands off his keyboard and gave Jackson his full attention. "But she was only a young child when she was adopted. How could they turn her?"

Jackson pointed to his star student. "Exactly. That's where the clever bits come in. According to sources, the daughter would go away to camp every summer. I would postulate that the camp she attended was summer camp in Russia, where she was trained and indoctrinated. The parents probably did it under duress, fearing that their daughter would be taken away if they didn't."

Engrossed in the tale that Jackson had spun from the shards of information, Stas inquired, "But how did they use her? What happened?"

Jackson deadpanned, "She grew up."

Stas threw a couch pillow at Jackson, and missed. Jackson continued, "Groomed to be a military and intelligence asset, she served in the Royal Air Force as a communication technician and, shortly after her honorable discharge, joined MI6."

Stas observed, "So *she* could have been the one tapping into all of our communication."

Jackson gave Stas an affirmative pat on his shoulder and responded, "Exactly. Yes."

***

Elda and Tosh marched in step into James' office. A haggard looking James motioned them to the chairs. Elda shut the door behind her and held her finger to her lips while she walked around the room holding a small piece of equipment.

Tosh sat down and addressed James. "*Privet*, James. How are you?"

James looked at Tosh in bewilderment but decided to play along. "I'm fine Tosh, how can I help you two today?"

Tosh held two fingers towards his eyes and then pointed to his chest, signaling, *watch me.* "We just wanted to say goodbye. We're leaving from Heathrow tomorrow morning. There's no sign of Sophia, nor of Snezhana, so we are assuming they have moved on to follow whatever trail they had picked up."

Elda held up one finger and pointed to the office landline. She held up another and pointed to James' computer. She gave James her best *don't you dare do it* schoolteacher glare as he opened his mouth to swear.

James nodded, took a deep breath and stated, "Well, I can't say I'm sad to see you two Yanks go, although I do have to admit you were right that we had had an issue here at MI6."

"Was the person who attacked me the extent of it?" questioned Elda.

"Yes, fortunately," answered James. "We gathered information on all the leads that you gave us and we have no current employees who were part of that network."

James handed Elda a piece of flash paper on which he had written: THE CUSTODIAN WAS AFTER THE THUMB DRIVE WE GAVE YOU.

Elda wrote back on that paper, ANYTHING ELSE FROM THE ATTACKER?

James scribbled, UNFORTUNATELY, HIS HEART GAVE OUT DURING INTERROGATION.

"Well, it's great to know we can trust you again," said Elda, handing James a thin folder. He opened it up and nodded.

"Yes, you can. We always clean up our messes." James burned the flash paper in his ashtray and mouthed a *thank you* to Elda and Tosh, who turned and quickly left his office.

***

Three orderlies, two female and one male, walked into Snezhana's room at the hospital, pushing a gurney with an empty body bag on it.

Snezhana sat up in her hospital bed and pointed to the body bag, "You want me to be in that? *Nyet blyat' put'!*"

"Yes," responded Elda curtly. "By the way, I like what you've done with your hair."

Tosh added, "When I told you to cut your hair Snezhana, I meant all of it, not just one side."

Sophia glared at Tosh and Elda, adding consolingly, "Don't worry Snezhana, you'll have a small tank of oxygen with you, and, if you keep your eyes closed, you won't feel claustrophobic at all."

Snezhana shuddered. "And then what happens?"

Tosh explained, "We go get Oliver and put him in a second body bag and then use the ambulance waiting downstairs to take you and Oliver to the undertakers."

Snezhana rolled her eyes and sassed, "Is cremation part of this too?"

Elda, locked in her serious operation command mode, gave Snezhana a sharp look, and responded, "Since they will be on the lookout for all of us, we will all five be smuggled out on a transport plane."

Snezhana shook her head, asking, "How, if they are looking for us?"

"In coffins," Elda stated.

Snezhana put her hands to her head and muttered, "*Lisus*."

Chapter Thirty-Six

Five wooden coffins with United States flags on them were wheeled across the tarmac to a RAF cargo plane. They were promptly loaded in and tied down.

Inside one of the coffins Elda whispered, "After takeoff and on my command."

From each coffin came the responses over Elda's earpiece,

"*Da.*"

"*Da,* ma'am"

"Righto."

"Bob's your uncle."

Elda breathed deeply from her oxygen tank and fought the urge to panic. She closed her eyes, so she couldn't see how close the walls were of the coffin. She felt the plane start to taxi and started to say a prayer for a safe takeoff. Her father had been an airline pilot and had told her the most dangerous times were takeoff and landing. She had never forgotten that and at times wished he hadn't said that.

A whispered voice spoke in her earpiece, "Elda, are you praying?"

"Hush, Tosh," Elda demanded.

Lying there, she hugged her Kriss Vector submachine gun tightly, until she felt the wheels retract and the plane level out for the flight back to the States.

She instructed the team, "Unlock."

In return Elda heard a series of small clicks, signifying that the internal locking mechanism inside all five coffins had been turned off.

She commanded, "Exit."

Elda, Tosh, and Sophia popped out of their coffins with their guns ready. Snezhana and Oliver were sitting up holding their weapons. No one else was in their space.

Elda lowered her gun and stated, "Good. We can breathe easy until just before landing, when we'll need to prepare for the next leg of transport and re-enter the coffins."

Tosh walked over to Elda's coffin and peeked inside, coyly observing, "Aw, Elda, your coffin has pink silk inside."

"That's because I'm so sweet," remarked Elda hitting Tosh on his arm, landing her fist right on the bruise that was still there from Newburyport.

"*Chert*!" Tosh drew back his arm. Elda looked at him quizzically and he pulled his punch. "Just wait, Elda. We won't always be on the same side."

"I am looking forward to that, Tosh," she stated.

Chapter Thirty-Seven

"I think I may have something, Jackson." Stas, bent over his laptop on the living room coffee table, called over to Jackson, who was sitting on a living room chair with his computer on his lap.

"Great! I'll be there in a minute." Jackson paused and stared at the pantry and asked, "What is Anatoly doing?"

Stas lifted his gaze from his screen and looked across the room at Anatoly, who had the door to the secret passageway open and was sizing himself against the walls and trying to squeeze in sideways. He removed his shirt and tried again.

Jackson frowned and yelled over to Anatoly, "Anatoly, what on earth are you doing?"

"I am about one-half inch too large for this passageway, Jackson. No amount of Crisco will push me through."

Jackson, set aside his computer, walked over and tried pushing Anatoly into the passageway.

Anatoly yelped, "*Oy!*"

Jackson stopped pushing and eyed the lack of clearance, observing, "You're right Anatoly. This was built for people more Stas' size."

Anatoly rubbed his arms, answering, "*Da*, At least we know. Yuri might just squeak through, and the rest of you will fit, but I won't."

"We'll cross that bridge when we come to it," said Jackson, turning back to Stas, inquiring, "What do you have, Stas?"

Stas looked at his screen and scrolled down, stopped and summarized, "Henry Davies is the manager of the communications team for James' division of MI6. His background check turned out fine, but there's something interesting in the additional information that James gave to Elda. He has a son."

Jackson smiled and quipped, "Well breeding isn't against international law, you know."

Stas took a deep breath before responding, ""Yes, but his son, Nigel, is married to a Russian woman and lives in Moscow."

Jackson walked over to Stas, adjusted his glasses, and leaned over to verify the information on Stas' screen. "Ah, that *is* an interesting tidbit!"

***

Henry stomped into the communications center at MI6, rubbing his chest. His secretary rose from her wooden desk near the door and stopped him, saying, "James wishes to see you now, Henry."

Arabella looked up from her station, watching the interchange.

Henry instructed the secretary, "Tell him I'll be right there."

Henry wandered by Arabella's station and, pretending to view her screen, whispered, "I will text you if you need to run."

Arabella nodded, grabbed a small black Mountainsmith bum bag from her desk drawer, then rose and strolled to the ladies room. From the hallway outside the ladies room she could view her station and see if anyone was coming for her. It also had a direct line to an exit door.

Henry rode the elevator up to James' office. James' secretary waved Henry into the inner chambers. James looked up, "Oh hi there, Henry! So good to see you. Have a seat. I'm going to need some help from you."

Henry breathed deeply in relief, flinched and coughed. "From me? On what, James?"

"Sit, sit." James motioned Henry to a chair. "I'm going to read you in on an operation and I will need you to help find some folks that have gone missing."

"Anything you need, James." Henry sat nervously on the edge of his chair and took out his cell phone to take notes.

James held up his hand to stop Henry, instructing him, "Please, no notes. This is highly confidential information. I fear that Sophia and Snezhana have been seriously injured and may even be dead. Tosh and Elda were just over here looking for them, and found no trace of them. I'd like you to check all of the commercial flights out of the UK, to see if two young women have boarded. One or both may be injured."

"Certainly sir." Henry returned his cell phone to his pocket.

James continued, "Also, Elda and Tosh have lost track of Anatoly and Yuri since the time of the attack in New York City. There was a lot of blood found there, but no bodies. They also fear these two could be injured and holed up somewhere in New York City, or perhaps even dead. Can you have someone check the NYC morgues and hospitals?"

Henry exhaled and grimaced, stating, "That will be somewhat difficult sir, but perhaps we can hack in and get lists of patients names. What dates are we talking about?"

James paused a moment and then instructed, "Look at the 27th of March until today."

Henry acknowledged the information and inquired, "Anything else, sir?"

James shook his head. "Not at this moment, Henry. I expect an update the minute you have any information. I have to go back to the drawing board. This mission has been brought to a screeching halt."

"So sorry to hear that." Henry pretended to sneeze and covered his mouth to hide his satisfied expression.

"That is all for now, Henry." James made a dismissing motion with his hand.

"Very well, sir." Henry stood, waiting to see if there was anything else. James looked up from the papers on his desk and waved Henry out of his office.

Henry left James' office elated, his feet skimming along the linoleum floor. Suddenly he slumped against the concrete hallway wall in relief. He texted Arabelle. ALL OK. WE ARE NOW PART OF THE OPERATION.

***

Mid-air, in route to the United States, Elda read the duplicated text diverted from Henry's phone via the tiny transmitters that Tosh had placed inside MI6. She compared it to the information coming from the bugs she had planted in James' office. She nodded her satisfaction. The trap was working.

***

"*Chert*! I may have screwed up," exclaimed Yuri, as he rushed in through the apartment door, slammed it behind him, and threw the grocery bags on the coffee table.

"*Chto*?" inquired Anatoly. "And, I hope you didn't buy eggs."

Stas and Jackson, startled, looked up from their computers. Stas carefully pushed the nearer bag away from his computer.

"What happened?" demanded Anatoly.

Yuri held one arm across his abdomen and bit the cuticle on his forefinger of his other hand. He then held that hand palm up towards Anatoly and answered, "I was going to the grocery store and I got turned around. So I stopped at a coffee shop to ask for directions back here."

"Did anyone overhear you?" Anatoly interrogated.

Yuri rubbed the back of his neck and looked down at the floor. He shook his head as he answered, "I'm not sure. Sitting at a table with his computer was a man who seemed to perk up when he saw me. I should have been in disguise. Elda told us to, but I figured I was just popping out and right back."

Anatoly took a step in Yuri's direction, inquiring sternly, "Did you mention the apartment number, Yuri?"

Yuri backed up a step. "Of course not," he stated.

Anatoly scratched his head and then turned to address the room, "Let's go to lockdown mode anyway. Stas and Jackson go to the other apartment through the tunnel. Take some food with you. We don't know how long you'll have to be in there and we can't go out again. Yuri, if you can fit through the tunnel, go with them."

Yuri objected, "No, Anatoly. I am not leaving you here alone."

Anatoly dismissed Yuri's concern, "They don't know what apartment we're in, so no one is safe. Stas and Jackson will need you to protect them." Anatoly handed Yuri Elda's Kriss Vector short barreled pistol caliber submachine gun. "Do you know how to use this?"

"*Da*," Yuri remarked as he took the gun.

"Just suck that in while going through." Anatoly gave Yuri's flat abdomen a gentle punch, slid the couch against the front door and sat at the table with his Vityaz-SN submachine gun. "*Idti, idti, idti! Seychas!*" He unfolded the 9 inch stock ready to steady his weapon against his shoulder.

Stas picked up a grocery bag and ran through the passageway.

"Are there enough groceries here for you?" inquired Jackson politely.

Anatoly responded without turning, "*Da*. Go now."

Jackson picked up the second bag and walked into the passageway. Yuri saluted and said, "*Qui nos morituri te salutant.*"

Anatoly looked at Yuri quizzically, asking, "*Chto za blyad'*, Yuri?"

Yuri informed him, "It's a Latin saying I learned from Elda. It means: *We who are about to die salute you.* The gladiators used to say it before going into battle. I'm surprised you didn't know that, Anatoly."

"I like that." Anatoly saluted back. Closing the pantry door, he shook his head at the vision of Yuri, shirtless, wiggling his way through the passageway. He said softly, "*Qui nos morituri te salutant.*"

***

"Bollocks!" James slapped his hand over his mouth when he realized he had spoken out loud. He was looking at his second computer that he had bought and set up himself, with a lot of remote advice from Stas.

"Damn spellcheck." He hoped that would cover up his slip to those who were listening in. He was viewing a private channel for emails diverted from Henry's account that Stas had also given him access to. Staring back at him was:

WE HAVE ACCESS TO JAMES' INFORMATION. ANATOLY AND YURI FEARED INJURED OR DEAD. SOPHIA AND SNEZHANA ALSO. WE ARE FOCUSING ON FINDING ELDA AND TOSH. NO THREAT TO DC OPERATION ATT.

***

Anatoly knelt on the hard cloth covered cushions of the couch and peeked out the door's spyhole. A man was wandering from door to door, knocking, displaying a badge when the door opened and then showing his cell phone. Anatoly shook his head and muttered, "No brains there." He slid the couch away from the door and stood waiting for the knock. The man knocked on the apartment next door and, receiving no answer, made a note of the apartment number and moved on. He sharply knocked at Anatoly's door. Anatoly shouted, "Yes, I'm coming."

Anatoly threw open the door and yanked the man inside, kicked the door shut, tossed him to the ground and zip-tied his arms and legs. It was over in seconds. Anatoly rolled the stranger onto his back and growled, "Who are you?"

The man stared up in terror at Anatoly looming over him and shook his head. Anatoly took Stas' Bose noise cancelling headphones from the coffee table and placed them over the man's ears. He placed a towel in his mouth and duct taped the headphones and the towel to the man's head,, inquiring, "Can you still breathe?"

The man nodded. Tears welled up in his eyes. Anatoly picked him up and slung him over his shoulder and threw him down onto the bed and closed the bedroom door on his way back to the living room. He then slid the couch back against the door.

Just in case there are more of you.

***

Elda unlocked the door of the apartment and pushed the door, but nothing happened. She glanced at Tosh who shrugged. She heard someone from inside yell, *"Odna minuta."* She listened to the sound of a large piece of furniture being dragged away from the door.

Anatoly's head peeked out. "Hurry in," he ordered, holding the door open.

Elda stepped in, followed by Sophia helping a hobbling Snezhana, and Tosh half dragging a pale faced Oliver. Tosh commanded, "Let's get Oliver into bed."

"Ah, there may be a problem with that," Anatoly said, as Elda opened the bedroom door, peered in and closed the door again.

"Who the hell is that, Anatoly?" she snapped.

Anatoly shrugged and smiled disarmingly, answering, "It's a long story, Elda."

"We have all day," Elda responded, then instructed, "Tosh can you put Oliver on the couch? Sophia please help Snezhana to the comfy chair and give her something for a footstool. Okay, Anatoly – spill. And where are Yuri, Stas and Jackson?"

Tosh demanded, "What happened here while we were gone?"

Anatoly pointed to the passageway, stating, "Yuri is with Stas and Jackson in the other apartment. I had them go there for their security. That man in the bedroom was going door to door looking for us."

Elda frowned and quizzed, "For us? Are you sure?"

Anatoly held up the prisoner's phone for Elda and Tosh to see. "Yes, he had pictures of us on his phone."

"*Interesnyy…*" Tosh took the phone, scrolled through a few pages and then handed it back to Anatoly, telling him, "Give the phone to Stas and Jackson. Have them analyze the information on it."

Elda asked of Anatoly, "What did you find out from him?"

Anatoly shook his head in the negative and stated, "The prisoner is not talking yet. I was waiting for you and Tosh to get back before putting the pressure on the interrogation. Here's the information that Jackson and Stas pulled from facial recognition and his files. Apparently, he's an attaché at the Russian embassy here." Anatoly handed a number of pages to Tosh.

Tosh quickly reviewed them. "*Interesnyy.* He's had plenty of opportunity to activate a poison pill if he had one, but he hasn't, which makes me think he's a bit player." He handed the papers to Elda.

Elda briefly scanned them and declared, "Crap. That means diplomatic immunity. I'm glad you didn't hurt him, Anatoly. Good thinking." Elda quickly scanned the sheaf of pages. "Good, got it. Let me speak to him for a while." Elda marched into the bedroom and closed the door.

Anatoly directed Tosh over to the laptop on the counter. "Tosh, while Elda's in there with our prisoner, you may want to look at some pictures that Snezhana took while Sophia was meeting with Emily."

Tosh looked at the video screen where Stas was conferencing from the other apartment. He stared at the pictures that Snezhana had uploaded from a thumb drive. He frowned at the screen. "Snezhana, what made you go to this park?" Tosh inquired.

Snezhana poked her head around Stas so that she was seen by the camera. She answered, "I remembered all the stories that you told me when I was growing up about Gorky Park and the clandestine activities that went on there and I thought, what if this operation is being run by someone of that era? Might not he also use a park as a drop and meeting spot?"

"Good job, Snezhana. We'll discuss this when Elda is through in there." Tosh stared at the screen for a moment longer. "Bastard. I will handle you personally."

***

Elda strode out of the back bedroom, removed a pair of blue medical gloves and washed her hands in the sink. Tosh stopped his pacing and demanded of Elda, "Well, what did you get out of him? And why the gloves?"

Elda threw the gloves in the trash. "It's psychological. Inexperienced players usually cave pretty quickly when they see me put the gloves on, because they fear I am going

411

to perform a medical procedure on them without anesthesia. The gloves are just a useful prop to soften the victim."

Tosh narrowed his eyes and spoke, "*Interesnyy…*"

Elda ignored Tosh's probing into her techniques and informed him, "I learned quite a bit during the interrogation, and not enough. It seems like junior there in the back bedroom was looking to make a name for himself. He regularly intercepted Alexei's emails to see how he could ingratiate himself to Alexei and get transferred back to Moscow to work for him. He saw that we were on Alexei's most wanted list and downloaded our pictures. In fact, he was doing that exactly at the moment that Yuri walked into the coffee shop."

Yuri came into view on the computer screen and apologized, "Bad timing. I'm sorry Elda. I should have heeded your advice and gone out in disguise."

Elda shook her finger at Yuri in mock reprimand, declaring, "Hopefully you have learned something from this for future missions, Yuri. Actually, though, it was good timing. We now have his phone and laptop with a number of Alexei's emails on it. Stas can go over the computer and see what other information he can find."

"And we also have this…" Tosh handed Elda the laptop displaying the picture that Snezhana had taken.

Elda glared at the screen. She snarled, "How perfect. There *he* is with the MI6 mole. We have them both now."

Tosh took the laptop back. "I would appreciate it, Elda, if you would leave handling Alexei to me."

Elda looked at Tosh with a serious expression and deadpanned, "Well, Tosh, you know how hard it would be to extradite him from Russia for any trial here in the US. We, *of course* will submit all the paperwork, but we have *no* control over whether or not he lives long enough to comply."

Tosh nodded his understanding, and said, "*Spasibo.*" He placed the laptop back down on the counter.

Elda started pacing as she thought out loud, "Now, all we need to find out is what they are actually planning. All we know so far is that whatever will happen will be in the DC area."

"So what's next?" inquired the penitent Yuri.

"First we need to handle this mess," Elda declared.

Smiling, Tosh observed, "I'm sure, Elda, that you know a person or a place."

Elda smiled back at Tosh. She informed him, "You're correct, Tosh. I do. We need to squirrel this man away for a while, unharmed. We can't have him raising an alarm.

It'll be a bit tricky due to his diplomatic immunity, but I have an angle there." Elda picked up her phone and dialed a number. "Dan. How are you?" She grinned and nodded. "No, you're right. I didn't call just to find out how you are. I have a bit of a situation and can use your help. I'd like to intake a patient to your facility, just for a short while."

Elda glanced at Tosh inquisitively. Tosh nodded his approval.

Elda continued, "I also would like a second opinion on the readiness of one of my operatives." She listened and responded, "Thanks so much, Dan. I owe you one." Elda gave him the address and ended the call. She set her phone down on the coffee table and turned to an expectant Tosh. "It's all arranged."

"Good. When will he arrive?" Tosh asked.

"He'll be here in about an hour." Elda started pacing again, as she listed her todos, "I need to pop out and get the court order and fake IDs. I'll leave you to hold down the fort. The materials you need to prep the prisoner for transfer will be here shortly. You know what to do."

"*Da, khorosho.*"

Chapter Thirty-Eight

A short dark-haired woman paced nervously along the side of a runway waiting for a plane to land.

A man in a business suit walked up to her and informed her, "They'll soon be here to pick you up and take you to Moscow, Angelina."

She stopped, spit on the ground and spoke through clenched teeth, "I'd rather stay here and kill that ublyudok who pulled out my molars. I'm not like Borya. I refused the poison suicide pill."

The man consoled her, "You'll have your chance in the future, but for now your description is out and they are scouring the airports and train stations looking for you."

Angelina took a deep breath and tapped her fist on her chest. She declared, "I'm grateful that you didn't kill me when you killed Borya."

The man shrugged and waved his hand dismissively. He disclosed, "I had no reason to keep him alive. I did owe you for saving my life two years ago. Now we are even."

"*Spasibo*. We are even. And I will find that large bastard and even the score with him, no matter how many years it takes me to do so," Angelina vowed.

***

The secure desk phone rang shrilly. James glanced at the caller ID and held up his hand, stopping Henry in midsentence. "I need to take this," he uttered, picking up the receiver.

Henry stood and inquired, "Shall I leave?"

"Yes, please. Come back in five," James ordered.

Henry scampered out the door.

James answered his phone call, "Yes. I'm alone now, Ed. It's safe to talk…"

Ed filled James in on the status of the team, "We've found Yuri and Anatoly."

James frowned, pausing in mid swing in his desk chair. He asked apprehensively, "No! Really? Are Yuri and Anatoly alive and okay?"

Ed's answer filled him with relief, "No, not really. Yuri has serious mental deficits from being in the water too long. And Anatoly's hand is disabled."

James focused to keep his joy from reflecting in his voice as he replied, "Tut, tut. Poor Yuri. So we've lost two more agents? Bollocks. Who is left? And, where are they now?"

Ed replied, "I have no idea where the rest are. You know Elda never fills me in."

James' smile threatened to break his face in two. Then Ed added, "But I am suspicious Sophia and Elda are back in London." James dropped his smile. He put his feet up on his desk and sat back in his chair, and probed, "Uh huh… Quite. So, Sophia is alive? London? Interesting. What do you think they are doing here? Do you have any information you can give me to help me locate them?"

Ed responded, "I wish I could, but that's all I have. I'd appreciate it if you can find them for me."

James swung his feet down off his desk, spun in his chair and looked out his bulletproof window at his view of the River Thames. "Right. We'll be on the lookout for them. Please let me know if you get any further traces of their whereabouts." He spun back to his desk smiling, then buzzed down to Henry's department, leaving a message that Henry could come back up to finish their meeting. He tapped his pen on his desk blotter and muttered, "This little piggy went to market… I've always fancied ham."

***

417

Henry and Arabella were crammed into the small closet sized room in the bowels of MI6. Henry said in a soft voice, "Basically they are down to Sophia, Elda, Tosh and Stas, if we have all the current information right. Stas is not an operative and Tosh is an old man. I doubt they can harm the operation in any way, so not to worry if we don't get them. Elda and Sophia are thought to be in London. We have no more operatives left here, Arabella, so it will be up to you and me to take them out. We'll need to at least get rid of Sophia. I think eliminating her and leaving her entire team in broken remnants will take the wind out of Elda's sails. Can you use a gun?"

"Yes, Henry, I can shoot rather accurately too," Arabella declared.

Henry responded, "Good. Now look for any signs of them. Check airport video feeds, traffic cameras, underground cameras, and anything else you have access to. Run facial recognition for all four of them in case Ed's information is incomplete."

Arabella asked, "If I fail to find them?"

Henry sighed and scratched the back of his neck. He muttered, "In that case, we are both obsolete. Find them."

***

Ed pushed back his chair in his tiny DC office. Standing up and stretching he looked out his window at the daily traffic jam. He wondered where the team really was. He wistfully looked at the cars below and fantasized that they were all down there in a van waiting for traffic to move. Frustrated from the lack of reports and information, he took his Samsung Convoy 4 burner flip phone out of his pocket and pressed a, by now, familiar key sequence.

He was pleased that Elda picked up. He spoke rapidly, but was careful to not speak any words that would trigger a trace. "Operation *Dezinformatsiya* is on. Over to you guys now. You know they will check the feeds?"

"Of course," Elda replied.

Ed acknowledged that Elda had it under control, "No problem? All handled? Great. I assume you are not really gone over the pond?"

"That's for me to know and you to find out," quipped Elda.

Ed rolled his eyes at Elda's answer. "Yes, yes, I know. That would be telling. Good luck." He flipped his phone closed.

Ed sighed and looked at his phone for a few moments before placing it back in his pocket. He kicked his trash can and then retrieved it and cleaned up the litter. He hated it when she went solo. Despite his confidence in Elda's abilities, he took a moment to bow his head and say a short prayer.

Yuri twisted his head to one side. He pouted, "*Moy Bog*! I can't see a thing."

Elda gently turned his chin back into position and requested, "Yuri, it's only a tiny light. Sit still so the doctor can finish examining you."

Yuri blinked his eyes and glared at Elda, but sat forward on the apartment's living room couch and let the psychiatrist shine his light in Yuri's other eye. Tosh stood nearby, observing the interactions between Elda and Dan.

The doctor finished his exam and informed Elda and Tosh, "Excellent. There are no signs of neurological impairment. His oral and written tests are also solid. I see no reason for concern."

Elda shook the doctor's hand and commented, "Thanks, Dan. I appreciate you coming out here on such short notice."

Dan the doctor smiled at Elda and said, "Any time for you, Elda. I miss working with you."

Elda returned his smile with a warm one of her own. She added, "I miss working with you too, Dan. Now to our other issue. Here are the court orders for the patient to spend 30 days inpatient. Anatoly will help you transport him to the Psychiatric Institute of Washington since his psychosis at times tends to violence. We have had to subdue him and he's strongly medicated."

The doctor reviewed the papers Elda had handed him and inquired, "Will we need to extend his stay at all?"

Elda shook her head and declared, "No, I'm pretty sure with the rate things are going here that 30 days should be fine."

Just then Anatoly came out of the back bedroom supporting a wobbly, drooling prisoner.

Elda signed the admission form and then handed the last bit of paperwork to Dan, who co-signed and said, "Thank you Dr. *Ulrich*. It's always a pleasure doing business with you.

Elda winked, "My credentials will hold up."

Dan chuckled and observed, "I expect they will. Did you get all the information you need from him, Elda, or shall I get more?"

"We're all good there, Dan. Thanks for offering. Just don't let him contact the outside during his stay," Elda instructed, moving over to one side to let Dan escort the prisoner out.

Dan gave Elda the thumbs up, "Don't worry. He'll be in lockdown with the other psychotic patients. No one will know where he is."

"Perfect," Elda acknowledged.

***

Henry leaned over Arabella's desk while she searched the feeds. She turned slightly and glared at him and sneered, "I could do this better if you let me work."

Henry growled back at her, "This is my number one priority right now. Put up with it."

Arabella sighed and went back to work. A few minutes later she said in a low voice, "I have them."

"Where are they?" Henry demanded.

"Definitely in London. I got a hit off of the Heathrow feed and this woman here matches with Sophia." Arabella tilted her monitor so Henry could see better.

"Are you sure?" he asked.

She pointed at her screen and explained, "Yes, look at the number of points that match. It's an extremely high probability."

Henry shook his head and admitted, "It's all confusing to me. I'll take your word for it. And Elda?"

422

"She's harder to spot, but," Arabella said, referencing her computer again, "I think this hooded person in Victoria Station may be Elda. I'll have to pull more feeds to see if I can get a better shot of her face. These are both from today."

Henry squinted and leaned in towards the screen. He postulated, "That one doesn't look at all like Elda."

Arabella agreed, "I know. The height is off by an inch, but she could have done that with inserts or special hidden lifts. It's unclear if that person is a small man or a female, but I'm chasing down all the leads that don't match to someone else. The hood hides a lot of the face but that could be deliberately done too."

Henry pursed his lips and clenched his fists. He exclaimed, "Drat, I wish we had more resources to tail the Sophia one. Keep me posted. Let's keep this information to ourselves as far as MI6 is concerned right now. But do let *him* know what we have found out. They have to light somewhere. Then we can get them."

Arabella put forward, "If that is Sophia, then she is bound to show up at one of the places we know to be associated with her, especially her apartment. Sophia's records don't show her to be extremely creative as an operative."

"I hope you're right. I'll let you get back to it," Henry offered, turning to leave.

Already typing quickly, Arabella absently nodded and continued searching the feeds. Henry strolled away humming to himself. Once he was out of sight, Arabella unlocked her bottom desk drawer and took out her Mountainsmith Tour bum bag. She peeked inside, nodded her satisfaction and snapped it around her waist.

***

"Can't you at least keep the coffee table clean?" Sophia complained gesturing at the table.

Stas looked up from his computer screen and glanced at the littered candy bar wrappers and empty coffee cups that were strewn across the wooden coffee table. He shook his head and explained, "*Nyet*, I need to keep my concentration. The wastebasket is too far away."

Sophia stomped into the kitchen and brought back a small metal wastebasket and started cleaning the table, tossing anything her hands touched. She reached out and picked up Stas' laptop.

Stas screamed, "*Nyet*!" and held out his hands for his precious computer.

Sophia laughed at the look of abject horror on Stas' face and put his laptop gently back down and placed his hands back onto the keyboard. "Let me get you something decent to eat. You can't keep going on that junk." She strolled back into the kitchen and began pulling food out of the refrigerator and clanging pans.

Yuri came lumbering out of one of the bedrooms. "Food?" he asked. His face was lit up, anticipating of a good meal.

"Yes, now bugger off so I can cook," Sophia ordered, shaking a frying pan at him.

Yuri sat heavily on the couch next to Stas. "How's it going, Stas? Found anything yet?"

"It's almost impossible to work under these conditions," Stas pouted.

"I know food and companionship. How horrible," Yuri said, giving Stas a half hug.

Stas grinned and then pointed at his screen. "Can you wake Jackson up? I've been analyzing the prisoner's emails and cross checking them with other data I've found and I think I may have discovered something, but I need to bounce this off of his brain."

"Da." Yuri bounced away, strode back into the bedroom and pounced on Jackson. "Wake up you sloth!"

"Argh! This is like living in a zoo," Jackson complained.

"Stas has something to show you," Yuri said, getting up and walking back into the living room.

"Tell him I'll be right there," grumbled Jackson, rubbing the sleep out of his eyes and searching for his glasses.

Jackson stumbled out of the bedroom wearing a black and white checkered robe. Sophia walked up to him and held out a cup of coffee.

Jackson took the cup and breathed deeply to inhale the odor. He smiled and took a sip. "Thank you. Just what the doctor ordered."

Sophia looked Jackson up and down and grimaced. "Where *did* you get that robe?" she wondered out loud.

Jackson looked down at his robe and put his arms protectively around his waist. "I *borrowed* it from Tosh. I liked it AND he told me that I could keep it," he explained.

Sophia shook her head and exclaimed, "Blimey!"

Jackson ignored her comment and sat next to Stas. He asked Stas, "What do you have?"

Stas excitedly explained to Jackson, "Before I forget, they did take our bait. We have confirmed the mole at MI6 and traced it to the Kremlin. Now, let me show you the trail that I have found. I think it is cohesive, and if so, I know where they may try the attack."

***

Arabella grabbed her office phone and dialed Henry's extension. He immediately picked up. "Can you wander over here? I think I have where they are staying."

Henry jumped up from his desk, knocking over his chair. He left it there, ran down the stairs and jogged heavily over to Arabella's station. Once there he inquired, "What do you have?"

Arabella told him, "It looks as if they are staying at Sophia and Oliver's apartment. The alarm that we had left on the door has been triggered."

Henry clapped his hands and pointed to the door, proclaiming, "Let's go."

Arabella held out a hand to stop him and asked, "Now, Henry? What's your plan?"

Henry filled her in, "We'll each sign out a gun from the armory to go to target practice. Instead we head over to the apartment. I know that the keys to all local employee's abodes are kept here in case of an emergency. You distract the desk clerk while I lift the keys to the apartment. We let ourselves in and start blasting before they have a chance to react."

Arabella frowned, paused, and asked, "And then?"

Henry explained the rest of his plan, "We lift the weapons from the bodies, and fire their guns as if they were firing on us. You shoot me in the leg. You said you were a good shot, so please make it just a graze. Then we wipe the grips and triggers and put the guns back in their hands. Our story is that we went there to check on the alarm system, since it had triggered, and they started shooting at us and we returned the fire. Elda's known to be a rogue warrior and Sophia has been distraught about Oliver. We can spin it as they were both rather unhinged and you can plant an electronic trail that backs that story up."

Arabella stared at Henry for a moment and then nodded her head. "Surprisingly good, Henry. Yes, yes, that could work. Fine. Give me an hour to straighten up some things and plant the information. Then I'll text you and we'll go get those keys."

***

Tosh and Elda sat in the DC apartment on the couch with Stas, staring at the computer screen. "Perhaps we can blink on alternate minutes? My eyes are killing me from staring at this screen."

428

Tosh chuckled. He reached into his pocket and took out a small bottle of Visine and passed it to Elda.

She held out the bottle and checked the label. "You travel with a bottle of Visine in your pocket?" she inquired.

Tosh shrugged.

Elda tilted back her head and put a drop in each eye. "I hope this really is Visine."

Tosh shrugged again.

Elda looked at him with apprehension in her face.

He reassured her, "*Ne bespokoysya, eto.*"

"Whew." She blinked rapidly and grabbed a pink Kleenex from the large yellow and gray box on the coffee table. Just then Henry and Arabella came into the camera's view.

"Who is she?" Elda inquired, blotting her eyes again.

Stas ran a quick facial recognition on her and answered, "Her name is Arabella Johnson and she works for Henry in MI6 communication. She's the deep plant."

"Ah." Elda held the tissue to her nose and sneezed.

Tosh spoke into his microphone. "Stand by. Wait until we know for sure their intention."

Arabella crouched at the door, out of view of the spyhole, and inserted the key while Henry stood to one side, gun in his hand. She opened the door and they jumped in firing and immediately stopped.

"Bloody hell! There's no one here!" Arabella exclaimed. She twirled around and ran back down the hallway just before a man in black fatigues took Henry down. A second soldier ran after her. He soon returned panting and spoke into his comms, "Sir, I lost her – she had a motorcycle parked outside and was gone in a flash.

The man listened in his earpiece to his instructions from Tosh and then commanded, "Take him to James."

Chapter Thirty-Nine

Anatoly asked, "Can we engage at will or do we have to wait for orders?"

Tosh, Elda, Anatoly and Yuri gathered together in the living room. Elda took charge. "Downtown DC is a densely populated area. There will be many tourists around. You are all pros. I expect you to use your best judgement. Kill, evade or capture as you see fit. Let's try to coordinate as a team when we can. What are you bringing for weapons?"

"I have my favorite knives. Thank you, Elda, for the new ones," answered Anatoly showing the throwing knife that was secreted up his sleeve, and another attached to his belt and hanging inside his pants, and a third in his sock. "And I am bringing my MSS Vul silent." He opened his jacket to flash a sliver squat gun nestled in his leather under arm holster. He straightened a tie that was loosely hanging around his neck.

Elda gave him a thumbs up. "And, I see you have another weapon just in case too, Anatoly. Good." She then turned to Yuri, asking, "Are you bringing a weapon, Yuri?"

Yuri grimaced and held out his weapon, explaining, "Although I dislike guns, I am carrying a small pistol. These folks deserve no mercy. Thanks to Tosh insisting that I get extra target practice, I am now a reasonable shot."

Anatoly corrected him, "Reasonable? No, I'd say you are good."

"*Spasibo*, Anatoly," Yuri said, with a smile.

"Tosh?" Elda inquired.

"I have a Vityaz-SN submachine gun in my backpack that Anatoly can grab easily in an emergency. He's a master at that weapon. And a PSM pistol as a sidearm in my back holster." Tosh pulled out an angular looking gun and then replaced it. "Plus I have my OBS-3 survival knife in my pocket."

Elda raised her eyebrows and quipped, "Remind me to stay on your good side. That OBS-3 always reminds me of a large version of a Swiss Army Knife."

Tosh replied, "And you, Elda?"

"I have my Ontario 6141 MK 3 Navy Knife in a sheath under my jacket, as well as my new favorite pistol, thanks to Anatoly." Elda opened her jacket to show the M&P 380 SHIELD EZ pistol in a shoulder holster. Anatoly wolf whistled.

Elda gave Anatoly a wink and went on, "OK. Here's the plan. We are going to go scout out DC, especially the area around the White House, so we can be intimately familiar with it, and also, with possible areas where the attackers could come from. We will take the metro to the Smithsonian Institution Offices. We will walk up 7th St NW so we can survey the National Mall, and cut over on Madison Dr NW to 15th St. NW to the White House. If anyone gets cut off or lost, we will reconvene at the International Spy Museum. I figure *that* should be easy for us all to remember. Here are your maps so we can hopefully look like a tour group wandering around. Ready?"

They answered in a chorus: "*Da*."

Elda ordered, "Head out."

***

The heavily armed tour group ambled along taking pictures, following the few routes the President had taken within DC. Their surveillance didn't take long. Mostly he had left from the White House lawn by helicopter.

They stood across the street in front of the White House, chatting, pointing and taking photos.

Elda pointed with her nose to her right. "Tosh, look at that group of soldiers heading our way."

Tosh looked in that direction. "Interesting… They walk like Russian soldiers, but they are dressed like American Army troops. I don't see any insignia, however. Yuri, just in case, take my backpack. They are carrying bags and probably have weapons." Tosh passed Yuri his backpack.

Elda held up her hand. "We can't have a shoot out here, Tosh. The Secret Service would be on us in a jiffy. Also, look at how many tourists are around here."

"*Khorosho. Ostupat?*" Tosh requested.

"Yes, retreat slowly and stay in character as a casual group of tourists, for as long as we can," Elda directed.

As they strolled away, Elda checked over her shoulder and spotted one of the soldiers looking down at his phone. He tapped another on his shoulder and gestured in the direction of Elda's team.

Elda observed, "Uh oh, we may have been identified. Let's pick up the pace a notch." She started walking more quickly and the group kept pace with her.

They strode quickly to the Mall. Tosh turned and observed that the squad behind them had formed up and were now marching in double time.

"They are definitely on to us. *Idti, idti, idti*!" Tosh commanded.

The four of them started running, weaving their way around tourists. The soldiers kept pace with them.

"Where are we going, Elda?" inquired Tosh. "Perhaps we should split up? Divide and conquer?"

"Yeah, that strategy hasn't served us well in the past, has it?" Elda sneered and suggested, "I think we should stay together. Strength in numbers and all that rot. Seriously. We don't want to get picked off one by one. We're heading to the Spy Museum. It has a number of displays we can use as shields and there are fewer people in there than the other museums."

"I don't like this being chased by a mob of soldiers. Missions should be clean and targeted. This new generation is far too messy and noisy at what they do. There's an art to being a spy. Sneak in, accomplish your objective, and, if needed, kill efficiently and quietly, dump the body, leave no trace," Tosh complained.

"I totally agree with you, Tosh, on that one. Team, let's go full speed to the Spy Museum," Elda directed.

The team accelerated to a full run, weaving around tourists, on their way to the museum. Behind them they heard curses from the following squad cutting off tourists.

"In here." Elda ordered, taking a sharp left, pulling Tosh along. She ducked into the Spy Museum. Anatoly and Yuri were right behind. Footsteps echoed in the stairwell as they pounded up the stairs. They paused halfway up and listened. All was quiet behind them. They continued on up to the 5th floor and entered a room with glass display cases.

Passing a display case with brass knuckles in it, Anatoly smashed the case and grabbed them.

Elda turned and scowled at him.

Anatoly commented, "What? Did you want me to grab you the rectal tool kit?"

"Shithead. This is NOT a shopping spree. Try not to destroy the place too badly, Anatoly. It's one of my favorite museums," Elda grumbled.

Anatoly shrugged and pocketed the brass knuckles.

Elda stopped and pointed ahead of her position. "Duck behind that display, Anatoly. If they come up the other way, we will try to lead them to you. Yuri, see if that door over there leads to a secret passageway in the ceiling, where you might be able to see down and pick off a soldier or two with your pistol. It's a bit like the modern-day version of the Vasari Corridor, Tosh."

Anatoly hunkered down behind one of the displays with his machine gun braced against his shoulder. Tosh walked back to the doorway and motioned for him to tuck in just a tad more.

Yuri opened the door that Elda had indicated and stepped in, closing the door behind him. Elda could hear his footsteps as he traversed the walkway to find a peephole. The sound stopped, indicating that Yuri was in position.

Elda motioned for Tosh to come over to her. She was standing at a kiosk that displayed a map of the museum. "There is only one set of staircases in and out."

Tosh nodded, "There is also the emergency exits, but to get to us here, they would have to come into this room by one of three ways, and we have Anatoly and Yuri positioned well to cover that."

Elda pointed at the Briefing Center. "I've been in this room before. The lighting is disorientating. And there is only one way in and out."

"Excellent," Tosh commented, "We can go in there, get acclimated to the lighting and choke point them in there."

Elda added, "Or be trapped…"

***

Tosh and Elda dashed into the briefing center. Their eyes quickly adjusted to the dark of the room, which was punctuated by glowing areas of red and blue lighting. They motioned to each other and smoothly split off to position themselves on opposite sides of the room so they could see in either direction.

"Comm check," whispered Tosh.

One click. "Okay, Anatoly."

Two clicks. "Okay, Yuri."

Elda added her three clicks. Tosh clicked four times.

"Okay. All comms okay," observed Elda, giving the thumbs up to Tosh.

Soon, they heard the sound of army boots clomping up the staircase and voices talking in Russian.

Then silence.

They waited.

Elda's comms clicked twice. Anatoly had them in his sights.

A man in green, brown and white camouflage poked his head into the briefing room to be rewarded by a bullet hole in his forehead and blood streaking down his face, as he fell over dead. Elda gave Tosh two thumbs up for his shooting, then signaled for him to leave with her.

Tosh and Elda sprinted from the room. Shots rang out and shards of glass from the overhead monitors sprayed down on them as they ran. They zigged and zagged and rolled across the floor to evade the bullets. A bullet zinged pass by Elda's head and hit the soldier behind her. "Thanks Yuri!" she shouted at the ceiling.

Elda and Tosh ran past Anatoly and positioned themselves back to back, guns covering both directions.

Silence.

"That was only two of them," Elda muttered to Tosh. She felt his head nod in response.

They waited.

***

Another camouflaged man skidded into the room, firing his submachine gun. His head exploded, peppered by bullets from Anatoly. Anatoly stopped shooting.

The sound of footsteps retreating down the stairs filled the silence.

Tosh yelled, "*Idti*! After them."

The three threw themselves after the assailants. They stopped in the stairwell to listen. Nothing.

Elda whispered, "We're on the 5th floor, Tosh. We should still hear footsteps."

In hushed tones Tosh suggested, "Let's go to the 4th floor. It also has exhibits so they could be in there."

Having found the way out of the ceiling area, Yuri joined them in the stairwell. The four of them quietly crept down the stairs with their guns ready.

Tosh motioned for Yuri and Anatoly to go through the exhibits backwards, while he and Elda went toward the rotunda. He whispered to Elda, "There are six rooms off of this circular room, all to the right of us." Elda felt grateful for Tosh's photographic memory. One glance at the map, and he had the entire floorplan in his brain. They hugged the wall, as they slowly and silently walked forward.

Suddenly a man jumped out of the *License to Thrill* room, firing at them. Tosh pulled Elda into the *Why Spy? Theater*. He motioned for her to cover the exit door of the room while he stood at the entrance.

Elda dropped to the floor and waited.

Tosh threw himself out the door onto the hallway floor and killed the approaching soldier.

Elda spotted another man jumping out from the doorway of the *Top Secret* room and cut him down with two shots to his legs. As the soldier reached for his gun, she put another round into his head. "Damn, I was hoping we'd be able to take prisoners."

Again silence.

They waited. Hearing nothing, they continued along the diameter of the circle, each one taking alternate rooms to check. When they met at the exit from this part of the exhibit, they positioned themselves on either side of the doorway to *An Uncertain World*.

Suddenly they heard firing from within and dashed in and nearly mowed down Anatoly and Yuri coming the other way.

Elda stated, "We got two more. And you?"

"We also got two," Anatoly offered, smiling.

Elda nodded her approval. She observed, "There are more...," and added, "Dead?"

Anatoly raised an eyebrow and smirked at Elda's question, then answered, "Yes."

Tosh spoke up, "There are two ways to get to the exit, both of which go through the museum store. We will split up at the Debriefing Room and meet again in the Lobby."

They all checked their ammunition and readied their weapons.

Tosh motioned them on, "*Itdi*."

***

Anatoly jumped over the railing near the bottom of each flight to speed his descent. Yuri ran down the stairs behind him.

Tosh and Elda took a more controlled descent, checking the doors of each level to ensure no one was hiding there.

As Anatoly jumped to the last level, he summmersaulted over the blue and silver metal railing and landed on his feet, rapidly firing at the man hiding behind a rack of clothing. Yuri stopped in a crouch halfway down the last flight of stairs and returned fire with a second man behind a shelved display. Splinters of composite wood flew into the air with plastic and metal pieces of souvenirs.

Three more men escaped from their hiding places and ran out the door.

Joined by Tosh and Elda, the four of them flew out the open door of the museum and Skidded to a stop as they viewed the soldiers hightailing it away.

"We can't catch them," Elda observed, continuing, "Let's get out of here. I'll call Ed to have him straighten it out with the museum and clean up the mess."

"I so had my eyes on the courier shoes," deadpanned Tosh. "Seriously, Elda, there was a lot of good stuff in there. I remember a lot of it well. Do you think we could have MI6 make some modern-day equivalents of some of these devices?"

"Good idea, Tosh. I'd rather enjoy a flashlight pistol," Elda remarked, pantomiming shooting with her right hand's index finger.

"I would have thought you would like the lipstick pistol," quipped Tosh.

Elda slapped him on the arm. "You would look absolutely dashing with the tobacco pipe pistol," she retorted.

"I know." Tosh put the pipe in his mouth and then gestured dramatically with it.

"You didn't!" Elda rebuked, fighting the grin threatening to reach the corners of her mouth.

Tosh winked at Elda.

She sighed and motioned up the street. "Let's get out of here before the police nab you as a common thief."

"Common?!" exclaimed Tosh. He turned and addressed Yuri and Anatoly, "*Idti! Seychas*!"

Chapter Forty

Elda, followed by Tosh, emerged from the passageway that connected the two apartments. "Gads, do the windows open in here?" Elda held her thumb and forefinger on either side of her nose.

Stas and Jackson looked blearily up from the computer screen. Jackson threw a candy wrapper at Elda.

The table was again littered with candy wrappers, joined by a number of empty coffee and tea cups. Yuri had his shoes off and feet up and was watching TV. Sophia was back in the other apartment tending to Oliver. The living room had the aroma of a locker room.

Elda coughed and reprimanded the three men, "Seriously, you guys need to wash your socks and to shower."

Yuri took his feet off the hassock, removed a sock and sniffed it. "*Lisus*! You're right, Elda." He removed the other sock and padded off to the kitchen.

Elda yelled after him, "Not in the kitchen sink, Yuri. Wash them in the bathroom sink!"

"*Da*, Elda." Yuri reversed direction into the bathroom.

"Stas, Jackson, anything before I send you two to the showers?" Elda inquired.

Jackson spoke up, "Yes, actually. We think we have pieced together a location where they are going to make their attempt on the American president." Jackson turned the screen to Elda and Tosh and started pointing at lines of code running in one window. "Stas wrote a simplistic AI algorithm that matched…"

Tosh cut him off. "*Chert*. Jackson, *enough*. Just cut to the chase and tell us where and when."

Jackson looked disappointed that neither Elda nor Tosh seemed interested in his discussion of how he and Stas had connected the various pieces of the information, and sighed heavily.

Elda quickly jumped in to mollify him, "I'm sure that you and Stas did some wonderful things finding this and connecting the dots. But that's why you're both here. You're two of the best at doing that type of work. So please tell Tosh and myself the conclusion about what you have found."

Jackson puffed up slightly and nodded. "We believe it will be next week, here in DC. There is an interfaith council meeting with the president in the Oval Office. We suspect that one or more of the religious men in that group is an assassin."

"See, that wasn't hard, was it?" sneered Tosh.

Elda reached out to put her hand on Tosh's arm. "It's been a long road for all of us here. We need to be gentle on each other for now. Okay, Tosh?"

"Yes, Elda. You're so right. My apologies, Jackson." Tosh snarked, patting Elda's hand.

"No harm done, Tosh." Jackson held out his hand for Tosh to shake.

Tosh slapped it away. "*Bog*! When did we all get so touchy-feelie and civilized? Enough. Let's get down to business."

"Okay, Tosh. So how do we get ourselves invited to that interfaith council?" asked Elda.

Tosh raised his forefinger upwards and exclaimed, "*Aga*! Leave that one to me."

"You, Tosh? I never took you for the religious type."

"I am full of surprises, Elda."

"Ah yes, yes you are, Tosh."

***

446

Tosh marched into the apartment and dumped two garment bags onto the couch. He glanced at Sophia and Oliver making out in the living room recliner. "Can't you two stay off each other for a moment?"

Sophia removed her lips from Oliver's for just long enough to say, "I nearly lost him. I'm going to enjoy every moment I have him around. After all, we're still newlyweds."

Tosh sighed heavily and threw up a hand in Elda's direction.

"Don't look at me, Tosh. I'm not the morals police."

Tosh shook his head, opened a garment bag and threw two long brown robes at Anatoly.

"I think these are large enough. I need you and Yuri to try these on." He reached into the bag again and extracted two pairs of leather sandals. "And these too."

Snezhana looked up expectantly. Tosh shook his head. "No, Snezhana. I need someone here who can guard this sorry lot. Sophia and Oliver seem to be locked together at the lips. And you are too gimpy still. It will only draw attention to us." Snezhana appeared downcast, but nodded and went back to her book. Sophia threw Tosh a finger.

Anatoly walked out of the bedroom in his monk's outfit. "Like this *duratskiy* outfit won't draw attention to us?"

Tosh looked him up and down. "Good. Once we shave the middle of your head you will look perfect."

Anatoly recoiled and held his hands to the sides of his head. "*Chto*?! I like my hair."

Tosh responded, "Too bad. It will grow back. Call Yuri and have him pop over to try on his outfit."

"Ah, the pleasure of seeing him wiggle his way through that passageway is cheering me up already." Anatoly picked up his phone and texted Yuri to come over. "May I shave his head?"

"*Nyet*. I will take care of both your haircuts." Tosh unzipped the other garment bag and threw an orange robe and sandals at Elda.

She looked at it and smiled. "Good thing I like very short hair," and went into the bedroom to change. An orange flash slipped from the bedroom into the bathroom. The sounds of a shaver filled the room.

Tosh pointed at the bathroom door. "See, Anatoly. Elda realizes what we need to do."

Anatoly clasped his hands on top of his head. "*Der'mo.*"

***

"Where is she?" Agitated, Ed booted up his laptop and scanned his messages for something from Elda. He muttered to himself as he typed, "Damn that woman. If she weren't such a good operative, I'd have her hide. The life of the President of the United States is on the line here. She should keep me *somewhat* in the loop."

He threw a wadded-up piece of paper into the small basketball hoop hanging over the wastebasket and watched as it bounced off the rim onto the floor. He continued to berate himself, "But you ninny, Ed. You are the one that told her to trust no one. But she knows me. We've worked together for many years and are friends. I do not want to have to tell Dawn that her wife has been killed in action."

He crumpled up another piece of printer paper and threw that one after the first. "Damn, I'm a bad shot today." He stomped over and picked up both pieces of paper and threw them into the wastebasket. Twirling, he grabbed his cup of coffee and gulped the rest of it down. "Not like I need any more caffeine right now." A phone ringing in his desk drawer made him jump. He ran to pick it up.

"Where on earth are you? Okay, okay, I know that's the wrong question to ask you. But I'm your boss. Help me here." He sighed and listened to Elda laugh, "Did you miss the wastebasket again?"

He smirked and answered, "Yes, I missed the wastebasket, as usual." Calmer, he sat down at his desk chair, swiveled to look out the window, and listened intently.

Elda explained, "We need backup but I don't want the assassins to be tipped off."

Ed reassured her, "No, Elda, I will not alert the Secret Service. We are suspicious that they have a mole there too. Plus, it will only spook the assassin and they will try again, and we may not know when or where. However, we both have trusted contacts within the Secret Service. I'll see who will be on duty that day and arrange to have those we know and trust alerted."

He waited as Elda mentioned, "You know this is the only real opportunity we have to get the assassins." He responded, "I agree this is the best shot we have. I will also have a hand-picked SWAT team ready to go at a moment's notice. They will be outside and our Secret Service agents can cover him on the inside."

He listened again and started laughing as Elda said, "We will be disguised as A Hassidic Jew, a Buddhist monk, two Catholic priests." Tears ran down his cheeks. "A Hassidic Jew, a Buddhist monk, two Catholic priests? It sounds like the beginning of a bad joke. Oh, I definitely wish I could see that one! Are you sure that lightening won't strike all of you?"

There was silence on the other end of the phone. Ed checked to ensure they were still connected. "Elda?" Her voice echoed in the phone and in the air. He swiveled his chair around to see Elda standing there.

***

Tosh sat on the couch next to Snezhana. She glanced up at him from her book and asked, "May I speak to you as my uncle?"

Tosh's face softened, "I would like that. We haven't had that opportunity for a long time."

Snezhana put her book down and turned towards Tosh, explaining, "I have always wanted to be like you. I'm so afraid that instead I do nothing but disappoint you."

Tosh reached out and held her hand. "Niece, when you were young, I thought, oh dear, this poor one is going to be like me. And, you *have* been like me all of your life. I've tried to clear the path for you at times, but you had to find your own way, just as I did."

Snezhana removed her hand from his and sat up straighter. "But I have made so many mistakes. Are you

451

really sidelining me because I'm injured or are you going to remove me from the team?"

Tosh chuckled, "Snezhana, do you think that I haven't made my own mistakes? I have screwed up royally in my time. I just didn't have someone watching me as closely as you do. You have learned from your mistakes. I'd like to say don't worry, but it is part of your DNA to fret, and, it's what will make you improve and be even better than I am." He patted her hand and stood up. "Now I must assume my professional veneer again. For your information, I am not removing you from the team. However, I am not reactivating you until you are in tip top condition, because less than that puts us all in danger."

Snezhana sighed in relief. "Yes, sir.'"

***

Elda slipped down her hoodie and removed her baseball cap, revealing her shaved head. "Hello Ed."

Ed looked at Elda quizzically, but was used to seeing her in different guises. "Hello Elda. I gather you're the monk? What brings you here today?"

Elda rubbed her head, and explained, "I really only needed to see an old friend. And that gave me the excuse to fill you in face to face. Shall we take a walk, so I'm not discovered here?"

Ed looked at Elda standing there biting the sides of her fingers. With her shaved head, she looked smaller and more vulnerable. "Let me grab a hat to blend in better."

Elda, in t-shirt, hoodie, jeans and sneakers, slowly glanced up and down, scanning Ed's apparel. "Really Ed. Take a good hard look at us."

Ed looked down at his shiny Corfam shoes, sharply pleated and pressed slacks, and reached up to feel his starched button up white shirt and tie. "Oh. I see. I have sneakers!"

He ran around his desk and kicked off his shoes and put on a pair of light gray sneakers. He then removed his tie and unbuttoned the top button of his shirt.

Elda laughed, "Let's go wild man."

The two friends and co-workers strolled along side roads. Ed waited. Elda spoke first, "I once asked you, Ed, if anything happened to me, for you to ensure that Dawn is taken care of."

"Yes, and I assured you I would take good care of her."

Elda turned and looked at Ed imploringly and placed her hand on his arm. "Can you also tell her why I do this?"

Ed stared at Elda in dismay. "It's hard enough for me to explain why *I* do it, Elda. What would you like her to hear?"

They continued walking, while Elda thought out her response. Finally she replied, "That I love her more than anything and, that she, and Vee, and the cats, are my family. Tell her it's not anything to do with her why I had to do this. It's all me. I never could trust anyone in my life and this job suits that part of me so well. It gives me focus, purpose and meaning. It uses all of who I am. And I'm with others like me. Others who have been broken by something early in life. I have done it for so long that I don't know who I am without it. Just as I need her in my life, I need this."

They walked along for a bit. Ed stopped and asked, "Do you fear losing her?"

Elda motioned for them to continue walking and replied, "Yes, I do Ed. I would hate for that to ever happen. But most of all, I fear losing me."

"Have you ever told her that?"

Elda stopped, turn to Ed and held out her hands palms up. She implored, "How do you say that to someone who hasn't seen what we have done and what we have seen… someone who hasn't been marred by life?"

"I understand." This time it was Ed who moved them forward.

Elda walked with her head bowed and her eyes looking down at the ground. "I know. That's why I am asking you to do this, if I don't make it back home."

Ed stopped and held out his arm to stop Elda. His eyes searched hers, as he beseeched, "Tell me what worries you about this mission."

Elda sighed deeply and responded, "I no longer fear Tosh or Anatoly. Sure they are both lethal in their own ways, but for this mission, we are on the same side. But, we are going to be with a lot of people in a small space. We don't know anything about the assassin, or if there are multiple assassins. If there is shooting, some of the Secret Service won't know who we are and will take us out, if they think we are a threat in any way. This entire mission has resulted in injury and deaths. And, all of us are operatives who, except for Yuri, are most comfortable working alone. I don't feel good about this one, Ed."

From where they stood they could see the Potomac River and the bridges over to Georgetown and to the Lincoln Memorial. Ed reached over and put his arm around Elda, holding her close in their years of friendship. "Believe you will succeed my friend. Have no doubt. It's when we doubt that we hesitate and make mistakes. You are one of the best. You will survive and you will tell these things to Dawn in person."

"I hope you are right in that Ed," Elda murmured.

Ed barked, "I didn't hear you."

Elda stood up straighter and snapped out, "You *are* so very right in that, Ed." She saluted him.

Ed returned her salute. "Much better. Now go save the world."

*****

"Hurry up Elda." Tosh was standing by the apartment door motioning her in.

Elda stepped through the front door. Still working on context switching her brain from her heavy conversation with Ed, she stood in confusion. "What? Why?"

Tosh gestured for her to hurry up. "We're in. Come. Let's go get Anatoly and Yuri."

Still rooted by the door Elda stammered, "We're in where, Tosh?"

Tosh grabbed her by the arm. "I'll give all the details when we're assembled." Tosh nudged Elda through the passageway into the other apartment. He motioned to Yuri and Anatoly, who had previously entered the second apartment via the hallway, to sit on the couch with Elda and addressed the team. "You all know that we needed a way to get into the White House. Well, we have it. My rabbi friend has added us to the Interfaith Council for the audience with the President."

Elda joshed, "Your rabbi friend? Your collection of *friends* would make an interesting cocktail party, Tosh."

"I'll invite you someday, Elda. But now, Anatoly and Yuri, it's time for the clippers!"

Anatoly grabbed his head. "*Der'mo.*"

Elda wondered, "Tosh, do we know how many are part of this Interfaith Council?"

"I don't have much information, Elda. I didn't want to tip our hand by asking too many questions."

Elda grimaced and observed, "So basically we'll be going in blind?"

"*Da.*"

Chapter Forty-One

Elda heard the unmistakable click of a magazine being loaded into a gun. She rolled out of bed, grabbing her Smith and Wesson from her bedside table, and landed in a crouch by the door. She silently opened it a crack. The smell of bacon wafted in with the tuneless sound of Anatoly humming. Opening the door fully, she saw Anatoly sitting on the couch methodically cleaning all the guns.

He glanced up at Elda. "Good morning, Elda. Your reflexes are rather slow today. It took you five seconds to open the door."

Elda rolled her eyes and lowered her gun.

Anatoly held out his hand. "If you give me that gun I'll clean it too."

Elda turned the gun around and handed it to Anatoly. "It's loaded."

He nodded, "*Da*. I would expect nothing else."

Elda wandered into the kitchen and took two forks from the drawer and flipped the pieces of bacon. "Don't let it burn. I'm going to grab a quick shower."

Anatoly grunted his affirmation and then went back to cleaning and humming. Elda sprinted for the shower. Five minutes later she was back and dressed. Anatoly had removed the bacon, and was now spooning scrambled eggs into a bowl. The rest of the group, drawn by the smell of bacon were starting to gather. Elda grabbed plates, forks and coffee cups, and lined them up on the counter, with a roll of paper towels set by them. She grabbed a piece of bacon on the way by the pile. Anatoly slapped at her hand. A calm voice came from behind her, "People have been shot for less than that."

Without turning Elda said, "Good morning, Tosh."

Stas and Jackson came through the passageway. Oliver hobbled out of the back bedroom, being helped by Sophia.

Tosh inquired, "Where's Snezhana and Yuri?" Just then his cell phone rang. "Chto? You're behind Yuri? He's stuck?"

Elda jogged into the kitchen and grabbed a can of Crisco off the pantry shelf and disappeared into the passageway. Soon after, she emerged, and right after her, Yuri popped out, with Snezhana pushing him from behind.

"*Chert!*" A Crisco smeared Yuri rubbed the scrape on his shoulder.

Anatoly was shaking with laughter. "I told you to stop doing those daily pushups, Yuri."

Yuri stuck his tongue out at Anatoly, replying, "Yes, Lord and Savior."

Elda put her plate down and pulled out the medical bag to put antiseptic on Yuri's scrape.

Yuri yelled, "*Chert*, Elda! That stings!"

"Sorry Yuri." She returned to her breakfast. Soon all of the bacon had been gobbled up. Elda reached under her plate and pulled out a piece of bacon, taking small bites and making exaggerated sounds and faces as she relished each bite. Nine sets of eyes were following every bite. She finished and mopped her plate with half a slice of toast and sat back with a satisfied look on her face.

Tosh reached under his plate and went through a similar routine. Elda frowned watching him. A long pause followed. Tosh shrugged and did it again.

Elda threw Tosh a finger and declared, "Damn it, Tosh."

"Sometimes you just get bested, Elda," smirked Tosh.

"Yes, but not this time." Elda reached under her plate and took out the last piece of bacon.

"*Touche*," sighed Tosh. Yuri peeked under Tosh's plate and then raised Elda's arm to declare her the winner.

"Now that we're done playing games," growled Tosh, "let's talk about today's operation."

It was a bright and sunny day. Two Franciscan monks, one Buddhist monk and a Hassidic Jew strolled across the National Mall on their way to the White House. They casually chatted with each other.

Elda looked down at Tosh's well shined shoes and remarked, "Hey sticky fingers. Aren't those the courier shoes from the Spy Museum?"

Tosh wiggled his eyebrows and nodded at Elda coyly, "Good eye, Elda. I had wondered where they went to. They still are a perfect fit."

Elda smiled and shook her head. She commented dryly, "I would love to hear *that* story," then added, "We will have to go through an x-ray machine, you know?"

"Yes, no worries," Tosh reassured, "Anatoly, I've noticed you have two sashes holding in your gown…"

Anatoly growled, "It's called a habit, Tosh. And, yes I do. You never know when one will come in handy."

"Are those metal tipped sandals too?" inquired Elda, admiring the black leather and silver rivet combination.

Anatoly smiled, replying, "*Da*. Tough, hey?"

Elda winked and in her best husky contralto joked, "Tremendously tough. I love the rivets. And such a large cross you have dangling there, my boy."

Anatoly winked back at Elda.

"And what are you hiding, Elda?" inquired Tosh.

"Nothing that an x-ray will detect."

***

A man with short dark hair buttoned up his clergy shirt and adjusted his collar. He added a long black jacket and a large gold cross. Lifting his foot onto a nearby chair, he polished his shoe, and then switched to do the other. He adjusted the crease in his black slacks and ensured they hung properly. A Catholic nun, wearing a black and white habit and a beautiful filigreed cross around her neck, walked into the room.

"Ah, there you are sister," he declared. "Are the others ready?"

"Yes," she stated, "They are in the other room."

He motioned to the door. "After you…."

***

Elda held her breath as the team's personal items went one by one through the x-ray machine and each person walked through the body scanner. Anatoly placed his cross in a bucket for separate scanning. The changes they had made to eye color, hair and facial structure had allowed them to defeat the facial recognition scans. Yuri was piously standing waiting his turn.

The guard held up his hand to stop Anatoly from proceeding through. Elda saw Anatoly take a deep breath to calm himself. On the other side of the equipment Tosh took one step forward and stopped from advancing further. The guard fiddled with his controls and then waved to Anatoly for him to step up. Anatoly sauntered through, picked up his cross and rejoined Tosh.

Yuri stepped up next and laid his cross in the plastic bucket. The guard looked at him and then at Anatoly. "Sure wish I had had you two on my high school football team. I think you've picked the wrong vocation." Yuri smiled politely. The guard motioned him forward and through.

Elda came last. The guard looked at her curiously. He turned to his fellow guard and commented, "I do think women should have long hair, don't you Frank?" Frank took off his hat and rubbed his own bald head. The two guards laughed. Elda stood quietly waiting. "Sense of humor must have gone with her hair," muttered the guard and he waved her through. She also successfully passed the scan and joined her team.

Tosh pointed at a Catholic Bishop who was standing to one side. "There he is. Let me introduce you all."

After introductions, the bishop outlined the day's agenda. "We will wait here for the others to join us. Then we will go on a brief White House Tour before our meeting with the president. When it is time, we will be escorted into the Oval Office. I will sit near the president and you all will stand where you are instructed to. I expect there will be a photo done with me beside the president and everyone else in the background."

Tosh inquired, "Is it possible to get a list of each person who is joining us? I would love to be able to keep in touch with them."

The bishop shook his head in the negative. "Unfortunately, I don't have my cell phone in here with me, so I can't access it. But I can send you that list afterwards."

Elda spoke up, "How many of us will there be today?"

The bishop looked upwards as he calculated the answer, "There will be eleven of us total."

"It will be rather crowded in the Oval Office then?" Elda observed.

Tosh added, "Yes, especially when you include the Secret Service agents, who will also be there with us."

Elda rubbed her shaved head, sighed and muttered, "Tight quarters…no comms…" Tosh nodded. The two of them studied the people coming in.

Two nuns and two priests walked in through the White House entrance together. One by one they handed over their crosses and rosary beads and strolled through the metal detectors. Gathering up their metal, they joined the Bishop and the assembled group that had grown to nine members.

The bishop smiled and welcomed the newcomers, "Ah, there you are. We are just waiting for a few more to join us."

Elda sized up the four that had just joined the group and touched her right eyebrow. Tosh looked carefully at each one and touched his right eyebrow. Anatoly took one look, coughed and touched his right eyebrow. Yuri looked puzzled.

Soon they were joined by the last two members of the council. Elda again assessed them and put her index finger up to her left eyebrow. Tosh replied by pointing at his right one. They both agreed that the two Catholic priests and the two nuns were the possible assassins and the last two were harmless.

The interfaith council members were joined by a tour guide and a member of the Secret Service. His eyes widened when he spotted Elda. She narrowed her eyes, glared at him and then motioned with her head that he should follow them. He nodded. Tosh observed the interchange. He raised one eyebrow. Elda touched her right eyebrow and tugged her right ear to signify that he was a friend. Tosh scratched his right eyebrow.

The tour guide started chatting and led them off into the White House.

***

Deep in the Kremlin a hand picked up the receiver of a desk phone and dialed a private number. "Is it on?"

The answer he wanted came faintly through the receiver. "*Da*. They have started the tour. It will be happening in a few hours. All is set."

"You know the price for failure." The hand replaced the receiver onto the phone.

***

"Wait here." The tour guide left to see if the president was ready for his audience with the bishop and his entourage.

The group, having finished their tour, stood quietly waiting to be let into the Oval Office. Elda felt her heart rate leap in anticipation. She noticed Tosh was holding one

466

palm over the other with his fingers on his wrist. Elda was glad to see that he also got pre-show jitters. Anatoly stood impassive and Yuri started fingering his rosary beads. Elda noticed that his strand seemed to be slightly shorter than before, as did Anatoly's. She also noticed that Tosh was now sporting a ring.

Elda reached inside her robe and slid up her sleeve a plastic knife that had been hidden inside her front hem. She glanced over at the two nuns and two priests and saw that their crosses were missing. She cleared her throat and Tosh turned in her direction. She discretely held her right hand to her throat. Tosh touched his right eyebrow.

The bishop stood near the door rocking slightly back and forth. The sounds of habits rustling, small coughs, and nasal breathing filled the expectant silence. The door opened and Elda noticed one of the priests snap to attention.

"OK. Please walk slowly inside where we will wait for the president." The tour guide held the door open. They silently filed into the Oval Office. There was no information as to the timing of the president's arrival.

The group stood awkwardly waiting. Elda twisted her neck to the right and held her hand to it and again to the left. Tosh moved to the right to get into position to cover one of the priests, Anatoly moved backwards and to the left until he was next to one of the nuns. Yuri frowned and his eyes narrowed. He slowly moved into a position where he could best cover the president. The bishop waited, smiling, happily anticipating his audience with the president. The tension in the rest of the room was palatable.

Another door opened. Two secret service members entered, swept the room, and then spoke into their comms. Elda spied her friend from the Secret Service standing armed in the hallway with three others.

The president waddled slowly into the room, followed by another secret service agent. The president looked disappointed at the lack of reception by the press, who were waiting to take pictures of him with the bishop. He stood by his chair and beckoned the bishop to him.

Elda maneuvered to the back of the group to better observe any sudden movement. The bishop warmly greeted the president and was subjected to a hand crushing handshake. The photographers started taking pictures.

At the first click of the camera shutters, the assassins reached into their habits and shirts and ripped away from their bodies the plastic weapons, that had been secured there by Teflon tape and filled with rosary bead bullets from their crosses. They immediately cut down the two Secret Service agents who were rushing to protect the president. The photographer's screams filled the room as people scrambled for cover.

The president reached out and grabbed a female reporter as a shield. She screamed and struggled to get free. He held her tightly in front of himself. A bullet pierced her abdomen and continued through her into the president. They both fell to the ground.

An assassin stormed up and climbed over the bodies to get the president. Yuri shot out his kneecap, felling him on the spot. The remaining Secret Service agent tackled the priest, disarmed him, and cuffed him. Having used his one bullet gun, Yuri was now defenseless. Anatoly threw Yuri his gun as a backup.

Anatoly lassoed one of the nuns around the neck and pulled her close to his body, tightening the noose. He could feel the rise and fall of her breath, the warmth of her body through her habit. She struggled against him, her feet tapping vainly on the ground, as the life force left her. He tenderly lowered her dead body to the ground.

Shots rang out. Tosh grabbed at his arm and his hand came away covered in blood. He leapt forward and managed to lash out with his ring at the face of the second priest, who immediately toppled over dead.

Elda jumped onto the remaining nun, pushing her down to the ground, and stabbed her in the neck with the plastic knife. Blood spurted everywhere. The nun struggled to fight Elda, but she was bleeding out too quickly and soon collapsed. Elda looked down in disgust at her blood covered orange robe. Her artistic sense was offended at how the red color clashed with the orange. Then she realized that not all of the blood came from the nun.

The chaos was over in seconds.

The Secret Service backup team had piled into the room and were yelling for everyone to drop their weapons. Elda, Tosh, Yuri, and Anatoly immediately knelt on the ground with their hands clasped behind their heads. While kneeling, Elda noticed that the president had peed himself.

Elda wobbled on her knees and fell forward on her face.

Chapter Forty-Two

"So, tell me what happened Henry," James requested, with uncharacteristic softness in his voice.

Henry gulped and stood in James' office in as much at attention as the cuffs would allow. He glanced at the two Russians who had captured him.

James, sitting on the edge of his desk, nodded at the guards. "He's safe with me. You can leave him here. It's MI6's problem now." The door clicked shut behind them.

Henry cleared his throat and began, "Well, as we know now, the Russians also had a watch on Sophia's apartment."

James waved his hands dismissively, "Yes, yes, but how did *you* end up there? Do you even *know* how to shoot?"

Henry flinched at James' tone, but continued, "Not well. But Arabella told me she could shoot."

James rolled his eyes and sighed, "Go on…"

Henry drew in a deep breath and continued, "Since we had heard that Sophia was back in town, I had Arabella monitoring the apartment, in case she showed up there. She also was monitoring the computer that Sophia and Oliver had in their apartment. She came to me and told me that someone had entered the apartment and was on the computer, and she would like to go there and access the computer, after whoever it was left."

An aggravated James ran his fingers through his hair. He barked. "I get *that*, but why on *earth* did you two feel the need to have guns?"

Henry went on the offensive. "*You*, of all people, know how many bodies have been found during this operation. Arabella thought we should have some way of defending ourselves and I agreed."

James took a deep breath and controlled his reaction. He spit out between clenched teeth. "Who were you shooting at?"

"Apparently, no one. Arabella entered the apartment first and started shooting, so I joined in." Henry gave a feeble grin.

James pounded his fist on his desk, making Henry jump. "My God! You're both prats. This is why nerds shouldn't use guns. So where on earth is Arabella?"

"Probably scared out of her mind. We were attacked by Russians!" Henry's voice finished in a squeak. He stared at James wide-eyed.

James shook his head and sighed heavily. "Right. You're a moron, but you're my moron. Let's get those cuffs off of you and get you to a safe house. We'll locate Arabella and get her there too. You two will lie low until this whole thing has blown over. Understood?" James unlocked Henry's cuffs.

"Yes sir." Henry mopped his brow in relief.

"I'll personally drive you there and then we'll send your things over later today."

***

The forest loomed darkly before them. James veered off of route 121 near the Epping Forest and parked the front of the car nestled against a tree. "We have to walk from here. The safe house is deep into the woods. You will be well hidden here."

"Thank you, James," said Henry sincerely.

"It is my pleasure."

They walked single file into the dense woods for a short distance, their footsteps making muffled noises on the dirt and gravel path, the sunlight casting dappled patterns through the tall trees, the birds calling in dismay at their habitat being entered. Suddenly James stopped and turned to Henry with a pained expression. "Can you please keep a lookout for me, Henry. I am afraid that nature is calling."

Henry chuckled at his boss's obvious distress. "Certainly, sir."

James walked off into the woods and Henry stood watching the path they had walked in on. He breathed in the fresh outdoor air and was overcome with relief and happiness at being alive. He started whistling "Happy Days are Here Again." The sound covered the faint crunch of footsteps advancing from his rear.

Suddenly two hands came from behind him into his peripheral vision and a plastic covered wire rope was pulled tight around his neck. He struggled against the noose, ineffectually trying to pull it away. Finally, he slumped to the ground.

James removed the noose from Henry's neck, checked Henry's pulse to ensure he was dead, and dragged the body deeper into the woods and propped it against a tree. With gloved hands he took a needle out of his pocket, uncapped it, and, using Henry's fingers, plunged the contents into Henry's arm. He splashed some vodka onto Henry's clothing, placed the half empty bottle into Henry's hands and closed his fingers around the bottle. He removed Henry's shoes and walked backwards, erasing his own footprints and the marks of the body being pulled. He then put on Henry's shoes and walked back to the body, leaving Henry's footprints. He removed the shoes and put them back on Henry, tying them neatly.

James covered his feet with a slipper-like shoe and softly pattered in a large arc back to the spot where he had left his shoes on the main trail. Humming, he walked jauntily back to the car.

On the way back to London he dialed a number and then spoke into the phone.

"It is done."

***

A small plane landed in a remote airfield in Russia. A short dark-haired woman standing on the side of the field followed the metal stairs being rolled up to the airplane door. The door opened and a woman stepped down to greet the first woman, "*Privet*, Angelina."

"*Zdravstvuy*, Arabella. How was your flight?"

"*Khorosho*, Angelina. I wish I could say the same about my mission."

Angelina said kindly, "Don't worry. There will always be another mission. I'm here to take you to your new home. Let's put your bag in the trunk of the car."

"*Spasibo*, Angelina." A feeling of relief and fatigue swelled within Arabella. She unclipped her Mountainsmith belt bag and lifted her carry-on bag. She stepped forward to the waiting black sedan. Turning, she threw her bags into the trunk. Suddenly she wondered if she was making a mistake in being so trusting. "Oh, I screwed up. I'm really tired. I need to get my belt bag back." She reached into the trunk to get it, and the gun it contained.

* * *

Angelina shot her in the back of the head and flipped her body in after the bags. She then closed the trunk. She waited for the plane to taxi away, then got into the driver's seat and drove quickly away.

While driving, she dialed a number and put the call on speaker. A deep electronically disembodied disguised voice reverberated through the car speakers. "Is it done?"

She responded, "Yes. I will leave the car for body pickup and call to let you know the location."

"*Khorosho*." The phone went dead.

Chapter Forty-Three

"Well done, Elda. It was lucky we had informed the Secret Service about the potential attack or we could all be dead. And, I am glad you survived. If you die, I'd rather it was at my hand."

Elda surveyed Tosh's face to determine if he was joking or serious. She decided he was sincere. She started to respond, but the pain stopped her. She took a deep breath, winced and began again, "Thanks… I think…. As for me, the damaged part of my liver will regenerate, so all is well. However, I'm still wondering where they found a vest big enough to protect the president."

Tosh chuckled. He acknowledged, "It's lucky he had that on. The bullet went directly through the hostage and into the vest. All he'll have is a bad bruise. I am glad to also report that the female he took hostage will be fine. The president is blaming it all on his predecessor for not being friends with Putin."

Tosh and Elda stood facing each other in the apartment living room. Elda was clenching her toes and biting the inside of her mouth to try and keep from crying. Tosh had one arm in a sling and was clenching his other hand into a fist and rocking back and forth on his toes and heels.

Elda finally offered, "We made a good team. I hope to work with you again and not be pitted against you."

Tosh deflected, "Same here, fellow old-timer."

Elda joshed, "Watch who you're calling old, Tosh." She then sincerely stated, "So true, though. The Cold War never stopped, did it?"

"No, it didn't," Tosh agreed.

Elda bit her lip, blinked her eyes and held out her hand. She stated, "Until we meet again, then."

Tosh bypassed her offered hand and gently hugged Elda. He abruptly turned and marched out of the apartment. Elda plucked a small object off her shirt. "Damn it Tosh! Another micro-transmitter?"

Laughter floated back in from the hallway.

Sophia and Snezhana were also saying goodbye. "I thought you were a wanker when I first met you, but you turned out okay. Thanks for saving my life, Snez."

Snezhana frowned and then snorted, "I'm not sure what you just called me, Sophia, but I was surprised to see that once you were no longer glued to Oliver in mouth to mouth resuscitation, you were a competent agent. In fact, I learned a lot from you. *Spasibo*.”

Snezhana and Sophia were standing near the front door of the apartment. Oliver wheeled in from the hallway. He was sitting in a wheelchair with both his and Sophia’s bags on his lap. “Come on Sophia. We have to catch our flight to London. The taxi’s waiting.” Sophia waved her goodbyes and followed Oliver out.

Jackson walked up to Stas who was standing forlornly in the living room. He put his arm around Stas’ slender shoulders. “Stas you’re tops. I hope to work with you again someday.”

“*Spasibo*, Jackson. I can pull the raw data, but I learned so much from you on how to analyze it and was hoping to learn more. I am sorry we will not be working together longer.”

Anatoly came jogging in from the hall. “Stas, grab your bag. We have to leave too.”

“Anatoly? *Vas*.” Elda handed Anatoly a paper bag full of pastries. “For the ride to the airport,” she added with a big grin.

“*Spasibo*, Elda.” Anatoly took the bag in his left hand and held out his right. Elda and he shook farewell and he disappeared out the door.

Yuri was shifting his weight side to side while waiting.

Elda recognized him, "Farewell again, Yuri. Thank you so much."

Yuri grabbed Elda in a bear hug.

"Ouch!" she yelped.

"*Chert*! So sorry Elda. I forgot about your wound." Yuri turned sharply away and stomped out the door.

Snezhana had hung back slightly. She held out her hand to Elda. "Thank you for your advice. I have learned much from you and from my uncle during this mission."

Elda warmly took her hand and shook it. "Take care, Snezhana."

Elda and Jackson stood silently in the emptiness. Elda turned to Jackson. "Thank you Jackson. I hope to work with you again."

"And I you, Elda." Jackson shouldered his bag and stepped from the apartment.

Elda plopped down on the couch and let the familiar sense of loneliness creep in. She took in and released several deep breaths and then stood, picked up her bag and marched out the door, closing it with the solid click of finality.

***

Tosh, gray eyes shining with anger, faced Anatoly in Tosh's Kremlin office. "He's mine, Anatoly. He betrayed us all. He put you and Snezhana and Yuri in danger. I *cannot* forgive him."

Anatoly held up his hand, and rebuked, "I know that Tosh, but you are more valuable than I am. Mother Russia needs you. Killing Alexei puts you at risk. If I do it, then you can cover for me, in the rare chance that it gets traced back to me. Worse case, I can hide for a few years until it all blows over. You have operations to run and more people relying on you than I have. Let me do this for you, *ser*."

Tosh sighed. "You're right, Anatoly. Killing should never be done in an emotional state either. I will gratefully accept this from you. *Spasibo*, my son. I will always ensure you are well protected."

Anatoly strode out of the office.

***

James grabbed the secure line in his office as it rang, put it on speaker and leaned back in his chair with his feet on his desk. "Yes, Ed?"

Ed's voice floated up from the speaker, "You owe me $1000."

481

James nodded at the phone, "Yes I do. You were correct. The mole was here in MI6."

Ed advised, "You should redo all your background checks to ensure you have ferreted out all the leaks."

"Don't you worry, Ed. I have it all under control."

"And my money?"

James swung his legs down and took a checkbook from his desk drawer and quickly wrote a check out to Ed. He stuck a sticky on it with Ed's name and put it in his outbox for his secretary to mail out. "Like a true Brit, I always honor my debts. Expect a check in a few days."

"Thank you," Ed said. "I look forward to our next bet."

"As do I, Yank."

They hung up.

James ran his fingers through his hair, kicked off his shoes and put his feet back on his desk. He settled back in his chair and opening the drawer again, selected a burner phone and dialed a number from memory.

A voice came over the phone, "You do not know how close they were to finding us."

"Yes, yes, I know how close that was. But I'm still in place. I will have to rebuild a network here, however. We lost all of our assets. I will call you when I have more information."

James took the Sim card out of the phone and pocketed both it and the phone for later disposal. Swinging his feet down again he opened his bottom drawer and took out a bottle of Glenlivet and a whiskey glass. Pouring himself two fingers worth, he settled back into a comfortable position and sipped his scotch.

To my future.

***

With a bounce in his step Yuri headed home to his apartment. He passed by an alley on his way and spotted a bedraggled kitten eating out of the trash. He tiptoed toward it, speaking softly to the scared orange and white ball of fur. Once within reaching distance he grabbed and shoved the hissing kitten under his jacket and ran home. He skidded in the door, and, shutting it behind him, quickly unzipped his jacket. An orange streak flew past him into the bedroom. Yuri headed to the kitchen and opened a can of tuna. The sound of the can opener and smell of fish brought his new find into the kitchen.

Yuri smiled broadly and exclaimed, "There you are, baby. Welcome home."

Yuri put a scoop of tuna and juice into a bowl and mashed it to make it easier for the cat to eat. He filled another bowl with water and then backed slowly out of the kitchen to let it eat in peace. He headed into the bathroom to clean his scratched chest. Still smiling, he thought, *I'll have to think of a good name for him or her.*

***

Alexei entered his apartment and switched on the living room light, only to find it won't work. "*Der'mo*! I will have to replace the…."

Alexei reached to vainly remove the noose around his neck. He struggled against the man holding him tightly. His chest vainly moved to bring in air. Eyes bulging in his head he opened his mouth wide to attempt to suck in any available oxygen. His fingers clawed at the noose, slowing as his system started shutting down. The world went dark.

***

Anatoly held the noose tight for a few more minutes and then let the limp body slump to the floor. With gloved hands he checked for Alexei's pulse. "None. *Mertvykh*. Job done."

He looked around the room to ensure he had left no trace. He pointed to each area and repeated, "*Proveryat', Khorosho, Ochistite*," his mantra of, "Check, Okay, Clear." He shut the door quietly behind him.

***

484

Snezhana reluctantly slogged her way to her apartment. After such excitement her day to day life seemed so dull. She aimlessly wandered around each room, wondering what she had made of her life and where she was going. *I have to get out of here.*

She plodded into her bedroom to change into an outfit suitable for bar hopping and noticed a card with a number on it on her bedside table. She picked it up and turned it over to read the scrawled handwriting on the other side: *Safe, but not boring. Enjoy, T.*

***

A knock startled Stas out of the depths of his video game. He opened his apartment door to see a pile of assorted sized boxes stacked there. "*Chto?*" He looked up and down the hallway but saw no one. "Hummm…."

One by one he dragged in the boxes and opened the biggest one. Securely surrounded by foam sat a T-Platforms rugged laptop machine. He was beside himself with joy. *Oh, I hope it has the Elbrus-8S chip in it and the ultra-secure Astra Linux Operating System, Special Edition. If not, I can rebuild it. But it would be great if I have access to the military version of Linux.*

He picked up a card that had fallen out of the box when he grabbed the computer out. Turning it over he read: *I hope this replaces the one you lost. Enjoy, T.*

485

***

Sophia and Oliver marched and hobbled into James' office without knocking. His frantic secretary trailed them. "I'm so sorry sir. They wouldn't wait." James nodded and dismissed her with a wave. He stood up and welcomed them warmly, "Oliver, Sophia! Shouldn't you both be home? You have a week of leave coming to you."

Oliver leaned on his crutches and announced, "That's why we're here, sir. I would like to extend my leave. I'm not sure if I'm coming back to work or not."

James ran his hands through his hair and looked puzzled. "What about you, Sophia?"

Sophia smiled sweetly at James and assured him, "Oh don't worry, James, wild horses couldn't chase me away. Oliver will be quite sick of me being at home in a week."

James grunted, "All right then. Per gra. But do let me know if there's anything I can do to help persuade you to come back, Oliver."

"Thank you sir," stated Oliver.

Oliver and Sophia left hand in hand.

Sophia squeezed Oliver's hand. "Ready to go home and check out our apartment? Especially the bedroom?"

Oliver gave her his sexy crooked grin and winked. Then he replied, "I can't wait. However, there is one errand I want to do on the way back to pick up something for my leave."

Sophia squinted at him. She inquired, "Where and what?"

Oliver jauntily replied, "The hardware store, my lovely. I want to get some yellow paint for the spare room."

***

Jackson paced back and forth in front of the large lecture hall at Harvard University. He wrote in block letters on the whiteboard: *Disinformation and Operation Bittman.*

***

Ed stood on the banks of the Potomac River watching a body being fished out. The face had been chewed so was not readily identifiable, but the body dimensions fit the man, from the Russian Embassy, that Elda had sent away to the insane asylum. The medical inspector examined the remains. "I will need to get this back to the morgue, but the most obvious cause of death is the bullet hole between his eyes."

Ed asked, "Would the timing fit with post the assassination attempt on the president?

487

"Yes."

***

Nigel recoiled from the spyhole in his front door. His heart raced. Beads of sweat broke out on his forehead. A man with a gun was standing there. *If I don't open the door he could shoot his way in. If I open it, perhaps he'll see he has the wrong place.* With trepidation--knowing he had no other options—Nigel Davies slowly opened the solid metal door of his large apartment in Moscow. He stepped back on shaky legs as the man pushed his way inside and stated, "Your father, Henry Davies, is dead."

Nigel sunk to his knees onto the marble floor and wept out of fear for his own future.

"You were our leverage against your father. And now you are useless." The man raised his pistol.

Nigel held out the palm of his right hand and implored, "Wait. Please. I can still help you."

The man dropped the pistol barrel downwards. "How?"

The assassin listened and at the end responded, "*Da.* You will still be useful. You may live. For now." The assassin exited the apartment.

Nigel dried his eyes and looked up a phone number on his computer. He dialed. "Yes, I would like to send a huge bouquet of flowers."

***

"Hi Honey, I'm home!" Elda strode into her house, expecting to be bowled over by her small dog, Vee, and hugged by Dawn. She was greeted by silence. The house smelled stale.

She went from room to room, searching the entire house, wondering where Dawn, Vee and the cat were, her anxiety growing by the minute.

Nothing.

The emptiness and quiet hung heavy as she trudged back through the house to the kitchen. Her heart dropped when she saw the note propped up on the kitchen table. She dropped her bag and plopped down in a chair to read it.

Please call me when you get home and I will have Vee and your cat dropped off for you. I love you, Elda, but I need a break from all of this. I have rented an apartment month by month while we sort this out. I will go to therapy with you and I do want to talk with you. But I just cannot be living my life with long stretches of not knowing if you're okay, or if you're even coming home again.

Elda put her head down on her arms and wept.